BROTHERHOOD

"Sometimes, when two warriors became close friends, they would call each other brother. I believe we are close friends like that."

If he expected any reply to that one, he was disappointed, because I was for once in my life speechless.

"So we're brothers," he said, puffing his pipe furiously, then passed it to me and I did the same.

"Now, brothers among The People have a special thing between them. In the old days, brothers sometimes shared their wives with one another. It was a thing that came with The People from their life in the far northern mountains."

He must have noted my pained expression. I could feel it like a mustard plaster pulling at my face. The faintest of smiles twitched at the corners of his mouth.

"Of course, we don't do that anymore," he said. "And even though we may be brothers, I wouldn't offer you one of my wives, because I know it's a thing that might not settle well in your thoughts. In the old days, I would have offered you any one of them. But these are not the old days."

BOOKS BY DOUGLAS C. JONES

The Search for Temperance Moon
This Savage Race
Season of Yellow Leaf
Gone the Dreams and Dancing

Available from HarperPaperbacks

GONE THE DREAMS AND DANCING

DOUGLAS C. JONES

HarperPaperbacks
A Division of HarperCollinsPublishers

This is a work of fiction. The characters, incidents, and
dialogues are products of the author's imagination and are
not to be construed as real. Any resemblance to actual
events or persons, living or dead, is entirely coincidental.

HarperPaperbacks   *A Division of* HarperCollins*Publishers*
10 East 53rd Street, New York, N.Y. 10022

A hardcover edition of this work was originally published
by Henry Holt and Company, Inc. It is reprinted here by
arrangement with Henry Holt and Company, Inc.

Cover illustration by Harry Scharre

First HarperPaperbacks printing: June 1995

Printed in the United States of America

HarperPaperbacks and colophon are trademarks of
HarperCollins*Publishers*

10 9 8 7 6 5 4 3 2 1

For Mary
Who has heard the singing

———◆———

AUTHOR'S NOTE

———◆———

It is difficult now, standing at modern Fort Sill, to imagine how a people once came, defeated and their culture destroyed by Manifest Destiny, misunderstanding, and greed, and how some of them rose above their misfortunes to become in later years productive citizens of a new state in the heart of America.

Most of the Indian reservations are gone. But once there were many. What follows is the story of one band in such a place. The principal characters are fictional but the setting is described with the intent of depicting reality.

—*Douglas C. Jones*
Fayetteville, Arkansas

GONE THE DREAMS AND DANCING

1

As I looked back, it seemed simple and concise. Maybe like one of those Asian puzzles with the pieces slipping into place unexpectedly, yet exactly. But that was afterward. At the time, it was disturbing and never simple or concise. It was walking wide awake into a dream, those first years I came to know them, sometimes comforting with images that come in sleep of loved ones and familiar places. But then the next moment like the mysterious shades of darkness that leave one waking in a cold sweat of confusion.

And me not always a willing part of the dream, either. But drawn in without the power to stop it, as though there were some magnet beyond all comprehension pulling me. Maybe that was the reality of it, a white man among a people foreign in every sense. A people of dreams and dancing. Dreams and dancing from some distant past to which there was no bridge. And me a man who always loved bridges.

Many's the night I have lain awake and alone, before I became one of them, realizing that I was being drawn closer to the tones and texture born of some other world. And thought often of what my friend Phil McCusker said. He knew them as *well as any white man, I suppose, having learned their language as a youth and spent many hours in their lodges.*

"Morgan," he would say, puffing noisily on his clay pipe, "no matter how long you are among them, you will never understand them!"

Well, defining them in these sorry notes I make for my children is not the purpose. The purpose is only to tell the story of how one man who understood the dreams and dancing led his people through their most difficult period—more difficult than the raids of Pawnees or Utes in the buffalo days, more difficult than the times of smallpox and cholera—and besides that, retained his dignity and honor. And besides that, like an expert at the loom, wove me into the fabric of their lives by placing on me a great mission. At least it was great for him. And then giving me the means of having any children to write for in the first place.

In fact, he didn't give me that chance. He forced it on me. So all my progeny owe him the debt of their living.

Many said it was an honor to be there at the end of a way of life for an entire people. But maybe they were wrong. Maybe shame was a better name for it. I've never been able to get it straight in my mind what it was, and after all the years to think about it before setting down the details in my own hand, I'm still not sure. Except that it made the gooseflesh come in ripples, and still does on reflection.

They'd been a proud people. Still were, even that day, knowing it was the finish of something that had started for them when they first acquired the Spanish horse so long ago and moved into the Southern Plains below the Arkansas to claim dominion over all opposition. Lords they were to be, of a land covered with buffalo and good grass and high winds blowing over it and the sun in summer like a fire of the spirit, the snows in winter like the cooling calm of clear water.

And defiant still, I thought that day as I waited for

them to come, in some ways akin to my own ancestors in Wales with the English industrialists sucking out the life-blood. And maybe a little knowledge secret in their minds, as with my own people, that no matter what came, their *being* was inviolate. Their communal soul would live on if only in song and story, the old men sitting around the winter fires explaining to the children how it once had been.

It's doubtful that most of them realized nothing would soon be left of their old life except those stories. And with the passage of the old ones who lived them, the stories, too, faded from memory.

After the war in Virginia, I had come to this place, this Western frontier in the middle of the continent. And had seen in many places the wild tribes. First when I was a wagon teamster at the great treaty meeting on Medicine Lodge Creek in Kansas. A while ago that was, 1867. And already at that time a full life of adventure and romance behind me, at least by most reckonings.

And the taste of it was good, this frontier. The movement of settlers, the building of railroads, the clash of cultures. And a last chance to see what it had been, but would soon never be again.

So I stayed. There were many years spent in the company of Phil McCusker, the interpreter who taught me the dominant language of the South Plains in that time when various tribes were coming in to start reservation life. And then I was with Mackenzie in the Red River War. Which was not much war at all for one such as myself, who had stood against the metal at Sharpsburg and Devil's Den and the Bloody Angle at Spotsylvania. And with holes in my hide to prove it, too.

But they called it war, nonetheless. It had one virtue: there was little killing, except for horses, and when it was finished the last warriors on Llano Estacado saw the signals in the sky, as Mr. McCusker would put it, and so came in to surrender at Fort Sill and begin reservation life. And follow the white man's road.

Many had come and were already in their small tipi and log shanty settlements, overseen by an agent provided by the Federal bureaucracy and also watched by the army. But now it was the last of them, the most warlike of a warlike tribe who had never touched the feather at any treaty meeting.

They were feared, these latest arrivals to the white man's pasture. Feared by all the roving bands and squash-growers along the streamlines in the old days, feared by the Spaniards and the Mexicans and the Texans, and finally by the white men from the North and East, who sent diplomats in black suits and string ties that seemed to choke off truth from their mouths, and then sent the soldiers in blue coats. Much like those coats I had seen in Virginia and Tennessee and shot a few who wore them.

In self-defense, of course, and in the heat of battle. But it gave me a sense of closeness to these wild tribesmen, all of us having taken aim one time or another at that hated cloth. But bygone now and mostly forgotten, a hard thing to swallow. And for these tribesmen as well, I suspected.

While I waited that windswept day, standing on a sandy knoll south of the fort compound and looking toward the western rolling country from whence they would come, the same feeling came that was always there when I expected to see them or heard the white man's name for them. A quickening of the heart. A sharpness of breathing. A prickly sensation along the spine at the very thought of them. Comanches!

Fort Sill, in that June of 1875, was not what most Easterners would have recognized as a fort. There was no stockade around the sandstone barracks and officers' quarters that formed a long rectangular pattern with a parade ground in the center dominated by a flagpole.

Other buildings, such as stables, ordnance, quartermaster and commissary warehouses, the hospital, the guardhouse, and the trader's store were arranged about the outer edge. South of all this was a large stone corral, a hayfield, a woodlot, and a garden patch. This was the civilian garden. On the far side of the fort was the one for officers' wives and a soldier from each of the troop messes. Why such a distinction, only the army knew.

There was a growing community around the fort, a cluster of off-post, unofficial structures: houses and stores, a tailor shop, a smith shed, a holding pen for cattle. And a small photographic gallery where a Mr. William Soule made his wet-plate impressions of Indians, who sat before his camera with a prop bow across their knees looking like a window-blind slat and of no earthly use to any hunter.

There was always at least one trader to the tribes, licensed by some Federal court or other agency to sell his blankets and beads with perhaps a little illegal whiskey hidden behind the bolts of brightly colored cotton yard goods.

There were no saloons, of course, that being against the policy of the government on reservations. But liquid refreshments were not difficult to find. It was a thing both agent and army tried to stamp out, but never could. And because of it, there were occasional shootings or knife fights, often lethal and almost always involving white men who hung about the reservation, making no effort to do anyone good.

The post proper was constructed on a small lift of ground that overlooked most of the surrounding prairie. But not by much. It was treeless and desolate and dusty. To the north were the gray ridges of the Wichita Mountains. Hills they were, rather. Having campaigned in high ground many times and hunted elk west of Denver, I knew what mountains were, and suspected that the Wichitas had been called so by someone who had been over-enthusiastic in naming them.

East of the fort, at some distance, were the buildings

of the Kiowa-Comanche Indian agency. James Harper, a good Quaker, was headman there and my employer on a part-time basis. There was the agent's house and my own, and those of other agency employees. They were no great shakes. My own was a two-room slab-side, having a single window in each room with glass shipped in from St. Louis and framed in curtains by my wife, Augustina.

God rest her!

All that white muslin grown gray because it had been two years since the typhoid came and took her and hence the end of any effort to keep much of anything clean.

Augustina! I had called her July because it was short and because it had an Indian sound to it that I thought to tease her with, but she always laughed her wonderful laugh and said, "At least you're close, Liverpool Morgan, and it's better than September!"

God rest her!

The agency had the usual trappings. There was an Indian goods warehouse, a sawmill powered by a Chicago steam engine, a shinglemaker, and a corn grinder. The last was an exercise in frustration. For although local Delawares and some Wichitas used the grinder, few of the former wild tribe hunters ever showed much interest in it.

All this had been built by the black soldiers of the Tenth Cavalry under the direction of dear old Colonel Ben Grierson, who, if one were to want a Yankee officer to admire, was an excellent selection.

And all the while that brick and mortar and lumber were being molded in fashion and form of an army post, the troopers were called out on various occasions to run down red marauders. Many of these were already sup-posedly living in peace on the reservation, but some could not always resist the temptation to join their wild brothers south of Red River in Texas, there to ply their old trade of horse-stealing, ranch-burning, and general hell-raising in reprisal for what they considered an invasion of their country. Not an unfounded assumption!

But all that was past now, as I waited for the coming of the last of the South Plains hostiles. Grierson was gone, along with his buffalo soldiers, and commanding the fort was that same Ranald Mackenzie of the Red River War. The combat garrison at Sill was the Fourth Cavalry, two troops of which were drawn up into line now, waiting too, sitting their mounts with carbines held butt-down on right thighs. They were near the new icehouse just east of the main post plateau.

As yet, there was small semblance of an icehouse about the structure, because there was no roof. Bare rock walls without windows, and only one door of heavy oak cut at the agency sawmill. It had the look of a fortress prison, and at the moment that was the purpose it would serve.

On the sloping ground behind the quartermaster warehouse were many members of the garrison—soldiers not on duty elsewhere, and officers with their wives. The women wore long white skirts that whipped out in the wind, and some were holding parasols against the late-afternoon sun. Most of the civilian employees of the fort and the agency were there as well, the men, like myself, wearing their usual drab garb: wide-brimmed hats, collarless shirts, dark coats, duck pants, and boots. It was not a colorful assemblage. Everything had a sepia tone. Looking at them, I half expected a crack to appear across the scene, as on one of photographer Soule's glass-plate pictures.

To the south, across one of the many post roads, was a band of Comanches, come to watch also. A few of the men were dressed in buckskin, but most wore what the white men wore except for moccasins with long fringes at the toes and heels. The women were mostly blanket-wrapped, stoic of expression, their loose hair fanning out at shoulder length. The men's hair was done in twin braids along either side of their faces, with a long scalp lock at the back, a style not particularly appreciated by the agent because of its warlike connotations, but a fashion the Comanches refused to abandon.

The brown faces were set in hard lines, flat and reflecting the sun, black eyes squinted almost shut. I heard not a sound from them as they stood motionless, their children behind them as quiet and somber as the parents.

These were some of the people who had been on the reservation for a time. From central Texas they were, a Paneteka band. Behind them at some distance was a cluster of tipis, many still covered with buffalo hide but some with canvas because these people had had little opportunity to take buffalo on the hunt since arriving at the agency. Those great beasts were almost gone, on the reservation and off. Their monument was acres of bleaching bones left by hunters who took only hide and tongue and left the rest to rot. And sometimes, now, even the bones were being scavenged to make fertilizer for growing the crops that these old hunters of the humpbacked animal so detested.

We waited. There was a hush about it all, the only sound a harsh cawing of crows in a stand of timber to the east, near Cache Creek. A lugubrious moment it was, for white and red alike, as though everyone waited for the funeral procession of a departed one, troublesome in life but mourned nonetheless in passing.

The leader of this band coming to surrender was known by name to us all. He was Kwahadi, war chief of the Antelope band whose name he bore. In the final days of the Red River War, it had been he who so frustrated Mackenzie, hiding his people like shadows in Palo Duro Canyon, coming out at night to steal the Indian ponies the army had taken during the day. Until finally Mackenzie knew what the Texas Rangers had known for a long time and what I had heard stated in grim tones across many a low campfire along the branches of the Brazos:

"When you capture a Comanch' pony, kill it quick,

before the bucks have time and opportunity to take it back right from under the noses of your night guards!"

Oh yes. They were good at taking horses, better even than the Crows, a high compliment. That was why they always had bigger pony herds than any other tribe on the plains.

The first indication of their approach was a small dustcloud to the southwest. We stood immobile, eyes turned in that direction against the slanting sun. Nothing sounded but the whisper of the wind and, from Cache Creek, the crows.

They came, the first of a long cavalcade, led by Mr. Horace Jones, Fort Sill interpreter and scout. And then a section of the troop of the Fourth Cavalry that had gone out to meet them. There was a small space between Jones and the first Comanches. Then the wild tribesmen, with other blue-clad soldiers riding along either flank in single file.

On the instant of seeing him, we all knew who he was, and not only because he rode at the head of his people. Kwahadi was an imposing man. Tall for a Comanche, he rode without effort, even though the calico pony beneath him was nervous and prancing wildly. His hair was loose, flying in the wind. He was naked to the waist, except for a bright yellow bandanna knotted at the throat. His leggings and moccasins were thickly fringed but with no decorations, plain and without color. But his horse was painted in various designs of red and white, in many ways matching the paint across his face, red and white stripes that ran from his nose back to the exposed ears.

On his left shoulder was a small rawhide shield and, suspended from it, four feathers. They looked a little frayed, as though they'd been hanging there a long time. At the center of the shield was a painted outline of a wolf's head, in black. He carried a lance in his right hand, point up, fully ten feet long and streaming with human hair.

He was much as I had pictured him in my mind

during those long, dusty rides with Mackenzie while we chased him and his people across the plains and through Palo Duro Canyon. We never caught any of them, of course, but only some of their horses.

When the sunlight struck his head just so, I could see the glint of copper color in his hair and knew the stories were likely true, stories spread across Texas and the Indian Territory that there was a chief growing in power and respect who had a white captive mother. White captive mothers among them were not unusual. But a white half-blood growing to the full stature of honored war chief was another matter.

It was a tribute to his courage and initiative against enemies, as McCusker told me many times, because no Comanche ever became a war chief without those things. And it started young, this rise to power, when he was not yet of voting age in the white man's world. Some of the yarn-spinners and a few Eastern newspaper writers attributed such leadership to his mixed blood. But McCusker never said such a thing. He knew there had been great chiefs among them who had come to their authority just as young and without benefit of a white mother.

That day, looking at him for the first time, I saw no white man in the features of his face. High, flat cheekbones and crescent sculpted lips. Eyebrows plucked clean and a long, square chin. But then he turned his head toward the watchers on the slope above the road, and I saw the hint of gray in his eyes.

In that instant, I felt his gaze touch me. I had never looked into such eyes before. There was a depth and intensity much like that seen in the eyes of men in battle. A brittle viciousness. But somehow a difference. A subtle defiance that challenged me to measure him, at the same time showing disdain for any judgment I might pass.

That exchanged look lasted only a fleeting second, no longer, and then he turned his face away. But in that moment I felt naked, as though he had judged *me*.

Immediately behind Kwahadi came the others I assumed to be the headmen of the band. Some were old and there was one woman, old as well, her fierce face painted black. From her saddle hung a short Comanche quiver with bow and arrows vaned with white feathers. Owl feathers, I assumed, because they retain their form and texture even when soaked with blood.

Then the young men, the fighting strength of the band, brave and recalcitrant. Then the elders, and after them the women and children riding the travois ponies. The trailing poles of the travois along the road spun up little plumes of dust that were quickly lost on the wind. Finally came the pony herd, with young boys keeping them well bunched in a long column. I estimated the herd at about two hundred horses—a tribute to Mackenzie's effectiveness, for in the old days such a group of Comanches would have had five times that many.

Altogether, man, woman and child, there were about eighty of them. I didn't try to count the mongrel dogs trotting alongside. There were too many to tally.

Those Comanche dogs fascinated me in some strange way. They were an ugly crew. They went along, heads lowered, beside the ponies of the band, taking no notice of these new surroundings, no single glance that I could see them make toward the people on the slope, who must have given off foreign and hostile scents. They trotted unperturbed into the white man's world. And I thought, They don't know. They don't know that they're just Indian dogs.

A dreadfully silent parade it was, with no talk among them and no call of recognition from their kinsmen who watched them pass, as though all of it was unseen, only felt, making the flesh crawl along skin turned cold.

The column passed well beyond the fort and then turned north to the unfinished icehouse. There, one of the receiving troops of soldiers broke ranks and moved to take the shields and weapons from the men and the old woman with the black-painted face. It was quickly done, the Comanches still on horseback and Horace Jones riding along their line, explaining what was expected. There was no sign of resistance or disturbance, and I heard no single word from any of them.

After the arms were collected, the men were told to dismount and were herded like goats through the door in the west wall of the icehouse. With the last of them inside, the door was slammed shut and barred. The rest of the band were instructed to move off a short distance and pitch their camp until further arrangements could be made for locating them out on the reservation.

The women guided their travois horses well toward the east and began slowly to unpack gear. Soon the skeletal lodgepoles were going up, almost without effort, it seemed, just appearing suddenly. Everything was done in bleak silence. The children stood out of the way, some naked except for moccasins, their gazes turned toward the slope where the white people were. Even the dogs sat calmly by with hanging tongues, their bony haunches on the ground. There were a number of cradle boards, and beneath their canopies I could see the small coconut faces with eyes as bright as polished black glass.

The horse herd was turned back by the troopers to the stone corral near the hayfield. Other soldiers waited in the growing camp to take the ponies of the women as soon as the travois were unloaded. I knew that a few of the horses would be returned to the band, but most would be sold at auction, the proceeds credited to the band's account at the agency store.

A detail of troopers carried the collected weapons to the ordnance warehouse where they would be stored. Some of these might later be returned so the men of the band could hunt. Of course, there was little left to hunt on the reservation. Perhaps they would be allowed to go off reservation to Llano Estacado, at the agent's pleasure. But I knew they would find little game there either.

At one corner of the icehouse a small fire had been kindled, where the soldiers were burning the scalps from

Kwahadi's lance. When that was finished, a trooper rode away toward the warehouse area with the ironwood weapon, holding it above his head and grinning. It looked terribly naked without the hair.

In that moment I recalled some of my reading and imagined the spectacle of severed heads, dripping, being carried through the streets of Paris during the days of their revolution. It seemed to me that these scalps, heathen trophies of hard-won victories, perhaps, were more tasteful, more easily stomached, being oiled and brushed and groomed and gleaming in the sun, showing respect at least for those who had once worn them.

An amazingly short time was required for all of it. A thing I was sure would be marked in history had been consummated within the time it would take to smoke a small bowl of pipe tobacco.

Colonel Mackenzie had been represented at the icehouse by his adjutant, Lieutenant Oscar Weslowski, who supervised everything with the efficiency of good adjutants. The following day, Mackenzie himself would formally accept the surrender at his headquarters and turn matters over to the Indian agent, even knowing as he did the habit of Congress to be laggard in appropriating funds for Indian food. And hence, in the coming winter, as in the past, the charges of the agent would be often fed on army rations or else starve.

So it was over. The whites began to disperse, going back toward the fort compound, talking loudly now, some laughing with relief, I suspected. Across the road, the Panetekas had disappeared as quietly as they had come, going into their tipis, their campsite now showing no sign of life. Even the children were tucked inside the lodges at this time of late day when they should have been playing and laughing and running with the dogs in the lowering sunlight.

So it was over. The end of a short, flashing culture. That riding to the hunt, riding to the joyous contact with traditional enemies, the Utes and Pawnees and Lipans and Tonkawas. Over, the dancing for victory, the singing to the buffalo, the nights of vaning arrows with owl feathers, and the old men telling stories of the strange men called Spaniards in their metal hats, driven back from the high plains in the days of the grandfathers. Over, the power of the wolf and the hawk. Over, the cedar flutes played in freedom.

And on that Fort Sill post, all was normal again, with the sound of a bugle at the parade ground, the notes of recall and troopers going to the stables and some, in their best bib and tucker, falling out at the flagpole for guard mount.

I heard the steam engine start up again at the agency, a harsh, unreal sound coming all the way from Europe. And I knew the agency millyard man expected to slice out a few more slabs of oak before the night came full on.

The crows had stopped their infernal racket as evening drew down, but now there were the mockingbirds, singing their varied songs from the jack oaks behind the Paneteka camp. With the dust settling, there was a clean smell, not so sharp as that at sunset on the holdings of my Da in the Ouachita Mountains in Arkansas, where the pines scented every thought. More like the odor of prickly pear after a new spring rain.

I stood against the wall of the quartermaster warehouse, smoking my clay pipe and watching the purple shadows running across the ground toward the east. And thinking about those men in the icehouse. There seemed some requirement to remain for at least a little while near them.

No guards had been posted, so confident was Mackenzie in Kwahadi's assurance that the war trail was ended. A mutual faith among warriors, I supposed. All the troopers were gone and Horace Jones as well, and the icehouse stood with its west wall against the lowering sun like a gray flag before firelight. Like the battlements of some castle in Wales, I thought, or more like a giant's tombstone fallen on its side.

Then I heard them singing. A low, throbbing sound that had no words I could translate. Just a moaning chant from the men inside the walls of the unfinished icehouse. As the singing began, the women completing their camp stood as still as the jack-oak trunks behind them. The children turned their heads toward the sound of their fathers' voices, and the dogs lifted their heads and pulled in their tongues and rose to sniff the direction of the chant. But it lasted for only a moment and was finished and the camp flowed reluctantly back into evening movement.

Finally, then, I could hear the commands barked on the parade ground at the fort as the new guard was posted, and shortly afterward, mess call from the bugler. It was almost dark when two wagons pulled away from the commissary storehouse, soldiers clucking the mules along and slapping them gently with leather lines.

One wagon creaked into the new camp behind the icehouse, where conical lodges had taken form. There were a number of small fires there now, running their blue-gray smoke toward the darkening sky in the lull of wind before sundown.

The second wagon pulled to a stop at the icehouse wall. One of the soldiers remained on the seat with the reins loosely in his hands. The other climbed into the box and began to lift bloody chunks of freshly butchered beef. These he threw over the icehouse wall. Even at such a distance, I imagined I could hear the raw meat striking the ground among the proud Comanches.

The scene came vividly to mind then, like an oil painting lighted on a museum wall. From a long time past, myself a youth full of the vigor of innocence and ignorance seeing the sights of the City of Brotherly Love on my way to cross the great ocean to join Giuseppe Garibaldi in Sicily. It was the zoo that came down the years in hard memory. And here it was again, now. Feeding the lions in their cages!

Some measure of tranquility should be expected when there's a peace treaty and an end to war. In my innocent days, before they signed that paper in the McLean house at Appomattox, it was a natural assumption. Later, all such illusions were dispelled for me, what with hearing men like my Da raging over what was happening to a lot of our people during the years the Federals called Reconstruction. So there was no surprise in those things that the Comanches inherited with peace.

Not that there were any more Texas Rangers or state militia or United States troopers riding through their villages, shooting hell out of everything in sight. But there were more subtle kinds of injury. Something that might be called violence to the spirit.

Once launched on the white man's road, whatever they expected may have had a sudden shock in their first full day of civilized life. And first impressions are sometimes hard to overcome.

That morning after Kwahadi had come in, when Horace Jones and a small detail of soldiers under the command of Adjutant Weslowski came to the icehouse and set the men free and escorted the chief and a few of his elders to the fort for their talk with Mackenzie, I was in foul temper. Because they were doing all this without asking me to come along as one of the interpreters. Not so strange, of course, interpeting being only a part-time job for me. The army had their own man, Horace Jones. And the agency had Jehyle Simmons, and a sour bastard he was.

So Toothpick Jehyle, as he was often called due to the lack of flesh on his long bones, accompanied Agent Harper and the chiefs to see the army boss and then later to escort the band out to their new home, leaving me out of all arrangements. I was on a contract job for the army, along with a number of other civilians, a tough breed of reservation men who hung about for purposes hard to understand. Surely not for the meager dollars they had from Weslowski's hand in return for their sweat.

Many of these army contract men were rough-talking and unschooled, at least to casual observation, with the single common characteristic among them being that they were usually drunk and belligerent. Or else they had such painful hangovers from terrible whiskey that their dispositions were even worse for having no alcoholic lubrication.

It was just such a lot I worked with that morning. The job was hauling sandstone from one of the creek bluffs east of the agency for the completion of the icehouse. It was hard and dirty work. But because of my high standing with the good Weslowski and with the contract foreman, Mr. Joel Stoddard, who was a partner in the general mercantile on the reservation, my hands never touched a single grimy rock. I was a wagon driver, which indeed was my major contribution to the army on the plains in those days. As all the others grunted and moaned, lifting the heavy stones in and out of the wagon, I sat in lofty detachment on the wagon seat, smoking my clay pipe and watching the cardinals working through the small stands of cedar that were scattered about the agency like green sentinels waiting for Christmas.

Where we loaded the sandstone was well away from any of the white man's installations, but at the other end of the haul we were in the middle of things, there beside the icehouse, with the fort all in view as well as the civilian enterprise buildings. The Panetekas who had come in to watch the surrender parade had broken camp earlier, leaving with the dawn. But as we creaked up to the east side of the icehouse with our first load of the day, we were close by the camp of Kwahadi's people, and the children came to the edge of their circle of tipis to watch, curiosity overcoming timidity.

The women of the band were beginning to take down tipis and make travois bundles, because Horace Jones had already told them that as soon as their chief finished talking with the soldier boss, they would be moving to their new home along Big Beaver Creek. The men who had been released from the icehouse sat in a tight group on the far side of the camp, smoking and, I supposed, talking about what might happen next.

While I sat sucking my pipe and making what I imagined to be friendly faces at the Comanche children, a heated argument broke out behind me between two of the workers. I paid little attention to it. Arguments among contract men were as endemic as griping among soldiers, and both were of small substance. This particular disagreement seemed to concern itself with a woman called Rabbit Rachel, who lived at one of the Red River crossings, on the Texas side, about thirty-five miles south of Fort Sill. I assumed she was not one of the local Sunday school teachers there. Such women held no interest for me any longer, nor did arguments about their available favors in return for a two-dollar consideration.

But this little discussion suddenly took on sinister and ugly tones as the contract men began to shout.

"Clean the little bastard's plow!"

"Kick his skinny ass!"

"Tan his hide, Albert!"

When I looked around, there was this Albert, a veteran around the fort and sometimes in drunken brawls in Stoddard & Blanchard's back room, grappling with a young lad only recently arrived on this wild frontier. A full-grown cur dog manhandling a pup, so it was time to get involved, I figured. But before my foot touched the wheel to step down, there was a dull report and a great cloud of gray smoke, and the lad collapsed like an empty grain sack.

The contract men scattered like chickens before a charging dog, going off in all directions, Alfred among them, the pistol still in his hand, running headlong toward the trees to the south, where the Paneteka camp had been the day before, and the poor lad thrashing around in the hard chips of sandstone at the tailgate. At the Comanche camp, all the children were running wildly but silently back to their elders, where the women had stopped their work and stood motionless, staring, and beyond them, the men had risen from their squats, their smoking forgotten now. All the Comanche faces were immobile, and the children took refuge behind the rawhide skirts of their mothers.

It was only a fleeting glimpse of that Indian camp, because I was running to the boy. But a glimpse I would not soon forget, all those black eyes wide and staring and uncomprehending.

The ball had entered the lad's body just below the breastbone, dead center, and his shirt was burning, set fire by the muzzle flash. It was finished for this one. I'd seen enough wounds in the old Army of Northern Virginia and in Sicily to know. A torn vessel just below the heart and the blood splattering as I slapped out the smoldering fire on his shirt. He tried to say something, his eyes not seeing me, then choked and shuddered and stiffened. He made a harsh gagging sound and the flesh on his face began to shrink in across the bones of his cheeks.

The others, except for the one with the pistol, began to come back then, in twos and threes, looking at the boy and at me holding him, and at the blood and the smoke from the shirt. It was a good shirt, not one of those rough things sold in Stoddard & Blanchard's. The fabric was only one of the little things that dance through the memory when catastrophe comes unexpectedly, a punctuation to all the rest that a man remembers. That smoldering shirt stayed stronger in my mind through the years than the features of the poor boy's face.

"Come on, you bloody ruffians," I shouted. "Onto the wagon with this lad."

We passed his body up onto the wagon bed and lay it on the stones not yet unloaded. All of them were now eager to help, trying to show their great compassion toward the boy for whose hide they had been screaming only a moment before.

I drove the wagon to Stoddard & Blanchard's, not far distant, the other contract workers coming on behind like a string of paid mourners. As I reined the mules along, I glanced back toward the Comanche camp, and they were all still there, watching. Even their dogs, noses up, sniffing, but unmoving.

The boy was laid out on the covered front porch of the mercantile store and Mr. Stoddard came out and clucked like an old hen, and bent down and closed the boy's eyes with his fingers. Then back inside he went and reappeared with a small tarpaulin and covered the body so that only the legs and feet were showing. The feet in new, rough leather work shoes and pointed toes-up. People had begun to gather, all men in rough garb except for the wife of the photographer, who was wearing a sunbonnet and carrying a walking stick. They came from all along this short street where the store was centrally located, and they stood back in a wide circle, looking at those upturned work shoes.

"Who did it?" Mr. Stoddard asked; he was expected to take the lead now, being the unofficial mayor of the

Strip, which is what we called the sorry street that ran before his store.

One of the contract workers mentioned Albert's name.

"Well," said Stoddard, "we know it wasn't an Indian, then, don't we?"

Which meant that every time something dreadful happened on the reservation, the first assumption was that an Indian had done it.

It didn't take long for the soldiers to appear. There were about seven of them, mounted and armed and with ammunition in their belts for revolvers and the big .45-50 Springfield carbines hanging from their saddles. Lieutenant Tracy Shadburn was leading them, which everyone expected because he had become a kind of reservation policeman. The army was the only law-enforcement group we had then, and Adjutant Weslowski, with his usual sound judgment of men, always selected his meanest troop commander to handle such affairs. And maybe the meanest troop commander in the whole Yankee army was Tracy Shadburn.

He never said very much. When he did, his words came sharp and to the point of things. No ruffles and flourishes.

"Where's he gone?" Shadburn asked, sitting like a slouching recruit in his saddle.

"I reckon he lit out for Texas," said one of the contract workers. "He's a mean one, Lieutenant."

Like so many of us, here was a man who had changed sides once the tide of advantage turned. Only a little while ago he had gleefully encouraged our fugitive to commit mayhem on the boy, and now he was the first to point the finger. Well, obviously now it was better to be on the side of justice, and more importantly on the side of the armed troopers, none of whom looked too kindly on any of us for creating such unpleasant duty for them. And our being only dumb civilians.

"Mounted?" asked Shadburn.

"Afoot."

So the cavalry patrol wheeled around the buildings along the Strip and started for the Texas fords and the rest of us went back to our work and soon an army wagon came down from the fort and carried the body to the hospital morgue. Shadburn and his men had the fugitive in tow and in the fort guardhouse before mid-afternoon.

The story was soon circulated that Albert made no resistance, surrendering meekly as soon as the soldiers overtook him. Which proved the man still had his sanity, at least. No rational being embraces the prospect of fighting with a handgun an antagonist who can stand out of his range and puncture his hide with large-caliber carbines. They said the prisoner looked a little fagged out when they brought him in, bleeding profusely from mouth and nose.

"Bastard fell off the horse," Shadburn explained. But it came out later that the troopers had made the killer come back to Fort Sill the same way he left it. On foot.

Lieutenant Tracy Shadburn. A tall, dark-faced man with flinty eyes and a slash of mouth below a well-clipped mustache. When Adjutant Weslowski called, old Tracy was off on the job, no matter how unpleasant. Some said the more unpleasant the task, the more Tracy enjoyed it.

Even in an army of old lieutenants, Shadburn was an ancient. Rumor had it that during the war he had been a colonel of cavalry, but had been reduced in rank for mistreatment of his men. And now he was still waiting out his years as subaltern, little prospect in view for promotion and already having more than twenty-five years of service behind him.

We often had a sip or two, Shadburn and me, sitting on the porch of the bachelor officers' quarters where he had his room, him being unmarried all his life. We would talk about the war, comparing memories of how our two opposing armies had gone about the business of slaughter, and listening to the mockingbirds singing in the darkness. I liked him. Maybe it was my life-long inclination to feel some uneasy kinship with scoundrels and outcasts.

Although Tracy Shadburn never uttered a word of complaint about having to police civilians, every other soldier on the post, from Mackenzie down to the lowest dog robber, hated it. The army had no authority to try civilians, so whoever created a hazard was arrested and put to languish in the basement of the guardhouse until word could be got to the Federal court in Fort Smith. And sometime after that, a deputy United States marshal would appear to return the prisoner to the mercy of Judge Isaac Parker.

Compared to some of those marshals I saw from Parker's court, Tracy Shadburn was a Mormon church choir director. The killer was eventually taken away by one such man, and we all expected to hear that one of Parker's ropes would have him before the first snow fell.

The poor lad's body was embalmed at the fort mortuary and left lying in an oak casket until his old daddy came for him, driving all the way down from Missouri in a spring wagon. It was a little remarkable that Weslowski had taken the trouble to notify any of the lad's kin about the shooting. Most such victims were simply planted in the growing boot hill on a slope behind Stoddard & Blanchard's store.

Afterward, it was always referred to as the icehouse killing. There was enough lethal mayhem around in those days that there had to be some way of distinguishing one incident from another. The most infamous one was called the Picture Scalping. A white man was found out on the western edge of the reservation, dead of many puncture wounds and his hair taken. One of Mr. Soule's photographic associates went out and took a picture with a trooper and a civilian scout kneeling beside the body.

Everyone said it was a Kiowa or a Comanche who'd done it, but I was never sure. Maybe so. Maybe the corraled wild tribesmen watched such things as the icehouse killing and figured that was the way things were done in the white man's world.

In all my years with them, I never heard what any of them thought about such things. Most particularly, none of Kwahadi's band ever mentioned what they had seen that first day after coming to their open-air prison called reservation, a young man shot down for no real reason. Phil McCusker had always said the Comanches didn't murder one another very often. The men were a headstrong, weapons-wise bunch and they rubbed against one another pretty hard sometimes in their quest for tribal status, but McCusker said it seldom came to fatal consequences.

Well, the icehouse killing gave them a vivid impression of what things were like on civilization's road, I'd guess. The irony was that they had little to fear from white men's knives and guns. What they had to fear was starvation.

The night was cool and dark, no moon due until the wee hours. After eating some army hardtack and a chunk of the pan-fried beefsteak I had cooked for breakfast, I sat on my little yard stool beside the door of my shanty, smoking and letting the gears of my mind go into neutral like the agency sawmill when the blade stood idle. The lighted lamp on the table inside cast its fuzzy yellow glow through the open doorway and I could almost hear the sound of Augustina's humming as she cleaned the dishes. My coffee sent its pungent aroma out from the cast-iron cookstove where the pot sat muttering, almost like that whispered humming had once sounded within those poor walls.

It seemed the longer she was gone, the more clearly I could see her. Not a tall woman and well on the hefty side, plenty for a man to hold when he took her in his arms. And my arms the only ones ever to do that delightful duty, so she told me. And she seemed so small when we stood side by side, the top of her head coming only to my shoulder. What a head it was, her deep brown hair piled up and her blue eyes shining beneath those dark brows, smiles coming quick as lightning, all enough to make my heart stop just to look at her.

She wanted a child so desperately, and sometimes in bed at night she would lie tight against my side and cry and say that she was imperfect and would never have a baby. I tried to console her with the thought that we'd been joined for so short a while and that such things as babies took time. And reminded her that we were doing everything we could, at every opportunity, to make it happen and that eventually it would. But she'd sob and say that we could never enjoy children between us.

Maybe she knew something I didn't. Because she was right, not through her own inadequacy but because of the typhoid that came so soon. But on the mornings after her despair, I'd find her at the stove, smiling and shining as she made my grub, looking at me with those marvelous eyes and saying, "Never you mind, Liverpool Morgan. Just a wee bit of self-pity last night, me so anxious to start our brood."

Oh, she could blaze up like fire in the piney woods. And those tiffs between us became as dear to me as the shining times. One night I came in from Stoddard & Blanchard's back room a little the worse for having sampled too much whiskey. Augustina never begrudged me a sip now and again, knowing the Welsh taste for such things. But on that night I managed to knock her china sugar bowl off the table, and it shattered into a thousand tiny white shards.

Like a cat she was up, going for a cast-iron skillet, and I made a hasty withdrawal through the open door and into the dark. Her raging voice, no longer soft and coming very close to teamster swearing, followed me. I was sure everyone on the agency could hear it.

That night I spent in the mule shed. It was miserable. Then the next morning when I cautiously peeked through the doorway of our shack, there she was at the stove as usual, smiling at me over her shoulder as she made my breakfast.

"A worthless man you are, Liverpool Morgan," she said. "But too precious to throw away yet. Come in and have your biscuits."

"I don't want biscuits quite yet," said I, and she giggled, and later, in the bed, the bread growing cold on the back of the stove, she scolded me for being such a naughty man, doing things in broad daylight that decent people did only under cover of darkness.

The memories of Augustina were bitter, but sweet as well. I allowed them to go their course for as long as I could stand it, then would try to force my thinking into other channels. And that usually meant the recall of days spent in armies when I was young and looking for adventure. I knew a man once who was a farmer and a religious zealot, before that got shot out of him during the war, and he always told me I was a soldier of fortune, going from one war to another. Well, I made no fortune at it and collected many aches and pains that stayed with me all my days.

Why was it, I thought, that some things came so vividly to memory while others remained lost forever behind the curtain of time? I could still hear the conversation of my messmates around cookfires in Virginia on those good evenings when the commissary department had sent down fresh meat for a change. Or the Christmas Eve when I was in that hellhole prison pen at Fort Delaware, singing the old carols.

Yet all I could remember of Tennessee was the rain and cold and shoes rotting off our feet and the drummer boy shot down in the charge we made at Chickamauga. Sometimes I wondered how many of the others had made it through that war, the ones I'd come so close to and knew so well. But after the Yankees captured me I lost all track of them and after the shooting stopped I never tried to find them. For which I feel considerable shame.

Some people say that old veterans recall only the good things from their service. I remembered a lot of the bad times as well, and on that night after Kwahadi's people had come and were already out, settling into a new camp on the Big Beaver, I wanted to think of Indians. But on the first thought, there was Augustina again.

When I first brought her to the reservation, sometimes after sundown a few of the Paneteka men would come to my shack and we'd sit in the darkness and smoke and talk. Always she brought coffee for them, and the many tin cups we had for just such an occasion. She would pass among the squatting warriors and pour their coffee and offer the sugar bowl and each would slowly, methodically dump at least a dozen spoonfuls into his cup.

And always the most highly regarded man among them would wait until she had returned to her kitchen and then say, "That's a good woman you got there, Liver."

It delighted her that they shortened my name. Liverpool held no meaning for them, but liver they understood. So to them I was Liver.

Then I'd sing a few Welsh ballads, and the Comanches knew enough of English to realize this was a different tongue. After a few songs and after they had finished their pipes of my tobacco or the rolled cigarettes, and after they had licked the last of the deposited sugar from the bottoms of their cups, they would rise and go away.

Once more the headman would speak, standing in the light of the door.

"That's good singing, Liver. Your gods must be pleased with such singing."

Then he'd be gone, too, disappearing into the darkness as silently as a footless ghost.

No one had come since the Antelope band came in to surrender. I hadn't expected them to come. So that night I sat alone in the cool night. I sang a little to myself, soft as the spring breeze so as not to wake my sometime boss, Agent Harper. Only to myself it was, and maybe at that the best kind of singing there is. Finally I heard from the direction of the fort the bugle's notes, a mournful call to sleep. Tattoo. And a little later, taps.

Well, thought I, now all the good young soldiers are tucked into bed for resting sleep, and only the guards marching their posts, dreaming of soft bodies and counting down the hours to beans at breakfast. Soldiers always dream of the same things. Women and grub and maybe a little whiskey now and again.

Still not ready for sleep, I wondered how long they had been here, those brave red people. Kwahadi's people, and not the white mother, either. The spirit singers. How long?

Tracy Shadburn said that old people spent a lot of their time sitting around thinking about the things that had happened to them in the gone years. He told me about his father, who had been a veteran of the War of 1812, and how the old man would sit in his favorite rocking chair, muttering about the British, all the while soiling the front of his shirt with escaped tobacco juice.

Maybe it was true. With old age creeping forward on me to make its final assault, the inventory of my own life seemed to creep into most of my woolgathering.

Da and Mother came to these shores, as they put it, in 1835, sailing in a rotten ship that smelled of sweat and rats, and myself born on the eve of departure and named for the city where the journey began. Perhaps my first days spent on the sea gave me the notion in some wee part of the mind that life was nothing more than roving about from place to place. Well, roving aplenty I'd done.

We settled in the pine hills of western Arkansas in the first year of statehood there. Da hauled in a steam engine from Fort Smith, bought with money he'd saved from his days in the Welsh collieries. He flayed and cursed that old machine as though it were a recalcitrant mule, but made it work, running the saw that sliced out those beautiful white planks, smooth as the crusts on Mother's pork pies.

Maybe that's why listening to the agency sawmill always made a small shiver in my soul. Because it was the sound of Da's blade in the few young years I stayed at home and had the opportunity to hear it.

When did I stop hearing that old engine coughing in the Ouachitas? Seventeen, maybe sixteen, and already a bulldog of a boy, buxom and full of strong vinegar. So off to the nearest river, for in those days the rivers were highways where people and adventure waited. I soaked it up.

Many's the task I took on to keep bread in my belly and cloth on my back. Stoking steamboats on the Arkansas and the Mississippi, herding mules, loading cotton on slimy decks, learning the smithy's art and developing my arms so that before I was ever known to any woman, the biceps bulged as did my Da's from his years of swinging a pick in some black hole.

There were things to learn then. From Fort Smith to Helena, from Cairo to New Orleans. Games of cards to master, and dice, and sometimes a month's pay gone on a single roll. There were finally the women, too. Some saintly, some wicked, but all good. They liked my black beard and hair, grown to manly proportions before I was twenty. All those faces were lost, but the softness and warmth recalled.

And the use of fists in heated discussion. I became very good at that, perhaps an inheritance from my Da, who before we sailed for America was shunned by all bullies in the old country because it was said that he had a left hooking blow powerful enough to shatter a tree stump. I spent a few nights in various jails from this inheritance.

It was in Natchez. Or was it Angola? There was this lot of us young lads working the docks, sweating in summer heat and raising all kinds of liberal hell at night in the saloons and bawdy-houses along the waterfront. Everything smelled of rye whiskey and fish scales.

There was one among us who was Italian, and he spoke constantly about this man Garibaldi. The upshot was that some of us decided we'd set out for the far Mediterranean to help in the fight. We had no idea what the fight was about, but it didn't matter.

Then came the great war of Northern aggression. At least so called by some of my friends. And us hardly bloodied in Sicily. So back home again to join whichever side we chose, as carefree as boys about to do a game of mumblypeg. I ended with the Third Arkansas Infantry, C.S.A. Because, like my Da, I found meddling in local affairs by the Yankee government distasteful, it was the South for me.

Before it finished, it was a war to free the black slaves, and that at least, said my Da, was good. He never held with human bondage. But he never before or after lost any love for the Federal government, either. Often I'd thought it broke his brave heart when his eldest son ended up working for that same government.

That war, better forgot! It was more than just the killing of horses. All I ever wanted to recall was that during its course I was close enough to see General Lee at least three times, and once, in the Wilderness, just before we went in, close enough to touch the bridle of his horse.

The war took the spunk out of me. Maybe it was the wound at Spotsylvania. My collarbone was shattered, and through the years it pained me. Maybe it was the slaughter all around. Maybe it was just the time to change. There was a dash of cold water on the old fires, for whatever reason.

But the wanderlust was still strong. I was always sorry I hadn't made the gold rush in New Zealand, but by then I was involved with Bobby Lee and Virginia. Then the Federals bought Alaska from the Russians and I wanted to go there, but the Indian frontier already had its

grip on me. That was a love affair, next only to the early
hell-raising days and then, later, Augustina.

I met her on one of my infrequent visits back to the
Ouachitas. A fine Welsh girl who struck me like a bolt the
moment I saw her, although my mother always said she
was plain and lacked a spark of fire. I didn't agree. It was
a Sunday dinner on the ground at the little hillside Methodist church where Da had become a member of the
Board of Stewards. It was after I'd been to the great Medicine Lodge peace treaty meetings and seen much of
Texas and New Mexico Territory, at least as much as
Taos.

I was a rough-looking lot that day, uncombed beard
and a buckskin shirt with fringes like the native savage
wore. And a Navy Colt revolver in my saddlebags, although I don't think anyone knew about that. And I
likely smelled strongly of horse sweat and woodsmoke
and a few more things impossible to wash out with simple
bathing.

By then I'd already established myself at Fort Sill,
I.T., as a pretty good interpreter, having learned the Comanche language from Phil McCusker. Just about any Indian found on the South Plains could speak Comanche. It
had been the trade language of that area for a long time,
like Swahili in some parts of Africa. I was general roust-
about for the Kiowa-Comanche agency and contract
worker for the army, expert with the lines, driving either
mules or horses.

Augustina was impressed with my credentials, none
of which I failed to mention, adding a few for full measure. So it was marriage, no hope for me of anything short
of that. Then the honeymoon on the road into Indian
Territory, hard wagon seats during the day, bright fires
and the wagon bed at night, with a pallet thrown across
the bags of grain I was hauling out to Fort Sill from Fort
Gibson for the army. There were seven wagons plus my
own, and a small detachment of escorting cavalry. But for
us, Augustina and me, there were only ourselves alone.

I told her about the harsh beauty of Sicily and the blue waters off Gibraltar and the snow-topped mountains along Raton Pass. And of course, there were the small whisperings of love in close embrace. Things that made me blush to think of, with the coming day. It's wondrous strange how a man can say things in the darkness that would never occur to him in sunlight.

She made no single complaint when she saw the miserable shack that would be home for us. She set to work with broom and scrub brush and needle and thread, and many's the time I took a ragging from the ruffians at Stoddard & Blanchard's store when I went in to buy flowered cotton bolt cloth for curtains and table covers and such.

Then the typhoid. A terrible time. Five people at the agency died. It was an empty terror because of the helplessness after Augustina and the rest were gone. It lasted a long time, my knowledge that a treasure was lost, never to be found again. A man must shed a tear now and then, especially the Welsh, so said my Da. And I shed more than a few and drank too much bad whiskey and managed to start a few fistfights, the first of that in a long time.

But finally the sun began to shine again.

There was the hint of coming moon in the east. Faintly I had heard the calls of sentries with each passing hour, their voices floating down from the fort compound like distant murmurs out of fading memories. So I knocked out my pipe and took a long stretch and looked once more through the darkness toward the fort and thought of those proud men who had been jailed in the icehouse. For only one night, but jailed just the same, like common criminals waiting for one of Judge Parker's marshals.

And on that night, with Kwahadi and his band out there somewhere in the dark, beginning a new life, there was a bit of the old sensation. Gone a treasure, never to be found again.

Taming of wild things had always disturbed me, maybe because I suffered the pangs of change from head-strong, impetuous youth to solid middle age. On that night in the stillness beside my shack, I had yet to perceive that some spirits are never really tamed. Only redirected in their power. At that moment I would have told anyone that I knew a great deal about Comanches. But my education had hardly begun.

3

It was four days after Kwahadi came in, and I was spending my leisure on a cool early morning at the Fort Sill stables, jawing with two of the troop sergeants. The bell in the fort chapel had just announced the beginning of Sunday services for those inclined to attend, mostly officers and their wives. The men I smoked with that morning were old soldiers and not too enthusiastic about sermons and hymn-singing.

I liked old soldiers such as these. Between them they had more than fifty years' service, and it showed in the scars and weathered faces that they wore. They were professionals, as cloistered in their way of life as monks, and they had low regard for the normal run of short-term soldiery and viewed with equal disdain those who rushed to the colors only in wartime.

"So you seen a little action?" one of them sometimes said to me when we were enjoying a sip together in the back room of Stoddard & Blanchard's store. "Well, you're just like the rest of them, Morgan. You never was a soldier. Just a Gawd damned armed civilian."

"True," I'd say. "But at least I came without being hauled in by the bureaucrats."

"Yes," he'd say, and snort. "Conscripts are worse than lice in hot summer!"

We were enjoying the quiet of that Sunday morning, my sergeants and me, smelling the wondrous perfume of fresh horse manure and sweet hay and the smoke of army-issue tobacco. But we'd hardly finished with our first pipeful when Toothpick Jehyle Simmons appeared, walking into the stable as though he were stomping poisonous spiders, glaring with his mean eyes and his mouth in its usual pattern of stern disapproval. He spoke without greeting or preamble.

"Morgan, those Antelopes who come in," he said. "They want a palaver with you."

"With me? To what purpose?"

"Yes, with you, and how the hell do I know to what purpose?"

There was an edge of anger in his voice, as there always seemed to be when he addressed me. A flavorless man, this Simmons, as though the sun had boiled all the juice from his bony frame. I never liked him much and often noted to myself that sometimes in sessions with the Panetekas he would tell Agent Harper things the Indians had not really said.

Simmons was one of a kind, in my experience. Most of the interpreters were either half-bloods themselves or else fully in sympathy with the people whose language they transmitted. But Simmons seemed to take it as a personal affront, always holding his long nose in the air when they spoke, as though there were a foul smell about. I had come to regard him as just another bureaucrat grubbing for his Federal money, not at all like Phil McCusker or Horace Jones.

Nor was I alone in my estimation of him. I was happy to see that as he stood there my two sergeant friends eyed him with distant hostility, as they might a skirmish line of enemy infantry.

"Then I'll ride out now," said I. "The good Weslowski has me scheduled for a run to Fort Gibson in the morning, so today's the day, and no waste of time about it."

"We want to know what they're up to," Simmons growled, shifting his feet with discomfort, the stares of the two soldiers unsettling him.

"Who might 'we' be?" I asked, already knowing the answer.

"Mr. Harper and me," he said.

And having finished all he had to say, he wheeled about in a flurry of straw at his feet and stalked out of the stable.

"That son of a bitch," one of my sergeants muttered, then leaned toward me and waved his pipestem in my face. "Look, Morgan, you be on the lookout, goin' alone amongst them red savages!"

"You think they sent me a special invitation to be scalped?" I said and laughed.

"Don't take it lightly," he said, still waving his pipe under my nose. "You never know what them heathen is gonna do."

It was clear and splendid that day, with summer coming on fast. The smell of things was exciting, and still more the prospect of seeing at close range the fierce and handsome face with the hint of gray in the eyes and a copper shine in the hair.

It was a pleasant ride on Deacon, my mule. My personal mule. That is to say, a mule not owned by the army or the agency, but by me alone. I never trusted horses. So it was always a mule for me when saddle riding became necessary and a choice possible. Mules are so much smarter than horses and certainly stronger, although with some of them there is always a problem of explaining who's boss. This can be successfully accomplished with a barrel stave. Discipline is not so difficult with horses.

There had never been any such problem with Deacon. He was a large dun mule whom I had bought from a Delaware. Deacon had been almost two years old then, and from the first we were friends, on a gentle basis with one another and no barrel stave necessary. For a year after I bought him, I half expected somebody to appear from the Nations claiming he had been stolen, but no such person ever came.

Kwahadi's encampment was about eight miles from the fort, and it was near midafternoon when I came in sight of it. I paused on a lift of ground some distance away to give them a chance to have a good look at me before I rode in. It was safe policy not to take these people by surprise, and most important when they had been so recently on the high plains and were sensitive to intrusion.

Looking at that camp was like a window opened to all the time of their life on the South Plains, because thus far they had not become diluted with white man's culture. No canvas. No log houses. No wheeled vehicles. The conical buffalo-hide tipis were strung along a branch of the creek, set among the small patches of post oak and blackjack. Many of the lodges were decorated with paint in various hues, circles and stars and animals. Not so imaginative as the Kiowas, I thought. But then the Kiowas were more taken to artistic endeavor, as with their sun dance calendars, now gone for all practical intents, because the sun dance had been outlawed by the bureaucrats.

There seemed no pattern to the placement of lodges. Among them I could see drying racks for meat, where a few pitiful strips of agency or army beef had been hung like wash on a clothesline. And pitifully few horses, too, and none looking any part the grand hunters or war ponies I knew these Comanches so valued. Their herd had been picked over to weed out the good ones, leaving them only the nags. I could almost hear Simmons croaking to Agent Harper and Colonel Mackenzie about the dangers of Comanche mobility.

It was a good campsite. There was sweet water and grass. This place was on the western edge of the cross timbers and marked by low trees, scattered along the streamlines. There were jays fussing from somewhere downstream, and over the more rolling country to the east was a single redtail, wings unmoving as he slid along the air currents, everything about him motionless except the turning head. He was hunting, looking for anything large enough to see and small enough to kill.

Even though still some distance from their camp, as soon as I started in easily and at a slow gait, the dogs came out yammering. I could see the women and children scurrying like waterbugs to the lodges, and soon all out of sight. The men came to stand motionless and blanket-wrapped even in the sun, watching my approach with the stillness of a tight-wound spring.

Before I came to the first tipi, an old man walked out to meet me, moving slowly and with his hair loose. Of all the men, he was the only one who did not hold his blanket over his head. His hair was not gray, but it was thinning, and I saw how old he really was when I drew near, the wrinkles about his eyes and lips like the eroded gullies running down into brown riverbeds. His eyes were dark, but with the glow of age rather than the sharpness of youth, and they were so bloodshot that there seemed no whites at all. His brows had been plucked, giving his round face the appearance of a wet and weathered disc of sandstone.

I drew Deacon in a few paces short of him and raised my right hand, palm forward, and spoke Comanche.

"I'm Liver. I've come to speak with you."

"I know who you are," said he, and I wondered how he knew. "Come smoke and have food with me."

I dismounted and the old man turned and I followed, watching his short-legged walk, a waddle like some blanket-covered duck. As we came near them, the half-circle line of men drew back, their feet not seeming to move. Among them I tried to find Kwahadi, yet did not, and knowing never to be too inquisitive on first acquaintance, I made no obvious effort at it.

Despite the old man's friendliness and the warm sun and no sight of weapons of any kind, I felt a tickle of foreboding run along my back. One did not walk alone among Comanches without such a thing happening. There was a certain smell to it all, plain to the nose, of smoke and cooking meat and horseflesh and something else impossible of identification, seeming dangerous only because it was the breath out of some other way of living.

And there seemed a certain embarrassment among them, at not being able to welcome me in the old way, with many ponies and war trophies at their back.

The old man led me to a newly constructed brush arbor, and there on the sandy soil we sat facing each other with legs crossed before us, and a woman came with the pipe.

When she handed down the pipe to the old man, stooping, I looked into her eyes, and I had never seen such cold fire in any eyes before. She was old, yet it was impossible to tell why I knew. For her skin was smooth as polished walnut, and the same color, and her hair shining black as a crow's wing. Maybe the hands, which were long-fingered and somehow clawlike and not so dark as the face, the flesh between skin and bone melted away. There was no friendliness in her gaze, yet it was as bold as any look I had ever had from an Indian woman. As her arms extended beyond the buckskin smock she wore, I saw the harsh scars across her forearms and knew she had mourned many of her people in the years gone down, and cut herself to prove it.

In that moment I knew she was the one who had ridden with the men, face black-painted, on the day they came in, and knew she was a powerful woman in this band. There was no trace of paint on her face now, only the hint of ocher in the part of her hair.

After that one steady look into my face, she turned and moved back through the line of men standing near the brush arbor and was gone. The old man before me slowly filled the pipe from a leather pouch that appeared between his crossed legs. His fingers delicately pinched out the tobacco and tamped it into the bowl, his head lowered, his eyes hooded.

"My name is Otter Tongue," he said, still working with the long-stemmed pipe. "We'll smoke a little now, in the shade. Then we can talk."

When he had the pipe bowl filled, he lit the tobacco with a sulfur match, his cheeks pulling in like a bellows. The dense blue smoke issued from the corners of his mouth, a moving veil, and after the tobacco was glowing red he lifted the pipe toward the sky and the four directions. He smoked a puff or two, and handed me the pipe. I offered it to the spirits, too, and he nodded his head in approval, a short, single jerk that made his hair quiver.

Like this village, he showed no sign of the white man. He wore a short deerskin shirt with fringes, open down the front for most of its length, and leggings to match. No decorations. It was a drab sand color. But his moccasins had tassels front and rear, probably buffalo tail ends, but maybe the hair of enemies, though I had never heard of Comanches wearing trophies of conquered enemies on their feet.

About his neck was a red bandanna secured with a polished joint of buffalo backbone, and hanging below that, yellowed with age, a pipestem-bone breastplate. It hung just above the protruding belly, like the half-raised curtain on a stage. About him was the smell of fat meat and a certain scent of sage, only faintly, a wisp of transparent smoke off some high plains fire.

"This is good weather," he said, which I expected him to say, knowing as I did that Comanches always talked of many things before coming to that which they really wanted to speak of.

"Yes," said I, "and the water still flowing well."

"Yes. It's good water here. Not much, but good. Not so long ago, our people came here often in the summer, during the hot seasons. And sometimes with the Kiowas, our friends."

"Yes, I know many Kiowas. But I have never mastered their speaking."

"It's a hard speaking to master," he said. "The Kiowas always talk to us in our own tongue. And often with signs."

He raised his right hand, short-fingered and somehow fat-looking, suspended as they were from bony wrists. He made a quick movement with his fingers beneath the right ear.

"Kiowa," he said, interpreting his own hand language, and there was the hint of a smile on his face.

"Yes, I know that sign." And I made the same movement myself. Then, with my own right hand palm down, I moved it across my belly, waving the fingers gently, like a snake crawling. "And Comanche."

"Oh yes. The Nermernuh." The smile was broad enough now to be called a smile, and in his old eyes there was a shine of friendship. "Like a snake going backwards, maybe. It's the same sign for the Shoshone, to many it's the same sign. So some white men called them Snakes, I understand."

"I have never known the Shoshone."

"They were our cousins," he said. "The grandfathers told us we came from the Shoshones' high mountains, and out onto the plains. You know that, of course."

"I've heard it said many times."

"It's strange, isn't it, how men sometimes go away from their cousins?"

"Yes, with white men as well."

"Cousins can be a hardship sometimes. Even enemies. The Utes, they were our cousins. But that was a long time ago. In the memory of this band, Utes have been enemies."

"It happens that way among white men, too."

"Yes, I've heard it said. You have many times fought among your own kind. As we have."

"Yes. Even brothers against brothers."

"I know of that time among you. But so far as I know, we have never fought brother against brother. It's a bad thing."

"So it's been said."

As the occasion presented itself, I looked behind Otter Tongue and along the line of men who stood immobile and watching. Still, I saw no one I could recognize as Kwahadi, even though I had the sense of his eyes on me. It was like standing near an unseen fire, feeling the heat without finding the source.

The old man smoked for a moment in silence. A wind had come up and it rustled the leaves in the arbor above our heads, little whisperings that he seemed to hear as though they were a part of the conversation. Then he lay the pipe across his knees and straightened his old shoulders and I knew the serious part was about to begin.

"I was a close companion of the great Iron Shirt. When I was much younger, of course. I served him as bodyguard and crier," said he. "And after that, the great His-oo-Sanchess. And then Kwahadi."

The names, as he spoke them, sent that wee shiver down my back once again. They conjured the image of horses running and war lances and feather-decorated shields.

"I've heard of those chiefs."

"We've heard of Liver, too, from our brothers, the Panetekas," he said. "We've heard that Liver is fair."

"I have always tried to be fair," said I, knowing now where he had heard my name.

"Our headman wants a request made of you. He has asked me to make it."

"I am ready for it," I said, wondering why he did not mention Kwahadi by name now.

He lifted the pipe from his lap once more and puffed it and handed it to me and I did the same. There was intensity in his old eyes and his jaw was hard-set. The sunlight filtering through the brush arbor cast stripes of brightness and shadow across his face.

"There was this lance," he said. "Taken on the day we came in. It's a very important thing to our people. It has much history. We would like to have it back. We have given our word to Mackenzie we will no longer travel the blood trail, so it would be harmless for him to give us that lance. And it would mean much to us."

"The hair from it was burned."

"I know. Our women saw that." There was a glitter in his eyes then, I couldn't tell of anger or humor. "The hair was important, too. But it's gone and doesn't matter now."

"The white man doesn't understand the taking of hair," I said, and knew the shine in his eyes was from something he found amusing.

"Some do. And other things worse. But now the hair doesn't matter. It's gone. But the lance. It was of the great Sanchess, and our people would like to have it back. It holds power for us."

"I understand that," I said, although I wasn't sure I did.

"It was a weapon carried by the man who leads us now, when he was a boy. I gave it to him with my own hands after the great Sanchess was killed by white men. It was a good medicine for that boy, and all the Antelopes recognized its power. Even before the boy went out on the mountains to seek his own medicine, the Antelopes knew that he would become a leader.

"He was a serious boy. He didn't play with the girls in the pony herd at night, as the other young boys did. And he was a good dancer. When the men and women danced, he would always be there close by, dancing alone and very serious. He had only fourteen summers when he killed his first buffalo, and later he was the best man in the band at taking buffalo with a lance."

Otter Tongue paused to refill the pipe, as though it

were a ceremony that required silence. Then he began again.

"On his first war party, he showed much bravery. Everyone knew he would become a leader. And he did. He was fearless, carrying the lance of Sanchess, and the other young men followed him when he set out on raids against the Utes and the Pawnees and the white men. The hair on the lance was beautiful, shining in the sun, making it a very special thing."

"Well, the hair has been burned."

"Yes, I know. But the lance is the important thing."

"They may have burned that, too."

"Did you see them burn it?"

"No."

"Sometimes the white man likes to keep trophies, as do my own people. Perhaps they have not burned it because they think it is the lance of Kwahadi. They saw him carry it in. But it was of the great Sanchess. We would like to have it back."

There was a long time of silent smoking then, and I took the opportunity to search for Kwahadi along the line of men, trying to keep my hatbrim low over my eyes. But I think the old man knew what I was doing, and there was the hint of a smile in his eyes, if not across his lips.

"Would you like to take some meat with me?" he asked.

"I would rather you fed the meat to your children."

"Aw," he said, obviously satisfied with my answer. "Yes, there's not much meat here, is there?"

"No. I would rather the children have my part."

"Yes. Children sometimes get very hungry."

Otter Tongue began to gaze intently at his moccasins, frowning, as though he were trying to phrase his next request. Perhaps he was allowing me the chance to look at the young men again, without embarrassment. Finally he spoke, without lifting his head.

"Now, about these horses."

He looked then toward the west, where the low jack-oak trees stood in the sun like dark green toadstools, frayed about the edges. It came to me that he was looking far beyond that, maybe as far as Llano Estacado and Palo Duro Canyon. Perhaps seeing in his old mind the buffalo, like a sea of dusty brown waves on a restless sea.

"There are not enough for our people," he said, his voice as far away as his vision. But then, almost suddenly, he turned back to me and there was a heated glow in his eyes and his white teeth shone as he peeled back his lips in speaking. "Not enough for everyone to ride. And too many mares. No stallions at all, only mares and a few geldings."

"I'll speak with Agent Harper. Maybe they've already sold your other horses."

"The Panetekas tell us this is not so. They are still in the stone corral. We need some of those horses. Our leaders should not be ashamed to ride among the people. They should have stallions."

"I'll do what I can."

Somewhere nearby, a cock cardinal made his sharp call, and Otter Tongue turned his face toward the sound.

"Soon he will be with his wife," he said. "The red bird is like our own young men used to be, with black paint on their faces for war."

He let off a short burst of laughter, as though he had made a great joke. Out of courtesy, I laughed with him.

"But then, the red bird is not brought into a place by the white man and told that he cannot make war again. Sometimes he does, you know, when another black-faced warrior comes on his ground. A good fighter, that red bird, when he has to be. But we are not talking of birds, are we? We're talking of men."

Abruptly he rose, as though I'd offended him in some way. He moved from beneath the arbor and I scrambled to my feet, thinking how awkward I must seem to this old man, who, despite his fat, moved with some secret grace.

A Comanche boy brought my mule, leading him

with distaste plain on his face and perhaps hatred in his eyes. The boy handed me the reins, careful not to touch my hand, then quickly ran back through the line of watching men.

"You like to ride that mule?" Otter Tongue asked.

"I find him good enough for me."

"We find horses better." He stood facing me, his arms folded across his ample belly and telling me with his eyes that this talk was finished.

"I'll see about those things for you," said I, and feeling embarrassed to have been dismissed so suddenly, me and my mule together, I mounted.

"Remember, Liver," he said, standing at my stirrup. "We are not like those birds. We have put aside the black paint. You must show us the right road. But we'd like to have that lance and those horses."

So I turned Deacon back toward Fort Sill, feeling until I was out of sight those eyes on my backside. The mule felt it, too, or maybe it was my own nervousness that made him pull hard on the bit, trying to break into a run. But I held him back. To the Comanches I wanted to appear as calm and self-assured as that old man had been under the brush arbor.

That night in my shack at the agency, I lay awake for a long spell, thinking about my little talk with Otter Tongue. And in my mind there was a vision of him as a young man, riding with loose hair and paint on his face, riding beside those chiefs he'd mentioned. There was a kinship between us, because I knew how he felt about those headmen. I knew the quality in his voice as he mentioned them, for it was much the same with me when I spoke the names of Bobby Lee or John Bell Hood.

I wondered what had lain behind those bloodshot eyes as we sat smoking. He had been direct with me about Kwahadi's request, as direct as any man can be. Yet there was something unsettling about it. As though things were hidden, his words and the impassive face, except for the little smile, a barrier set up between us clear on the surface but something concealed beneath, like sharp stakes below calm water.

When I slept I had the old dream I'd thought was long since gone. Back in the prison pen at Fort Delaware, my toenails rotting off from working all day in poisonous mud, the wound in my shoulder aching as the splinters of bone worked their way through the skin. I dreamed of the fat river rats that came onto the island in winter, and of how we killed them with clubs and roasted them.

I woke in a cold sweat and rose and went outside in my underwear to have a small pipeful of tobacco. Leaning against my doorside and watching the stars in the warm sky, I heard the chuck-will's-widow calling from the cedars across the road. He was there every night in season.

So, I said to myself, tomorrow, before I head out for Gibson, there has to be a small talk with Mackenzie about that lance and those horses. Straight to the real source of power around here. No need to make any argument with Agent Harper, with Simmons bending over his shoulder, hissing. I would jump the chain of command as any undisciplined soldier would do, and to hell with the bureaucrats.

Old Fort Gibson, on the Arkansas, was not too far distant from my Da's holdings in the Ouachita Mountains. It was no longer a real fort, but the army had established a commissary and quartermaster depot there. Some of the teamsters, as was their way in making names fit the case, called it the Coffee House. Of course, coffee wasn't the only commodity we hauled from there in our big-bed army wagons. There was feed for the Fort Sill garrison horses, salt and sugar, imperishable foodstuffs, either canned or dried. Without dry beans, many a good soldier would go hungry. And there were shoes and uniform coats and tentage, all used up by the army in quantities that would have shocked my old mother. But then my old mother always thought a pair of pants was something to be worn until there was nothing left to patch.

Gibson was almost two hundred miles in a straight line from Fort Sill, and a mite farther by wagon route. Our road skirted the Arbuckle Mountains on their north, and forded the Washita, then the Canadian, where the Shawnee Cattle Trail crossed the river. Sometimes in spring or summer when we were there, cattle up from Texas would be crossing, too. A more motley crew was never seen than those drovers. But God bless them all, I said, because I fought beside many a one from Texas in the old brigade of John Bell Hood.

After the Canadian, it was a beeline to the northeast and the mouth of the Neosho on the Arkansas River. And there was Fort Gibson.

A small detachment of cavalry always rode with us to discourage anyone who wanted to steal our mules. There was seldom any trouble, except that made by the teamsters themselves, getting into squabbles about a fifth ace coming from somebody's boot in the evening games of poker at fireside. These were usually settled after a few hardy licks were exchanged, with a lot of oath-making and empty threats. In only one instance that I recalled was there any bloodshed, and that minor, when one of the army contract men unsheathed a knife during a discussion about whether four of a kind beat a straight flush. He managed to slice himself along one thigh when the rest of us grappled with him to take away the blade and his unfair advantage.

Sometimes we were visited by Chickasaws or Seminoles and Creeks, whose countries we passed through. They were a different lot from the plains tribesmen. Most of them dressed like white men, except that a few wore blue jay feathers in their hair and mussel shells in their pierced ears. Most of them could speak English better than some of the teamsters or soldiers.

There were even a few now and again who claimed to have fought with the Confederacy, and with these I most naturally struck an immediate spark of friendship, because we were, as I explained to them, old comrades-in-arms.

All of which sat rather badly with my teamster mates, because they were mostly from Iowa or Illinois, and they or else their fathers had worn the blue. But my Yankee friends among them never gave me more than evil looks. My reputation with the left hook was known among them, and even though there were streaks of white in my beard, they respected the legend if not the man.

I did find it politic at times to soothe them all, along with the visiting redmen, with a few ballads sung at the campfire. Nothing calms the spirit like a good Welsh melody. Or, for that matter, nothing so much inspires the courage to combat. So much for contradictions.

The singing! It was strange to observe that among those of the civilized tribes, which were called that because they had taken the white man's road as no other Indians had, there seemed less affection for my singing than with the men of the wild tribe bands, most especially the Comanches. There were those to whom singing touched only the ear and not the heart.

But the singing. There was among the teamsters a young lad named Allis Featherman. No more than seventeen, a towheaded boy with eyes blue as the sea off Sardinia, slender and bony but with large and capable hands. He came from Sioux City, where his Da had made his way in late years selling and shipping such things as lumber and coal tar to the various army posts across Nebraska.

He had taken the wanderlust, much as I had in my youth, and come to the Indian Territory south of the Arkansas to make his fortune and find excitement. He lived in one of the shacks near Fort Sill, as did most of the army contract civilians. He was a natural tenor to my bass. He knew not a word of Welsh, but caught the tune each time and hummed behind my deep lead.

We had become fast friends, young man and old. It had begun one night in Stoddard & Blanchard's back room, where there was a pool table and games of dominoes and eucher and bluff. In one of these card games, Allis had become involved in an unfriendly manner with some of the ruffians who were always hanging about, he holding three queens to one of the other players' three knaves, and there was ill feeling when Allis pulled in the considerable pot of thirteen dollars.

So, on the evening in question, he found himself in peril of bodily harm until I suggested to the other players that all his winnings had been on the up-and-up and that he was, after all, only a tad. In the process of this explanation, the nose of one Rufus Tallbridge was broken and bloodied.

Rufus went about carrying two large Colt revolvers with bone handles, but everyone said he only used them in the dark of night, and then against unsuspecting victims. There were a lot of rumors about where his money came from, but he always had plenty, it seemed. Rufus was an ugly one, on sight and in soul, and looked even worse after his nose was rearranged.

So Allis became my good partner, following me about, and we often talked of things men talk about. I had the uneasy feeling that I was a replacement for that father he'd left behind in Sioux City.

He had been a favorite of Augustina. In fact, after he began to appear regularly at our shanty for the evening meals, it was her kindness toward him that helped dispel the terrible homesickness he suffered from, and I supposed at the time that had it not been for her, he would soon have left the wild frontier and gone back to Iowa. In time, he began to follow her about, too, and when he was in our home his eyes devoured her. Like a faithful dog or else an expectant lover. I thought many times that he likely loved her almost as much as I did, and there were flinty moments when I suspected that he would take whatever opportunity he might have of testing his manhood with her. But then, after such thinking I had to laugh at myself, imagining him at the mercy of her blows from the cast-iron skillet if he made such an advance.

At her funeral, when we buried her in the civilian cemetery west of the fort, not in the boot hill behind Stoddard & Blanchard's store, Allis wept as though it were his mother and sweetheart combined that we passed on to her glory. On that day I was ashamed of myself for ever thinking that he might have tried to force himself on her good disposition.

So Allis became a strength for me against the loneliness after Augustina was gone, just as she had been for him before. I began to teach him the Comanche tongue on evenings when he would come by, and we'd fry a pan steak and boil a potato and smoke. I suggested that maybe he should learn at least enough Welsh to support me in my singing in a grand manner, but although he took to the Comanche language quickly, he said Welsh was too much, and humming behind my lead would have to be enough. Allis had a head of his own, and once it was set, there was small chance of changing his mind about anything.

On the Gibson trip, after my talk with Otter Tongue, there was no singing, even though we were visited once by some Creeks at our second night's camp. I didn't feel like singing. I felt myself to be in the wrong place, and I could only wonder what was happening back at Fort Sill after my having gone to Adjutant Weslowski about the lance and the horses.

"Morgan, you act like you've got a bellyache," Allis said to me the first night out. We were unhitching my mules, Allis already having completed that task with his own team.

"Leave your elders to their proper thoughts," I said, grouchy as Toothpick Jehyle at his worst and feeling like hell for it as soon as the words escaped my mouth. I could see the hurt and humiliation on the lad's face.

"Well, hell's fire, you don't have to bite me so hard,"

he said, and stomped away, leaving me to do my own un-hitching.

It was a dismal, murky trip, as unpleasant as any march I'd known except maybe the one me and my comrades made from the Wilderness to stop Grant's flanking move at Spotsylvania. At least, on the day after our return to Sill it was ration day, an occasion that usually meant good feelings and festive activity.

4

Ration day! It was a carnival that happened once every fortnight, on a Saturday, when all the tribes came in from their settlements on the reservation. They came in long columns, the men in front and the women and children behind on the travois ponies. Everything was under the watchful eye of the army, of course, because it had been learned a long time ago that when a bunch of young Comanches came together, a little visible armed force was sometimes necessary to maintain proper order.

There was never much trouble. Just the soldiers being there was enough. Comanches seemed to understand fighting men, even though many of them never came to appreciate agents and other mufti-clads. Appreciating efficient enemies is an old soldier trait, as with us of the Army of Northern Virginia and the respect we had for the Army of the Potomac. A class to themselves, soldiers, and civilians are never wise to their thinking.

And Comanche men were all soldiers. Every boy born to mother among them was a warrior from the start, trained to protect and nurture his people. There was no other vocation available. It was the profession of all their men, and their pastime, too. Hunters and fighters, their men, as Phil McCusker always said to me.

So perhaps there was not so much freedom as we white men liked to think. No chance to be other than their fathers before them. But at least the wide space to do it in. The vastness. And until recently no intrusion of such things as railroads and coal smoke.

Isn't it strange, I always thought, how maybe if we'd had a little more space among us, we might have gone on being Welsh, there across the blue sea?

But, God, that's long past. And no comparison, really. Yet it was hard for me not to compare, being as solid-headed as I was about the English.

But now, ration day! In the early morning they began to come, so that by noon everyone had congregated. The travois ponies were aligned near the agency wagons, where the issues would be made. The women stayed there, just to the south of the agency buildings, for it would be they who took the rations and clothing.

Everyone waited, the women talking together and some showing off their new babes. Bright scarves everywhere and trade blankets and hair greased and combed. The men stood in clusters across the pasture, farther from the agency buildings, or squatted in circles where they gambled with dice or cards, a thing they had quickly picked up along the course of the white man's road.

Farther still across the pasture, short of the line of post oaks, the young men raced their horses. Wagers were made on each contest, even though they had precious little to wager. These young ones dressed much as they had in the old days, in buckskin leggings and moccasins and naked to the waist except for bandannas and a few with pipestem-bone breastplates. The older men wore hide smocks with fringes, and some were in white man's clothing. Their hair was mostly braided down each cheek with a war lock in back, unlike the younger ones, who wore their hair loose, defiantly, with only the single small scalp-lock plait flying out behind as they rode.

The horseraces were straightaway, for a quarter-mile. The little Indian ponies were very fast at this short distance, some looking hardly large enough to hold their riders. As the races became more exciting, some of the younger women moved down close to watch and, with their eyes, encourage the riders of their choice.

Children were everywhere, flashing among the travois ponies and the skirts of the women and the dice games, their white man's clothes flapping, always too large for them. Dogs, too, yammering and chasing after the children, fighting among themselves, and copulating.

That was most distasteful to Mr. Harper, but although he might explain the white man's way to the people, he had no success with their dogs, so they went on as they had from the beginning, propagating their own kind in sight of all.

I'd heard Simmons say it many times: "Why don't they eat some of those damned dogs? Like the Cheyenne. Always complaining about not enough meat, and all their camps like kennels!"

"There is a taboo against dog meat among them," I always said, even knowing as I did that he was aware of it. But I liked him to think I was trying to instruct him. "Dog is cousin to Coyote, and he a small spirit god to these Comanches. You don't want them eating their spirits, do you?"

"Spirits be damned! They'll eat some of those dogs this winter, when the rations get short." He would glare at me, chewing on his bad teeth. "And the rations always get short in winter."

I could never argue with him on that.

But ration day! When the time came, usually about noon, Mr. Harper and Simmons and myself and other agency people came out with little army folding tables, which were set up at the tailgates of the wagons. There the women queued up, chattering still, but looking with their deep, dark eyes at the stuff stacked in the wagon beds, as though they hadn't been eyeing it all morning.

There was corn—which they would likely feed to their horses, despite Mr. Harper's best efforts to teach them to grind it and make bread—and sugar and coffee and salt and soap. And sometimes salt pork, which they would eat only if there was nothing else. And sometimes clothing.

That clothing the bureaucrats gave them was a disgrace. I had seen Confederate regiments long on campaign fitted out with better stuff, and nothing could get much worse than that. The men's suits were all the same size. They were very large, and of material hardly worthy of the name, like shoddy that would fall apart as the first raincloud approached. It came to me each ration day that profiteering by unscrupulous men was not relegated solely to wartime.

They were good in taking white man's clothes and turning them to their own way of dressing. The sleeves were cut from the coats, making vests. And the sleeves were then used as leggings for the children. The bottoms of the trousers were cut out, making leggings for the men. The bolt cloth issued for women was simply wrapped around the body, without hint of needle and thread, so that many of them looked like ladies of India. A strange irony, considering the name we had given these people.

Stockings issued to children were cut as well, making more leggings for the wee ones, and what was left provided mittens for little hands. Men's hats were given them, but they threw these aside. The time had not yet come when Comanche men would all wear hats.

Then the beef issue, the highlight of each ration day. Usually, the beef was issued on the hoof, thanks to the good Agent Harper's recognition that they needed some symbols from their freedom days.

In a large holding pen east of the agency buildings the cattle waited, along with the young Comanche horsemen, finished with their racing now. When the time came, all the people gathered to cheer on their own favorite hunters, and somebody from the agency or the fort would release the cattle one at a time.

Often, the brute wouldn't run. Wall-eyed and obstinate, it would stand there bellowing, and had to be hazed and kicked and blankets waved in its face. When the steer was finally set in motion, one of the young men would ride alongside, pretending it was the old days, pretending this rust-colored Texas cow was a buffalo.

They weren't allowed to use arrows or lances. I never understood why. Only pistols. And they were not so effective with these as they once had been with their own weapons. So there were times after a chase, and five or six shots discharged into the flank, when a cavalryman had to ride out and finish off the work with his heavy-caliber carbine.

As was the custom with Comanches, the men skinned out their own kill. Then the women finished the butchering and hauled off the meat. And then the feasting.

Feasting was an important thing to these Comanches. But it worried Mr. Harper. Because sometimes the meat that was supposed to last for two weeks was gone in a single afternoon, the roasts and steaks and ribs spitted over fires already set and waiting before the first of the cattle were released.

Well, at least on one day out of fourteen, everybody was happy and the bellies of the children were filled.

That first ration day after Kwahadi's people came in, I looked for him again. But in vain. He had stayed in his camp on the Big Beaver, or else so expertly concealed himself among the others that he became invisible. I suspected he had not come, his pride keeping him away. And maybe still sitting silently before his lodge fire, staring into the flames with those metallic eyes, the fury still hot in him for having to bring his people to the reservation despite all his best efforts to avoid it.

But Otter Tongue I saw, standing back from all the melee, watching with a frowning face, and I wondered what was going through his mind, to see his people reduced to paupers.

After my few duties, helping with the rations and the cattle and assisting Simmons in explaining to the new Antelope band exactly what was expected, I went to old Otter Tongue and raised my hand as I had on our first visit. A quick little smile played along the edges of his lips. He lifted his hand in greeting.

"Not much meat there to feed so many people," he said, directly to the point.

"The headmen in Washington are sometimes stingy with the money," I replied, but decided not to mention that some of the money meant for the reservations was siphoned off along the way by grasping bureaucrats.

I looked about for sight of the old woman who had brought the pipe that day in the brush arbor, but she was nowhere to be seen. Back in the Big Beaver camp with her chief, I thought.

Otter Tongue was dressed as he had been before. He held a blanket about his waist with one hand, and the old pipestem-bone breastplate was bulged over his belly. But now his hair was braided down either cheek, and at the back alongside the scalp lock hung a single hawk's feather. I knew that had been won against some enemy.

After his first sally about the lack of cattle, we spoke for a long time about things that didn't matter: the lack of rain and the heat so soon in the year and the great numbers of red-winged blackbirds that had appeared around the livestock to feed off the droppings.

Then I told him about the lance and the horses.

That had been a nervous task I undertook on the morning of my departure for Gibson. But it was not so difficult as I had supposed it would be. Lieutenant Weslowski was less stubborn than his reputation in dealing with civilians would suggest. But then, Weslowski had always been favorably inclined toward me because I was an old soldier. He was Polish, with corn-tassel hair and light blue eyes, and was built like one of the beer kegs kept secreted in the back of Stoddard & Blanchard's store.

And the lines of his face were as hard as the hickory staves of those kegs.

"The colonel's busy," he snapped when I requested permission to see the commanding officer. "What's your business?"

So I told him about the lance, holding back on the horses until I'd tested the temperature of the water.

"They've got a fair share of pistols and rifles for hunting," said he, glaring at me from behind his desk, which sat beside the door of the colonel's office in the post headquarters. "Why do you want to give them that old stick?"

"Their headman seems to think it has great power for his people."

His eyes widened and he stared at me for a moment. It was a cold and wintry look, hard as the saber hanging from a peg on the wall behind him.

"You talked to this Kwahadi? He's a man does little talking, from what we saw when he came to surrender to Colonel Mackenzie."

"Not exactly to him. But talked to one of his elder statesmen, I did."

Weslowski grunted and finally turned his eyes back to the papers on his desktop.

"I see little merit in it."

"A token it is, sir," said I. "To rest in a chief's lodge and remind them of the glory days."

"Glory days, hell! The glory days are finished for 'em, and it's the last thing we want to remind them of."

"The memories of such times do not fade with the posting of new rules and regulations," I said. "As with me. I can still see the lovely beard of John Bell Hood."

Weslowski was older than he looked, and had served with the Yankees' Iron Brigade before successfully transferring to a safer occupation. The cavalry! I was playing on his soldier's sensitivity for service long past.

"What's Harper say? Why come to me?"

"Because the Comanches said I should speak to the

soldier chiefs," I lied. "Because they said you would understand how a warrior feels about old and honored weapons, even when not planning to use them any longer."

"Harumph!" he said, or some sound like that, and pulled the white handkerchief from inside his tunic, where it was always waiting. He wiped furiously at his runny nose. Lieutenant Weslowski's nose was always running in the days of dust and flowering blossoms. "All right. I'll have a word with Harper."

He bent his head back to the stack of papers lying before him, stuffing the handkerchief out of sight with one hand, lifting a quill pen from a well with his other.

"Well, there's a wee mite more, Lieutenant Weslowski," said I, and his head snapped up and his blue eyes popped beneath those ragged corn-tassel brows.

"Reb, I don't have time for all of this." He always called me that.

"It concerns an important matter. Horses. The Antelopes think they've been given short change on the ones they have. From what I've seen, they're right. A gaggle of nags, not enough for all to ride, and no stallions."

"Sure, you'd give them their whole damned herd back, I suppose, so they can slip down south of the Red and do a little burning and cattle-stealing."

"No such thing," I said, and lied again. "They say they want a few stallions so they can breed a herd. Long-time horse breeders, they are. And a way to help them in the new life. Make a little money selling off stock to the Texas drovers."

Weslowski glared at me a long time. So long, indeed, that he had to retrieve the handkerchief once more from its place and blot the moisture from his mustache, corn-tassel, too, with the ends waxed and sprouting upward like tiny horns toward his eyes. I could almost see him thinking about how such a proposition would sit with Colonel Mackenzie.

"How many horses are we talking about here?"

"I'd say at least twenty," said I, boldly. "All stallions and young enough to stand stud!"

"Harumph!" he said again, daubing with the handkerchief. "More like two or three, I'd say."

"Surely not enough to breed a herd, that," I said.

He waved his hand impatiently, turning his attention back to his stack of administration.

"We'll see. And next time on something like this, go to Harper. You work for him."

"Aw, but I work for the good Lieutenant Weslowski as well, and for the army, struggling with those contrary mules of yours and those beastly supply wagons."

"Get the hell outa here, Reb," he said without looking up and in a gentle tone. "And next time, go to Harper. It's his job, taking care of those people."

"I'm here now only because those poor savages said soldiers would understand, being men who know courage."

"Harumph!" But very softly and not looking up.

"Oh, one last thing, Lieutenant Weslowski," said I. "If we're all still on this green earth come Christmas, I'd be glad to come 'round and do a few fine old carols for your annual officers' ball. A mite better singing than you'll get from any of these dough-mouthed cavalrymen around here!"

He leaped up, face aflame, his temper completely gone with all my soft soap, scattering the papers before him like autumn's dead leaves.

"Out, God damn it, out," he shouted.

"Yes sir, yes sir," I said, bowing with the same sort of obedience I'd have shown Bobby Lee himself. "But remember the carols, Lieutenant. A natural beauty of sound you can add to Colonel Mackenzie's ball. And no charge for the service."

I got out before he could yell again, hoping to have left the spirit of Christmas in his wicked Polish heart.

It took four days, so I heard later, for my request to filter down to the agency. And when I returned from

Gibson, I found a curt note left with the commissary storehouse sergeant, telling me to report to Mr. Harper with no delay. And there the gates of hell burst open and Simmons was on me like one of its skinniest demons.

"What do you mean, Morgan?" he screamed, spittle spraying from his harsh mouth. "What do you mean, going over there to the army and making such a fuss?"

"Not a fuss. A request," I said, giving him my brightest smile. "A request from the Antelope band."

"Don't you ever go to the Gawd damned army again on agency business, you hear me?" He was bent forward, his face near mine, and I could feel the hot air rushing from between his teeth.

"Mr. Simmons," I said, my smile gone now and placing a hand gently on his chest. "I have never enjoyed having a man breathe on my face."

Simmons saw the change in my expression and gauged it properly. He stepped back quickly, like a bird hopping, taking himself out of range of my left fist.

"Well, by Gawd," he sputtered. "They won't *get* twenty horses. They'll only get ten!"

Throughout all this little exchange in the agent's office, Mr. Harper sat uncomfortably, squirming in his desk chair. Everything about him and his office seemed to smell of oats and prayer books. I liked Weslowski's office better, where the odor was of sweat and leather and gun oil.

"It's a thing I should have thought of myself," Harper said, with no hint of reproach about my going to the army over his head. He was a gentle man, with his bald pate always shining and his brown beard constantly in need of a comb and scissors. Maybe he was too gentle to be in control of such men as the young Comanches. "They shall have their horses. Ten stallions."

And he agreed on the lance as well. With my own hand I took it from the ordnance warehouse that same afternoon and placed it in my shack to await the appropriate time. And the horses I selected myself with the assistance of Allis Featherman, for although only a lad, he was a good judge of livestock. Each horse was a young stallion, each well formed, and we tied a ribbon about the necks of those chosen, to show the ones not to be sold at auction.

So on that ration day, the Antelopes' first, I had news for Otter Tongue that I was sure would make him happy.

After the cattle had been distributed and killed and the roasting had begun at the various fires around the agency, I escorted the old man to my shack. My coffee was cold and harsh but we drank some anyway, Otter Tongue with a lot of sugar in his. Then I produced the lance from my back room and told him that his horses were waiting in the stone corral.

He stood for a long time before taking the lance in his hand. There was a gleam of moisture in his eyes that reminded me of many an old veteran I'd seen standing before his regimental colors. Then he accepted the lance and placed a hand on my shoulder.

"My people will always remember you as their friend," he said. "Forever!"

They liked that word, forever. Yet, often as I'd heard them say it, each time there came a slight lump in my throat. And each time, too, I believed they meant it. I have often thought that a white man doesn't really understand the meaning of that word. But the day in my shack when I gave Otter Tongue the lance of Sanchess, I was sure he did.

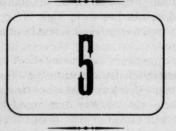

It doesn't rain much in August at the edge of the high plains. But it was raining that night as though the fates were doing what they could to mark it as something special in my life. It had been raining all day. Low clouds rushed across the land from the west, and the Wichita Mountains were lost in the dull gray of falling water.

I'd spent the day with Agent Harper and Simmons, going from camp to camp among the Comanches and Kiowas, doing our visiting duty and trying to keep our hats on our heads in the gusts of high wind. We were out on the reservation to see if everyone had enough to eat. Most of the bands didn't, and it upset the good Agent Harper almost to tears. He offered credit at the agency storehouse for those in bad need. On what collateral I had no idea.

Cornmeal and flour and dry beans were about all the agency storehouse could offer until the next consignment of contract beef was driven in from Texas. And the people living out on the reservation had little stomach for cornmeal or flour or dry beans. Sometimes I thought a Comanche would starve rather than eat like a dirt farmer.

It was sad, those people out there in their scattered settlements and huddled in damp tipis. They were a sun people, accustomed to good meat and bone-marrow soup for the children.

So by the time I got back to my shack at the agency, the day finishing off, I was wet to the skin and chilled even in August, and needed the inner strength provided only by a pint of bad whiskey from Stoddard & Blanchard's back room. It was my habit then of keeping such a commodity always on hand in my kitchen cabinet.

The fire was hard to start in my little cast-iron cookstove, obstinate until I dashed a dram of coal oil onto the wood and almost singed off the end of my beard in the flare-up of flame. There were fresh eggs procured the day before without requisition from the army's commissary warehouse, where such things appeared only in a blue moon, and then were mostly rotten. Cracking an egg at Fort Sill in those days was always an experience, waiting to see what odor issued forth.

With the eggs there would be a large beefsteak, well covered with pepper, along with hard sourdough biscuits left over from the night before. Making preparations for all of this, I was a little ashamed at the prospect of such grub, and all those red people under wet hide roofs with nothing. But in the army I'd learned that you eat what's at hand and worry about the other fellow only in prayer.

Nothing had ever been so sweet and secure as an evening coming into dryness after a day in the wet and wind, all snug against the elements and smelling coffee cooking and hearing the meat sputter in the pan and knowing the bread in the oven was growing hot. And on that particular night I was looking forward to the prospect of an hour or so reading the well-thumbed book *Hard Times* by Mr. Charles Dickens. The book had come to my hand from Lieutenant Weslowski after making the rounds of officers and their wives at the fort.

Weslowski knew that I enjoyed reading about the outside world. Sometimes I thought maybe he envied my having been to Europe in my young days and having developed a taste for letters. Mr. Dickens had become one of my favorites in the business of story-telling, even though he was English. But after all, I assured myself, the best writers cannot all be Welshmen like my friend Mr. Henry Morton Stanley, late of the *New York Herald*.

Mackenzie's adjutant was sensitive to others' needs. Everyone at the agency knew it was he who often took a collection of money from the officers of the regiment to buy foodstuffs from Stoddard & Blanchard's or the army's own commissary store to pass out among hungry tribesmen. Maybe he would be as kind to them now, in their need, as he was kind to me in providing *Hard Times*. It was a title appropriate for the Comanches, though they lived in an environment very different from Mr. Dickens's London Town.

But as it turned out, Mr. Dickens would have to wait, for after I had my supper brewing and my clothes changed and a drop or two of whiskey in my belly, the Comanches came. There was no knock at the door, only a low voice calling from the darkness.

There were three of them standing in the rain when I opened the door. Each held a buffalo robe over his head in the manner of a hooded monk, but as soon as the feeble light from my lamp struck them, the nearest pushed back his cowl and I saw the face of old Otter Tongue, his eyes shining.

"We've come to have a little talk, Liver," he said, and once more I saw that hint of a smile across his face, so elusive and hardly recognizable as an expression connected with humor. Rather as though on sight of my hairy face, he found something secretly amusing.

I invited them in, and Otter Tongue moved immediately to one of my straight-back chairs and seated himself, a little awkwardly, and let his robe slip to the waist. Unlike white men, he did not place his hands or arms on the table before him, but sat with his back straight, the lamplight shining on his round face, making the drops of rain running from his hair little glistening jewels.

The other two moved to the corner farthest from the lamp and squatted there. One of them slipped his robe back from his face as Otter Tongue had done, exposing high cheekbones, wide-set black eyes, and a large, thin-lipped mouth. He was a very hard-looking Comanche and in the strength of his manhood.

The other one kept his robe over his head, and it was impossible in that poor light to see his features. But I could see his hands, and they were slender and the fingers long, veins standing out like cords under the skin.

"I'm glad to see you," I said, taking a few black cigars from my kitchen cupboard.

"Well, it's raining," Otter Tongue said, taking three of the cigars placed on the table before him and turning in his chair, handing two of them to the figures in the corner. The other he clamped between his large teeth, peeling back the wrinkled old lips. I provided sulfur matches and we smoked, creating a dense cloud of blue in my small room.

"I have meat," I said.

"A little of that coffee I smell, maybe."

Bringing out cups, I poured a considerable quantity of sugar into each, along with the black brew. I offered them to Otter Tongue, and he served the two behind him—his bodyguards, I supposed, brought along to protect this old man against whatever dangers stalked the reservation. Not a bad precaution, what with some of the wild white men who hung about, stealing Indian horses from time to time and shooting off their pistols.

"I'll give you something to eat," said I.

"That might be all right," he said, blowing on his coffee to cool it. "Something to eat never hurt on a night like this one."

The old man placed his cigar delicately on the edge of the table and the smoke from it curled up past his unblinking eyes, lifting slowly like a pencil mark. I cut the steak into three equal parts, put each in a tin plate, and gave the whole of it to Otter Tongue. He passed two of the plates back to his men, and I sat down to watch them eat. This is no casual thing, I thought, coming out into such a night. So I waited as patiently as I could for the purpose of the visit to be revealed.

The steak was very rare and soon gone. Otter Tongue chewed a long time on his last bite, the muscles along his cheeks working slowly, then he licked his fingers and nodded, his eyes blinking rapidly.

"That's good meat," he said, picking up his cigar once more. "Not buffalo, but good meat."

A sudden burst of windswept rain rattled against the shingles overhead, and Otter Tongue gazed up, a trace of irritation on his face, as though the bad weather was a particular annoyance to him at that moment.

"We were glad to see the agent today," he said finally.

"He's a good man."

"So we've been told."

We smoked and sipped the coffee, and the fire in my stove made a rushing sound as wind gusted across the chimney pipe that ran in a black column from the stove up through the roof and into the night beyond.

"It's a long ride from your camp in such weather," I said.

"Yes. A long way on such a night as this."

"You can sleep here the night on the floor."

"It's not necessary. Our people are accustomed to moving about even in this kind of weather."

In the room was that familiar odor they always brought, a pungent but not unpleasant smell of smoke and cooked meat and horses. And I was sure they could detect some particular redolence of white man about me, too.

Without further preamble, Otter Tongue took from some secret place in his robe a long feather. He placed it on the table before me.

"I have a gift for you," said he. "It comes from the hand of our chief. Because of the horses and the lance."

It was from the tail of a Cooper's hawk, shining gray in the lamplight, with bands of black. The vane looked polished, as though it had been oiled and groomed carefully by one of the band's women. I lifted it in my hand.

"This is a good gift," I said, turning the feather so the light struck it. "I know the value your people place on feathers."

"Yes. To show courage. There are many kinds of courage, and not all of them have to do with facing an armed enemy. Sometimes the unarmed ones are equally dangerous."

"It was a small thing."

"No, horses are never small things to my people. Nor was that lance of Sanchess."

"I'll hang it on my wall to admire," said I.

"No, wear it in your hat. I have seen some of the white men with feathers in their hats. Although I don't know that these signify courage, as this one does."

He lifted his cup to his face and sipped loudly, then turned it up and finished the coffee. Slowly he placed the cup on the table, staring at it as though saddened. Then, with the tips of his fingers he dipped out the remaining sugar that had settled to the bottom of the cup and ate that.

"I have more coffee," I said, starting to rise, but he lifted one hand and shook his head.

"No. We thank you for hospitality already shown us. Now it's time for a little talk."

He sat back straight in his chair, head up and eyes focused above my head, as though he were about to speak to a large council of his people.

"A long time ago, we went to visit the Kiowas in the season of their summer celebration."

"Their sun dance," said I.

"Yes. It was on the Washita, I think. It was a long time ago and my memory is not what it once was. The

Kiowas called it the Sun Dance at the Bend in the River. Or something like that. Sometimes we have trouble making out what the Kiowas are saying."

He bent toward me, a twinkle in his eyes.

"We have never had a sun dance," he said softly. "We have always believed a man must come to his power in his own way, not under the eyes of many bystanders."

"It's my belief as well," I said, remembering Da's disappointment when I did not become a regular member of the chapel, or whatever it was he called it. Maybe I should have explained it to him as Otter Tongue had just explained to me.

The old Comanche seemed pleased with my words, and once more he leaned far back in his chair, his eyes still shining, his belly protruding under the buckskin smock and the pipestembone breastplate.

"Well, all white men don't think as you do," he said. "We have these priests coming among us, the ones who want us to worship their gods and in a large group, with singing and reading from a big white man's book."

"Missionaries," I said. "They mean well and have your people's interests at heart."

"I'm not so sure about that. They don't understand anything about my people and even less about our gods. But now, that sun dance."

He drew a long puff on his cigar and blew the smoke gently toward the ceiling, as though offering it to the spirit of the night outside.

"In that season, we had a child with us. She was a white captive child taken by the great Sanchess the year before."

Now he'd hooked me like a fish. Until then, I had supposed this was just more idle conversation. And the uneasy thought came to me that maybe the hawk's feather was only an opening gambit, like one of those I'd seen made with chess pieces when a Mississippi river captain taught me the game of knights and castles and bishops before the war.

Otter Tongue was watching me closely, and I knew he could feel my anticipation. He laughed—a short, hard cackle that was gone almost before it started.

"You people are always very concerned about white captive children, even from a long time ago."

"Of course," I said, recalling some of the lurid accounts I'd read of whites who had once been held captive by the Indians. "Weren't you concerned about your own children captured by the Pawnees?"

His eyes widened and he laughed again.

"Yes. Or the Apaches or the Utes or anybody else. We understand that. But now, the sun dance."

He puffed furiously on his cigar, and it burned down almost to his lips. Then he stared at it a moment and dropped it in my ash bucket beside the stove.

"That sun dance was a few seasons after the year the stars fell. I don't remember how many seasons. But after the stars fell. And this child grew into the band and became one of The People."

He paused and looked into my eyes with a hot intensity, and I knew he knew my heart was thumping. I had no idea why I was so affected, but maybe it was because of the strength of his voice when he spoke of the white captive child.

"This child who grew to womanhood among us became the mother of our last great chief. He was a fine child and was soon playing in the pony herds and learning to use the weapons of his grandfathers. I've told you about him before."

"Yes. He carried the lance when you came in."

"That's the one. Kwahadi. Now about that white captive child who grew to womanhood in our band. She was recaptured, we think. In a white man's raid on our camp. We were Nakoni then, but those of us who were left after that raid, we went to the Antelopes and have lived with them ever since. It was good, because our headman, who was only a boy when we joined the Antelopes, bore their name. And still does."

"Kwahadi!"

"Yes. Kwahadi."

"I had heard his mother was a white woman," I said, and somehow my voice was thick. Immediately a thousand questions came to mind, but before I could ask the first one, Otter Tongue was up, quickly, as though to forestall me.

"She was born white but she became one of The People."

The two men behind him were on their feet, moving to the door so quickly they left me sitting there on my arse, glued to my chair, it seemed. They were out into the night then, except that in the open doorway, Otter Tongue turned as he adjusted his robe over his head. And now there was no doubt about it. He was smiling.

"Our headman would like for you to find out where his mother is now!"

I jumped to the doorway, but looking into the rain I saw nothing of them going, only the darkness; they had disappeared as quickly and quietly as large shadows. I didn't even hear their horses as they rode away.

Mr. Dickens was forgotten. Even the fresh eggs were forgotten. When captured? When retaken? Where? Otter Tongue had mentioned the year the stars fell. Everyone on the frontier knew when that was: 1834, when there had been a large display of meteors. And he'd mentioned the name of a Kiowa sun dance. Bend in the River. I found a small pad of paper in my kitchen cabinet and wrote down all I could remember of what he'd told me. There wasn't much, so I gave it up in disgust and went to bed without any supper.

The next day, Jehyle Simmons found me hauling some lumber to the new icehouse. He told a story of an old Comanche coming in during the early hours of the morning to talk about the ration rolls. Each man in the various bands was listed by name. The women and children were identified only by number.

"This old man asked us to change the name of his chief on the rolls," Simmons said sourly. "Kwahadi's name."

"What change?" I asked.

"Not a change, really. An addition. He said his chief wanted to be known from now on as Kwahadi Parry. Trying to curry favor, that red butcher is, using a white man's name just because his mother was white. At least, that's what they say. And the old man said it, too. He said his chief wanted to take his mother's name. Son of a bitch, just trying to curry favor. Mr. Harper wanted to know what you thought about it, you being so cozy with that outfit."

"He can take any damn name he pleases," I said. "Others have done the same thing."

And said no more. It wasn't a time for me to be talking or thinking about those Antelopes. Not even this little game of Kwahadi, playing hide-and-seek with his mother's name and Liverpool Morgan being "it." I could almost hear Otter Tongue saying, "You're it, you're it." Like a precocious child trying to make a fool of some doddering, senile old man.

After Simmons and I parted, it suddenly came home to me. I had no idea why. But the evening before, with Otter Tongue sitting in my shack and drinking my coffee and eating my beefsteak, there had been the whisper of some wind I couldn't put my finger on, a sound unheard. But now I knew, as sure as my name was Morgan, that the man squatting in the corner with the blanket over his head had been Kwahadi! It infuriated me, his coming to my place and watching me talk without ever raising a voice of his own.

And I recalled yet again what Phil McCusker had always said: "You'll never really understand them. The longer you work at it, the more you'll realize how much you don't know."

6

In the old Texas Brigade of John Bell Hood, there was a man named Burton who claimed to be an Indian fighter. There were many such men in the Texas regiments. This one was also a barber. Often at night, in the winter quarters behind Fredericksburg in sixty-three, he would come to the poor huts of the Third Arkansas to cut our hair and talk about Comanches.

A dozen years later, I recalled some of his words. He said the Comanches tested their captives for strength and endurance and courage to see if they were fit to become members of the band. Those who failed the test were kept only as slaves or else sold off to other tribes or to the white man, so Burton claimed. We never knew if what he said was true or if he was only spinning frontier yarns for the benefit and amazement of those of us who then had never seen a high-plains buffalo hunter.

Later, many accounts of Comanche captives were published and each of these seemed to confirm the barber in what he said.

At Fort Sill, they were past the time of testing captives for the qualities they wanted in their own people. But the impulse surely remained, perhaps inborn, as natural to them as their black eyes, stringing out a person to feel the texture of his fiber, *like the prophets of old stirring the entrails of goats. And they were stringing out Liverpool Morgan to see if he was really worthy, with more substance than the mere ability to have a few horses and an old war lance returned to them. So the feather was only payment for something still due.*

Yet there was honor to it. For they had not approached some bureaucrat or white soldier to gain their ends. And these were important ends. Kwahadi would never have gone to so much bother or spent so much time planning, had it not been of intense concern to him. And because of him, to the rest of his band as well. They were not looking for a white woman, either. To them, and most especially to Kwahadi, she was not white. She was a Comanche, and perhaps that was even more important than the fact that she was his mother.

The old man had told me very little. Certainly he knew more. So they were paying out only a little line to see what might be caught, before revealing any more.

It was in that time, after the affair of the feather and my feelings bruised at being so used and still angry with them, that I came to some small appreciation of their chief. It was elusive, like smoke so thin it cast no shadow. And even though I began to comprehend a small bit of it, there was no comprehension of the depth of Kwahadi's intensity in searching out his mother's joys and sorrows after she had been recaptured and the two of them separated.

Yet, even though I began dimly to perceive these things, it was very disturbing to have my entrails examined.

And therefore I could appreciate what that white child had gone through, although mine was no ordeal at all compared to hers, I was sure. And perhaps because he understood what had been required for his mother to pass the test before she could become his mother, Kwahadi felt himself to be not half-white, but whole Comanche.

It was a long time after I tacked the hawk feather to the wall of my shack before I saw Otter Tongue again or any of his people, because Fort Sill was busy that fall and me with it. And there was one personal affair that took me away for a time.

It was not only busy but eventful. The sensation at the fort that season was when some of the wild tribes' young men stole all the horses and mules the army had in the stone corral. There were sentries posted that night, but all they could tell of it afterward was that suddenly the gate was flung open, the bar obviously slipped off from inside the walls, and everything ran out, hurried along by parties unknown who rode skintight against the animals' necks and making little yipping noises.

Rumor had it that the Kiowas had done it. But I suspected that a few of those horses ended up in the camp on the Big Beaver, spirited away to hiding places in the breaks along the creek when anyone from the agency approached.

Agent Harper and Simmons made some visits to Kwahadi's camp that fall because of the horse raid and because there was the belief between them that some of the young men were riding south of Red River to take cattle.

There were the usual alarms raised in Texas about Indian rustling, but nobody ever proved Kwahadi's people were involved. A hard thing to prove. Each time Mr. Harper and Simmons appeared to make a census of young men in the band, they were frustrated through one ruse or another.

"They've gone out to hunt," the elders would say.

Or, "They're all visiting our cousins, the Tenawa."

And Toothpick Jehyle would gnash his teeth and spit.

"There's always meat hanging on the drying racks," Simmons complained to me once, after a fruitless trip to the Big Beaver. "Where the hell does it come from, if not from Texas?"

"Sure it is that you people at the agency don't issue them much," said I.

"We issue them what we've got!"

"And never enough," I said. "What's the harm if they take a few cows in Texas? They're not down there taking hair."

"By Gawd, they're not supposed to leave the reservation without Mr. Harper's say-so."

"For the sweet sake of Jesus, man, if you saw your children hungry, wouldn't you drift off to find them meat?"

"Corn, Gawd damn it," he shouted, turning away from me in disgust. "The damned heathens have got to learn to eat corn!"

Had the chance come my way during that period, I would have warned old Otter Tongue about the trouble they might be making for themselves. I was still considerably miffed at their placing on my shoulders the responsibility for finding a recaptured white woman, but not upset enough to want some of their young men ending in a white man's jail.

But the chance never came, because the letter did. It was from the Ouachitas and it meant quickly settling my affairs with Weslowski and Agent Harper for a short spell and taking Deacon from his stall and making a beeline for Arkansas.

The letter was only a week old, which was better than usual. The mail service to Fort Sill from the outside world was not the best. The Missouri, Kansas & Texas railroad was already in operation along the old Texas Trail through the Indian Nations, from Chetopa, Kansas, all the way south to the Red at Colbert's Crossing. There was a stop at Boggy Depot, not far from old Fort Washita, and that was where most of the Fort Sill mail went into a stagecoach for the rest of the journey west.

Fort Washita had been abandoned a while ago. It was established back in forty-one to protect the newly arrived Chickasaws from marauding Comanche bands. I suspected that old Otter Tongue knew all about it.

But the mail. Stoddard & Blanchard, of the mercantile business, ran a weekly coach from the front porch of their store to Boggy Depot, carrying various passengers. These were usually replacement officers and maybe their wives, a few drummers, and some missionaries coming to save the savages from perdition. And on each trip, this coach carried the Fort Sill and agency mail. Stoddard & Blanchard had a contract for mail hauling, showing their friendliness in high places, which had brought them their license to trade with reservation Indians.

Sometimes one of their regular drivers would be holed up with a woman or have a rock-splitting hangover, and they'd hire me to drive their coach. Some coach it was! A regular wagon without springs and fitted with a tarp covering and rough oak seats. But the horses were top rate, so even though the journey was a little over a hundred miles, with changes of teams twice along the way, the round trip usually took only a week, precluding tornadoes or high water at the Washita crossing.

The officers at the fort maintained a subscription to the *New York Herald,* and when I took the run for Stoddard & Blanchard, the newspaper provided good reading in the evenings when I stopped on the way back from Boggy Depot. It was strange how old acquaintances leaped off the page of that newspaper to delight my eyes. There was, for example, Mr. Henry Morton Stanley, a good Welshman. Some said he was only a bastard, which I said was no blink on a man, his having had nothing to do with it.

I'd met Stanley at the treaty councils on Medicine Lodge Creek in Kansas. That was in 1867. He was part of the large press corps who'd come to the wilderness to report on the talks with all the wild tribes south of the Arkansas. The quartermaster for the peace commission had a special tent raised for them, which he kept well supplied with canned lobster and small kegs of whiskey.

Each night the newspapermen would gather there and talk and smoke and drink. They told tales of how they'd ridden out onto the prairie to find an old Kiowa sun dance lodge, which they had pilfered of ornaments.

Or of how the Indian women came through their camp each day to collect letters and other paper to be placed in the shields of their menfolk, thus providing depth and strength. Or of how Major Joel Elliot of the Seventh Cavalry escort took his task so seriously. Elliot would die the next year at the Battle of the Washita.

It was a place toward which I naturally gravitated each evening, that press tent, where I could enjoy the company of literate men. But, maybe even more, to enjoy those wee kegs of whiskey, since in those times I was addicted to such things. It was at Medicine Lodge that I learned there is no better companionship than that of newspaper writers, if one wishes to imbibe.

The other news writers called Stanley "Spooner." I had no idea what it meant, but knew it was a demeaning handle. Spooner was somehow not a part of them. He was a quiet, standoffish man. As the others displayed their talent at jokes and tall tales each evening, he sat on a camp stool in one corner of the press tent with a quill pen, writing his long reports on page after page of foolscap, of which he had an inordinate supply. Then, in the morning, as sure as the sun, he would hand his packaged sheaf of papers to the mounted army courier who rode each day to Fort Harker, where the Kansas Pacific railhead was. Only then it was called the Union Pacific, Eastern Division.

Stanley worked for the old *St. Louis Democrat,* but he sent copies of his stuff to Mr. Horace Greeley and it was published in the *New York Tribune,* and there seen by James Gordon Bennett, who ran the *Herald.* So, after the treaty councils were finished, Stanley was invited by the elder Bennett to become a *Herald* man, then was dispatched to Abyssinia and other African places to report on the various wars there, and in his spare time to look for missionaries lost in the jungles. He found one, too, whose name was Livingstone.

Old Spooner liked the smell and taste of new places, just as I had in my youth. It put us close together, so I always reckoned, and many's the time I thought maybe I'd just sail off to Africa and join him in his search for rivers and lakes and mountains no white man had ever seen before. The *Herald* continued to describe Stanley's travels, even after he joined some English geological society. Once a *Herald* man, always a *Herald* man.

Newspapers and periodicals kept me aware, in those days spent in the wilderness, of what was happening in the outside world. Mr. Tweed of New York City carried off to the penitentiary. The Eads Bridge, of steel and concrete, being built across the Mississippi at St. Louis. The assurance that worms could be cured in humans as well as horses by daily doses of Dr. Morse's Indian Root Pellets. Most of all, though, they kept me in touch with old enemies and friends, such as U. S. Grant in the White House and Bobby Lee at that college of his in Virginia.

And Spooner. It made a good feeling inside me, knowing that this strange Welshman had made a go of things, bastard or no.

It was amazing to be among a people like the Comanches, who until so recently were as they had been for centuries, without metal or wheels or domesticated food animals. And meanwhile, all the marvelous things happening to the rest of the world, like the construction of bridges and big buildings and railroads and steamships. All signs of great industrial progress.

Well, maybe not so great to the Comanches, who had other ideas about progress than the white man did.

As chance had it, I was on the mail run when my letter came; it was in one of the gray canvas bags until taken out and passed over to me, along with the rest of the agency mail, by Mr. Stoddard. It was postmarked in Fort Smith and it told me that my Da was dead and business required that I come at once.

So it was Deacon and the saddle and a long ride in autumn's chill, knowing I would not be there when they laid him in the ground.

There was a strange excitement about going home. Even though it had not been my home since I was a tad. Yet there was an excitement, riding up into the hills after we crossed the Poteau River. Everything was sweet-scented, and the pines left so much of themselves on the ground that Deacon's hooves made not the slightest sound in the needles. The air was brisk in that pungent-smelling shade, and the earth dappled with the light sifting through the branches like crystal shards fallen from the cold stars.

But any exuberance at homecoming faded swiftly. It was a nightmare, in fact.

Mother laid everything on the panic and collapse of seventy-three that brought hard times, and Da disillusioned and heartsick about the dream of his America gone to hell. She said he'd never been the same after the election to the Presidency of that damned Yankee, Grant.

In truth, he'd died of old age. He was almost ninety at his passing. And it was time to die, I thought, and a lot better doing it in the piney hills on the earth's green surface than in some flaming pit in Wales. No panic in money had laid low the man of the famous left-hooking blow. It was his time. He was fully twenty years older than my mother, and when I was born he'd been a man of fifty summers, and had fathered four more sons after me. Like one of his Old Testament heroes, some of whom, I'd been told, were still impregnating their various wives after passing a century.

But so much for Scripture.

I tried to console my mother, but I was like a stranger in that family where I had spent no time at all since a wee youth. And my four brothers seemed to blame me with their eyes for not having been around to help manage things, as though that might have stayed Da's course for another ninety years. Had I been, they would have rebelled against that, I supposed. Had I been, everything would have sunk quick, because figures and inventories and sales were always things as foreign and distasteful to me as Turks.

I visited Da's grave. He was buried in the little plot beside the church where I'd married Augustina.

And her family? They looked on me as though I were a visitation of the Black Plague, having taken their shining daughter among the savages, and her dying there alone and in misery. How could I explain to them how happy she had been? How can a man tell a father such things about his baby girl, when the die is already cast in his mind?

The mill was running well again, at least one portion of gladness, my brothers hard at it. A close-knit group, said I, and no real place for me, even had I wanted to stay.

I did stay for some time. There were a lot of legal things to tidy up. Deeds and claims and inheritance. Old Da had left no will. So it turned out that my siblings were wetting themselves about my showing up some day, maybe, to claim my share, destitute and ragged of trousers. No matter the assurances I made to the contrary, they wanted it all on a piece of paper.

And even Mother muttering, "A legal settlement there should be, it's true."

Where she came to think about things legal I didn't know. But I had some strong suspicions.

So we were off to Fort Smith, my brothers riding around me as though they thought I might try to escape. There was a document drawn in some musty office, with a lawyer behind his desk using words I couldn't understand, and finally I placed signature to the statement that I would hold no claim to anything called Morgan in the future. All that had been Da's would be shared by my brothers.

On the evening of that ritual, they turned home with faces dreary as priests at a sacrifice, even though I'd offered to buy them a good meal with some of the small money I had from the transaction. So it was a night alone

in Fort Smith, where I had started my wandering life.
The saloons along Garrison Avenue were boisterous and
lively, but I felt more lonely than I had since Augustina's
leaving, more devastated than I had been since watching
old comrades first begin to fall at Sharpsburg.

It wasn't because of the loss of a fair share of my
Da's holdings. I didn't give a good damn for any of that. It
was because of my reception among brothers who
seemed to regard me as a world-ranging felon who went
about setting fire to barns and molesting little children on
the street. We'd never been close, my brothers and I, because I'd flown from their nest when they were very
young, but blood is blood. It was galling to think that people who had come from my father's loins had less appreciation for such things than did a bunch of heathen
Comanches living penned up on a reservation in Indian
Territory.

In such a state of depression, I naturally found my
way into one of the houses of ill fame on Commerce
Street, and there sat in the parlor and listened to an Irish
piano player and marveled that a man in such a profession
didn't know a single Welsh ballad.

There was a young woman named Henryetta who
sat with me and we sipped costly brandy until dawn was
marking the windows with gray light. The old vinegary
spirit to do other than talk had somehow vanished, like
the fire and thunder from some forgotten battlefield. Of
course, I had to pay the house for the young woman's
company throughout the night, and it was very expensive. It was embarrassing, too, having that crowd of
whores eye me with suspicion because I wasn't randy for
one of the upstairs rooms and the activity that went on
there. But Henryetta seemed to understand, and I
marked her as a woman of great compassion, bound to go
a long way in her chosen avocation.

So much for my inheritance.

I returned to the hills after two days in Fort Smith,
to take on a little more of my mother's cooking before

departure. With Welsh hardheadedness, I insisted to myself that I was in no hurry to return to my Indians. That I
didn't care what was happening there and that old Otter
Tongue's charge to find some long-lost white captive
meant nothing to me. No compulsion of some savage like
Kwahadi would intrude on my civilized thinking, I said.
My concerns were only with that new steel and concrete
bridge in St. Louis and the coming Presidential election,
I said. But it was a lie.

I was itching for Deacon and the ride west, even as I
enjoyed Mother's rich squirrel stew with the tiny morsels
of red meat and the chunks of white potatoes.

When the time came, Mother melted into tears, putting up a terrible fuss about my going. It was a dismal
sight and hard on the ears, her wailing that I should be
close by to protect her from the savages across the line in
Choctaw Nation. And her surrounded by four other sons
weighing among them almost half a metric ton and own-
ing everything in sight besides. I didn't know what she
expected me to do if I stayed, except to beg for bed and
food from my betters.

It was the way of all mothers, I supposed, or at least
of mine. But I broke away from the tears and scolding and
departed, even shaking hands with each of my brothers
and telling them I admired their taking after Da in marry-
ing and having children late, but that whichever of them
had my first nephew, I would bring back a Comanche
scalp for the lad. That left them in shocked silence, giving me time to mount Deacon without further fuss and
get the hell off their mountain.

Just short of the Poteau River, I stopped at the shack
of a whiskeymaker I knew and purchased three half-
gallon jugs of white refreshment. He came from a long
line of whiskeymakers, and his product was the best I'd
ever tasted. He was a tad to the west of the Arkansas border, and hence living illegally in the Choctaw Nation. It
didn't adversely affect his efforts at the still.

Actually, I didn't *buy* the jugs. Rather I won them in

a five-card stud game in his lean-to kitchen, where we played through the night, the old man, his son, and myself. From the son I won a new .45 Colt pistol, a single-action with ivory handles. The old man took it all with good humor, but the son was beginning to act sullen and pugnacious by the time the sun came up, so I made my departure from there as quickly as possible.

Then it was on in a hurry, the jugs swinging across Deacon's rump and the revolver tucked snugly into my waistband under my overcoat. It was cold as hell that day, with high scurrying clouds that looked suspiciously like ice crystals shining beneath the sun. But I gave nature little of my attention and slept in the saddle as the good Deacon found his way toward the west.

When Deacon and I arrived at the agency about dusk of the third day after leaving Arkansas, Allis Featherman was found to have taken up residence in my shack. Only temporarily, he explained, so he could be there to welcome my return. He had a small slab of sugar-cured bacon and a stack of army hardtack hoarded for the occasion, and when he showed this provender to me, it was as though he had stolen the Crown Jewels of Queen Victoria.

"I didn't know if you'd ever come back," he said, grinning and fidgeting and pushing up the hank of yellow hair that hung in his eyes.

"Such small faith in me, then," said I, "that I'd leave old friends like you and the good Rufus Tallbridge alone without my company!"

"Rufus?" he asked. "That son of a bitch. He likely hoped you'd sunk in quicksand along the way. I bet his nose still aches from that night. You remember that night?"

"I'm afraid I do. And with small delight, letting my temper take charge of better judgment."

"Better judgment, hell," he said. "Rufus needs his nose touched a little bit more, if I see the right of it."

"Well, slice the bacon and start cooking, you young barbarian, before I waste away from hunger."

While the scent of cooking meat filled the shack, I did my unpacking and went to the shed to rub Deacon down and grain him. I wondered where Allis had come by that bacon and the army hardtack he was laying in the pan grease to soften. But sometimes it was better to leave questions unanswered. Yet I offered silent thanks to Weslowski's commissary warehouse for providing a homecoming supper.

Before we ate, there was time for a few sips of the white whiskey. Two of the original jugs of the three were left, the third having gone the way of good spirits on the road back to the reservation. As we drank, I cautioned Allis about the hardships brought on by good whiskey and bad women, teasing him to see his ragged-tooth grin and the ducking of his head in pleased embarrassment.

There was something he held back. I could feel it in his sidelong glances as we sat at Augustina's table, chewing the rubbery bacon. But I wouldn't give the little scalawag the satisfaction of asking, and after we'd finished and were having a second cup of coffee, it came clear.

"Ol' Toothpick's gonna come in here any minute," he said, and his eyes held a knowing glint.

"Simmons? To my humble palace? For what, then?"

"Oh, I guess he'd best tell you. He's been watchin' for you all the while."

"Well, it's nice knowing so many of you even realized I was ever gone."

Simmons came while we were still on the coffee. He didn't bother to knock, but opened the door to a cold blast of air and glared around like a bear disturbed in his sleep. Slamming the door behind him, he stalked in and sat down without invitation and plunked his bony elbows on the table. Allis was still grinning like one of those apes

I'd seen in the Philadelphia zoo on my way to Garibaldi, his eyes darting back and forth between Jehyle and me.

"Sorry to hear about your father passin'," Simmons said without looking at me.

"It was his time," I said.

I took another tin cup from the kitchen cabinet and Simmons poured himself a full dose from the pot that sat on the table. The whiskey Colt I'd won lay in full view on a wall shelf, and Simmons looked at it and grimaced.

"Going armed now, are we?"

"Only a small trophy from a game of chance," I said.

Simmons lifted his cup and blew into it and made a loud slurping noise as he sucked the coffee over his bad front teeth. In the process, his eyes met mine for the first time, hard and brittle, both of us knowing there was no love lost here.

"Good trip?" he asked.

"Not much of it."

"Shame about your father," he said.

"Only to be expected, with his years."

Simmons drank again, noisy as a sow at the trough. He was as unsightly as ever, peeling back his lips like a snarling mongrel.

"Well, you missed it," he said, placing his cup before him and gently pushing it away.

"Missed what, Mr. Simmons?"

"That bunch you make so much of. The Antelopes."

There was a small tightening in my gut because my first thought was that Simmons and Agent Harper might have caught some of those Big Beaver people with stolen cattle or maybe something even worse. But then I dismissed that, because under such circumstances I knew Allis Featherman wouldn't be having so much fun with all this.

"All right. What about them?" I asked.

"There was these young bucks," Simmons said, then drew a deep breath before he went on. "Half a dozen of 'em. One afternoon right after you'd left, they came into the agency store."

He glared at me squarely, as though I was supposed to make something out of what he'd just said. I felt an urge to grab his scrawny neck and squeeze until the seeds popped out.

"They were a little rowdy. Then they went away. But the next day they was back, painted up good, feathers in their hair, half naked, even after everybody's told 'em they gotta wear clothes like civilized people. They were doing a lot of yelling, insulting Mr. Harper. He said he'd call the soldiers, and so they left again, riding good horses, too."

The tip of his tiny red tongue flicked out, wetting his thin lips.

"Were they drunk?" I asked.

"Hell yes, they couldn't hardly walk, some of 'em. Painted like savages, loudmouthed."

"Where'd they get whiskey?"

He stared at me a long time, unblinking, as though I were some kind of simpleton.

"Damn!" he finally said. "How the hell do we know where they got it? But the day this all started, Stoddard & Blanchard had two fresh-butchered beeves out for sale."

Allis couldn't contain himself any longer.

"Stoddard & Blanchard's always got whiskey," he said. "Everybody knows that."

"Yes," Simmons said, fixing the lad with a harsh look. "But it ain't for the Indians. Anyway, they come back a third time," he continued, looking at neither of us now, but gazing off into the distance above my kitchen stove as though baffled, as though he couldn't believe what he heard his own mouth saying. "This time they raised hell. Wrecked the store, and Mr. Harper trying to get them out. They dumped stuff and pulled out all the bolt cloth."

Allis Featherman snickered and said, "One of 'em pissed in the dry beans!"

"Well," I started, but could say no more. Allis Featherman's delight was infectious, and as I drew a mental picture of that Comanche with the dry beans, it was all I could do to keep from laughing in Simmons's face. He ignored me, still staring off into space.

"Then the damnedest thing happened. Right in the middle of all that yellin' and tearin' up, in walks this Kwahadi. Just walked in holding a blanket around his shoulders and his hair all oiled and slicked down in braids and a white mark of paint on one cheek under the eye, like a big tear."

"Kwahadi? He came to the agency store?"

"I just told you. Gawd damnedest thing I ever seen. He didn't say anything, not a word. Just stood there in the middle of the floor. Didn't have a weapon on him that I saw. Just stood there and looked at all the stuff scattered around on the floor—"

"And the wet beans," Allis said.

"—and you never seen such a look as he give them bucks. They was six of 'em, and right then and there, they just ducked their heads and got the hell out in a hurry."

"But you're sure it was Kwahadi?"

"Well, hell yes," Simmons snorted, now glaring at Allis and me in turn. "I seen him the day he come in, and I was with him and that bunch of old men of his the day we talked to Mackenzie. It was him! And after the bucks had left, he still stood there a minute, looking at me and Mr. Harper, never said a word, then he just turned around and walked out. Not a Gawd damned word."

"What did you say to him? You or Mr. Harper?"

He shook his head, and the bewildered expression was back again as his eyes wavered from face to face.

"We didn't say anything. It was all over so quick. It was like . . ."

"Like what?"

"Like he wouldn't have heard anything we had to say. Like me and Mr. Harper wasn't even there."

It finally came to me that Jehyle Simmons needed a little more than coffee after recounting this strange tale. He was badly shaken, I couldn't imagine why, as though some door had opened and he'd seen something terribly frightening beyond. I even felt a twinge of compassion for the son of a bitch. So I took his cup and emptied it in my slop pail beside the stove and poured him some white whiskey.

Of all the people at Fort Sill, Simmons was one of the few I'd never shared a sip with. But now his need was apparent. There was nothing social about it. Allis and I watched him have his drink in silence, seeing the dance his Adam's apple did up and down the stringy neck.

"Well," he gasped. "You know those people better than me, so what do you think of all that?"

"I don't know Kwahadi. I've never talked to him."

"The hell you say." He was glaring at me, his eyes watery from the strong spirits. "Well, there's a lot more. Coupla days after this happened—"

"When they pissed in the beans," Allis repeated.

"—Stoddard's up at the fort, raisin' hell about this big Indian who come to his place with a whole string of young bucks behind him. All painted. Stoddard says this big one who had a spot of white paint under one eye walks into his store. All by hisself. So this big one says to Stoddard in English, if he ever gave any of his people whiskey again, the whole bunch would ride in and burn down his place."

"Kwahadi said that?"

"It had to be him. Stoddard was off the reservation when the Antelopes came in to surrender, so he'd never seen this Kwahadi before. But the way he told it, there ain't no doubt who it was. He just left his escort parked outside like a troop of cavalry and came in and talked English!"

"A lot of them know a little English nowadays," I said. "What did Mackenzie do?"

"Nothin'! And Weslowski did the talkin' and he told

Stoddard if he sold any more whiskey to the Indians, his license would be revoked. And Stoddard claimed he hadn't sold any whiskey to 'em. And Weslowski said Stoddard & Blanchard's was the only sure source he knew for whiskey on the reservation and that the next time any of that bunch from the Big Beaver got drunk and raised any hell, Stoddard would likely lose his license anyway and get his store burned down besides."

Now I laughed outright. Weslowski said that? Silently, I blessed all Poles.

There was no restraint left now. Allis was on the floor, laughing, tears running across his cheeks. Simmons acted as if he were beestung.

"I like Mr. Stoddard," Allis sputtered, "but can't you just see his face when that Comanche came in and told him he'd burn his store?"

"Shit's afire," Simmons shrieked, and jumped up and charged out of my shack, leaving the door open.

Allis and I got ourselves in order then and had some more coffee, half cold, but each time our eyes met we laughed like children caught in mischief. He told the whole story once more, and almost lost control again, and said it was a story all over the reservation now.

"It's a thing that should bring smiles to Comanche faces," I said, "in a time when there's not much for them to smile about."

"One thing I don't understand," Allis said, serious now. "The army knows about Stoddard's back room. And that it's illegal."

"Sure, but closing off all supplies of such things as whiskey and beer is bad for the morale of the soldiers," I said, having some wisdom in such things. "And Kwahadi knew he could make that threat about the burning, because he knows about that back room, too, apparently. So he saw the chance to show the white man that he's not a house dog trained to mess only outside."

"He what?"

"Hell, lad, look here, he had Mr. Stoddard in a vise.

And the army, too, in a smaller way. Nobody can take much action against him when all he's doing is threatening to control something the army and the bureaucrats should have been controlling all along."

"But how the hell did he know about that back room and what's legal and illegal?"

"You ask too many questions, lad. But I'm beginning to think that man might know a lot more than anybody around here gives him credit for. Now take this pot of coffee and set it on the stove and let's not hear more about it. My head's beginning to hurt, just trying to work it all out. But the best of it is that old Toothpick Jehyle is beginning to see some chinks in his armor of authority."

After Allis left for his own digs, tottering a little on legs made shaky from the white whiskey, and my lamp out and the fire in the stove going down with a last few dying sputters, I lay awake in the darkness, thinking about that Comanche chief. I tried to structure the features of his face in my mind but made a bad job of it. And it came to me that if he was intent on finding his mother, he would, whether I helped or not. Well, I'd always liked a man strong in his convictions, so maybe it was time to let the Big Beaver people know that I was hot for the search. At least within my limits and capabilities.

Before I slept, I noted that my chuck-will's-widow was no longer singing from the cedars across the road. He was long ago gone, and with good reason. The wind from the west had begun to make harsh little whispers under my eaves, the first messenger of the hardest months of winter just ahead.

Well, at least I felt that I was finally really home.

7

It was a hard winter that year, and the last of what came to be called *Mackenzie's Folly*. He wanted to make shepherds and woolspinners of the wild tribesmen. He saw the short grass across the land surrounding Fort Sill and believed it would be good for sheep.

A large flock was shipped into North Texas from New Mexico, driven by contract herders to the reservation, and then distributed to all the camps and settlements. It became a strange and somehow sad spectacle, all those disgruntled soldiers and agency people herding the shaggy beasts out to their new homes. The sheep were no less out of place on the terrain of western Indian Territory than were the white men playing drover to them.

In less than a single lifetime, that would change. But in the late 1870s, the land there was still pristine and from over every horizon one could imagine the great herds of buffalo appearing, grazing and almost indifferent to the half-naked people who followed them with bows and lances. And so both the cloth-clad men and the driven sheep with lineage back to Wales and Spain seemed to be searching for their time, like a clock whose face had been set spinning under the slowly advancing hands.

It was quickly apparent that the Comanches and Kiowas

were not interested in sheep. They didn't like the meat. They had no idea of how to go about woolgathering or weaving, and had no inclination to learn. Within a few days after delivery of the woolly creatures, the young men were using them for target practice, riding them down on ponies, bow and arrows in hand. The carcasses were left to rot where they fell.

Da often told the story of his time as a lad, already working in the mines, and coming home to the Morgan cottage, where the only food for the evening meal was a single baked ram's heart. He'd vowed that once on the shores of a new land, he would never allow mutton in any of its forms to pass his lips. So it was easy for me to understand my Comanches' loathing for sheep, even though their experiences were completely unlike those of a boy black and grimy from the Welsh collieries.

When Adjutant Weslowski learned what was happening to his commanding officer's sheep, he was furious and made many utterances about the savage redman. Yet there was nothing he could do about it, outside of providing each shaggy animal with a permanent cavalry escort. When it was suggested that he might send foraging parties out to collect the slaughtered sheep and bring them back to the Fort Sill messes, he explained with profane language that soldiers seldom had any more appreciation of mutton than did the Indians.

Before the first thaw of spring, all the sheep were gone. The wild brothers of the Comanches, the wolves and coyotes, harvested whatever had escaped the target practice.

During the warm seasons, there were cattle drives passing along either side of the reservation. The Chisholm Trail on the east and the Western Trail on the west, great unmarked highways along which the Texas drovers herded their charges toward the railheads in Kansas. It was a thing that created many a headache for Agent Harper, because these cattle were often grazed on reservation grass that everyone hoped would be saved for Indian horses and beef. But even more serious was the temptation placed before the tribesmen of a little close-at-hand moonlight looting.

It wasn't a bad situation, I thought, for with that many cattle so near, it wasn't a problem for the bands to steal a brute now and again. And sometimes the drovers paid duty of a few cows to any menacing bunch of Comanches or Kiowas who lurked about, thinking rightly that to give up a steer or two without shooting was better than getting the critters stolen anyway, and with the possibility of bloodletting.

My young friend Allis Featherman told me how it worked, having seen it once, firsthand.

"It was a lank day for work at the fort," he explained. "I was out on the eastern trail, gabbing with some of those Texas cow drovers."

"A bad lot, that," I said. "All wearing those big revolvers and taking unkindly to a Yankee like yourself."

"Well, anyway, this day I'm talkin' about, they was passin' along not far from that Big Beaver camp and I was with some of 'em and we were just jawin' and lollin' along beside the two wagons most of them drives has. The cattle was off to one side, movin' north, and then all of a sudden there was a lot of excitement and the cow boss came back with a couple his men and they took rifles outta the tack wagon.

"On this little ridge a quarter-mile off was a bunch of Comanches, about ten of 'em. Just sittin' on their ponies and watchin' the cattle pass along. So the cow boss and a couple his drovers rode out there to see what the hell they wanted, and I went along to talk for 'em. I'm not too good at it yet, but I can speak Comanche better than most of them Texas boys."

"You're progressing handsomely in that language," I said. "But on with this hair-raising tale."

"Well, there's not much hair-raisin' about it," Allis said, ducking his head and grinning. "Anyway, we all sat there on our horses and had a little smoke. Then this one Comanche buck I've seen a few times with Otter

Tongue—mean-lookin' man—he says he allowed there was a lot of cows down there and that his people were pretty hungry and maybe the white man could spare a few.

"Well, this cow boss looked it all over and decided it might be a good idea. He looked at their bows and arrows, and a few had old pistols and one a rifle, and some were painted and wore feathers in their hair.

"So the cow boss says he'll drive out a couple cows for them if they give their word not to come messin' around after dark and maybe causin' somebody to get hurt. So this head Comanche says they'd all stay in their camps after sundown, where they belonged, and the cow boss had a couple head drove out and the Comanches went off with 'em. And that was the end of that."

"Well, it's a fine story, Allis, and glad I am that you're a part of such things."

"Well, I don't think the army or Mr. Harper would like it."

"True, but then the children of the army and Mr. Harper are not sucking old bones for sustenance."

Then the cold weather came and the drives stopped until spring, leaving the bands nothing much in the vicinity to supplement their government beef rations. There were a few deer still being taken out on the reservation, but even a big deer wouldn't feed many hungry children.

The tribesmen knew where the cattle were, once the drovers stopped coming. So now and then a few of the young men would ride south of the Red and take a head or two in the still of night, a practice they'd perfected over their past years in taking horses right from under the noses of their various enemies.

It was a constant weight on Mr. Harper's mind, because he was afraid that at any time he might hear such a mission had turned into a blood raid, with smoke rising from white men's ranches and a few dead bodies scattered about on the Texas grass.

There'd been some of that kind of trouble in the

past. Mostly from Kiowas, who went south to hunt white men and not livestock. Old General William T. Sherman himself came out once to look into the situation and in the process very nearly lost his own hair. A sad trophy that, because by then Sherman's hair was a bristling gray-red and not much of it to boot. And the old bastard's head was so tough that no scalping knife would dent it.

In this first winter of Kwahadi's coming, there was little chance of any serious bloodshed. The braves who bundled themselves in buffalo robes and rode to Texas were after beef to keep their people from starving. So they were there in a hurry, back in a hurry. And often I said to myself that if the Federal government wouldn't ration them, it was only to be expected that the wild tribesmen would take their beef direct from the citizens. And from whom better than the Texicans, their bitter enemy these many years.

Poor Mr. Harper! He had other problems, inhuman to think of, not only trying to keep the braves on the reservation and seeing that everyone had something to eat.

That winter there was a lot of rustling, white men coming into the small Indian herds and sometimes, we suspected, felons from one of the Civilized Tribes, because, civilized or not, they had their share of thieves and ruffians, as do all peoples. It caused many a wrinkle in the bald pate of Agent Harper, for he had little control over his charges and even less over the ones who were stealing from them.

In the month of February, a Kiowa band on the northern fringes of the reservation was hard hit, losing a number of their valuable ponies. Mr. Harper and Simmons and I rode up to have a look, escorted by a detachment of cavalry. Tracy Shadburn was in command of the troopers, and on the journey we rode side by side and he made his opinions known.

"Hell," he said, the breath from his mouth making a white cloud before his face. "This is an arse-blistering cold ride for nothing. You could station the whole Gawd damned army out here and the horse thieves would still run off the stock!"

His disposition, usually foul anyway, was made worse by the presence of Toothpick Jehyle Simmons, who constantly rode abreast of us to grouse about one thing and another. Until finally Tracy gave him a good barracks-room stare and spit his words like bullets from a Gatling gun:

"Fall back in the column and think about fornicating with pigs, as we all know you do, you weasel-faced civilian offal!"

Old Tracy, good with the best of soldier's language. But we were no longer pestered with Jehyle's obtuse comments.

"Take no offense, Morgan," Tracy said to me in a rare concession to my service to a flag. "There are civilians and there are civilians. And at least you are distinguished by having had your hide perforated by some of our lead."

"No offense taken, in view of my having perforated some of your boys, too," I said, and Tracy laughed, a caustic sound like ice breaking.

Maybe I liked Tracy because he reminded me so much of another old man who had been my company commander in the Third Arkansas, before he was invalided home with a hand shot to pieces. He'd always worn a stovepipe hat in battle, and his language had been the pride of all unrighteous men who ever heard him.

There was little we could do about the stolen stock. A new snow hid the tracks. We knew that whoever had taken the horses likely ran them north through Caddo country and on into the Unassigned Lands and maybe all the way to the Cherokee Strip. They were all places where there was a market for horses, no questions asked. These predators were taking a page from the wild tribes' book, stealing away into the night with the most important thing of the Indians' life, preying like wolves on sick cows and knowing the bands were restrained in their response by fear of punishment from the bureaucrats.

Perhaps that gave Mr. Harper the biggest headache of all, constantly worrying that soon some band of Kiowas or Comanches would grow tired of being victimized and ride out with black paint on their faces. All men can come close to violent action if pushed to the border of their patience, even those with the most peaceful of intentions.

During the Medicine Lodge peace councils, I had seen old Satanta, the Kiowa chief, raging about some of the white men in the peace party killing buffalo only for the tongues. Had such a thing happened a second time, I was sure Satanta would have left the treaty negotiations, which would have meant hard times for isolated whites caught by war parties.

So we talked to the Kiowas, trying to soothe their hot tempers. They were as angry as men can get without falling off the deep end and going out to seek blood. Maybe they were most angry at the fact that their hands were tied.

"If we killed some of these people," one of them said to me in Comanche, because that was the only way I could communicate with them, "Your Great Father would have us all put in one of those Iron Houses like the one in Texas where they sent the great Satanta."

"I knew Satanta at the big treaty meetings on the Timbered Hill River," I said. "He was a hot-tempered man. But the men he killed in Texas had not stolen any of his horses."

Of course, I didn't speak in such a manner within hearing of Agent Harper. He might conclude that I was approving Indian retaliation. And maybe I was.

One of the old Kiowa elders, named Bear, seemed to take it all philosophically. As best I could judge, he was of an age with Otter Tongue, but it was hard to tell. He was not fat, yet there was about him a certain substance. His face was remarkable, unlined and full-fleshed, with eyes that had a definite Mongolian slant.

Phil McCusker had always told me there were Kiowa men with faces as beautiful as women's are supposed to be. In Bear's features I could appreciate such a thing.

I asked him if he had ever known the Nakoni chief Iron Shirt, and he said he had, and Iron Shirt's son Sanchess as well. He said he knew Iron Shirt's grandson Wasp, who had taken a Kiowa wife and lived a long time with his wife's people. Wasp, Bear told me, had been killed in a big raid on a freight outfit on the road the white man called the Santa Fe Trail in the year before the white men fought each other over the black man.

"I remember that raid well," Bear said in Comanche as fluent as my own. "We lost one of our young men, too. A man named Skull, who had been taken as a white captive in Texas while he was still a child. He grew up among us and became a feared Kiowa warrior."

Everyone on the frontier had heard of Skull. Stories about his cruelty still circulated. Phil McCusker had told me about whites becoming wild-tribe warriors, and he said they were often more brutal than their red brothers.

It was only on the ride back to the agency, suffering in the sharp wind that my heavy overcoat failed to turn completely aside, that I realized I should have asked old Bear about Kwahadi and his mother. He likely knew the story. So I filed his name in my mind for a possible future visit.

It was in this time that I finally knew Otter Tongue was not coming back to speak more to me about Kwahadi and his mother. For whatever reason. The thing had been eating on me since that rainy night of the old Comanche's visit to my agency shack. Thus far, call of duty had prevented my digging into their genealogy. Now, maybe, with the worst of winter past, and few freight hauls for the fort in the offing, there would be time for a ride on Deacon to the Big Beaver.

But so much for good intentions. All went astray as they had so many times in my sinful past. There was in that time an impelling urge to sit at one of the backroom tables at Stoddard & Blanchard's store and match my wits and cards against all other players.

A few days after the Kiowa horse-stealing, I sat at a gaming table under coal-oil lamps, and in the company of a rough lot. One of them was the ugly Rufus Tallbridge, whose nose I had once encountered with my left fist. He had more money than he usually did, and the devil of a thought came to mind that maybe our Rufus knew something about all those Indian ponies being stolen and sold to the Civilized Tribes.

That back room at Stoddard & Blanchard's had a quality about it that brought out wicked thoughts. The players showed great diversity in dress and language. There were always a few soldiers there and the various drummers passing through, the army contract workers and the agency roustabouts. And often those who could not be identified by occupation because they had no apparent one, like Rufus.

That place had a smell like few others I'd encountered. There was the thick, oily scent of kerosene, the sweat of hard-working men, the rank presence of bacon rind, thick tobacco smoke, and spilled beer, all adding their own tone to the medley of odors. Into the evening, the hanging lamps cast a light the color of orange peel, and even that seemed to touch the nose rather than the eye.

Rufus got drunker than usual that evening, which is to say very drunk. So I managed to take about thirty dollars from him at five-card stud poker, my young friend Allis Featherman sitting behind me, laughing happily whenever I pulled in a pot.

Later that same night, much later, as I was about to bed down in my modest shack, someone rode past in the darkness and fired two shots at my window. It was from about twenty rods off, as near as I could guess from the reports, and the heavy slugs plowed into the walls well below my window glass.

Well, Rufus was reputed to be a bad loser. It didn't bother me much. I knew that once his temper had had its airing, he'd ride off to Texas or wherever it was he rode off to, and sulk a while before returning once more to soil the landscape around Fort Sill, laughing his ugly laugh and acting as though he were blood brother to all in sight, meanwhile picking out the spot in every man's back where the suspenders crossed as a likely target for one of those big Colt pistols he always carried.

So much for vermin.

The snow was barely gone, but there were already plans for celebrating the Centennial birthday of the Federal Union. Lieutenant Weslowski was overseeing the construction of firecrackers and other things in the ordnance warehouse, a dangerous game where no smoking was allowed. The soldiers there pulled the slugs from .45-50 carbine ammunition, dumped the black powder into cardboard cylinders, and fused it with more powder wrapped in oil paper, like a rat's tail.

The army of the Yankees never had enough ammunition for proper target practice, a condition well known to me in the forces of the old South, and now the lovely Pole was taking some of that away. A little each month, he maintained, to make a display and rousing noise in memory of the Declaration of Independence in 1776. It was small matter to me, though I had to admit that if things hadn't turned out as they had, we might all be paying homage still to some English monarch like Queen Victoria or similar Germans.

In that time of Mackenzie's adjutant making his firecrackers, I went back to the Big Beaver. It was March or thereabouts. The months on the plains seemed to arrange themselves in memory as hot or cold, and nothing in between.

The Antelope camp was a desolate-looking place. There was no green to break the monotony of sandy soil where the tipis were scattered about, and the trees were black and leafless. They'd made a small brush corral for their horses, located in the center of the encampment to be carefully watched, no longer allowing the herd to wander free for grazing in the surrounding area. They knew that now there were many white men about like Rufus Tallbridge who would be glad to take their livestock wherever offered, but without bill of sale.

There were crows along the creek making their harsh language, well suited to the cold and windy day. They were in the bare branches of the jack oaks, like black leaves fluttering, announcing with each caw the fact that all warmth was gone forever. I'd disliked crows since the first time I saw them picking at the dead on Virginia's battlefields.

Otter Tongue received me in his lodge, where I was led by one of the young boys of the band. A few women scurried about to avoid me as I passed among the tipis. When I was ushered into his presence I knew he had expected me, some scout having warned him of my approach when I was far out on the reservation and away from the village. He was sitting on the far side of the tipi, and behind him the young Comanche who had been in my own place that night of the rainy visit. His name was Hawk, as it turned out, and my first assessment of him had been correct. He was a very bad-looking Comanche, with eyes like dark flaming coals that searched out each particle of my being, outside and in, as he sat behind old Otter Tongue and listened to our casual talk.

"Liver, it's a hard day for riding outside in the cold," Otter Tongue said.

"Well, your lodge is warm enough."

It was a typical Comanche tipi, the poles holding the hide walls reaching to their apex at the smokehole above us. Various items of clothing were hanging about, and even a few weapons. I suspected that Otter Tongue and the other elder men of the band had been busy during the winter months, making bows and long, straight arrows vaned with owl feathers and tipped with the old standard tin warheads obtained over the years from the Mexicans.

There was a small round hole in the ground at the center of the lodge, where a fire of oak branches burned. Otter Tongue complained that there were few buffalo chips nearby for the making of good lodge fires. Along the edges of the tipi were the robe beds and the rawhide bags filled with all the family truck and clothing and soup ladles and such. Within that buffalo-hide cone, there was a warmth unknown within wooden structures, as though it were living like a heartbeat.

"I have a little food for you," Otter Tongue said.

We ate a few mouthfuls of beef, roasted in some past moment but cold now. There wasn't much, and each time I swallowed I could feel Hawk's gaze on my throat. I wondered if he knew that I was myself thinking about all the young men who had risked their lives taking this meat in Texas.

"You'll forgive me," the old man said, "but I have none of your coffee to offer."

"I have no need of it."

Otter Tongue brought out a long-stemmed pipe decorated with paint and feathers. After he'd loaded it with coarse Mexican tobacco and lit it, he offered it to the sky, the earth, and all four directions. Then we smoked silently, enjoying the aroma of the tobacco and feeling the warmth of the small fire on our faces.

"It's good tobacco, don't you think so, Liver?"

"Yes. It's very good."

Their eyes were on me, and I knew they expected me to open the real business at hand. And I knew they knew what it was.

"I'd like to talk some about the white captive child you told me about before," said I. "And about what happened to her."

There was no change in the expression on their faces. Slowly, Otter Tongue took the pipe from my hands and passed it to Hawk and the young Comanche puffed a few times, still watching me with that cold, hard gaze. The thought crossed my mind that here was a man who would be a poker player among poker players, for there was never any hint in his eyes that might betray what lay behind. Across many a table I had sat, but never seen a solid wall of blankness such as he gave me. It made the cold tingles go up my back. A hard man, this young Comanche. If I held a flush, I would hesitate to bet a nickel against him, just from his look!

"You changed your chief's name on the ration rolls," said I. "I think maybe it all has something to do with the same thing. Where did you get that name?"

"It was his mother's name," Otter Tongue said, holding his pipe again now, the smoke moving lazily up past his slitted eyes. "That white captive child I told you about."

"Maybe you could tell me some more about her."

"I don't know any more about her. I never knew all the details. Only the woman knows the details."

"The woman?"

"Yes," Otter Tongue said. "She is an old woman. Maybe older than me. She remembers that white captive child well. Maybe you ought to talk to her."

"I wanted to talk with your headman," said I.

The little smile began on his lips, and he shook his head.

"No, no, I think not. Our headman is out hunting with some of the young men." He turned his face back toward Hawk. "Isn't this true?"

"Yes, he's out hunting deer," Hawk said, and his voice had a flat, metallic sound, like the tapping of a hammer on a cold anvil.

"This is a very important woman you should talk with," Otter Tongue said. "She's like a chief in the tribe. Past menopause, you see, and with great power. Her name is Sunshade, and she was the favorite wife of the great Sanchess."

"Who took that white child captive?"

"Yes. Sanchess. I've told her you might come, and with much persuasion she has agreed to speak with you. But Liver, you have taken a long time to come. I expected you much sooner."

"There are many duties with the army and with Mr. Harper."

"It doesn't matter. Some things require speed. Other things do not. You are a friend and we knew you would come. Now I'll have her come here, if you want to talk with her. She spends much time here in my lodge at night, sitting with my old wife and exchanging gossip. Or sometimes, when the children come to hear the stories, Sunshade comes to listen. But she knows those stories as well as I do. Maybe better. She told them to Kwahadi when he was still going naked through the camp and playing in the pony herd. Stories about the grandfathers when they came down from the mountains and had the horse and fought the Spaniards and the Apaches."

Without any signal that I could detect, Hawk suddenly rose and moved quickly from the lodge, and Otter Tongue and I continued to smoke as though nothing had happened. But with the last puff of the Mexican tobacco I felt a cold blast of air and knew the tipi door flap had been pushed back again. Then she was there, moving behind Otter Tongue and squatting and looking at me with the same interest she might show if she'd seen a large bug on a rock. Black eyes, but not shining, rather like coal dust, and I could smell the hostility as though an angry copperhead snake had come into the tipi.

"I need to look at the pony herd," Otter Tongue said, and with a loud grunt he came to his feet and walked out of the tipi, leaving me there alone with this woman of much power in the band. I knew what Otter Tongue meant. I could feel it.

She was no complete stranger. I had seen her last summer on my first visit here to the Big Beaver. She it was who had brought the pipe to us in the brush arbor. Once more I saw the deep mourning scars on her arms, and once more that flat, haughty face, smooth as calm water.

"I have a little gift for you," I said, taking a clay pipe from my coat pocket. That pipe was meant for Kwahadi, but it was plain now that I was not going to see him.

Sunshade took the pipe quickly, as though she were afraid of touching my hand by chance. And my tobacco pouch the same way, her hand darting for it. She loaded the pipe quickly, too, then lit it with a splinter from the fire. As the smoke drifted up before her face, she looked younger, and it was hard to believe she was as old as Otter Tongue. Maybe older. She had not taken on excess weight as some Comanche women do, coming into their late years. There was about her an air of strength and confidence, and she looked me directly in the eye, boldly, as though daring me to do or say anything of which she might not approve.

"You want to talk?" she asked bluntly.

"If you're willing."

"I'm not willing. A white man killed my husband, Sanchess, a long time ago. It is still on my mind."

She puffed on the pipe, billowing smoke from the corners of her mouth, watching my reaction to her words.

"But our chief has said I should do it. So I will. He told me you would come, to talk about his mother."

"That's true. Did you know her?"

"How could I talk about her if I didn't know her?"

"Good. Tell me from the beginning," said I.

But she waited a long time, smoking and watching me closely. My hands seemed suddenly awkward, hanging between my knees, and I took out my own pipe and smoked with her, wondering if she would ever say anything. But then she began to talk, in a monotone, like the recitation of a story by rote. And lowered her eyes to the small fire. Her hair, bobbed at shoulder length, fell along either cheek, reflecting the flicker of flame like a mirror.

"My husband, Sanchess, led a raiding party in the year of her capture. He had seen her before. There was

this white man's fort on the River of Broken Guns. I don't know what you call it. It is a small river and runs into what you call the Colorado. Sanchess told me all about it, but I don't know exactly where it is.

"In the warm season before this raid, Sanchess and his brother and some more of our men drove some horses there to trade for guns. They gave many good horses to this white man named Parry."

She said it as Simmons had told me Otter Tongue did, with the accent on the last syllable.

"This white man showed them some guns. My husband said they were fine guns. But the ones this Parry gave for the horses were no good. They wouldn't shoot and finally were thrown away. It made Sanchess very angry to be cheated."

Now she paused and looked at me without raising her head, a glaring look it was. I could hear her sucking on the pipestem, and outside I could hear the wind fingering the sides of the lodge. After a moment she looked into the fire once more and continued her story.

"While he was there, he saw this white man's daughter. Parry's daughter. She had eyes like the sky and hair the color of that red metal the Mexicans use to make bracelets.

"My husband vowed he would go back there and steal some horses and maybe some children, too, maybe that man Parry's daughter. And he did, the next warm season after the cheating, after the ponies were strong on the new spring grass.

"He brought the child to us. We were camped near the Conchos. She was very strong and high-spirited and brave. After a while, Sanchess gave the child to his father, Iron Shirt, who was our headman. She became his daughter, growing into the band. She became my sister-in-law and after a while she married my brother, Wolf's Road. Then the boy-child was born."

"Kwahadi?"

Her pipe was finished and she reached for my tobacco pouch lying between my feet, reloaded the bowl, lit it, and smoked again for a long time, in silence, and I tried to hide my impatience.

"The boy was born the year we went to the Kiowa sun dance again. We went often to watch the sun dance, because Iron Shirt had many friends among them. Sometimes we hunted with them along the stream they called the Timbered Hill River. It was near that country where the child was born, after the sun dance. The Kiowas called that their Dakota Sun Dance because some Dakotas came to watch it, too. We gave the Dakotas a lot of horses.

"Later she had another child, this one a girl and born feet-first and very sickly. The boy was always strong. I helped raise him up to manhood, being his aunt, and made him mind his mother and do the right things toward her. Sometimes I had to tie his thumbs to the lodgepoles and let him hang a while to settle his high spirits."

"How old was this Parry child when she was taken captive?" I asked.

Too many questions to suit her, I supposed, for she abruptly dropped her smoking pipe at my feet and was gone from the tipi before I could say any word in apology.

It was very strange to be left sitting there alone in Otter Tongue's lodge. Hidden Comanche things seemed to drift across my face like the smoke from her pipe. The spirit of long evenings when war parties might be going out, or when the elders of the band sat before a fire just like this and recounted the tribal history for the children, or when the warriors came home and lay in the bed robes with their wives.

I felt foreign and out of place and quickly moved out of there with a shudder, into the cold sunlight and wind, and saw the ice crystals hanging in the bare trees along the Big Beaver. Deacon was hobbled at the tipi door. There was no Comanche in sight. Only a few dogs watching me from afar and the ponies in the pole corral, watching too, the breath from their flared nostrils making dense clouds of white vapor.

As I rode away, there was a prickly sensation along my back, as though many pairs of eyes were on me. Once out of their sight, I had plenty of other things to think about. The Colorado. Somewhere along its course she'd been taken. Not much more real information than that, and a cold ride into the bargain. At least a start. And more talking to be done with that mean old Comanche woman before this was finished to the last draw of the cards.

Back in my shack for the night, I stood a long time gazing at the hawk feather hanging beside my door. And recalled that on his first sight of me that afternoon, old Otter Tongue had looked quickly at my hat and, seeing no feather there, smiled his little smile. Now that I remembered, each time he had seen me since giving me the feather, he had looked first at my hat to see if it was there before looking into my eyes. I hoped it gave him some sense of satisfaction that I had figured out his little game and would wear the thing on my person only after I'd won the right.

The face of the old Comanche woman kept coming into my dreams that night. A strong-minded woman she was, yet in her bearing there was some kind of elusive, fierce beauty.

8

Kwahadi had six wives. It was all there on the ration rolls. And ten children.

The eldest child was a slender little girl I judged to be about eleven years old. She was always there with the band when they came in on ration day, walking among the other children with regal grace, in her beaded and fringed smock. There was some kind of flashing loveliness about her, her teeth so straight and white, her eyes sparkling black, her ready smile. A favorite child, this one, even though a girl. Her name was Padoponi, which I interpreted to mean Deep Water.

My young friend Allis Featherman came to me with that knowledge. He'd seen the girl many times and made a point of it, I suspected. He began to give her sugar candy, the little red and green gumdrops to be had at Stoddard & Blanchard's store, which she accepted with eyes downcast but with that brilliant smile, then walked away from him with her head high, as though sugar candy was her just due, her hair fanning out as black as midnight behind her.

"Allis," said I, in my fatherly tone, "you look like a wounded calf every time your eyes light on that child."

"She may be a child now," said he, grinning and showing his big buckteeth below the tangle of freckles on his cheeks. "But she won't be a child forever."

"You'll be careful there, mooning around the young women of that tribe."

"Hell's afire, Morgan," he sputtered, eyes wide with indignation. "All I do is give her candy. And some to those other Comanche young'uns, too."

"Yes, but you never look at them with the same light in your eyes as when you look at her."

"It's only a little candy!"

"You're spending all your wages on candy," I said. "But I do admire your taste for quality."

This child was the daughter of Kwahadi's eldest wife, a rather squat Comanche woman of no real distinction I could see except for her name, which was Coming Back from the Pony Herd. This information from Master Featherman as well, for he had suddenly become an expert on the wives and children of the Antelope band's headman, due to his interest in the girl. I suspected that most of this intelligence came to him from some of the younger riders in the ration-day races, where he was always hanging about. After he'd handed Padoponi his sticky gifts, of course. Allis was becoming fluent in Comanche, thanks to my teachings.

Then I began to notice that on those days when he was not employed in some army contract job, Allis no longer lolled about near me, and it had become seldom that he appeared at my shack in the evenings for a bait of biscuit and gravy. So it came to me that he was riding out to the Antelope camp at every opportunity on the little bag-of-bones pony he'd bought from a Wichita buck. The nag was on its last legs but was good enough for Allis, so long as he didn't try to whip the horse into a dead run. He rode bareback because he couldn't afford a saddle, and his bridle was an old thing he'd wheedled from Mr. Stoddard for a few pennies, the leather of the reins old enough to have served in the Revolution that Weslowski was preparing to celebrate, all twisted about with twine string to hold it together.

In the games at the back of Stoddard & Blanchard's store each evening, Allis was no longer a permanent fixture behind my chair, even when I drew to busted straights. So he was out at the Big Beaver, I reckoned, learning the language. And maybe a little more besides.

I said nothing to him about it. A man's follies must remain his own. Then one evening we were helping the army stable crew to worm some horses in the Fort Sill stalls, and it came out clear and simple.

"Went out to the Big Beaver today," Allis said.

One of the sergeants sneered and shook his head.

"Yeah, Allis, you're a ripe one to be a squaw man."

It so embarrassed my young friend that I pretended I hadn't heard any of it.

No one had ever told me about Kwahadi's wives until Allis Featherman brought the information. It had never been a thing that crossed my mind. Certainly, Agent Harper knew, but I was on the outer fringes of his confidence, and Jehyle Simmons probably knew as well, but would rather die than give me the reading on his pocket-watch face. So he wouldn't say anything enlightening about the people he had begun to call my "pets," as though they were old mongrel dogs lying at my feet before a warm fire in winter.

It was a good indication of how much Jehyle knew about those Comanches. The idea that they could be anybody's pets was laughable to me. Otter Tongue with his hoarded wisdom of the ages, that tough young warrior, Hawk, with his hard eyes, and least of all Kwahadi. If anyone was a lapdog, it was me, and I found that very disquieting. Yet, on proper reflection, I knew they would never ask favors of someone they considered weak and condescending, but rather of a man of their own stature.

Now, all those wives became a problem when Mr.

Elander Gurk came on the scene. I should say the Reverend Elander Gurk, for he was a fire-eyed Baptist missionary sent to save the heathen—from the devil and from the Methodists. But in a way I was thankful to Elander Gurk, because through his efforts I first came to speak with Kwahadi. Well, not so much *with* him as *for* him.

Many things were involved, as is usual in such cases. First and foremost was himself, Elander Gurk. He had his own ideas about how to civilize the barbarians, and most important on his list was adherence to his own strict code of conduct. And that definitely did not include having six wives.

Then there was Mr. Harper, who had always admitted to an uncomfortable itch in his soul over the wild tribes' custom of a man, if he were any man at all, taking more than one wife into his lodge. Bigamy was not a thing sanctioned any more by the bureaucrats than by the Baptists, but Mr. Harper had never figured out how to do anything about it. Besides, he had many more pressing responsibilities.

And then there was Kwahadi, whose power among the bands on the reservation was growing with each passing sun, even though he had been the last of the headmen to come in. Maybe that was part of it; he'd been the last to carry a blood lance against the white man.

It had not escaped the notice of other chiefs that during his first winter on the reservation he had kept his people fairly well fed, and without getting any of his young men into trouble for stealing Texas cattle. What was even more impressive to everyone was that his band already had a small herd of horses, with many mares ready to drop foals.

He, the wildest of the wild tribesmen, had already accommodated himself to the white man's road, or so it seemed. And he'd done it without bowing and scraping like a slave to his master. So the word had passed along: Kwahadi was a good man to have around when dealing with the white man. And many of the other chiefs had gone to the Big Beaver camp to seek his advice.

All this came to a head, like a boil everyone had tried to forget, when Reverend Gurk marched into the agency office that spring and demanded that for the benefit of their souls, all the Comanche men had to rid themselves of extra wives, and the first among those required to do so was Kwahadi, because of his great influence on the others. Mr. Harper developed an acute stomachache, and by the time Simmons and I arrived in his office, he was red-faced and sputtering.

Gurk implored the agent, citing the proper scriptures and details of the holy circumstance of wedlock, with liberally sprinkled comments on the horrors of sin and a few threats of damnation for all involved, which I assumed included Mr. Harper, Simmons, and myself.

He was a regular brimstoner, and with each pronouncement the little gray beard that ran around the edges of his jaw bristled and came to a quivering point at the chin, reminding me of the raised hackles on an angry dog's back. Simmons noticed the same quality in the preacher, and afterward we agreed that he should henceforth be known as the Hound of Heaven.

The Reverend Gurk wore a narrow-brimmed hat pulled tight against his skull, and his eyes gleamed from the shadow of it. His coat was deacon length, coming to the knees and fanning out behind him as he whirled and danced back and forth across Mr. Harper's office, arms flailing and the words pouring from his mouth in a near hysterical stream. Of all the missionaries on the reservation, he was to me the most unattractive.

Everything was made worse by the heat in the room. Although it had turned warm outside, Mr. Harper's pot-bellied stove was stoked full and roaring as though we were in the midst of a howling blizzard. I could feel the sweat running from beneath my arms and collecting under my hatband. I noted that Gurk seemed incapable of sweat. Maybe such a thing was prohibited by another of his moral principles.

The outcome of it all was that Mr. Harper agreed to have the Antelope headman come in for a little talk, with Gurk in attendance, and I was dispatched to the Big Beaver to pass the message along. Rather, it was an order. It was fine by me to be out of there, with the heat and the Bible quotations flying about and a chance to take my mule on a little airing in open country.

The redheaded woodpeckers were about, and I saw a number of cardinals, too, feeding low among the oak trees. As I rode along, I was aware that in some places there were patches beginning to green, and each of the small streams I crossed was bank-full. There was a good fresh smell about everything.

I didn't see Kwahadi at the camp. I hadn't expected to. Indeed, I had become accustomed to his being more spirit than substance. But I related Mr. Harper's instructions to Hawk, who was working a horse on the near side of their village. I suspected someone had seen me from afar, as usual, and he was there by design. At any rate, he said he'd see what Kwahadi thought about it and would let us know.

"Mr. Harper is very serious about him coming in to the agency," said I.

"We'll see what he thinks about it," Hawk said in his sharp-edged voice, and turned his pony and rode back into the village, dismissing me as thoroughly as if I were a common soldier turned away by a general's aide.

It was three more days before Hawk rode into the agency to inform us that his chief would ride in that same afternoon to have his little talk with Mr. Harper. I hadn't mentioned the purpose of the talk, but I suspected the Comanches knew what was coming. Information spread across that reservation like oil on top of still water.

Mr. Harper gathered the principals, myself included. When I walked across the small porch of the agency office, Hawk was squatting against one wall, smoking a cigarette rolled in some kind of dried oak leaf, and he made no sign that he knew me. He made no sign, in fact, that he knew I was even there.

It was shortly after noon when we saw them coming in, and Simmons let forth a string of blistering oaths, which made the Reverend Gurk scowl with embarrassment and resentment. Kwahadi had brought his whole band, it seemed, all strung out in a line as they had been when he surrendered, him riding in front and the others behind, including all the women, children, and dogs. And damned if he wasn't carrying that old ironwood lance, warhead up in the sun. Only now it wasn't decorated with hair.

They reined up in front of the agency office, and I saw Otter Tongue and, farther back along the column, Coming Back from the Pony Herd, and Padoponi riding double behind her. None of them gave me any notice as I walked out onto the porch to welcome them.

Everyone stayed in his place along the column as Kwahadi slipped down from the little piebald pony he was riding. He moved slowly onto the porch, and Hawk took the lance from his hand, this stony-eyed Comanche now up and ready to do whatever his chief required. I held the door open, and without a single glance at me, Kwahadi walked inside. There, his eyes focused on Mr. Harper's face and the agent rose from behind his desk to bow and smile and generally look hospitable.

The Reverend Gurk, unaccustomed as he was to polite discourse among Comanches, wanted to plunge right into his business. But knowing it was best not to offend a man like Kwahadi with rudeness, Mr. Harper offered coffee. Simmons poured, not spooning nearly enough sugar into the cup. This thick brew came from a blue enameled pot that was always gurgling on Mr. Harper's sow-bellied stove.

Although he was offered a chair, Kwahadi remained standing directly in front of Mr. Harper's desk. The agent began to speak of the weather and of the band's string of horses and the mares ready to foal and other such trivia. Kwahadi said nothing, holding his coffee cup in both hands but never once lifting it to his lips, all the while keeping his eyes fixed on Mr. Harper's face as though there were some terrible fascination there.

Not expected to join in this conversation, I had the opportunity at last to study Kwahadi's face at close hand. It was a harshly handsome face, in a way that some might have said was cruel because of the wide mouth that turned down at the corners under the distinct bow of his upper lip. As though he never smiled.

Without the sun to shine on it, his hair now looked raven black, no hint of copper glint. It was done in braids down either side of his face, the plaits wrapped in some soft fur I didn't recognize. Along his back hung the war lock, the hair uncovered and well oiled. He held a light buckskin robe over his shoulders, and below that the fringed Comanche leggings and the moccasins with horsehair at heel and toe. These were brightly beaded moccasins, much too garish for Comanche taste, and I suspected they had come to his hand from some Kiowa friend.

The Reverend Gurk's impatience had finally reached the point of explosion, so Mr. Harper opened the sensitive subject of polygamy. No flutter of interest crossed Kwahadi's face. Gurk explained the seriousness of hellfire and the advantages of his own version of virtue, Simmons doing all the interpreting. Still, Kwahadi made no move to speak, to respond in any way. Gurk's impatience was turning to hot anger, and Mr. Harper made a few soothing remarks, himself becoming visibly restive as Kwahadi continued to gaze steadily into his face.

Simmons began to sweat, unaccustomed as he was to delivering what amounted to a sermon. Twice he looked frantically at me, imploring assistance, I supposed. But I kept my peace and my place at the side of the room beyond the potbellied stove.

"It's to show yourself as a good example," Mr.

Harper was saying. "A good example to your own people and all the others of your tribe. Leading along the white man's road. It is your responsibility as a great chief."

This seemed to bring the light of interest into Kwahadi's eyes and he bent forward slowly and placed his cup on the edge of Mr. Harper's desk. Once straightened to his full height again, he folded his arms under the buckskin robe, staring now at some distant spot above the agent's head.

"Living with more than one woman is a sin and an abomination," Gurk shouted, a finger pointed toward the ceiling.

Simmons didn't know any Comanche word for "abomination." So in Comanche he said "a fearful thing." But Kwahadi's mouth turned down sourly at the corners and I suspected he might know the word and it obviously didn't set too well.

"You owe it to your people," Mr. Harper said without much conviction.

Suddenly one of Kwahadi's long, slender hands appeared, palm down, demanding silence. Then he turned his face toward me, and for the first time looked directly into my eyes. I took that look as a demand, too, a demand that now he would speak and he wanted me to interpret. I wondered why he didn't speak in English, because I knew from the incident of the whiskey at Stoddard & Blanchard's that he enjoyed some command of it.

When he spoke, looking again now into Mr. Harper's face, his voice was soft and gentle, almost like a woman's, a crooning sound that seemed to flatten out the rough edges of his Comanche words.

"He says that among his people," I said, "anyone can take whatever religion he wants. Each man comes to his gods in his own way. As for himself, when he takes the white man's religion, then he will worry about the white man's hell."

As soon as my last word was spoken, Kwahadi went on, more quickly now, his words becoming sharper. And this time, before he was finished, his eyes had gone very hard.

"He says his wives are good women. They are strong and each has much power. All have given him healthy children. Each has been on war parties in the old days, and each has killed game, and each of them is sometimes very headstrong."

Once more he spoke, and now the words were biting and all the smoothness had gone from them.

"But, he says, if you think he should throw five of his wives away, then you are going to have to go out there right now and tell them which one he keeps!"

As soon as I'd dropped that among them like one of Lieutenant Weslowski's firecrackers, Kwahadi wheeled and walked out, leaving Mr. Harper and Gurk with popping eyes and no sound except a whispered oath from Simmons and the gurgling of coffee in the enameled pot.

On the porch, Hawk was up to meet his leader, handing Kwahadi the old lance. For a moment Kwahadi stood looking at his people, still mounted on their ponies, and their eyes were on him, every one.

I was beside him quickly, and once more he looked at me, and it seemed the corners of his mouth were not so drawn down as before and maybe a new light was shining in his eyes. We were of a height, and I returned his gaze squarely. On some impulse, I thrust out my hand, half expecting him to ignore my invitation, yet he took it and pumped it up and down elaborately, as though it were a movement completely foreign to him.

"Now soon," he said in English, "we will smoke together."

Then he was off the porch and up quickly on his pony and I stood there flexing the fingers where his firm grip had been. A sensation as though I had just taken the hand of old John Bell Hood himself.

All of them were looking at me. I saw old Sunshade with her young face, and she appeared no more friendly than she had on our last meeting. They were immobile as stone, only their loose hair moving in the soft wind from the west.

It was an uncomfortable position, under all those dark eyes, so I quickly retreated into the agency office, and there found the three white men at the single front window, bent over and peering out.

"What the hell are they doin'?" asked Simmons.

"Waiting for you to come out and decide which five wives Kwahadi's going to turn out of his lodge," said I, and laughed. From his expression, I had the thought that Mr. Harper was laughing, too, inside.

The Comanches sat there in the lowering sun for a long time, saying nothing, watching the door of the agency office. Then they turned finally and rode away, slowly, Kwahadi leading, the lance held warhead up, as though he were riding out to face old enemies.

The Hound of Heaven made some racket about writing a letter to Congress, but nothing ever came of it. In the following weeks he tried his hand among the Kiowas, with little success. He was beginning to discover that wild-tribe Indians did not take seriously anyone who tried to bully them into the white man's religion. In less than two months he was gone from our reservation, off to ply his trade among more passive aborigines, leaving the Comanches and Kiowas to less caustic shepherds.

The subject of Kwahadi's wives never came up again.

That smoke with Kwahadi was a long time coming. But there was the satisfaction of having had him offer it. Because it had been his initiative, I decided not to force it. Wait and see, said I. No need to irritate him.

It was my favorite time of year. The oaks were leafing out full. I've heard some say that jack oak and sandbar willow and black hickory and plains cottonwood are unattractive trees. But as they came to green, I could think of nothing more beautiful, standing usually squat and defiant against a shining blue sky in early summer. And among them the cardinals were staking out territory and mating, and in the short-grass prairie I could hear the golden voices of the meadowlarks.

The Texas drovers came early that year, on the Chisholm Trail, which ran close alongside the camp on the Big Beaver. Mr. Harper was distraught as usual at how they herded their cows across reservation land, taking their time about it so the beastly longhorns could eat their fill of Indian grass.

There were fines for such things, but a devil of a time to find a court that would levy them. It was in this period that Agent Harper came on the idea of Indian policemen and an Indian court, and began writing letters to Washington City to that effect. It took a long time to hatch.

The Comanches seemed little concerned about Texas cows on their reserve. Kwahadi's band was taking a heavy toll of the beeves and all of it aboveboard, not stealing them at night, but demanding and getting them in daylight from trail bosses anxious to avoid trouble. A few head were exchanged for the privilege of fattening the rest before the trail north to Kansas. It was a good trade all around.

And although most of the grazing was on that part of the reservation the Antelopes considered their own, they shared the proceeds of business enterprise with other bands and always had enough left over for considerable meat-drying in anticipation of winter. Phil McCusker had always said that even in the worst of times a Comanche would share what food he had, and it still held true.

Twice that summer I visited the camp on the Big Beaver, going about agency business. I saw Kwahadi both times, but he never came near me or spoke. I got only a nod from afar as he rode a little stallion among his livestock. Always close beside him was Hawk, looking like a dark cloud with his frowning face.

When I saw them together, I assumed they were

planning their next gentle assault on the Texas herds. More power to them, thought I. And no bloodshed in the bargain. It came to me then that this wild Comanche was running a fine lease business, as good as any Fort Smith real-estate hackster: so many head of cattle for so much time on Indian grass.

It was in that time that Allis Featherman came to my shack one night with a tube of pemmican, that pulverized meat mixed with various berries secret to all but the Comanche women, done up in a short section of beef gut and sealed with tallow. He had it from one of Kwahadi's wives while he was on the Big Beaver helping them with their foaling, being such a fine hand with horses.

It was very good, that pemmican, but would have improved a little with aging. It was like heavy bread, somewhat like that I had had in Sicily many years gone, and we ate it with a small drop of blackstrap molasses on each slice. A lovely treat, summer or winter.

Well, I told my young friend, if someone were looking for enterprise, there was no need to look farther than this.

"Yeah, and he's even started his own small herd of cows. Keeps 'em in the breaks along the creek," Allis said with some show of pride.

I gave him a look of mock horror.

"What is this strange interest you have in the father of a certain young girl?"

He grinned, bobbing his head, and I thought, Aw, Allis, my young friend, lost you are to the offspring of this wild barbarian. But what better place to lose one's heart than to a princess?

It was busy that spring, with all the talk of trouble among the Indians up north, in the Dakotas. The army across the frontier was in a high state of activity, which meant a lot of mule-driving for me.

But the hustle and bustle didn't mar Lieutenant Weslowski's Fourth of July celebration. Agent Harper proclaimed a special ration day and promised the issue of extra meat for each of the bands. Where the good man came by it, I never learned.

The tribes rode in and camped between the fort and the agency. They'd been told there was a show for the evening, so as the day wore down they sat about their fires, talking and chewing tough beef and waiting, telling the stories of their people and playing little jokes on each other. It was a time of full bellies, and there was much laughter among them.

Kwahadi had not come. He ignored ration day, remaining on the Big Beaver each time. But all his people were there except the old woman, Sunshade.

As soon as it was dark, Weslowski's dog robbers began shooting off the firecrackers, and the Comanche children squealed and ran among their people like frightened dogs and everyone laughed. Some clever soldier in the ordnance department had constructed Roman candles and pinwheels, and these displays were met with loud approval from the tribesmen. There was little wind that night, and the smell of gunpowder soon hung heavy across the assemblage, recalling to many minds other fields and other days, I suspected.

After the fireworks, the campfires continued to glimmer into the night, the people eating most of their meat ration and talking as the Big Dipper turned about the North Star. Some of my old Paneteka friends came to my shack and I entertained them with coffee and a few Welsh ballads. Before I was done I saw the shadowy figure of Hawk on the outer edges of the Paneteka crowd, and later old Otter Tongue, although neither of them came within range of my lamplit doorway.

It was as fine a celebration of the Federal Union's birthday as I had ever seen. I remembered the one at Gettysburg when, all day of the Fourth, we lay battered and wounded along Seminary Ridge, after the great battle, waiting for the Yankees to come or else at least set up some kind of racket in honor of Independence Day.

They did neither, and in the night we slipped back to Virginia in the rain.

The Comanches slept near the fort and the agency that night, but the next morning, by the time I was afoot, they were all gone, leaving their still-smoking fires across the land like the ghosts of their former lives. I wondered what they thought of all those firecrackers and flames spouting in the air. And knew without being told that no such display could ever take the place in their hearts of the old dances they had enjoyed in the confines of Palo Duro Canyon and on the high plains beyond, in celebration of a good hunt or a good victory or a good life.

Routine at the fort quickened two days later when word came that Lieutenant Colonel George Armstrong Custer and many of his men of the Seventh Cavalry had been soundly whipped by the Sioux in Montana Territory. Old William Tecumseh Sherman had got the news, so we learned, on the same day Lieutenant Weslowski had been shooting off his firecrackers. Sherman had been in Philadelphia with other bigwigs, celebrating Independence Day, when he received the first telegraph from the West. Hardly a thing to enhance his enjoyment of the occasion, I suspected.

The debacle was no great surprise to me, having heard all the stories in the late Army of the Confederacy that often Autie Custer had come close to being sacked by Rebel horse leaders like Wade Hampton and Fitz Lee. Actually, during the sectional conflict, I'd paid little attention to stories about cavalrymen, holding them in high disdain and seldom seeing any of them because they avoided infantry like the plague, for fear of being butchered by aimed rifle fire.

It was one of the disappointments of my career with John Bell Hood and Bobby Lee that I'd never had an opportunity to shoot at a massed group of mounted belligerents.

At Fort Sill, they had a retreat parade in memory of Custer and the brave lads who died with him. I attended and was much impressed by the pomp and circumstance, as I have always been by martial bands and flags and ramrod adjutants before the drawn-up formations of troops, barking commands that always set various things in motion. In the old Rebel army, we were never so colorful during such ceremonies, but we usually managed to hold our own when the guns began to shoot.

There was a sudden flurry of stories written in the Eastern newspapers about a general uprising. Similar stories in some frontier papers as well, mostly to encourage the Federal Congress to send more money and the President to send more troops, both of which were desirable for the economy. But most of us considered such scare stories utter hogwash.

The people out on the reservation heard about Custer almost as soon as the white men at the fort and the agency. It was a temporary dash of cold water on their spirits, because they had no idea how the army might react to such a disaster. They stayed near their lodges and for a long time none of them was to be seen around the agency store or Stoddard & Blanchard's.

I suspected there were a few glad hearts among them. Even though the Kiowas and Comanches had never been on completely friendly terms with most tribes north of the Arkansas, except maybe the Crows, it was a victory for their side. Few of them could know then that Little Big Horn was the beginning of the end on the northern plains, just as the Red River War had been in the south.

9

September was a mean month that year I spoke for
Kwahadi in the business of the wives. The rains hadn't
come all through August, and it was as dry as old snuff,
the land turned to gray powder and the air thick with hu-
midity. Skies had gone metal hard, with only a cloud
passing far above now and again, driven before high
winds as hot as a breath from one of Mr. Bessemer's fur-
naces. A good sweat could be worked up before breakfast
just from the effort of pulling on a pair of boots.

Tempers ran short. When I was near the fort I could
hear the harsh scolding of the noncommissioned officers
as they drilled the poor soldiers dismounted, a thing all
cavalrymen despise. Jehyle Simmons and the agency
sawmill operator got into a fistfight. Those who witnessed the affair said it was an outlandish display of futil-
ity, with no blood drawn and hardly a blow worth
mentioning struck by either party. In the back room at
Stoddard & Blanchard's each night, the players were sullen, their dispositions as ragged as a shard of glass.

Maybe the weather brought on the atrocity of the
season, although I doubt it.

It was a lonely time for me, what with Allis Featherman staying so much at the Big Beaver settlement, paying his court to the beautiful Padoponi. There was much
time spent on the trail to Gibson. And at the fort, much
contract work. Each night I was usually so tired, with
hands bruised from the heavy leather reins, that there
were only a few moments spent reading old issues of
Harper's Weekly before falling exhausted into bed, hoping
that morning would bring some resurgence of youthful
vigor. It seldom happened. With age, I found that I had as
many aches and pains on arising in the morning as I had
had on going to bed the night before.

There wasn't time to give much thought then to the
question of Kwahadi's mother and his obsession with
finding her. There were times when my butt was so sore
from the wagon seat, and my mouth so dry from September's dust, that I didn't really care if I ever saw a Comanche again. The hawk feather hanging on my shack wall
gathered spider webs with hardly a glance from me for
days on end.

But the Antelopes came back to my attention rather
forcefully and tragically as the result of Mr. Olin Crater.
Olin Crater showed himself to be a brute of a white man
such as the Eastern newspapers always ignored in their
stories about Indian reservation mischief. But on the
good side, he was the cause of showing that Kwahadi was
really on the white man's road. And the affair created a
most favorable impression on Agent Harper and other
bureaucrats who were eventually made aware of what had
taken place.

Olin Crater lived in a soddy near Anandarko, where
he claimed to keep himself busy helping the Kiowas
learn to farm. It was difficult to imagine Olin as a friend to
the Kiowas or anyone else, and even more difficult to vi-
sualize him with a plow in his hands and giving instructions on its use. The only reason he was allowed to stay
on the reservation at all was that from time to time his
services were required in repairing the agency sawmill.

Where he came by such a mechanical talent, nobody knew.

Olin was a little hummingbird of a man, a full head shorter than Allis Featherman, with no visible chin at all and eyes that seemed forever darting about, looking for a favorable place to insert his beak. He always smelled of sour sweat, the very worst kind, even after the times he bathed, which for him meant being caught out in a sudden rainstorm without his slicker. I had always suspected that Olin had a lot missing in his head, a lot of vacant spaces, and that was to prove correct. But he was a vicious little bastard, which was to prove correct as well, and a constant companion of Rufus Tallbridge when Rufus played the games in the back room at Stoddard & Blanchard's.

It began when September was going down into October and already a nip in the air, so welcome after the summer's beastly heat. A Texas drover came into the agency this day, thinking he'd seen another Indian massacre, as he called it, reporting a man and boy murdered and found in a grove of post oak just short of one of the Red River crossings.

Mr. Harper sent me off on Deacon to the fort with this intelligence, and there Weslowski's usual posse went into action: old Tracy Shadburn, looking grim as the death he expected to find, and a dozen troopers, all veterans and well armed, each looking as stormy as Tracy himself. I went along because Mr. Harper was convinced that we had an indiscretion of Indians and the agency should be represented.

I'd seen many a battlefield, from Sicily to the Wilderness, but never such a sad sight as this one, with great pools of blood blackened on the ground. There in the oak grove where the drover led us were the victims, a grown man and a child I guessed to be about eight. The man had been horribly hacked with a heavy blade, ax or hatchet, and the little lad shot in the back of the head with a large-caliber weapon. He must have been a fine-looking young man when alive, but now that was ended. His large brown eyes were half open, and the sight of it made Tracy and his hardened veterans grind their teeth.

Their pockets had been turned out. There were no boots on the man and he had a large hole at the big toe of his left stocking. There was no pocketbook, no weapons, no tools in the wagon. There were no horses and we could tell from the tracks that there had been at least three. In the wagon was a trunk, open, and inside a jumble of boy's clothing but no single item large enough to be worn by a full-grown man.

And worst of all, they had been scalped, but a rather ragged job made of it.

"Red hellions," Tracy snapped, stamping about and looking at the sprawled bodies, the other troopers staying well back and still mounted but growling wordlessly. "Well, they didn't take the boy's clothes because they must have been grown men, and unable to wear 'em."

"Lieutenant," I said, "you should have been a Pinkerton detective."

"It don't take detective work to see who did this," he said, scowling. "But whoever took that hair did a rough job of it."

We brought the bodies into the fort, a sad chore. Four of the troopers rode their horses hitched to the wagon, jury-rigged with rope, and the two forms, large and small, in the bed. On the way home, the soldiers did a lot of swearing about savages doing such things to a peace-loving man, although none of them had the vaguest notion of who this man might be. But it caused a rising of bile in the gut, just going along on Deacon while behind in the wagon lay those two people, mutilated, a lad and the man we assumed was his Da.

They put the bodies in a fly tent behind the post hospital, on view as it were, in case anyone could shed light on whom the man and boy might be. It was a tense time at the agency, with Mr. Harper preparing a report to his superior bureaucrats that someone had been slain by parties unknown. Simmons and I stayed close beside him that day, my going absent without leave from Weslowski's army duties arranged for me. We wanted to give the good man our support, knowing his distress, but there was little we could do to ease his obvious pain.

Before nightfall of the day after we'd brought in the bodies, a trooper rode down on a prancing horse, saying that the Antelope chief and a couple of his men had come in and seen the murdered pair and wanted a talk. And it was only me they'd talk with.

I got there as quick as Deacon would carry me, but Kwahadi was already gone. There was Weslowski and Tracy Shadburn and one of the regimental doctors and Horace Jones, the Fort Sill interpreter, and Otter Tongue, placid among them, wrapped in his usual buffalo hide and looking like a statue from the ages. But his eyes were alight with some inner fire as he gazed down at the two forms lying on door panels supported by sawhorses.

"This old man wants to talk to you," Weslowski said. He was wearing his saber, which I knew meant everything was very official.

Otter Tongue turned his face to me, and there was that enigmatic smile.

"My friend Liver," he said and offered his hand. He had never done that before, but I knew he'd seen me shake his chief's hand on the agency porch and that was good enough for him, fine retainer that he was, like one of Queen Victoria's generals. "A bad thing, this killing of children for no purpose."

It was no time for idle chitchat before getting to the meat of things, and I knew the old Comanche would understand. So I wasted no time and plunged into it for all our sakes to get it over, and most of all for my own sake because Tracy Shadburn appeared ready to work me about the head and shoulders with his pistol barrel had I not done so.

"Do you know this man and boy?" I asked.

"Yes," Otter Tongue said, with me interpreting all along. "But not his name. We never knew his name. Our chief offered the camp's hospitality to them."

"When did this happen?"

"Two nights ago. They came to our camp in their wagon and we gave them meat and smoked with the man, and the boy had a little pemmican and honey," Otter Tongue said. "Our chief invited them to pitch their camp near us, for the night, so no one would steal their horses. There were two horses for drawing the wagon. A set of geldings, all right for drawing such things, but not much good for riding."

"On the Big Beaver, two nights ago?"

"Yes. Going south of Red River, the man said."

"He knew your tongue, this man?"

"Oh no. He knew none of it. But our chief knew enough of his to speak with him."

"Where did they come from?"

"From north."

"Kansas?"

"Yes, I think that's the place. From Kansas, and going to Texas, this man and his son."

By then I had my clay pipe going and offered it to the old man, and he took it with a nod and puffed, his red eyes on me all the while. Then he looked down at the two still forms on the slabs.

"There was another man with them."

"A white man?"

"Oh yes, the man we've seen many times here on your ration day. The one with a face like a weasel!"

I looked at Weslowski and Shadburn and Horace Jones and knew from their expressions that we all knew the old man was speaking of Olin Crater.

"A little man? Wide hat and no hair on the face?"

"Well, that sounds like him. He's always with that pistol man, coming to look at our pony herd from far off. We've seen them."

"Rufus Tallbridge?"

"I've heard his name called, yes."

Otter Tongue sucked on the pipe without effect, it being burnt down, and with a small shrug handed it back to me.

"He was traveling with these two," said he. "And the next day when they left in their wagon, this man with the weasel face went with them."

"Was he armed?" I asked, thinking of the large bullet wound in the boy's head.

"I saw no weapon on him," Otter Tongue said. "But this man with the wagon, he had two weapons in his wagon, a long gun and a short one. He made no display of them, but they were there. Along with many of the white man's tools."

"Like an ax?"

"Yes, there was an ax."

"Son of a bitch," Tracy Shadburn muttered, his face working with emotion.

"And this young boy? The man's son?"

"Yes, he of the wagon, his son. He was very proud of his son, and our chief told him he was right to be proud of such a young man. The boy's mother had died a long time ago, so they had finally decided to go to Texas."

"And this other white man traveling with them, the one of the weasel face. What did he say?"

"Not much. He ate a lot, but said little. We knew from their talk that he had been traveling with these two for only a short time. Across the Indian country, the weasel-faced man said. He was with these two, he said, so they might protect each other in the dangerous country. As though it might be the trail to Santa Fe in the old days."

With that, Otter Tongue glanced at me with his little smile, almost wistful, but it was gone in a twinkling.

There was such conviction in Otter Tongue's words that Adjutant Weslowski apparently believed him on face value, and Tracy Shadburn as well. And therefore the cavalry posse rode off again without further discussion, leaving the old Indian still standing there beside the bodies on their door panels.

When Tracy Shadburn and his troopers rode out of Fort Sill, I went with them, although Deacon had some difficulty keeping up. I assumed that Mr. Harper would want me to go along as agency representative, but no matter whether or not that was so, I couldn't have been kept away for any amount of money. It was coming on night when we rode into the draw where Olin Crater's soddy squatted like a mud toad. The shadows under the stands of stunted trees were already dark purple and the last light was going from the sky above the gully. Tracy slowed his soldiers to a walk, the horses snorting and some of them blowing hard. The cavalrymen unholstered their revolvers with the seven-and-a-half-inch barrels.

"I never liked this little son of a bitch," Tracy muttered, loud enough for all to hear. "But if he tries to resist, avoid killing him if you can."

We rode right up alongside the soddy and dismounted and went in as though we'd been invited and found the bony figure of Olin Crater bent over a bowl of hominy and brown gravy, a great deal of the latter on his receding chin. His eyes widened when he saw the drawn pistols. He swallowed a mouthful of hominy and wiped his mouth on a sleeve.

"Howdy, boys," he said.

Tracy lifted Olin by the shirt collar and slammed him back against one wall.

"Been down along Red River lately, Olin?" Tracy snarled.

"I ain't been nowhere, boys, really I ain't."

"Don't stand there gawkin'!" Tracy roared at his men, and they jumped to rummaging through the place. "And don't forget to check the shed and corral out back."

It's difficult to understand how stupid some men can be, especially those who live by petty theft, as I suspected Olin did. Only this was more serious than petty theft. The soldiers found the pistol under the bed and the rifle leaning in one corner of the soddy. Pistol and rifle, just as Otter Tongue had said. There were clean clothes stacked on a small side table, incriminating evidence because few people had ever seen Olin Crater with clean clothes. And behind the house, in the horse shed, there were three horses, two of them obviously harness drays and both geldings. And leaning against the wall of the privy was a double-bitted ax that still had bloodstains on it!

Tracy Shadburn and two of his biggest troopers were very rough on Olin Crater, shoving him about and screaming in his face and threatening him with things unmentionable, like a quick lynching or maybe spitting him on a bayonet.

"We've witnesses who saw you," Tracy kept yelling.

Finally, with the promise that before they carried him back to Sill they'd pull out his toenails with wire pliers, Olin broke down and confessed all, tears running off the end of his nose. He'd killed the man first, with the ax, and then the boy with the pistol he'd found in the wagon, blowing away the back of the boy's head even as the lad was begging for his life. He was a sorry lot, and lucky to get out of that soddy alive.

I was proud of old Tracy that night. His restraint must have been a difficult thing for him, knowing as I did his urge to make a bloody mush of little Olin Crater's face. Even so, he looked the other way as a couple of his soldiers pulled out hanks of Olin's hair and kicked him in the groin.

All the way back to Sill, the soldiers cursed their prisoner, as much for their inconvenience as for anything Olin had done. It was a strange ride, all that hatred mouthing forth and yet off to either side in the scattered trees the last of summer's mockingbirds putting up their soft voices.

They kept this fine specimen in the basement of the post guardhouse until a marshal could come for him.

Then he was fetched back to Fort Smith and the hangman. Later we heard that Judge Parker had put him on the gallows along with three murderers from the Cherokee Nation, all dropped together in a bunch. Tracy Shadburn got a trip to Fort Smith out of it, as a witness to the confession and the other evidence. When he returned, he looked as though he'd enjoyed a two-week drunk.

"That Fort Smith's stout as sulfur and molasses," Tracy said to me, his eyes still bleary and his skin a pale green color. "Worse than old Cincinnati used to be. I had a hell of a fine time, Morgan. You shoulda been there."

The ration day after we got the news of Olin Crater's demise, I sought out Otter Tongue to tell him about the close of the case. He shook his head gravely, holding his blanket tight across his shoulders.

"That hanging you do," he said. "A bad thing. With a rope around the neck, how can a man's spirit escape to the land beyond the sun?"

In Olin Crater's situation, I thought it was just the right treatment, land beyond the sun or no. There was another good thing about it. For six months or so after Olin was carted off to the rope, his good friend Rufus Tallbridge was scarce around the reservation. The terrible thought occurred to me that maybe our Rufus had joined that little son of a bitch somewhere along the trail after the night spent on the Big Beaver and just before the final act near the Red.

Such things are nightmares made of.

We never did learn who the murdered man was, nor the name of his son. For of all the things he had taken, Olin had apparently destroyed only the man's pocketbook and any papers he might have had identifying him. We buried them, man and boy, on boot hill, to lie among all the scalawags and scum who already inhabited the place.

One of the reservation missionaries came in to say a

few words over the graves. Only he and Mr. Stoddard and myself were there, except for the four volunteer army contract workers who waited to lower the oak boxes into the holes and cover them. The wind was blowing very hard that day.

It's strange how old loves intrude at most unusual times, suddenly and without warning. After we'd laid that poor little lad to his final rest, with no chance to have made his own mistakes, I went home and thought about the son we had always dreamed of having, Augustina and me. She was so real to me then that I could almost smell the lovely fragrance of her skin. It ran the gooseflesh out along my arms.

A long time she'd been gone, yet in my lonely hut there was no day that I wasn't reminded of her, even knowing in my mind that she was gone. Yet I could not escape the thought that maybe she was somewhere, waiting for me. In the place beyond the sun.

I could hear old Otter Tongue's voice, saying it. The place beyond the sun. Well, it was a comforting thought late at night, when the wind moaned under my eaves, even though I didn't really believe it. Forgive me, Da.

That was the fall when Sunshade came to me with the clay pipe between her teeth, the same clay pipe she had thrown at my feet in Otter Tongue's lodge. I'd supposed she had cast it aside forever. I was sure she came on the instructions of Kwahadi, and at first I wondered why he did not come himself, now that we had spoken to each other. But then it came to me that maybe this old woman knew more of her chief's mother than he knew himself.

But no matter why she came, or that she still had my gift pipe in her mouth. Her old yet young eyes blazed at me as hard and hostile as ever. Then it came to me, too, that this was how she viewed the entire world, with that fierce glance, and me only a part of the whole.

What a grand portrait she would have made, leading

her people over the ramparts with a rifle in one hand, a flag in the other, and naked to the waist as was that Frenchwoman I had seen in a painting in Philadelphia honoring the spirit of the revolution against the Bourbons. But Sunshade had no revolution and no ramparts to attack, no flag either, and remembering the quiver and bow on her saddle the day they had come in to surrender, I suspected she would disdain any weapon that came from a white man's hand.

She and Hawk were awaiting me that day in a small grove of oaks just north of the agency buildings. They were sitting their ponies as immobile as granite markers in a city park, but I felt them drawing me to them as though they were shouting my name. When I rode up, pulling my hatbrim low to shade my eyes from the lowering sun, Hawk backed his horse away a few feet, making no sign that he knew me, and throughout all that followed he said not a word.

Sunshade's little mare seemed uncomfortable to be so near a mere mule, and began to fidget and roll her eyes until the old woman twisted a handful of mane in one fist. Then the pony quieted and stood, but continued to quiver along the flanks as though expecting old Deacon to bite her at any moment.

It was the time of first frost, each morning the glistening shine of it along the stubble of the hayfields and lying like a layer of milk glass across the tops of the neatly stacked Fort Sill woodlot logs. There was the smell of coming snow, although everybody knew it would likely be weeks before the first fall. But already I could see the winter coats of the two Indian ponies coming on, long and shaggy, and the horses' breathing was white in the low wind.

It was late in the day, the coming night's chill making the air sharp. I'd been at the agency office, helping Mr. Harper work out the details of an argument between two band headmen who claimed the same winter campsite along one of the reservation streams. It was impossible! We finally resolved it by telling them they should ride out to the Big Beaver and let the Antelope chief decide. We learned later that they had done so, and Kwahadi questioned them about their personal battle honors and then awarded the choice spot to the one with the most service to his people.

A good system, that, although of little value in a white man's court where such things have to be decided. It showed the value Comanches placed on warriors.

When I rode Deacon up to her and drew rein, Sunshade glared at me, clamping the clay pipestem between her teeth. I touched my hatbrim and made a wee bow.

"I'm glad to see you," said I, and produced my tobacco pouch, for I could see her pipe was cold. "Have some of my tobacco."

She took the pouch without a word of thanks and tamped the bowl half-full. I provided a match and she struck it on her teeth, and even in the blustery wind she had the tobacco glowing quickly.

"About that raid," she said abruptly, and I had the impression she was being rude intentionally.

"When the white captive child was taken?"

"No. I've told you about that. The raid those men made on our camp. Men with metal on their chests when they rode into the village."

I knew she meant badges when she cupped a hand and placed it over one breast.

"Metal," she said.

"Yes, I know those kinds of men. Texas Rangers, maybe."

"Maybe. They came on big horses. White man's horses. It was early in the morning. We were camped on one of the rivers that flows into the Red. I don't know what you call it. White man's names for rivers and other things were for the elders of the band to know, not the women."

She puffed the pipe slowly, her cheeks pulling in

with each draw, and watched me closely to see the effect of her words on me.

"Have you heard of such a raid?" she asked.

"Yes, I've heard of many such raids. This river you said flowed into the Red?"

"Yes. In Texas. They came shooting the guns you hold in one hand."

"Pistols."

"Yes, pistols. They set fire to the lodges. They had a bunch of Tonkawas with them and the Tonkawas ran off our pony herd while the white men with metal on their chests rode through our camp, back and forth. Our men were killed coming from their bed robes. The people ran everywhere to get away from the white men. And I caught him up and we ran into the river and across it and then walked for five days and five nights to Palo Duro."

"You caught up Kwahadi?"

"Yes. I don't know what happened to Chosen."

"Chosen?"

"His mother. She had a small baby girl. I told you that before. I don't know what happened to them."

I was aware now that she was not so irritated by my questions as she had been before when we talked in Otter Tongue's tipi. I suspected Kwahadi had told her to be civil.

"Chosen was her name?"

"Yes, Kwahadi's mother. Before that, when she was still white, her name was Parry."

"So I've been told. How old was Kwahadi then? When the men on the big horses came?"

"A few summers he'd seen," she said evasively. "I don't know. I didn't count the seasons. He was old enough to be riding in the pony herd, tending the horses. The year the men with metal on their chests came, it was the Season of Yellow Leaf. We had started to go to the Kiowa sun dance again during the summer, but changed our minds. It was good we didn't go. While they were having their ceremonies, their camp was attacked by the

Skidi Pawnee or the Osage or somebody. I don't know. But we were not there."

And something else suddenly came to me. Once again this reference to the Kiowa sun dance. And I knew it was a way of matching their years to the white man's. Unsure in their own minds about how Comanche seasons reconciled with the numbered years, she and old Otter Tongue had thrown out this clue, hoping that maybe one of the Kiowa calendars would tell more than they could.

"We walked for five days and five nights," she said, her words coming fast now. "It was very cold. It was raining the first two days and we had little clothing between us. We came to Palo Duro, and my people, the Antelopes. My husband and his band, they were Nakoni. But my people were the Antelopes. And they took us into their lodges, and there Kwahadi grew and became a man and a great war leader."

"And you never saw her again, this Chosen?" I asked.

She smoked, saying nothing, until the bowl was burned down. Then she slipped the pipe into some hidden place beneath the trade blanket across her shoulders.

"I dreamed about her," she said, and her gaze left my face and seemed to search out toward the westering sun, a faraway look shining in her eyes and the wind blowing the hair back from her face. "I dreamed she was dead and gone to the place beyond the sun, where people live after they die. It was a strong dream and it came many times."

"Tell me about the dream," I said.

"I dreamed she had gone to the place beyond the sun," she snapped, and I knew she had no intention of detailing any of her dreams to a white man. "I told him. I told Kwahadi his mother was dead, but he thinks maybe my dream was wrong. He wants her back where she belongs, with The People. To live in one of those wooden houses you white men are building for us."

"There will be many wooden houses," said I. "I'm

told the one for Kwahadi has already been finished, alongside Big Beaver Creek."

"Yes," she said. "And with a glass window. He keeps his horses in it!"

Then suddenly she turned and rode off without another word, Hawk falling in behind as he gave me a final look.

So it was back to my shack in a hurry to write down in the little book what she had said. That evening, smelling bacon cooking, I read everything I had in that book. Not much, really, but all any white man knew, I suspected, of what had happened to Kwahadi in his young years. But one good thing. There were three sun dances mentioned, so I knew that when opportunity presented itself I would have to ride north and talk with the old Kiowa, Bear. Maybe he could unlock the details from his tribal memories.

Otter Tongue had said he thought Chosen had been recaptured, but Sunshade said she believed Kwahadi's mother was dead. For a long time in my bed that night, I thought about Sunshade's dream. I had no more faith in dreams than I did in heaven, yet I knew from Phil McCusker that dreams were the real stuff of life to the Comanches.

It seemed that all my nights after talking with any of the Big Beaver people were restless, my mind working on the thought of a white captive child who grew to be the mother of a great chief. And now the great chief was conquered, but in his changed condition he was impelled to find his mother. Who had sprung from the very people who had conquered him.

I lay listening to the freshening wind, knowing it meant a cold day on the wagon seat tomorrow. In its whisperings I could hear the words of old Sunshade and in my mind see the eyes defiant and hard. And I thought of that great chief when only a boy, walking through the cold and rain, half naked, the woman beside him, walking all the way to Palo Duro Canyon.

We walked for five days and five nights.

And I supposed with every step that boy wondered what had happened to his mother, wondered whether she was alive or dead, wondered all the days into his manhood, and wondered still. Maybe the white side of his nature refused to believe in Sunshade's dream of Chosen's death. And maybe the Comanche side insisted that his own dream be to find the truth.

10

Looking back after all the years, one surely must despair that a diary wasn't kept, marking down the days' events one by one. So many changes were coming fast and later it was impossible to arrange things all in proper sequence. Perhaps that's why so many allow their recollections to die and go to the grave with them, casualties of the embarrassment of bad memory.

So it was with many of us, unable to arrange in order the emotions, much less the events.

Colonel Mackenzie was gone from Fort Sill, replaced by a man named John Davidson. Almost everyone hated to see Mackenzie go, such a fine man was he, even though in recent months going a little glassy in the eye and later an insane man, so it was told. Perhaps he understood the wild tribesmen as well as anyone because he had fought them so long. It drove him mad, some thought, or else the lingering dreams of slaughter on the battlefields of the War Between the States.

Davidson was a good man but never seemed so close to what was happening on the reservation as Mackenzie had been.

Weslowski remained on station as post adjutant, and it was he who became best known of all the soldiers who came and went. In later years, many would think of him, his pale blue eyes *watery and his hand constantly darting into his tunic for the handkerchief to wipe his running nose. It was only then, after long association was completed and gone, that men realized how Lieutenant Wes had grown in their affection, both white men and red alike.*

And out on the reservation, there were changes as well— many wooden houses being built, and fences to keep Indian ponies and cattle contained. More and more Texas drovers grazed their herds on reservation grass, paying tribute for it, all unofficial but now overlooked by the bureaucrats because it meant meat in the lodges.

And on each ration day, more and more of the Kiowas and Comanches appeared in white man's clothing. They seemed embarrassed at first, ill at ease in cloth that must have been flimsy to their touch after a lifetime of wearing animal skins.

The agency was running a school for their children, and some of the missionaries were doing the same. It was beyond understanding why so many of those schools tried to make the boys cut their hair to white man's length. Not the girls, but only the boys among a people where men valued their long hair more than the women did. It was hard to imagine what short hair had to do with making them more civilized.

It was as though someone were afraid of any semblance of the old life, when one had only to look into the dark faces and the black eyes and see beyond doubt that these were the children of those free-roaming days, the youngest generation of the Kiowas and Comanches. No bureaucrats' rules could erase such evidence of what they had been.

Many's the time in those early seasons of reservation life that food was scarce, little hungry eyes looking into pots that were empty. It was a miracle that so many endured. It was a miracle that many finally came to the fact that in the white man's world as paupers, one must eat what the white man eats: bread made from ground cornmeal or wheat, boiled beans, pumpkins and melons, and other such truck far removed from red meat and mesquite-bean mush.

The images that come on reflection! I hear yet the sounds of nightbirds along the streams and in the flat prairie grasslands, calling my memory back. But all of it so vague after these many years, the details lost on the wind and gone forever and only the overwhelming vastness seen or felt of the open plains and the great herds and the people, pure as packs of wolves then, but now struggling to be free again in a new world little understood.

The saddest season was the one when the hunters went out for buffalo. Not only the hunters but the whole band. And it all started when Kwahadi and I finally had our little smoke.

It was a flashing good spring that year when I rode out to the Big Beaver. Mr. William Soule, the photographer, had asked me to intercede with the Antelope chief on his behalf. He wanted a picture of Kwahadi and his various wives while they were still in plains garb and looking the part of wild Indians.

The camp had changed. It had spread out, and I knew that what Mr. Harper said was true. Tribal units were breaking up all over the reservation and living in little family clusters. This was brought on largely by the placement of the wooden houses we were building them, generally one for each head of family according to the ration rolls and scattered across the land in anticipation of their becoming farmers, each family having its own garden plot nearby.

Not that very many of them actually lived in the wooden houses. Like Kwahadi, most kept horses in the little slab-side structures and lived themselves in tipis alongside. Or, in summer, in brush arbors. Never had I seen a people so devoted to the brush arbor.

All through the camp, where it stretched along the banks of the stream, were women working over pots suspended from tripods of poles or sitting in groups in the shade of the lodges, gossiping and sewing. There were a number of children playing among the dogs, the youngest of them wearing nothing but tiny moccasins. *In puris naturalibus,* as Mr. Henry Morton Stanley might say. A state of nature that Mr. Harper did everything he could to discourage.

I was happy to see that on my approach no one ran to hide as they had in past times. The fact is, mostly they ignored me.

Kwahadi's family unit surrounded his wooden house, one of the biggest we had yet built, having two rooms and a glass window. Nearby was his tipi, painted with black wolf heads, and his brush arbor. Arranged in a semicircle around them were the lodges of his wives and of old Sunshade, and beyond that, a small tipi that I knew was the menstrual lodge where women were isolated during their time each month. And set in the center of it all was the horse corral where, that spring, when I visited him, they were gelding some of the colts dropped in previous seasons.

Outside the corral were a number of small boys, waiting astride older horses to tend the colts when they were released. Inside were three Comanche men, all of them wearing vests made from white men's coats, and one with a hat, high-crowned and black. It was the first time I had seen a hat on a Comanche head. There, too, was my young friend, Allis Featherman.

A fascinating operation, that, with Allis right at the center of it with his castrating knife, his hat pulled tight down over his mop of straw hair. He had told me that of any five colts dropped in the Comanche herd, only one was usually considered good enough for breeding, the rest being turned into eunuchs.

There were many birds singing that day and the land smelled of fresh weather, warm, and the wind not stirring any more than the usual amount of dust from the corral and the pastures beyond. A setting of peace and tranquility, if ever there was such a thing.

Kwahadi's eldest wife, Coming Back from the Pony Herd, greeted me in her chief's brush arbor, and a small boy who I assumed was one of his sons ran up to take Deacon's reins. She offered me meat and a tobacco pouch and asked me to sit in the shade before the man himself appropriately made his appearance after these initial hospitalities were offered.

"It's a good day for the young ponies," said I, pointing to some of the new foals playing beside the mares in an oak-edged field.

"Yes," she said, and smiled. She had a soft face, much unlike that of the granite-hard Sunshade, and there seemed to be no hatred burning from her eyes. Because she'd never had a husband killed by the white man, I supposed. She pointed to the corral. "But not so good for the older ponies."

She hurried away, giggling at her own boldness, and for a while I watched Allis Featherman and his companions working on the colts in the corral. It was all done quickly and expertly, with only a forlorn whistle from the young horses now and again when the knife sliced through. After each cut, the wounds were plastered with something that looked like creek mud, but I knew from Allis this was a secret kind of antiseptic grass mulch.

"They heal in two days," he'd told me.

"And lose their future as stallions," I'd said.

"The best gets the most," he'd replied, and I'd cuffed him roughly about the ears.

When Kwahadi came, he was wearing much the same garb he'd worn in the agency office that day with the Hound of Heaven. But now his hair was loose except for the scalp lock falling down his back, and I thought that good, his accepting me as a casual friend for whom there was no need of detailed grooming.

I'd hoped he might speak of his mother that day, once the unimportant conversation about the weather was finished. But he never came close to the subject. I had the feeling he avoided any talk of it because his mother was a shared secret so powerful that we could not mention it even between ourselves.

He had a direct way of looking at me when he spoke, and the speckled sunlight filtering from the roof of the arbor sent the gray lights shining through his eyes. Now and again, for no apparent cause, he would gaze toward his horse herd or watch a circling hawk, a distant expression on his face. I wondered at those times what he was really seeing. When he looked toward the corral, there was the satisfied half-smile of a commander observing that his subordinates were doing their job well.

"The young man Allis," he said. "A good young man. He has come to mean much to my people."

"And your people to him," said I, hoping it didn't sound too patronizing, though it was true.

When finally I mentioned the purpose of my call, a quick frown crossed his face, like a small passing flight of black birds, come and gone in the same instant. He smoked for a while silently, holding his long-stemmed pipe in both slender hands with the pronounced veins showing under the skin. It was a surprisingly delicate skin, almost like old parchment easily torn.

As I waited for him to speak, the slow wind moving his long hair back along his neck, I watched him and saw for the first time that his ears were pierced, each lobe with a tiny band of Mexican gold, like wedding rings. There was a sense of his knowing that I was inspecting him, but there was no resentment. It was like looking at the cover of a book, none of whose pages had yet been revealed. Some of these I knew he would always keep to himself.

"Why do you want the image of me and my wives on one of those pieces of glass?" he finally asked.

"For history. So that your own great-grandchildren may see how you appear."

"Does this have something to do with throwing away some of my wives?"

"No, it's not anything like that. Mr. Soule is interested in history. Not in converting you to his religion."

"What is his religion?"

"I don't know. I never inquire of a man as to his religion."

A quick smile played at the corners of his mouth and he nodded, puffing his pipe. "That's good. I'm not sure what religion is. Only that some spirits move certain men, and not others. But now I am told by some of the Panetekas that there is a law you've made that forbids our young men from taking more than one wife. And I am told that some of the older men have already taken this road and sent off all their wives but one. Are you sure this thing with Mr. Soule is not something to help the missionaries? To make me throw away a lot of good women?"

"No, it's for history only."

"Well, history is good. Someday I'll tell you about the Spaniards, as it was told to me by the tribal fathers. But," he said, "I'm not so sure your missionaries are good. There are some of them who have come with their wives and children and built a wooden house to sing to their gods just upstream from our camp."

"Yes, I know," said I. "The Mennonites."

"Well, they're not so bad, like that man with the long coat and the whiskers on his face stiff and dead. A few of my people have already listened to them. But it's not a religion I want to take."

It was amusing to me that the Mennonites, who disavowed all forms of war, should be cultivating their moral field among maybe the most warlike of all the plains tribes.

"This white man's road is very confusing sometimes," Kwahadi said. "In many things there's an argument about how to do it. Some say one way, some say another. Then when it's finished, everyone's supposed to do everything a certain way, each like the other.

"We know all about arguing. We've always been good at it. But when it's finished, everyone does as he pleases."

"It's confusing to the white man sometimes," I said.

"My wife you just saw," said he. "She says she's civilized a crow. A large black bird that comes and sits on the edge of this brush arbor each morning to eat corn she gives him. A strange bird. But very brave. Because he comes when the others of his tribe sit back in those oak trees yonder and only watch and make a lot of noise. But they get no corn. My wife says it proves anything can be civilized.

"Now you white people use that word a lot. Civilized. I don't know what it means. I don't think my wife does, either. I think maybe she believes it means learning to eat corn."

He laughed then and his expression was abruptly softened, a greater transformation than any I had ever seen on a human face. All fire and ice suddenly gone in a flash, but then quickly back. Except in his eyes, he continued to laugh.

"Liver, let's talk now," he said, as though nothing that had gone before was talking. He laid his pipe aside and bent toward me, and in the flat parchment of his facial skin I could see the tiny creases at the ends of his eyes.

"My people have always been traders. Now I'd like to see what kind of trader you are. I'll allow this Mr. Soule to take my image on his piece of glass. I've seen some he's done of the Kiowas. Very impressive for their great-grandchildren. But I'll not have any of my wives except one. Coming Back from the Pony Herd."

"I see no reason why Mr. Soule would not be happy with such an arrangement."

"Coming Back is my favorite wife," he said. "It's hard not to have a favorite, even though they are all fine women. There's no bitterness about it. All the others know she is my best wife."

"Mr. Soule will be happy."

"Well, there's something else," said he, watching me closely now. "Mr. Soule must come here. I'll not go into his house near that place where they sell the whiskey to have him do these things."

"That can be arranged. He has a wagon. Inside the wagon he can do his pictures as well as he can do them in his wooden house. There were many like him in the great war between the white men. They took their wagons along with the armies, making their images as they went."

"These men would have had a hard time keeping up with one of our war parties in the old days," Kwahadi said. "But that's good, if he can come here. He can make his picture. And now, there is your part of the trade."

He became very serious now, rubbing his chin with his fingers as he watched the work being finished in the corral, the gelded colts released to run in the pasture where the mares were grazing. The boys on the older horses rode beside them, reaching out to touch their manes and muzzles, speaking words softly to soothe the excited colts. I knew these young boys would watch the new geldings very closely to see that they did nothing crazy because of being cut.

"Those are good boys," Kwahadi mused almost to himself. "They know what to do. In the old days, the boys watched our herds all the time and there were many horses."

For one of the few times ever, I knew then what was in his mind's eye: large herds of ponies eating the grass of Llano Estacado. It was a good feeling for me, yet sad. And he wanted to keep that moment for a little longer.

"When I was a boy," he said, "I was watching the horses when I had only seven summers. And at night I played in the herd, and sometimes the older girls would come and teach us wonderful things about how men and women could be together. Sometimes we slept among the horses, in the cool seasons lying on their backs and feeling the warmth of their bodies."

He looked at me then and smiled gently, almost, I thought, the way a woman smiles when she thinks of the good years of her coming-to-age.

"Did you know that when The People first saw the horse, they thought he was a god? They thought he was a dog, brother to the wolf. But then they found that he was not a dog or a god but only brother to man."

It was no shame then for me to feel the skin along my neck ripple. These were powerful words. But now he was finished with such things, and squaring his shoulders, he took a deep breath and came back to the present.

"I'm going to tell you a serious thing, Liver," said he. "These people of mine are not yet ready for the white man's road. They talk always about the old ways. How we killed the buffalo to live. How we moved when we were ready to move, going even into Mexico. How we always went out to fight our traditional enemies like the Pawnees or Apaches. In their hearts, they are not certain that such things are gone.

"But I know they are gone. So if we could go out again for a large buffalo hunt, maybe they would be ready afterwards to take the white man's road without so much complaining."

He looked squarely at me, and there was in his eyes some deep sadness and a bitter downward turn of his finely sculpted lips.

"If you can arrange for this band to go off the reservation and make a big hunt in the late summer and fall, then I will allow your Mr. Soule to do what he does with his little wagon and his pieces of glass."

"Such things have been done before, for others," said I. "It might be arranged. But you understand that someone from the agency or the army will have to go with you."

"Yes, to keep my young men from scalping a lot of white people," he said sardonically.

"To protect you from wild shooters who aim their guns at anything," I said. "And you will have to tell Colonel Davidson exactly where you plan to hunt."

"Yes. I understand. Hawk will come to you when you tell him, and he will say these necessary things to Davidson."

"And, my friend," I made so bold to say, "you must also understand that you will find few buffalo."

He stared at me for a long time then, the sad gray still in his eyes. When he spoke, it was so softly I could hardly hear.

"Liver, have you ever seen a child starve to death?"

"No. I'm happy to say I haven't."

"I have. It's a very bad thing to see. With the old ones, it's not so bad. Their lives are over anyway, so it doesn't matter much. But a young child with his belly sticking out and his eyes large and nothing to put in his stomach, that's a very bad thing.

"Now, this is the part only you must hear. I know we'll find little game. Your white hunters with their large rifles have already killed everything. I know this. But my people don't believe it. And only by showing them can I convince them. If we stay out long enough, some of us are going to get very hungry. That's a hard thing for a man to do. To show his people something by letting a few of the older ones starve!"

"I'm sorry. But the old ways are gone."

"Yes. Forever!"

And so they went out, as they had done so many times through their short history, looking for the buffalo. But not the same. With them went the representatives of the Federal government in the form of Mr. Jehyle Simmons and Allis Featherman.

Allis made such a nuisance of himself in Mr. Harper's office that the agent finally agreed to take him on as part-time interpreter without pay, just for the occasion. So Allis went with them, but not I. I'd formed a contract with Mr. Stoddard to drive his new stagecoach for the summer months. The regular driver was in Forth Worth, trying to find a cure for the social disease he'd caught from one of the belles who sometimes hung about Boggy Depot, on the eastern end of the run.

That was a terrible time for me, having made the commitment and yet straining to break it and go with Kwahadi's band onto the high plains, looking for meat. But some better judgment prevailed and I decided I must make my word good. My good word was about all I had left in the world, and was worth protecting. So I didn't go with my Antelope friends, and it turned out to be just as well.

After I'd made the proposition to Mr. Harper, and he to Colonel Davidson, and the approval had been given, but before the band left for their off-reservation hunt, Mr. Soule drove his little boxlike wagon out to the Big Beaver and Kwahadi posed for him, standing beside Coming Back from the Pony Herd, who sat on an empty whiskey keg provided by the resourceful Mr. Soule. Young Allis Featherman himself was the sergeant major of this operation, myself being at the moment halfway between Sill and the Choctaw Nation in that strange new wagon stage of Stoddard & Blanchard, with its canvas roof and leather springs.

On my return, I went straight to Mr. Soule's establishment and viewed his handiwork. There they were, Kwahadi and his favorite wife, caught forever on the glass. Well, unless somehow it was broken by clumsy hands. They were in their plains garb and looked very Indian, he holding an eagle-feather fan in one of those delicate hands. She seemed on the very verge of smiling, a twinkle in her black eyes, but the chief was very, very grim. Looking at the image of his face, I remembered his words to me that day in his brush arbor. And I thought that the good Mr. Soule had well caught the spirit of this half-blood Comanche. The lines running back from his eyes were much like the many fingers of the forks of the Brazos where his people had lived and hunted, and the plucked brows barren and flat as the plain of Llano Estacado.

It left me much affected, and there were maybe a few tears as I went back to the little shack the agency people had been so kind to provide me. But I passed it off as only the wind-driven dust, and yet spoke most gently to old Deacon. Who didn't care one way or the other.

One of our crosses to bear, us Welsh, the tears coming from time to time in moments of sentiment. But, as my dear old mother always said, tears are a washing of the soul.

Rumors had begun to float across the reservation like maple seeds before the wind, as they always did when something new was afoot. Everyone soon knew that Kwahadi was going out again and murmurings were abroad that there was great menace in such a thing.

Two days before the band's scheduled departure, Mr. Harper sent me to the fort with the intelligence that the Antelopes were planning a dance, and maybe some troops ought to ride out to the Big Beaver to insure that the ceremony wasn't one of those many the bureaucrats had prohibited. So Lieutenant Tracy Shadburn mounted out a detail of his dog robbers and I rode along to do whatever intrepreting was required.

A cruel sight that, watching the soldiers issued forty rounds of carbine ammunition and a dozen or so for their revolvers, and their faces already set in a mask that spelled no nonsense. As though they could hear the distant mutter of artillery and were riding toward the battleground.

We were late starting, maybe by design, and it was dark before the fort fell far behind. A good summer night it was, with plenty of cicadas and other assorted bugs making their cheerful racket among the tree-lined watercourses. There was not much talk among the soldiers, Tracy and his troops being intent on serious business ahead.

Then from far off we could hear the pulsing of the drums, like great beating hearts. When we came into sight of the village, riding to the crest of the last rise of ground, there were the fires below us. A sight it was.

I drew in old Deacon and Tracy Shadburn close beside me, the troopers strung out behind, muttering at what they saw. There were least a dozen fires kindled around Kwahadi's lodges and wooden house. Red reflections wavered on the window glass. Near the largest of the fires were old men beating the drums, using switches and lengths of saplings as drumsticks. Behind them was a group of singers chanting the words of songs unintelligible yet somehow of a universal language.

Around the fires we could see dark figures dancing, men and women together, and on the fringes the children were dancing too. All of them singing, everything in unison, everything a moving part of the whole. The sounds of the drums and the singing filled the night, and here the insects and birds and frogs were silent, listening.

"Well," said Tracy Shadburn in his menacing voice, "let's go down there and bust this up."

"No need," I said, reaching out a hand to touch his arm in the darkness. "It's only a dance they have for celebrating the hunt. They always do this before they go out for the buffalo."

Whether this was true or not, I had no idea, but I suspected it was the case because these were a singing people who took every opportunity to celebrate with their gods.

"It looks pretty damned troublesome to me," he said, but there was indecision in his voice.

"No harm being done," said I. "Let them have their dance. It's only a natural part of the night."

"You better be right, Morgan," he said, and I felt him shudder. "That racket makes goosebumps on my back."

"They're only talking to a spirit world never known to us," I said.

"We'll watch awhile, just in case," said Tracy, although I had no notion what the case might be. I suspected he simply wanted to see and hear more. It was an addictive thing, that throbbing and chanting, maybe a whisper from the past for all of us.

The better part of an hour we stayed, noting that the intensity of the singing did not increase. Nor decrease either, simply going on and on through the night, the figures about the fires seeming to move without effort, without fatigue. Then finally we turned toward the fort and rode away, listening to the sound of it long after we could no longer see the fires, all of it beating gently in the night behind us and finally gone with distance. And through our whole ride home, not a word was spoken by any of the soldiers.

It was raining the day they left. Not a good day for travel, but I supposed they were anxious to be away on schedule, afraid someone at the agency or maybe even Davidson would change his mind.

They trailed their column down past the agency, riding out as they had always done, the young men at the lead, the older men and women following, the women on travois horses heavy with the burdens of tipis and the meat they had dried for the trip. Allis Featherman had informed me that they had killed off all their small herd of Texas cattle, stripped the meat, and hung it to dry, hoping there was enough to sustain them until they found the herds.

It was a dismal day, and I was not detailed for a run on the coach until the morrow. There was the prospect of staying dry inside my shack and reading a little in some of the dime novels that Stoddard & Blanchard were stocking by then. Not very great literature, but at least better than spending a soggy day killing the ants that had invaded my kitchen cupboard.

But weather be damned. As soon as I heard someone shout that the Comanches were coming, I slid into my rubber raincoat and out onto Deacon to watch them from some distance as they passed. Soon Mr. Harper joined me there, the water dripping from his hatbrim like liquid pearls.

"They seem to have accumulated a number of weapons," said the agent, sounding as though it were one more of the failures of President Grant's benevolent Quaker policy.

There were only a few rifles and pistols among them, but all the men, including the old ones and some of the women besides, had the short Comanche quiver and bow, and a few carried lances. Mr. Phil McCusker had always said that of all the plains tribes, Comanches were the best at taking buffalo with the lance.

Kwahadi was leading them, and close behind him rode old Sunshade, her face painted ocher but running like red sweat in the rain. Hawk was there, too, with the lance of Sanchess, carrying the weapon for his chief like a squire out of Mr. Scott's *Ivanhoe*.

Allis Featherman was well toward the head of the column, and when he saw us he rode over, grinning, and I saw the big Colt pistol in his belt, the same that I had won from that Arkansas whiskeymaker and loaned to the lad for this little journey.

"We're off to the buffalo ranges," he shouted, no amount of rain dampening his spirits, his teeth shining even in this lightless day.

"Mr. Featherman," Harper said, touching his hatbrim with his fingers in a very formal way, "do your duty well, and watch out for these people."

"I'll do the best I can, Mr. Harper."

"And try to keep that pistol dry," said I, and he laughed and wheeled away from us to rejoin the column.

Simmons had waited until the last possible moment, but now we saw him ride out from the agency buildings to fall in with the cavalcade, looking dejected and grumpy. I damned him for being there instead of me, and damned myself for driving that Stoddard & Blanchard coach instead of him.

Watching the band move toward the treeline to the south, I knew something was missing but it took me a wee spell to realize what it was. There were no shields.

Because shields were not required for the hunt, but only for war. When I pointed this out to Mr. Harper, he grunted and muttered something about a few shields likely being hidden in the travois bundles. Maybe he was despondent, as was I.

It was a glad day for the Comanches, rain or no. The people passing us held their heads high, and their ponies pranced and rolled their eyes; the children on the travois, or riding double behind their mothers or aunts, wore happy faces. Tagging along behind, the only ones in the whole group who looked dejected, were the dogs, heads down, tails tucked.

"They seem to have fewer dogs now," the agent said.

We both knew what had happened to those missing dogs, no explanation required. During the last winter, when rations had been short, there had been canine stew on the Big Beaver. Like anyone else, Comanches hungry enough would eat anything, taboo or no.

Then they were gone, winding like a retreating thread of Confederate cavalry into the gray trees. That analogy deepened my depression. Lost causes have a special spot in the hearts of old soldiers, enough to moisten the eyes.

Before we turned back to our dry wooden buildings for some of Mr. Harper's blue-enameled-pot coffee, a single horseman came riding back from the treeline and straight to us. As he drew near, I saw it was Hawk, wearing an antelope-skin headpiece and still carrying the old ironwood lance. He drew up abruptly before us in a shower of mud, the rivers of rain running off his great square chin. He raised his free hand in salute, but his eyes were as flinty as I'd ever seen them.

"My chief wanted me to tell you, Liver. He hopes you and the soldiers enjoyed our dancing."

Then with a sudden movement he turned his pony away and galloped off, the antelope-skin hood streaming out behind.

"What did he say?" Mr. Harper asked.

"He said his chief wanted to thank you for helping them make this hunt," I lied.

"That was considerate of him," said he. "They are a good people. If only we can show them the way."

His words turned sour on my ear, and I found myself detesting the idea of having any of his coffee. After he rode away, I stayed for a long time there, looking toward the south and Texas and glad I had not shared the dancing with Harper. It was certain that everyone on the reservation knew about the dancing from Tracy Shadburn and his soldiers. But not through me. It was as though I wanted those sounds to remain mine alone among the white men.

The rain was coming harder, making the distant trees blur to vision, and to the northwest there was no visible indication that the Wichita Mountains had ever existed. Toward Cache Creek a single crow made his wretched cawing, and it was a most mournful sound. And I thought of those people who had passed off into the somber mists and were now gone, I knew, for the last time on such a journey.

It all came to us from Allis Featherman. Simmons was so bitter from the experience he wouldn't talk much about it.

They came back on a day even worse than the one that saw them leave. Not rain, but a cold wind off the high plains, and a hint of snow in the low clouds rolling overhead like a gray feather tick gone crazy and running toward the east. A terrible late-September day, more like November.

Allis came straight to the agency office and there related the story to me and Mr. Harper. All the while the little potbellied stove muttered with its filling of burning oak, and the odor of the blue-enameled-pot coffee was thick as musk in the room. The lad took two cups of the scalding brew, seeming to relish the blistering heat of it, and then Mr. Harper went back to his wife's kitchen and brought out some cold pork roast and Allis gulped it down with hardly a chew to the mouthful.

"It rained on us for almost a week," he started, still eating pork and gulping the coffee.

They rode to one of the Red River crossings and forded to the other side and made their first camp. Not a good beginning, with all the tipi hides and bedding wet and hardly any wood to be had dry enough for burning. A cattle herd was crossing along the Western Trail, but the band had their dried beef to eat and none of the young men tried to steal any of the cattle.

"If we'd seen that herd later," young Allis said, a bulge of meat in one cheek like a cud of Tracy Shadburn's chewing tobacco, "Kwahadi couldn't have stopped their rustling it."

Kwahadi and Otter Tongue and Hawk rode over to reassure the drovers that everything was peaceful and aboveboard. They knew the chief, his fame already having spread among the Texas cattlemen, and everyone exchanged tobacco and had a little smoke in the rain. When they turned back to The People, the trail boss shook Kwahadi's hand.

"I was with them," Allis said. "They offered a cow or two. But Kwahadi said he didn't need it. I don't know why he said that. Maybe pride. I just can't figure why he didn't take a little beef from those people."

I thought I knew why, but said nothing.

They didn't travel a straight line, even though they knew exactly where they were headed. Kwahadi led them on meandering routes to avoid any contact with white ranches and settlements. At first that was an irritation to the hot-blooded young men, who wanted to go directly at it, but later, in country more sparsely settled, the problem solved itself.

They made no hunting camp until they reached the forks of the Brazos, almost one hundred fifty miles from their starting point. The first day there, the sun came out and spirits soared.

In the evening they danced, singing to the spirit of the buffalo, asking all their gods to bring meat within range of their weapons. And the next morning in dazzling sunlight the young scouts rode out, their hair loose in the wind. In the evening the young men returned. They had found many bones lying on the prairie, but no living game. They stayed there for more than seven sleeps, each day searching to more distant points, but found nothing to hunt.

There had never been a country so empty of game. Nothing but a few jackrabbits, and already the small supply of beef running out. They spent a long time along the Double Mountain Fork, because so many could remember the days when the buffalo ran there so thick they were like a brown cloud blown over the land, raising dust-clouds that could be seen from far off. But now there were no herds. As though all the buffalo had run across a great hole in the ground and fallen in and disappeared.

Finally they crossed the low divide to the White Fork of the Brazos and hunted there for days and killed only two buffalo, the only ones they saw, and very old.

"Every night we went to sleep hungry," Allis said, and there was a glistening in his eyes. "Those little children dreamed bad dreams and cried in their sleep, but when they were awake they didn't say nothin'. They just watched each day when the hunter scouts came in, and no game."

Then up the Running Water Draw and onto Llano Estacado, expecting surely to find buffalo there. They found nothing but pronghorn antelope. There were not enough horses to run the antelope down in relays, as they had done in the old days. So, using a red-flag bait waved on a lance, they managed to draw a pair of the little animals close enough to shoot, the pronghorn coming to see what this new flash of color was, and dying from their curiosity.

"Did you ever try to feed that many people with two pronghorns?" Allis asked. "Not a good mouthful apiece, brains, guts, balls, and all!"

They moved slowly up the Llano Estacado, south to north, camping frequently because the young men insisted from experience that there would be buffalo just beyond the closest horizon. They found bones again, and old white hunters' camps, and now and again empty brass cartridge cases from the huge Sharps rifles, the cases left lying in the short grass like specks of gold beginning to go green in the weather.

They avoided the old white hunters' outpost of Adobe Walls. That had been a place of disaster in their memories, where pony-mounted warriors had tried to oust invaders armed with long-range rifles and fighting from behind solid walls.

"He told me," Allis said. "He called me into his lodge and told me. Kwahadi said there was this medicine man named Coyote Droppings who told all The People that his power was so great it would turn aside bullets. And they rode against those white hunters at Adobe Walls. I knew about that before, but I never knew what happened, all of it. He told me. The bullets weren't turned away. And some Comanches and Kiowas died there. So we rode far around it because he said it was a bad time in his people's history brought on by a false prophet."

It was on Llano Estacado that the dancing and singing to the buffalo became nightly affairs. The elders met each day, but there was nothing they could do except ask the drummers and singers to come out. Once, they danced and chanted for a full night and into the dawn, trying to call forth the buffalo. After that one big dance, many of the people in the band stopped coming to the dances, stopped their singing because they were hungry and growing weak.

Sunshade went far out onto the plain to sing to the buffalo, but none came. Each morning the scouts went out and found nothing. The children began to make traps for prairie dogs and jackrabbits, both hard to catch. The girls searched for bird's eggs, but it was past the season for them. One of the older horses went lame and they killed and ate it.

An old woman died before they reached the Canadian, and they buried her in the usual way, in a sitting position and facing east and covered with rocks. That night there was a mourning for another of The People having gone to the place beyond the sun, but it didn't last long.

They moved slowly downstream along the Canadian, but it was the same there as everywhere else. Only now the short summer was going and the winds were hard and cold. They moved south again, to the Salt Fork of the Red, and found no game. It was a wet time, raining almost every day for a week, and they could taste snow in it as it came down in slate-colored sheets to dampen their clothes and their hides and their spirits.

Now they began to see a few ranches, and Kwahadi avoided them. Even with all his efforts and those of Otter Tongue and Hawk to prevent it, sometimes one of the young men would go out at night, and in the morning there would be a white man's steer in the camp, quickly killed and eaten.

From the Brazos onward, Simmons had been insisting that they return to the reservation, where they could be fed. But Kwahadi turned a cold eye on him and said they had not been out long enough yet.

"He kept saying that," Allis told us. "Not out long enough yet, and he'd look at the children standin' around with them big eyes, hungry and not runnin' and playin' with the dogs. Hell. There wasn't no dogs by then. We'd ate all of 'em. But he kept saying, 'Not long enough yet.'"

It turned scalding hot for a few days, and there were storms that blew away some of the tipis. The people were growing careless in pegging down their lodges because they were weak and some didn't seem to care anymore. They killed two more horses, but Kwahadi told them they had to keep as many as they could because they represented all the future wealth of the band.

Then, already back in Indian Territory and traveling slowly down the North Fork of the Red, Kwahadi said they'd go in; he'd been watching the children all along and finally gave up the hunt just before any of them starved.

"He sent me on ahead on the best horse he had," Allis said. "So I did, and thank God it's all over."

Mr. Harper had kept their normal ration of beef on the hoof in the agency holding pen, and Weslowski sent over half a dozen head of army cattle. When Kwahadi came, the cows were waiting but the band didn't slow their march. They herded the cattle right on past the agency and toward the Big Beaver before they slaughtered them and fed. Going home in their pride before they satisfied their hunger.

"And it is home now," said I. "They've finally been shown they have no other."

Allis gave me a funny look then, realizing only now, with my words, what Kwahadi had been doing in keeping his people out through all that misery.

I hadn't gone out to see them ride back through. It was a sight I had no desire to see, that forlorn band in their last hunt on the open plains, bedraggled and sore and hungry and red-eyed.

But I heard they rode still with great pride and dignity, even with the pain in their bellies.

"By the by, Morgan," Allis said, pouring himself another cup of Mr. Harper's coffee and looking as though he was glad the story was finished. "I loaned that big pistol of yours to Hawk for the hunt. He never got to fire it a single time. But I neglected to get it back. I'll ride out tomorrow and fetch it."

"No need," said I. "The mice in my wee shack are not yet vicious enough to be pursued with a .45-caliber weapon."

Later I came to appreciate my own generosity.

11

It was that winter, when I spent so much time along the northern tier of the reservation, that I came closer to Kwahadi's mother. I had not seen him for a long time, my other duties preventing me. But the thought of that white captive taken so long ago was never far from my thinking.

A lot of horses had been stolen that year in the north, close to the reservation boundary. The herds were widely dispersed to find fodder in the wintertime, and it was hard to watch them. Especially now that the bands did not bunch their ponies together but more or less scattered them in small family units. They were a tempting target for the rustlers, who were never far away.

"There are sure a lot of men around here who steal horses," Otter Tongue said once, when we were watching the ponies race on ration day. "Stealing horses is all right when you can go out and steal them back again. It's a good way for a man to show his power. But there's nowhere now the white man will let us go to steal any of them back."

"Mr. Harper and the army are very angry that there are so many horses stolen from your people," I said.

"Being angry doesn't help much, does it? In the old days, if somebody came into our herds and took a few, it didn't matter. We had so many. And then we could go out on a raid ourselves and everybody felt good. Now we don't have very many to lose, and there's no raid afterwards. It's a bad thing."

"We're doing what we can to stop it."

"Well, in the old days, it wasn't easy to steal The People's ponies. There were always children playing in the herds, all through the night sometimes. And they would give the alarm. And there were all our dogs, too. They'd set up a great racket if strangers came near, so we could run out and have a little fight with them. Now the ponies are scattered and there aren't so many dogs anymore. Have you ever eaten dog, Liver?"

"No, I never have."

"Well, it's nothing to look forward to." He was silent for a moment and then he said very quietly, "Here on this reservation, our children are afraid to go out at night and play with the horses."

Suggestions from among the harder citizens held that if we were to take Rufus Tallbridge out, tie him to a tree, and shoot him dead, much of the rustling would cease. But even though we were sure that he and some of his kind were responsible for most of the crime on the reserve, nobody was ever able to prove it. In the back room of Stoddard & Blanchard's store, it was observed that he never seemed without funds in one pocket or the other, and no apparent means of coming by such money in any honest endeavor.

Maybe we put too much on our Rufus and other reservation hangers-on. There were loose men always drifting across the land from the Civilized Tribes Nations, few of them of the sort who could resist taking a horse here and there to be run across the boundaries and east of the Washita for easy sale.

Most of that horse-stealing winter I spent near Anadarko, doing what I could to help. Which wasn't much.

We put up a few fences. We tried to get the bands to organize their young men into security teams, but such things were foreign to them. We suggested to Mr. Harper that he increase his efforts at getting an Indian police force started. Mostly, as the bloody English are always saying, we just muddled through. And horses kept disappearing.

But no wasted winter, that. I came to know the Kiowas, and old Bear, the medicine man. He and I had many a fine evening in his lodge, smoking tobacco I'd brought along and eating pemmican and Stoddard & Blanchard's honey or striped candy. And he told the stories of his people. Of their enmity with the Osages and Pawnees and of their friendship with the Comanches. He told me of the Ten Grandmothers, those sacred medicine bundles that were never opened except by one priest, and that only once each year. Even Bear himself did not know what they contained.

It was a great revelation, having the sense of how a human mind can work sometimes in tandem with another, even though the two are separated by half a world, one in some still unknown northern vastness of America, the other in the far sand-and-sun country east of my Garibaldi's Sicily. The Ten Grandmothers were much like the old Jews' Ark of the Covenant, which was opened only once each year, on the Day of Atonement, and viewed by a single selected priest. As Bear told of the Grandmothers I could hear the voice of my Da when in my childhood he related the stories from his Old Testament.

Bear was a reflection of his entire band, all outgoing and cheerful and showing me the greatest of hospitality. I liked them and, as I grew to know them better, pondered the tales I'd heard of how they were the most vicious and brutal warriors on the plains.

Having been on the frontier a considerable time myself, I knew that if I asked them questions, they might very well tell me out of politeness what they supposed I wanted to hear, not wanting to offend me. So I made a point of asking no questions until I had made firm friends of them, had established my position among them. It was a joy riding with the young men along the edges of the Wichita Mountains or through the low quartz hills bordering the Washita River. Even though sometimes the cold was beastly.

But the evenings in Bear's lodge were the greatest joy of all. Looking into his Mongolian face in repose before the flickering fire was like gazing back into the ages. Even more so than with Otter Tongue, because Bear seemed more inclined to talk freely, not so guarded as my elderly Comanche friend, more willing to reveal himself to me. And I truly believed that he enjoyed our little talks as much as I did.

His tipi was like others I'd seen, with all the truck hanging about the walls and bedding robes at the base of the lodgepoles. And in Bear's case there was a bed made of logs set in a boxlike pattern with cedar lining it, trade blankets across the top. There was always a nice fire, small but warm, in the circular hole at the center of the floor.

There was the odor of smoke in the lodge, and of dried meat and the faint hint of crushed cedar. And such silence, when we were not breaking it with our own words! Even the fire seemed to burn without noise, and from outside I seldom heard any sound except the wind, no other voice to intrude on us, as though members of the band were staying well away or else passing silently by because the old man was entertaining a visitor and should not be distracted.

Bear's clothing was very colorful, beaded in many places with tiny sections of painted porcupine quill or glass trade beads. Like all the men of his band, he wore a great deal of shining metal or glass in his hair or ears. I recalled that Phil McCusker had said you could always spot a Kiowa band from far off, so long as the sun was shining, because they sparkled with reflected light. He wore his hair loose and cut short over the right ear in the old Kiowa tradition, and at the back a scalp lock and a bushy sprig of finely brushed quills.

Often I was offered a bed in his lodge at night, and I would roll myself into one of the hair-on buffalo robes and sleep the sleep of innocence. There had always been something about lying in the dark under a hide tent, listening to the wind vainly trying to get inside, that brought a strange, distant peace.

It was one of those dreary January afternoons when the sun was incapable of putting anything through the thin clouds except a dim glimmer of cold orange color. Once, in the old army of the South, I had known a man who was a painter, and orange was a hot color, said he. Well, he had never been on a shivering mule along the Washita in dead of winter under a transparent cover of high cloud. It was orange and it was cold as a witch's heart!

In the company of a group of young Kiowas were Deacon and I, looking for tracks leading to the east, because the night before a few horses had disappeared from one of their jury-rigged corrals. But we had no luck and all spirits were at low ebb until somebody kicked up a big bobcat from a stand of low cedars. He was caught well away from the larger trees, where he might have taken refuge. So a merry chase ensued.

Anyone who has ever tried to catch a common domesticated cat that doesn't want to be caught can testify to how these strange creatures can run in seven different directions at the same time. The young Kiowas on their ponies found it vastly funny, trying to ride close enough to switch the darting cat with their long quirts. And never one I saw come close. They were chasing a slashing beam of gray, like dawn's light across a wavy mirror.

But it brought yipping and laughter and bright faces, a fitting end to what had otherwise been a dreadful day.

The bobcat finally disappeared into a small stand of post oak near the stream and was gone like the elusive smoke he was, but still the young men dashed about swinging their quirts, now at one another.

That evening the clouds thickened and it began to snow before darkness fell. Mr. Harper had been in Bear's camp that day and had left me a goodly supply of tobacco and two live chickens. I was staying through this time in one of the wooden houses we had built for the Kiowas, still disdained by them as much as by the Comanches. There was no stove, and I had to do what little cooking I did on an open fire, which I could never master completely, except for baking ramrod bread as in the old days in Virginia.

Trying to pluck feathers from a chicken without a boiling pot first, as I'd seen my mother do so often, is not the easiest job in the world. But before I was well started, I was rescued by some of the band's young women, giggling and shaking their heads, sent by old Bear, I suspected. They took the birds from my willing hands and chucked them into the fire, feathers and all.

"You go sit with Father," one said to me in Comanche.

And I went to Bear's lodge and he smiled at me and we smoked while he continued to laugh about my failure with the chickens. Then after a while, one of the women brought the birds and one peeled off the skin, taking with it all the black-charred feathers, then slit the little white bodies and scooped out all the entrails. She laid the naked chickens on a copper platter, which I suspected came from some long-ago raid along the Santa Fe Trail, and departed, carrying the guts in her cupped hands.

"I never liked birds much," Bear said. "But they are better than no meat at all."

"You're welcome to share with me," said I.

In my coat I had a small matter of salt and pepper and sprinkled the birds liberally with both. We ate them, one bird each, until the bones glistened clean of meat, and old Bear smiled at me and nodded his head.

"Well," said he, "it's better than corn!"

We smoked again, and one of the women came in to put a few more small twigs on the fire, making it blaze up brightly. I told Bear about the bobcat chase and we laughed together, his old face beaming in the firelight, his slanted eyes shining.

Well, it seemed as good a time as any. So I started with old Iron Shirt, a man large among the Comanches while Bear was still a young warrior. He said Iron Shirt was greatly respected among the Kiowas, and he told of the times he had seen him at the Kiowa sun dances, when Iron Shirt's band came to watch, as though he were giving me the thread to follow. So he opened the door to me, whether he knew it or not, but I suspect he did. And I tried to recall then all the notes I had made myself, lying now to the south in my kitchen cupboard.

"I am told," said I, "that your people make a record of sun dances on hide, so that you may keep the happenings of the tribe for each passing season."

"Not exactly," he said. "Only a big thing was painted on the hides so that when we told our history, it would remind the teller of that time and place and help his memory."

"I've never seen one of those hides," I said. "It would be good to look at one."

He smoked silently for a while then, his gaze going from the fire to my face and back again. I supposed at the moment that he would change the subject, as Otter Tongue had so often done at critical junctures. But he didn't.

Slowly he rose from the fire and moved back into the dark recesses of the lodge, near his cedar bed, and took from some secret place a long roll of buffalo hide. It was tied securely with rawhide thongs, and he undid these before coming back to the fire, holding the rolled skin in both hands as gently as though it were a Talmud. And to him, it was.

"This is only one of them," he said, sitting once more across the fire from me and placing the rolled hide to one side so we could both see it. "There are many more. But this is the one entrusted to me. Not many white men have seen it."

He unrolled the hide, and it appeared to be an entire buffalo robe, hair off, carefully fleshed and cured so that it was soft. At the center were the first symbols, and they were painted outward from there, radiating like a pinwheel to the edges. There were many finely drawn figures and colors of red and blue and black and white.

Never had I seen such a thing. The pigments on that hide were like living blood and the total effect startling and somehow complete, an end in itself. There were tiny human figures with wounds spilling blood, and some with spots I took to mean smallpox, and some with warbonnets or feathers in their hair. There were little horses running, and trees without leaves, and cactus plants with large spines, and circles representing Spanish coins taken in a raid on the Santa Fe Trail.

No one could have told me that a dead hide could speak, yet this one did, even before Bear began to explain its meaning. Like voices from the past years coming to me, and the painted figures reaching out to touch my face.

Regularly spaced were black marks I judged to be about three inches long by an inch wide, and between these a sketch of what appeared to be a structure of some sort, with a flowery design on top. Above these were the little figures that told the story.

"Winters," Bear said, touching one of the black marks.

"And summers," said I impulsively, touching one of the little houses which I now knew represented the summer sun-dance lodge.

"Yes. And all the other things that tell the stories of that time."

"It's a thing of great beauty," I said.

I'd had no notion of where to start in connecting any of this with the story of Kwahadi's mother. But then I saw the figure of a little man with a shower of stars above his head. These were not the six-pointed stars of David or even the five-pointed ones of some Christian symbolism. They were four-pointed and stood in a tight cluster above the head of the little man figure. I touched the drawing with the tips of my fingers, lightly, and felt them speak to me. It was the year the stars fell in the waning months of winter, 1834!

"The year the stars fell!" I said, a little breathlessly I'm afraid.

Bear smiled and nodded, seeming well satisfied that I knew such a thing and could read it from his calendar.

What a tingling in my fingers! Here was this old buffalo hide, crinkled at the edges with age, and on it the record of things that had happened years before I learned to speak my own language, much less the Comanche tongue, through which I was able to make my thoughts known to the Kiowas. The same Kiowas who, in the dim past, had started this pictograph, putting it all down as surely as if they had known of my arrival and inquisition.

Well, I brought myself up short on that kind of thinking. They had not done any of it for me, but for themselves, but now at least I could feed off it.

So, with my finger still on the figure with the stars, I thought, That was 1834! And from that I began to count around the circle of black marks and sun-dance lodges.

"I've heard of a sun dance you had in a great river bend," said I. "On the Washita, I think it was. Where is that?"

Without hesitation, Bear reached out and touched a symbol. There it was, as clear as anything Mr. Henry Morton Stanley had ever written. The sun-dance lodge with that flowery design above it, which I now took to represent the lodgepoles. And below that, a great curving double line.

"The Peninsula Sun Dance," Bear said.

Quickly I counted the marks from the year the stars fell, and knew the year of that particular celebration had been 1839. But I was not yet sure.

"Do you remember if Iron Shirt came to that dance?"

"Yes, do you see this?" And he pointed to a small wavy line below the river symbol, like a snake. "Comanches. I remember that he brought his band that year. It was a good year. The summer before, there had been no sun dance because we were too busy fighting the Cheyenne. And after that was the headdragging winter, when one of our warriors killed a Pawnee and dragged his head through the camp before the Cold Season celebration."

"That was 1838," I said aloud, not meaning to, really, but it came out as I recalled what Sunshade had told me. The year of Chosen's capture. The year of the taking of Kwahadi's mother when she was a child. But she had told me a great deal more, as well. More than I had realized at the time.

"There was a time when the Sioux came to watch a sun dance," I said. "Do you remember?"

"Here," he said, pointing. "The Dakota Sun Dance. It was on the Washita too. Not far from here. I remember Iron Shirt again that year. We had many good nights in the lodges, talking with the Dakotas. They gave us some guns. We gave them many horses. We spoke mostly in the sign language," Bear said, moving his hands eloquently before his face. "But there was also one of them who knew a little Comanche because he had often traded with them for horses. Almost everybody traded with the Comanches for horses. They had more horses than anybody."

My mind raced along with his words and I counted the black marks from the Peninsula Sun Dance to the

Dakota, and knew the latter was in either 1843 or 1844.
The summer before Kwahadi was born.

"Here is a time when you painted two sun-dance
lodges in a row," I said.

"Yes, that was the Double Sun Dance," he said.
"We had two that year, in the hot season. Some people
call it the Warbonnet Sun Dance because we had the
headdresses of feathers then, very impressive."

Old Bear suddenly laughed.

"The winter before the Dakotas came, there was a
big argument and a woman was stabbed in a fight. Some
of the tribe went off to Mexico to raid. But then the next
summer it was all right again and we had the celebration
when the Dakotas came."

"I see how the pictures help you remember what
happened."

I remembered, too, something else Sunshade had
told me, and brought up the most important question of
all, because its answer would tell me the year that
Kwahadi lost his mother.

"There was a time when you had a sun dance, and it
was interrupted by a war party of Skidi Pawnee. I don't
think the Comanches were there that year."

"Yes, I remember that one well. I got this that summer." He lifted the sleeve of his smock, and there was a
brutal scar shining in the firelight. "A hatchet wound.
You don't need pictures on a hide to remember such
things.

"But that summer I wish the Comanches had come.
They could have helped us. The dancing was at a campsite on the Timbered Hill River. I understand you white
men call it Medicine Lodge Creek."

"Yes, I've been there, at the great treaty meetings
many years ago."

"I know," said Bear. "I saw you there!"

I was speechless then, because in all my memories of
that meeting where I had come to know Mr. Henry Mor-·
ton Stanley, there was no face like Bear's that I could

recall. Maybe because I was too interested in the newspaper people and the whiskey keg in their tent.

But it was a time now for quick recovery from such surprises, so as not to lose the thread of things. So I put the question once again.

"That sun dance. Can you show it to me on the paintings?"

"Of course," said Bear, and touched the hide.

And now I counted quickly from the last known date, each black mark and sun-dance symbol alternating perfectly to the place Bear had indicated as the Skidi Pawnee summer.

"I'm trying to make this into white man's numbered years," I said, feeling I owed him that much at least. He only smiled and nodded.

"I know," he said.

It didn't surprise me. Maybe because I was too excited to be surprised, coming so close to my goal. And there it was, plainly written on the hide as if printed on the presses of Mr. James Gordon Bennett. Skidi Pawnee summer, 1854. And that same fall, according to Sunshade, Kwahadi's mother had been taken from them.

I needed nothing further from him, but for a long time he allowed me to admire the calendar. A thing of beauty, as I'd said, but much more. A book of the past for those who could read it, and with Bear's help I had read it well. And knew the next answers could be found only in Texas!

"I thank you for allowing me to see it," I said finally.

"Well, you're coming to think like a Comanche," he said, and laughed, offering me his tobacco pouch. "Sometimes they come at things from the side, indirectly. That's what you've done here, looking for that woman."

"You knew I was looking for a woman?"

"Of course. But I allowed you to do it in your own way. It's just as well. I could have told you much less than the calendar did. All I knew of her was the memory of seeing her once, standing beside her lodge with that son of hers who is now the chief of the Antelope Comanches.

"He was only a boy then. They were camped in Palo Duro Canyon and we were visiting them, a little war party of our brave young men. I was not so old then, you see." And he laughed once more, and I knew now he was enjoying all of this.

"We rode into their camp and she was standing there, watching us pass. She was a fine-looking woman. Not large, but fine-looking. I remember that red hair, shining in the sun like Mexican copper!"

And in my robe that night, hearing Bear's heavy breathing and that of his wife, the fire gone to ashes and the darkness swallowing me like coal cotton, I was unable to sleep. Thinking.

No wonder these Comanches and Kiowas had become such fast friends, no matter their language differences. No matter their different tribal customs. No matter their different views of the gods and how a band should be governed. They were cut from the same piece of rawhide. Bold and fierce and warlike, yet somehow gentle. And more than anything else, capable of seeing into another man's soul. And, I suspected, having a sixth sense to detect his motives.

Power! That's what they both called it. The spirit that guided each of them to his destiny. They had sung to gods I would never know, nor would they know mine, either. Yet somehow their fingers seemed always on the pulse of my thinking.

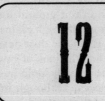

12

It was in a book by Mr. Charles Dickens. He wrote, "It was the best of times, it was the worst of times." Or something close to that. And maybe it wasn't even Mr. Dickens. I read so many of Weslowski's books by the good Englishman during that period, it seemed all printed words belonged to him, though that was an injustice, perhaps, to other authors lost to memory.

Whoever wrote it, I agreed. In all men I'd seen, whether red, white, black, or many shades in between, it had always impressed me that there was some good, some evil in them. And so in events as well.

It was certainly true in that lovely spring when my young friend Allis Featherman tried to become a member of the Comanche tribe. It had a tender start and a brutal ending. And thrown in for good measure, like one of old Bear's symbols on the sun-dance calendar to keep me from forgetting, the sewing machine.

Allis came to me one morning as I was lounging under the porch roof at Stoddard & Blanchard's, killing time until the next stagecoach run to Boggy Depot on the MKT line. All across the land were the sounds of the larks and, from the oaks along the edges of the fields and roads, the fussing of jays and the fluting notes of cardinals ready to mate and claim their ground for raising young. The wind blowing in from the high plains was gentle and smelled of fresh grass. Even the dust devils blown across the road near the store had the look of gay spring dancers.

Allis seemed to move with some hesitation, and his speech was at first reticent, as though he were about to admit pilfering some cookie jar and bring shame on his head for it. But his mind was not on cookies.

He hemmed and hawed for a while about nothing in particular. It came to me that he had been spending so much time among his Comanche friends that he was becoming like them in his talk, skirting the real subject until a reasonable amount of unimportant words had issued. But at last he came to it.

"Morgan," he said, "I've come to ask you to speak for me."

"And with whom?" asked I.

"With the father of the girl I want to marry!"

"It's come to that at last, has it?"

"Yes. And sometimes it's their way, to send a man to speak for the suitor, to make his case, you see?"

"Indeed I do see," I said. "But just to be sure we aren't muddled in what we're talking about, it's Padoponi, isn't it?"

"Yes. Who else?"

"I thought you might have found a fat Mexican who took your fancy, in heat as you are."

He flushed and started to say something as hot as his face, but then I laughed and he held off.

"Now tell me, my fine young lover, how old is that girl?"

"Why, hell, Morgan, she's at least fifteen!"

"No need to use a soldier's language when you're speaking of your love," said I, still grinning. "Then when must I speak?"

"The sooner the better."

"You see? As I said before, you're like a rutting boar."

"God damn it!"

"There, boy," said I, patting his shoulder rather roughly. "In such a situation you've got to expect a certain amount of hazing. Now. How many horses are you willing to give for her?"

At the hitch rail alongside the store were a number of ponies, switching their tails at the flies, heads down in the sun. Allis looked at them a long time, judging their value.

"I haven't got enough money for horses," he said. "They're so expensive now around here."

"No horses, no wife."

"Well, there may be something else."

"Then buy that instead."

"You can't buy one around here."

"What, then?"

"A sewing machine."

"A *what?*"

"A sewing machine. He told some of the bucks he wanted one for his wives. He saw that one in the agent's house, and Mr. Belton's wife using it to make clothes."

"Aw yes, our new agent's wife, teaching the wild heathen the trappings of a civilized world."

Our good Mr. Harper had gone, replaced by William Belton, who seemed not so gentle, but I had to admit he was perhaps better suited to the rigors of wild tribe administration.

"Don't call 'em heathen," he snapped, his anger starting up again. I squeezed his shoulder and asked further about this machine.

"For his wives, then, a nice sewing machine."

"Yeah. So, on your next run to the railroad, could you get me one? I've got enough money for that, I think."

"How much money?"

"Seventeen dollars."

"That should be enough. But do you think they have such contraptions at Boggy Depot?"

"No. But you could get one. You could order it. Or one of those train people you're always drinking with. They could get one up in Kansas or someplace."

I began to realize I had not been selected for this role of champion because of any grand reputation I might have among the Comanches, but because I could get the machine.

"And you'd want a few spools of thread, I take it."

"Well, whatever it takes to run one of those things."

The speed of commerce in that place was not outstanding, so it took a wee while, Allis Featherman fidgeting all the time and thinking about his little black-eyed love out on the Big Beaver. But patience was all that was required, because Allis had been right about my friends on the MKT.

One of whom was a conductor named Keims, and as soon as could be expected, which was well into summer, he had such a device in my hands, brand new and out of Cleveland, Ohio, by way of Fort Scott, Kansas. And a neat box of thread of many colors, like Joseph's coat. Not only that, but he placed two dollars in change back in my hand. I used that to buy a large bag of peppermint candy from a news butch on the MKT. I knew Kwahadi shared his people's craving for such sweets.

On the trip back to Fort Sill, the heat so softened the candy that it fused together like a mass of red and white striped sandstone. But no matter. The taste was still the same. All it needed was a little chipping with a hatchet.

For my own part, I bought a nice bridle well mounted with good bright metal, highly polished leather, and reins of braided hemp in three colors that looked like a snakeskin. I wanted Kwahadi to have something for his daughter that he could claim as his own—other than the candy, of course, which I suspected he would issue in large quantities to his children anyway.

It was a lovely little device, that sewing machine. It

worked with a hand crank that sent the needle up and down in a blur. Keims had been thoughtful enough to provide three packets of extra needles, explaining that his wife was always complaining about the needles breaking, and he showed me how to install them and how to thread the bobbin. The thing made a loud racket when the wheel was cranked, much like a miniature sawmill.

Allis Featherman was in a dither once he clapped eyes on the little instrument, asking silly questions about catching one's finger under the needle or touching it lightly here and there along its flanks, as though it were a newly castrated colt. Then he disappeared from the agency, and I assumed he had gone back again to his Comanches, so he could be on hand for my presentation.

The night before my planned pilgrimage to the Big Beaver, I pondered on the hawk feather given me so long ago, but discarded the idea of wearing it now for the first time. I had told nothing to anyone of the things I had learned of Kwahadi's mother, and no great deed had yet been done. So the feather would have to wait. After all, I reasoned, the chief had wanted to know where his mother was, and I didn't know that.

Maybe it was a touch of my Welsh hardheadedness, my keeping mum. They'd played closemouthed with me, so now I with them. But I felt guilty because they had likely told me as much as they knew.

Whatever. No hawk feather in the hat on this trip.

I had no idea whether Kwahadi was aware of my mission. Certainly Allis knew, and as I rode into the Comanche camp, there he was off in one of the far brush arbors, watching me as a cat watches a mouse and smoking all the while with some of his young Antelope friends.

The chief was on his new front porch, constructed by the agency carpenter at his request. He liked the shade and the efficient way the wooden shingles shed rainwater. He still wasn't using the rest of the house for anything except an elaborate stable, but he liked the porch. He was in an old rocking chair that Allis had salvaged from one of the Fort Sill trash dumps. Nails had been applied in obvious places to avoid having the thing crash down into splinters when a butt settled on it. Not the best furniture work I'd ever seen, but it worked.

Kwahadi was wearing a hat! The first time I'd seen him with such a thing. It was high-crowned, narrow-brimmed, and very black. It seemed more to emphasize the rest of his Comanche dress than to conceal it. Especially the earrings, which I knew he changed from time to time; on this day he wore Mexican silver pendants.

A hat on the head of the Antelope chief, thought I. So, that much further along the white man's road!

Some of his younger children were playing on the porch beside him, and one was sitting on his lap. At my approach he shooed them all away and they went somewhat reluctantly, eyeing me with irritation writ large on their faces for having come to spoil their time in the shade with their father.

Dismounting before the porch, I untied the large burlap bag from Deacon's saddle, the bag in which I had all the plunder to buy Kwahadi's daughter. Little Horse, Kwahadi's eldest son, came running from somewhere to hold Deacon's reins and scratch his neck, and he grinned at me, showing a mass of utterly white teeth. He had come to expect that each time I arrived he would take care of my mule. I winked at him to express my complete approval.

I placed my bag on the porch at Kwahadi's feet and sat on the edge of the rough board floor, and Kwahadi bent forward and we shook hands violently, as we always did, as if we were wringing chickens' necks.

"I'm glad to see you, Liver," he said. "It's been many sleeps. Is that hair on your face getting whiter?"

"It may be," said I.

"You should come around more often, to places where you're welcome."

"I've been driving that wagon back and forth to the railroad."

"I know. You spend all your time doing that."

"Well, I saw a lot of cattle grazing on my way here this time."

"Ah yes," he said with satisfaction. "That new thing they've let us do. We get a lot of money from the Texas men for letting their cows eat our grass. And we get some of the cows, too."

"The new leasing policy. A good thing."

Looking through the camp, I could see more wooden houses than before. And everywhere the packs of dogs were growing large once more, a good sign.

"I see you have many dogs again."

"Yes, dogs copulate more than anything I've ever seen, except some men," he said, and his features softened in that strange way as he smiled.

"Maybe you could sell some to those Texas friends of yours."

"Maybe so. Some of those Texas men have become good friends, all right," he said. "They come each year, the same ones. They looked strange at first, in those big hats and those leather boots with high heels. But now I'm becoming accustomed to them.

"They say that someday, if I go on helping them graze their cattle on our land, they'll build me a great wooden house with a lot of rooms. And a well under the floor so that water can be drawn into the place where the women cook. They say they'll bring me an iron stove."

"Iron stoves make cooking a lot easier."

"Well, that depends. When a woman has learned to cook on an open fire, she doesn't like to change, not if she's stubborn, as all my wives are. But maybe they'll see some advantages."

He told me about his horse herd and how it was increasing. And of the cattle he could now call his own. There was pride in his voice, and rightly so. Maybe now the winters of short rations from the agency would not be so hurtful for his people, with cattle grazing nearby and lease money in their pockets. I suspected most of the money was in Kwahadi's pockets, which was all right because I was sure he would spend it for the benefit of all his people.

"Now, you keep doing everything you can to get the agent to let us have our own policemen," he said. "It won't be easy, because men who wear badges have done a lot of bad things to The People. Maybe I can't persuade any of the young men to wear those badges. But I think maybe I can persuade a few."

He found that very amusing and he laughed silently, his shoulders shaking. I knew that if anyone could get young Comanches to wear badges and police their own people, this chief was the one. And he knew it, too!

Then we spoke of the weather and how the chokecherries had bloomed so well and how the frogs along the streamlines were so noisy this year that it was hard to sleep at night. The conversation seemed to drag on for a long time, and I had the feeling he was doing it intentionally. But finally he looked at the burlap bag lying at his feet.

"What's in that sack, Liver?"

"Gifts from another man," said I. "I've come to speak for him. He's asked me to bring his case before you."

"And what case is that?" he asked, and I knew from his tone that he knew exactly what case it was, and for whom.

"He wishes to have your oldest daughter for his wife."

Kwahadi rocked back and forth slowly, gazing out across his pastures and corrals and the tipis of his family. For a moment his glance flicked to the far brush arbor where Allis Featherman and the young Comanches were all watching.

"I'd better have a little smoke on that," he said.

I'd expected such a thing and was prepared. I took two of Stoddard & Blanchard's black cigars from my vest pocket and passed one to him and held a match for him as he puffed, the blue smoke issuing from the corners of his wide mouth. As I lit my own, he sat back, rocking once more, staring to the far horizons.

"My daughter Padoponi is worth a lot of horses," he said quietly. "But I don't suppose you've got any horses in that burlap sack."

"No, but I have something else," said I, and opened the bag and slipped out the little sewing machine and placed it at his feet.

"Aw," he said, leaning forward, a new light in his eyes. He reached down slowly to touch the machine, his long, slender fingers playing along the metal surfaces. "Do you know how to make it work?"

"Yes, I can show your wives how to make clothes with it."

"But it won't work on buffalo hide, will it?"

"No. But there aren't many buffalo hides left anymore."

"Aw," he said, settling back again in his rocker, smoking, looking at the machine as though he thought it might suddenly leap off the porch and run away.

"It's a very hard thing when a man's favorite daughter must go from his lodge," he said softly, almost to himself. "Padoponi is still very young but of marriageable age, because she has already begun to go with each passing new moon to the menstrual tipi. But to a father, maybe a daughter is never old enough to marry. A daughter is hard to lose, no matter how old she is."

"My young friend, for whom I speak, is a good man," I said. "He would treat her well."

"I know the young man you speak for. I like him. I'd expected him to come forward before now, the way he looks at her and moons around. If he could play a cedar flute, he'd have been playing it outside my door at night for a long time now, keeping me awake. And it's good, his sending you to speak for him. I like that. It's one of our old ways when sometimes a man sent somebody else to do his talking. Sometimes, when a young man is asking for a wife, he doesn't talk too well for himself."

He turned then and stared at me with his brittle eyes, and I could see the gray flecks in them.

"Usually the man sent was a respected warrior. And I've heard that you are a respected warrior among your people from the time you fought a long time in that battle between the white men over the black man."

"The fight was about other things, as well," I said.

"I only know what I hear about the white man's wars. They have never interested me much."

He rocked, smoking until the cigar was burnt down to his lips, then mashed out the fire on an arm of the chair. He seemed deep in thought, somewhere far from me.

"In the old days, we didn't allow the white traders to winter among us and take our women as wives or partners in the bed robe. As some other tribes did," he said. "But many white captives grew up among us and became of The People."

Now he looked at me directly, suddenly, like a whiplash, and there was a hint of hostility in his eyes, or perhaps challenge. And I knew he was thinking about his own mother.

"Blood didn't matter to us, but only custom, if someone grew to become one of us, no matter their color or their blood. But grown white men didn't ride into our tribe and claim wives."

Then for the only time since our first conversation together, he spoke to me in harsh and bitter tones, and his face had gone as blank as the side of a limestone bluff.

"Go back to Fort Sill," he said. "Come back here in two days, when the sun is going to the place where it sleeps. And when you go, take your young friend with you."

I quickly slid the peppermint candy and the bridle from the burlap bag and placed them beside the sewing machine, but Kwahadi refused to look at any of it again.

He continued to rock, his face set in cruel lines, his eyes now turned to the far brush arbor where Allis Featherman waited.

Nothing for it but to take up the reins of Deacon from the hands of Little Horse and move out of this camp. The boy, who was not smiling now, backed away from my mule and I could sense that the mood of his father had passed on to him and his black eyes were harsh.

I rode directly to the arbor and Allis ran out to meet me, his face expectant, eyes wide, and behind him his Comanche friends grinning like wolves.

"Come on, Allis," I said in English. "Catch up your horse. He wants the both of us out of his place."

"He said no?" Allis gasped.

"He said come back in two days. Catch up your horse, boy. It's back to the agency for us, and quick."

The agony and embarrassment that came into his face were painful to see. And with a loud groan, he turned to catch up his horse. Seeing the slump of his shoulders, at that moment I could easily have shot the Antelope chief!

It was the worst two days of my experience. Allis Featherman needed to be tied to a post and left there for fear he might wear out all his boots with his pacing back and forth. And such furious language! Straight out of the stables of Fort Sill it was, blistering the air around him.

I was equally irritable, running out of patience with my young friend and disillusioned with what I had taken for a close friendship between me and the Antelope chief. And turned out of his camp like an unwanted dog, with harsh words from taut lips.

The first night we stayed in my shack and drank some of Stoddard & Blanchard's brown whiskey, and it was terrible, but the both of us got drunk just the same. Allis finally passed away into a noisy sleep, and I sat drinking alone, a serious thing, thinking that I should take that damned hawk feather off the wall and chuck it into my stove. Although with the warmth of the night, there was no fire burning.

So what to take my mind off the day's events? Only a few days before, Weslowski had given me a number of old faded issues of *Harper's Weekly*. Sipping my scalding broth from a tin cup, I sat under my smoky lamp and leafed through a few pages. Nothing like keeping abreast of the outside world, me lost in this heathen land!

There were the cartoons of Mr. Thomas Nast, raising billy hell with all politicians of whom he didn't approve. Which included most of them. And the doings of President R. B. Hayes, a man who never impressed me much but who had at least withdrawn the last of the occupation troops from the defeated South. About time, too, after all these years.

And engravings of the buildings in a place called Menlo Park in the state of New Jersey, where somebody named T. A. Edison was trying to make a glass tube that would shed light by pumping electricity into it. What a lot of foolishness these inventors get involved with, but at least New Jersey was one of my favorite places, that having been the state upon whose shore I first stepped after escaping from the prison pen at Fort Delaware.

And the increase of railroads, spreading like spiders' webs across the middle plains, where once the wild tribes and their buffalo held dominion.

Aw, lovely pictures of the famous Delmonico's in the city of New York, and the oyster bar. The thought of eating these delicate morsels from the sea, along with boiled lobster, all washed down with dark ale, as I had once done in Philadelphia before going to Garibaldi, made me forget the torment of that snoring boy sleeping in my corner.

And the building of the bridge between Brooklyn and Manhattan in New York! Bridges had always fascinated me. A road over the roiling waters. Somehow poetic. Some of the writers were saying it would be the engineering marvel of the century if ever completed; an infirm man was the chief of its architects.

But even the thought of fresh oysters and great bridges could not keep my mind long off the distractions of the day. So I sat bitterly into the night, thinking of how poor Allis Featherman's suit had been turned down.

Well, maybe not. Kwahadi had said to come back. We'd soon see. If that sewing machine was still sitting on the porch where I'd left it, then all was over between my young friend and the maiden Padoponi. If it and the other plunder had been taken into one of their lodges, then it was another matter. We'd soon see.

Fuzzy-mouthed, we spent the next day as best we could, Allis and I, neither mentioning the thing most on our minds. We hung about the fort's blacksmith shop, watching a sergeant smithy hammering out the shape of horseshoes. Then a while observing a dice game between some Panetekas behind the stables. Then helping load some new-cut lumber at the agency mill, piling it on a wagon to be taken out onto the reservation, where some new house was being built for a chief or one of his favorites.

By nightfall, we were snapping at each other like old bears and should have parted company. But I didn't want to leave him alone or out of my sight for fear of some wild thing he might do.

We ended, of course, in the back room at Stoddard & Blanchard's, where there were a goodly number of players in a five-card stud game. Allis sat in long enough to lose what little money he had left after buying the sewing machine and then sulked in one corner, glaring at everybody, his lower lip thrust out like a slice of raw calf's liver.

I played on. Rufus Tallbridge was there, the worst poker player I'd ever seen, with plenty of greenbacks on the table. I expected to take some of those, but had little chance as it turned out, because of Rufus making some nasty remarks and in equal part because of my nastier temper at the moment. Which wasn't helped when Rufus drew a fifth heart in one hand, which has always been a hard thing to beat in five-card.

A little later, when my own luck was running a mite better, Mr. Stoddard closed his store out front and came back to watch the play and supervise rowdyism.

"Rufus, I see you've got a little playing capital," said he.

"Rufus always has playing capital," Rufus said, as usual referring to himself in third person, the bastard. He laughed, throwing back his head in the way he had that showed off his ugly tonsils. "A smart man always has money in his pockets."

"Make your bet," I said sharply.

Rufus threw a couple of bills into the center of the table, still laughing, hitching at the two big pistols in his belt.

"In the war, Rufus made a fortune," said he.

That drew my attention, although usually I paid little heed to anything he said.

"I thought you were a common soldier like the rest of us," I said.

"Rufus was no *common* soldier. Rufus was an *un*common soldier. Going from place to place and collecting bounty on the way."

I stared at him, strong bile rising in my throat. I knew exactly what he meant. I knew he'd served in the Yankee army, but I'd had no details till now. The Yanks, like our own poor Confederacy, had found it necessary to offer money to men for enlisting late in the war, when the ardor of fighting had cooled a little. And I'd known a few who had made a business of taking bounty money in one place, deserting, enlisting somewhere else, taking bounty once more, deserting again, and on and on, traveling across the country taking a profit because those poor lads who were doing the fighting needed comrades badly, the casualties mounting every day.

"A bounty jumper, then," said I, and felt my voice

going thick with fury. Of all things I despised, it was a bounty jumper I loathed most.

"A smart young soldier," he was saying, and took a long drink from the bottle he always kept between his big feet when he played.

"Rufus Tallbridge, you're a cheap, slimy son of a bitch," I said and hardly recognized my own voice. And knew that saying it wasn't enough. I had to feel the flesh of his terrible face against my fists!

Maybe it was my sour stomach from being treated as I had been on the Big Beaver. Or maybe it was the memory of all those men and boys I'd seen fall, from Sharpsburg to the Wilderness, brave enough to be there, and the likes of Rufus Tallbridge taking advantage of their deadly situation. No matter that he'd been cheating on the Yankees. Their army had been full of good, proud soldiers, too.

So, as he started to rejoin, never suspecting his peril, I reached across the table with my right hand and took a fistful of his shirtfront and yanked him toward me for the left hooking blow so favored by my Da.

Rufus went back with a crash, blood spurting from the nose damaged once before by my hand, cursing loudly as he went, chair and all. Everyone jumped back wide-eyed and I threw the table aside, scattering cards and money and bottles in every direction with a clatter. One of the big pistols had escaped its holster and I kicked it aside.

"You bounty-jumping son of a bitch," I yelled, and Rufus was struggling up to meet my charge, clawing at the remaining pistol in his belt. But I got to him before he could clear the gun, and slammed him back against the wall with another left-handed blow and kicked him solidly in the groin as he slid down. His eyes rolled back and he went limp but I lifted him to his feet and smashed the left in again, the blood splattering along my arm. His face was a red mash now, and a shining tooth skittered across the floor. For good measure, I gave him a solid right to the ear. Rufus sagged to the floor, legs wide apart.

They were all pulling me away, then, their arms around me, and it was a good thing or else I might have lifted Rufus once more for the final slaughter. Seeing his crimson face, I was suddenly ashamed of myself for acting as though I were still a wild young stag in rut. Yet there was a certain satisfaction about it all, in knowing that the left hooking blow of my Da was still working well.

So, finally restrained, I helped the others get our Rufus back into a chair. They washed the blood from his face, and his eyes began coming back in focus. He began to mumble about killing somebody, which I didn't take too seriously because he was always threatening to kill somebody. My concern was more for a split knuckle on my left hand, from coming in contact with the tooth, I assumed. I plunged the hand into a bucket of water Mr. Stoddard had rushed into the room when the rehabilitation began.

I took a great chiding from Mr. Stoddard in those moments while Rufus came back to this world. It was his right, being one of my employers, but even as he spoke I imagined the gleam of approval in his eyes.

Allis and I were out of there quickly, and I feeling little glory in smashing the face of such a ruffian, now that the action was complete. A man who feels he must carry two revolvers wherever he goes must have few other defenses. As the lad and I went into the night, Mr. Stoddard shouted after us.

"Bad man to make an enemy of, Morgan. You've got to stop banging him about."

"To hell with him and his kind," I said.

As we walked to my shack at the agency, Allis laughed all the way, slapping my shoulder. At least if nothing else, the little joust had taken the edge off our sour dispositions. Nothing clears the air so much as a little harmless bloodletting.

"I never seen hands move so fast," Allis chortled.

"A spectacle I made of myself. But a bounty jumper is the offal of all society."

"I didn't get that," he said. "What's a bounty jumper?"

"Someday I'll explain it all, lad."

Thinking of Rufus Tallbridge's chopped face, I felt a shame that would not leave my mind. But a little pride, too, for the old days.

13

The first thing I looked for when we rode out to the Big Beaver in the red glow of setting sun was that sewing machine on Kwahadi's porch. It wasn't there! My old heart must have skipped a beat or two, and I was embarrassed for my wicked thoughts about the Antelope chief, festering these past two days.

"Lad," said I to Allis Featherman, riding beside me, "you're about to take on the burden of wedlock!"

He couldn't say a word. He tried, but all that issued from his gaping lips was a mouselike squeak.

The camp seemed deserted. Even the dogs failed to run out in their usual manner to greet us. But I knew the people were aware of our approach. The empty rocking chair on the front porch was still swaying back and forth, as though someone had departed its seat in a hurry. I could feel a hundred eyes on us, but saw not a single face.

I had no notion of what might happen next or of how we should go about this thing, never having been involved with a Comanche wedding. But they made it easy for us. As we rode into the village and pulled in before the wooden house of Kwahadi, no sooner were Deacon's delicate hooves stilled in the dust, than they appeared from all sides, grinning and waving and some of them singing. All of them in this first wave were women, except for Little Horse, who ran to us and took the reins of Deacon and Allis Featherman's horse as we stepped down.

Then I saw Coming Back from the Pony Herd pushing her daughter from one of the chief's lodges, and the girl was dressed in fawn-white doeskin, long fringes hanging to her ankles where tiny moccasins peeked out. There was ocher in the part of her hair, and along one cheek a single white teardrop of paint such as I had seen her father wearing on the day he surrendered.

"Lad, I think you're supposed to go fetch your new bride," said I, giving Allis a gentle shove, for without that I don't think he could have moved a step.

Padoponi lifted her face to him as he came, and her expression was serious until he was close enough to touch her. And then the flashing smile, and she quickly cast down her gaze. Allis stood dumb before her, shifting his feet in the dust as though ready to bolt. All the women were singing now, setting up a great racket, and the sound of it seemed to unsettle my young lad even more than had the sight of Padoponi.

Then from another of his tipis Kwahadi appeared, and with him a white man whom I knew to be a Mennonite, dressed in black like an undertaker, in his one hand a large Bible. All the band's men were coming out now, their faces painted and their hair oiled and braided. They stood well off as their chief led the white missionary toward the waiting couple.

Kwahadi was wearing his black hat and now a white shirt and vest as well. But beneath that, the usual buckskin leggings with the hanging fringes and the Comanche moccasins, plain but with hair tassels at heel and toe and along the seam of the instep. In his ears were the largest dangling earrings I had yet seen among any of these people.

He glanced at me with that small, peculiar smile which so changed his expression. But then to the serious business of what was happening.

Quickly I moved over to take my place beside Allis where he stood redfaced and glassy-eyed, as though in a dream, and Padoponi before him still, with her face down but smiling just the same. The poor lad was wet as a muskrat with his own sweat. At least, thought I, he's had the good judgment to remove his hat.

It was over in a twinkling, the missionary saying a few words only, and then telling Allis to take the girl's hand, which he did with great fumbling and dropping his hat in the process but quickly retrieved and held like a pincushion before the belt buckle with his free hand.

I think I heard the missionary say something about man and wife. I could never be sure because the singing took up all the space for hearing. Coming Back from the Pony Herd was pushing the young couple off toward the river. And my young Allis, with his hat still clutched like gold in his free hand, being led away by the girl. To a new tipi I now noted for the first time, well back from the others and among the oaks of the creek bank, shining at the top with the lowering sun. It was made of buffalo hides, not canvas, and I knew it had been erected as a new home in Kwahadi's family complex. Buffalo hides, under which Allis would sleep his first night with his bride, and likely the last such hides in the band, painted around the bottom in great black wolves' heads and yellow circles and red stripes.

There should be more to it than this, I thought. Yet it was over, a wedding abruptly done. Without the missionary's part, it would have been done even faster. Direct and to the point. No folderol. Well, all right with me, simple and honest as was their way of speaking.

Then the occasion for hand-shaking. I felt every man's palm in that band on Allis Featherman's wedding day, beginning with Kwahadi, of course.

"I thought we'd do some white man things in this

wedding," he said very seriously, as he wrung my hand. "So I asked that religious man to come."

Then old Otter Tongue, who took my hand gently. "I'm sure glad to see you again, Liver," he said.

And all the others, including Hawk, who had my pistol, which Allis had given him on the buffalo hunt, thrust into the belt of his leggings. His eyes were as cold as the steel of that revolver, and in his hand the strength of a man in his full power who works each day with horses.

And after the men, even some of the women. Coming Back from the Pony Herd, smiling her soft smile. Old Sunshade, glaring and red-eyed. But it was a strange thrill, touching her for the first time, her skin like dusty paper, dry and brittle.

And even the boy Little Horse, who shook hands as he had seen his father do, with great violence.

"Now," Kwahadi said in a loud voice, after all the white man's social business was taken care of. "We'll have a big celebration as we did in the old days when there was an important wedding."

Somewhere among all those hand-shakers had been the Mennonite, a man with chin whiskers and a sour face. He may have told me his name; I was never afterward able to recall it, so lost was he in this sea of smiling Comanches.

The people had begun lighting fires. I had missed the piles of wood waiting for the match, prepared in advance and waiting who knows how long. They were hard to miss, set in a wide semicircle around Kwahadi's complex of lodges. I had failed to note that new tipi, as well, though I have always prided myself on the excellence of my ability to observe what is happening around me. So I knew my excitement had been exceeded only by that of Allis Featherman.

Allis and his bride had disappeared into the new tipi and there was a great shout from all the women. Now the sun had left the top of the bridal suite, and the conical shape of it grew dim in the dusk, and I thought of my young friend inside, a married man.

The fires began to flare up and the singing increased in tempo. Drummers came forward and thumped their instruments, the sound seeming to press in on my ears. Some of the women ran to the fires with chunks of freshly butchered beef and I knew that Kwahadi's herd was smaller by one cow. The meat was spitted over the flames, and soon the odor of roasting beef was going through the camp. The dancers formed circles, and the serious business of celebration began. The dogs were out in force now, yammering, and the children ran with them, laughing and jumping like little wisps of smoke in the flicker of firelight.

Kwahadi took his place beside the largest fire. No rocking chair now but sitting on the ground, legs folded in the old Comanche fashion. He indicated that I should sit beside him, and I felt myself to be the guest of honor. They gave me the choice cuts of meat from the loin, roasted to a pink color and with the taste of oak smoke in each bite.

Coming Back from the Pony Herd sat immediately behind her husband, a little forward of all the other wives. Her face was beaming, her eyes shining with delight. No sooner had I swallowed one hunk of steak than she pressed another into my hands. She was wearing a crudely made shirtwaist of agency-issue cloth, brilliantly purple, and I knew that with Kwahadi's help she had begun to master the little sewing machine.

Otter Tongue sat to the other side of me from Kwahadi throughout the evening. Now and again he touched my shoulder, smiled, and said the same thing over and over.

"I'm sure glad to see you again, Liver."

The missionary stayed only long enough to eat a single roasted rib. Then he took himself off up the valley to his mission and his own people. I was alone with them, then, and felt truly one of them.

It was a time of good memory, that wedding night of my young friend and Kwahadi's daughter. We ate and smoked and watched the dancers far into the darkness, until finally a new moon appeared.

"Moon Mother's come to see the celebration," Otter Tongue said, his hand lifted toward the sky. "That's good."

The dancers made circles about the fires, shuffling first in one direction, then the other, their moccasined feet making intricate patterns on the earth with a whispering sound that could be heard above the drums and singing. Then some of the circles closed to form a single line, men and women together. Well back from the fires but still in their light, the children imitated their elders, making little songs of their own to Earth Mother and all the other spirits that provided for living things.

Toward morning, Kwahadi made his gifts. He gave me a nice little blue roan gelding. His eldest son brought the horse to me at the fire, grinning and acting as though I were a favorite uncle.

"This is a good pony," he said, handing me the reins.

"Yes, Little Horse, I can see that he is," said I. "He's like a horse I once saw long ago, ridden by a great general in an army I served with. His name was Little Powell Hill."

I'd never served directly under A. P. Hill, of course, but I'd seen him many times and I hoped his name might please Little Horse. Which it did. His grin grew wider, although I don't know how, and he turned and ran back to join the dancers, yipping softly like a fox kit.

"This Little Powell," Otter Tongue asked. "Was he as great as Mackenzie?"

"Yes, better than Mackenzie. He saved the day for my people above the Antietam one day. Against the bluecoats."

"I never heard of such a place."

"It's a long way from here. A river in the white man's state of Maryland."

"I like the sound of that name," he said. "Maryland. I like the sound of it."

Kwahadi gave Allis two mares and a three-year-old colt, the best possible gift because it meant the new couple could start their own herd. These three ponies were led through the camp and then into the darkness beyond, Hawk walking ahead of them, the reins over his shoulder. Finally, I supposed, they were hobbled before the dark lodge where Allis and his young lady were sleeping. Or whatever they were doing.

At last, with many of the children already sleeping on the ground but others wide-eyed and waiting, Sunshade sat near Kwahadi and told the stories of The People. Of how they had split off from the Shoshone long ago, of how they had come into the Southern Plains with the Spanish horse and driven out the Apaches and made Llano Estacado their home against all transgressors. Of how they had found their power among the buffalo and fought their many enemies.

Sitting there among them, listening to the old woman create before me the fires of centuries lit from the great northern mountains to this oak-rimmed prairie, it was like an unknown, unfelt wind, blowing across all that land as it had in their countless summers, driving the seeds of buffalo grass before it. Blowing across all that land as it had in their countless winters, brooming the snow on the ground until it was smooth as sanded oak. A feeling of unreality. Here they were now, yet in this place empty of all they had ever been before.

Her old face shone in the firelight, the eyes glinting with passion, the hands moving like birds above the bright flame as the hard lips uttered the sacred words that told of The People's time of glory. Now gone. Now forever faded into memory, and even the memory among some of the younger ones beginning to disappear. And their chief before them wearing a white man's hat. A white man's shirt. A white man's vest. And across his flat belly a white man's gold watch chain!

14

The memories of that wedding celebration and the night around the dancing fires with my friends the Comanches had to last me a long time. I didn't see any of them again until well into the spring after the turn of another year, for, on the very next mail run I made to Boggy Depot, a letter was waiting for me. My dear old mother had gone on, taken by the same typhoid that carried away Augustina.

There seemed to me some evil prophecy in that. Of all the women I had known in this world, and in those spirited days of my youth there had been many, the two most dear had been taken off by the same malady.

So in a somber mood I took leave of absence after a wee wrangle with Mr. Stoddard, because he had no other drivers at the time. We settled the issue by having young Allis Featherman take my load until I returned, he being as good with wagon teams as I, and maybe better. And he had the need now, with his new responsibilities, of making a few dollars here and there beyond what the army paid him to wheedle their mules back and forth between Sill and the depots to the east.

Deacon was getting on in years, and I decided to ride the wedding gift from Kwahadi, the little blue roan. Deacon looked at me with mournful eyes on the morning of my departure, as though he knew it might be the last time he saw me.

So once more the long trip to the Ouachita Mountains, but a better visit than the last, despite the sadness with standing at my mother's grave. My brothers seemed more inclined to treat me as something other than a wild barbarian, maybe because after signing that document in Fort Smith disavowing any claim to Morgan property, I no longer presented any threat to their future.

It was so pleasant that there were long moments when I couldn't decide whether I would stay or return to my plains and the Comanches. I worked in one of the mills where the sparkling water of the mountain stream was cold and clear and had a voice like angels gossiping. And the smell of new-cut pine was a tonic stronger than lively spirits from glass bottles and not nearly so disastrous to a man's innards. It was sublime to feel good sweat on my face, and sore muscles not used much of late and me ready for bed quick after a steaming bowl of rabbit stew with thick gravy and little green peas no bigger than the pearls around a fine lady's neck.

And I enjoyed a little city life after seeing nothing but the back room of Stoddard & Blanchard's store for many moons. Twice I traveled to Fort Smith on the roan, who had proved to be a fine little animal of great strength and some speed when required, and good sense so long as he was kept from the grain shed, where, if he was allowed, he would eat himself to death like any ordinary horse.

On my second trip to the city on the Arkansas, I beheld a public hanging. Two ruffians who had done murder and rape in the Cherokee Nation were sent to their peace by Judge Parker's court. Actually, it wasn't as public as Eastern newspapers would have everyone believe, and all of Parker's hangings were reported. The gallows

was surrounded by a wooden fence, so that about all anyone except invited guests could see was the top of the
scaffold. I had no invitation to stand within the intimate
confines near the death machine, for tickets to such affairs were reserved for politicians and newswriters, victims' families and morticians. It was dreadful enough,
even with that.

I was close enough to see the condemned men as
they were marched to the rope. White men they were,
and as ignoble in appearance as anyone I'd ever seen. I
thought for an instant of Rufus Tallbridge, the last person
in the world I wanted to think of.

Attending the Garrison Avenue saloons on those
trips, I discovered what should have become obvious
some years ago, but I'd been too muddy-brained to see it.
I could no longer stand at a bar and drink the fiery liquid
for hours at a time with no more damage than a morning
afterward of splitting head. Each time I returned from the
city after those binges, it took me fully three days to re-
cover, my back aching and my bowels rebelling and my
poor lungs scorched from so much late-night cigar smoke.

I stayed on in the hills, eating and sleeping in the
house of first one and then another of my brothers and
telling them and their families about the Kiowa-Comanche reservation and the things being done there. Or not
being done. I didn't deceive myself that any of them had
any sympathy for my friends in Indian Territory, but at
least they listened with interest. All the households were
gurgling with children by now, but they were too young
to enjoy hair-raising tales of redmen and charging ponies—young enough, in fact, so that when I held out my
hand there was not one of them too large to sit on my
palm as though it were the seat of a split-bottom chair.

The fall came, and with it that sharp-tasting air in
the pines, where the needles seemed to grow greener as
the cold increased. It was a lovely time, hearing from
some distance the saws slicing through the soft wood, and
watching the great pileated woodpeckers hammering the

rough bark of the trees, looking for grubs. And sometimes, in the early morning, the sunlight coming to the ground in shafts of pale blue light, I saw a flock of turkeys caught along one of the streamlines, red wattles bobbing like Comanche fringes.

I might have stayed right there, down through my old age and all the seasons, if a letter hadn't come. Always a letter coming, dreadful in its contents, to interrupt the brightness. In my old regiment I can recall some of the lads fearful of opening messages from family, knowing that inside lurked tales of bad times and hunger on the home place, and they too far away to do anything about it. I was coming to understand that feeling.

It was from Allis Featherman, come by way of the Boggy Depot run on the MKT north to Muskogee in the Creek Nation, and from there by coach to Fort Smith, thence on muleback to my hills. Allis was much better with horses than with a pencil, but his meaning was clear enough.

The first news was bad. Old Deacon had died. From a broken heart, I thought, but then realized how foolish I was to think such a thing. Deacon was a smart mule, but not that smart.

The next news was even worse. Old Sunshade had thrown herself away.

During the first snowfall along the Big Beaver she had taken her favorite buffalo robe, now moth-eaten and tattered about the edges, and walked out of camp in the time of darkness. No one realized she was gone until the following night, and then Kwahadi organized a search party, but they looked in vain. She got as far as the Wichita Mountains, although at the time no one knew that. She was walking west, maybe thinking of her beloved Palo Duro Canyon, out there somewhere toward the sun's setting place. But she only got as far as the Wichita Mountains.

Two young Kiowas hunting deer found her body. They knew she was Comanche from her clothing and rode at once to the settlement on the Big Beaver with the news that led Kwahadi's men out to bring the old woman back. They held a great funeral mourning, the women slashing themselves on the arms with knives in the old way because Sunshade had died in the old way, feeling her time was up and going out alone to start her journey to the place beyond the sun, and on the final spot, lying on the ground, her buffalo robe wrapped tight, the snow drifting over her.

Her body had not been molested by the wild animals, and Allis reported that all the Comanches said it was because wolf and coyote understood her great power and were afraid to touch her.

They buried her quickly in the little ground set aside for that purpose beside the Mennonite mission house, now called Sycamore Mission because of the trees that surrounded it. Hence it was Sycamore Cemetery, and already a number of the older Comanche had been laid down there. Allis wrote that they buried her in the traditional Comanche way, sitting in the grave, facing east.

I spent many a long night under one of my brothers' lamps, reading and rereading that letter. It created an overpowering guilt, a new sensation for me, because here had been an old woman who did much to set me on the course of Kwahadi's mother, and I in my slovenly way had dallied about over the years, doing nothing about it until the casual notion struck me. And now it was too late for her ever to know what had happened to that red-haired captive woman whom I suspected she had come to love.

But maybe, I consoled myself, old Sunshade knew already. She had told me about her dream. Not much of it, but enough for me to know she believed in her heart that Kwahadi's mother was dead. And believing that, maybe she held no hatred of me for taking so long in the search.

But no matter how often I told myself such fables, I

knew they weren't true. I knew that old woman had hated me with a kind of intensity that seemed to focus all the various parts of her loathing for white men onto my head, like a magnifying glass under the sun, because I had not taken my mission seriously enough. Her dream had told her that this Chosen was gone and she took it as fact, almost as though she had witnessed the dying. But her chief, the man whom she had led to Palo Duro and then nurtured to proud manhood, didn't believe the dream. And maybe Sunshade had suspected as I did that Kwahadi refused to believe in any dreams, and so she wanted to prove this one, and in that way somehow wipe out his heresy and thus make him more Comanche than he could possibly ever be by blood alone.

It came to me that there was some jealousy involved in her not wanting to share him with the hated whites; she was savagely resentful of his commerce with them, jealous as only some mothers can be, even along with their pride in a son's accomplishments.

And that brought the most perplexing thought of all: that she had been his mother since the day the Nakoni band was destroyed, and wanted him to remember only what came afterward. Wanted him to remember that as she fed him and disciplined him and told him the history of The People, she was his only mother, then or ever. In his manhood as well, she was the only woman he should rightly claim as mother, for all time and all places. And finally, maybe some of the hatred that glowed from those fierce old eyes was fueled not by the memory of white men at all, but rather by the fact that Kwahadi had never believed her dream or accepted her as mother, and so part of her fury, at least, was directed toward his own compulsion to find this Chosen. And bitterest of all, Sunshade had been forced to help him in the search!

So maybe any affection she bore toward the red-haired captive had turned to malice because it was that red-haired captive who still, even after all these years of absence, was foremost in the mind of the man she held in her thinking as son.

I remembered a chance remark of Otter Tongue's on one of the Fort Sill ration days, a casual statement that had not attracted my attention at the time.

"That old woman has much power," he'd said. "She had no sons or daughters, either. There was a spirit in her so strong that it killed all her children before they could issue from her body."

Otter Tongue may have been telling me that he understood Sunshade's motherly possessiveness. But what he didn't tell me, because he didn't know, was that when Sunshade had the opportunity thrust on her by those raiding Texas men to have a child she could bring to manhood, she snapped at it like a fish at bait, then later grew to despise the idea that Kwahadi wanted to deny her motherhood by harping on that other woman, his real mother who wasn't even Comanche.

It was a time when I began to think I had read too much of Mr. Dickens and Mr. Scott and other intelligent men, and that such a pastime did nothing for me except to roil my mind and send my thoughts along roads I couldn't understand. There'd been a young comrade in the old Third Arkansas who could hardly read at all but who had managed to get through a countraband copy of *Uncle Tom's Cabin* when we were in the trenches before Suffolk, and it had set his mind along such new and unusual paths that he vowed he would never read another book again.

Well, one thing was clear: I had to get to Texas and take up the chase, for my own peace of mind if nothing else. Some of Kwahadi's obsession had worn off on me, it seemed, but it had taken a long time and the death of an old Comanche woman to spark it.

"Never worry about time," Phil McCusker had said once. "They don't think much about it. Not about tomorrow, anyway."

But it galled me that so many tomorrows had passed

with my laziness when those people on the Big Beaver had as much right to know what had happened to the red-haired captive as the bloody Highlanders had the right to know what had happened to Mary, Queen of Scots.

So I was off to Texas, riding little Blue as far as Boggy Depot, stabling him there, and then taking the MKT line south across the Red. And this time I would find her, I said. And for the first time in many weeks, those Kiowa sun-dance calendars burned bright in my head.

When I crossed the Trinity, it didn't impress me as much of a river; I'd seen the Delaware at its widest point and the Potomac after hard rains. But what it lacked in width it made up for in ancient history, for I'd heard the tales Comanches told of how their grandfathers had long ago traveled along its course into the flat regions of southeast Texas, sometimes not stopping short of Galveston Bay. Tourists they were, admiring the country along the way and taking a few horses here and there from white settlements, not bothering with bills of sale.

Fort Worth was a goodly settlement, even though mostly a cow town like some others I'd seen. Now there were a lot of railroad men about as well, because most of the people who laid tracks felt that Fort Worth was the logical place from whence to spray metal in all directions across Texas.

The streets were wide and dusty and there were sidewalks everywhere, some of hard surface but mostly planking. The traffic of excellent horseflesh was impressive, either saddle mounts or drays in span before various kinds of vehicles. But even these last were fine-looking animals. They ran to red, it seemed, from the amber of chestnuts to the deep blood color of bays. Any one of them would have made my friends still living in tipis north of Red River beam with delight.

I took lodging in a hostelry across the tracks from the

MKT passenger depot, where a clerk treated me with some suspicion as his eyes cast about for baggage and found only the roll under my arm—an extra pair of pants there, long flannel underwear, a new broadcloth shirt from out of Fort Smith, and a razor for trimming beard and hair, tied all together inside my yellow rain slicker.

But when I produced my wad of bills, the total of my wealth in this world, his appreciation of me increased to the point of garrulousness. He was obviously a Fort Worth booster. In rapid order he explained to me that the city had two newspapers, each with a circulation of more than a thousand, and that in Fort Worth could be found pleasure palaces outdone only by those in New Orleans. I bought a newspaper from him but excused myself from the other, saying that I was in no mood for physical effort now, except to have a short stroll to kill the rest of the afternoon and get my bearings in his lovely town.

A bay window in my room opened to a street running off through the business district, and I could see the spires of churches beyond that. And the courthouse, this being Tarrant County's seat of government, and citizens going in and out for the conduct of their affairs with Texas.

I threw my truck and the newspaper on the bed and went out then into the winter sun. There was more than sun. A stiff breeze from the west cut against my face, and my heavy winter coat was barely adequate.

There were shops for ladies, window displays of hats with plumes and dresses with bustles and Spanish fans and lace. Well-accoutred saloons, where I made some brief inspections and took small libations, for I felt more need of fire in my belly than had been left from that long rattling ride in the cars from Boggy Depot.

There was a drugstore where a man could get a seltzer water, flavored as he liked, that issued from a spigot shaped like a nickel-plated cow's teat. Or colored ices or a bottle of laudanum, that ghastly tincture of opium to which some of the poor doctors in my old army had become addicted. Or pills for all causes, from piles to falling hair to sour stomach, and salves for saddlesores on horses or heat rash on little children.

There were a number of general mercantile stores, one of which I entered and found a place that sold books. My taste at that moment for heavy reading was not keen, so I selected one of the current dime novels, garish in color and violent in content.

The people on the street were friendly enough, many nodding to me as I passed, although we had never clapped eyes on one another in this world. The women all wore bonnets against the Texas sun, even now in winter, and long dresses made more for utility than for style. The men were uniformly dressed in long coats and boots, some with jangling spurs. I saw no evidence of revolvers on any of them except two, who were peace officers, proclaimed brightly by the five-pointed stars on their coats. They seemed the only two people I saw who were in no hurry.

I located the headquarters for the Ranger company stationed in Fort Worth, my destination in fact. But the day had run too short to do my work this day, and so I passed on by and soon returned to my hotel, where I had a supper of chili soup and a slab of pecan pie as delicious as any sultan of Persia might desire. Well, it should have been fine fare, because it cost me twenty cents!

Then back to my room and under the gas lamp to read my dime novel, a thing called *Night Hawk George and His Daring Deeds* by a certain Colonel Prentice Ingram. Not much there! The good Colonel Ingram wouldn't make a small wart on the arse of Mr. Charles Dickens or Henry Morton Stanley. So I cast Colonel Ingram and Night Hawk George aside and took up my newspaper.

An item caught my eye at once. The theater house was presenting within the next few days a limited engagement of the Orion Opera Company's version of Mr. William Shakespeare's *Hamlet*, the leading role to be played by Mr. Charles Chapin. Of whom I'd heard. According to the advertisement, the company was running out their string on a greatly successful tour that had included such enlightened places as St. Joseph, Missouri, and Dodge City, Kansas. At the latter place, as I'd read before in the *New York Herald*, the esteemed Chapin had become somehow enraged with the comedian Eddie Foy, who was also playing the Kansas trail town, and took a shot at said Mr. Foy with a .45-caliber pistol. But, luckily for the Orion Company and Mr. Foy, he had missed and been discharged from jail with a five-dollar fine for disturbing the peace.

It suddenly struck me funny that here I was in Texas, on a mission to discover events of the buffalo days, yet contemplating Mr. William Shakespeare and those who spoke his lines on a gas-lighted stage. Here, in a city now catering to the arts, and me looking for a girl who had been abducted by wild horsemen not far away in either time or distance.

Expectations are seldom met. Sometimes the reality is smaller than anticipated, sometimes larger, and if neither of these, at least different. The first time I saw a Ranger office on that trip to Fort Worth, it looked like any ordinary drygoods store. Except there were no bolts of cloth on the shelves, but only record and ledger books, and no glass cases with buttons and thread, but only rifles and shotguns shining in a row and deadly looking. I assumed that out back somewhere were a barracks and stable and blacksmith shop, but I heard no clang of metal on metal.

Nor any hardbitten peace officer presiding, but only a lad who looked no older than Allis Featherman, with a brindle mustache that extended out from a small mouth like the awning over Stoddard & Blanchard's front porch. He had a pair of flat blue eyes that seemed incapable of seeing beyond the edge of the wide brim of the hat that he wore, even here inside.

He was frail, the biggest things about him being a

cartridge belt studded with the brass of ammunition, and a huge Colt pistol with ivory grips in a hand-tooled leather holster. His name was Nobis Chandler.

I reckoned he was descended from some of that tough Anglo-Saxon breed who first peopled this state, before it was a state, and fought the Mexicans and, before and after that, the ancestors of my friends the Comanches. But I bore him no ill will for it.

He was very cautious with me at first, and then I explained that I had been with the old Third Arkansas Infantry, which he knew had become a part of the Texas Brigade after Sharpsburg, and with that, teeth appeared below the brindle mustache awning and he looked even younger still, smiling as he was. So then, the questions.

"Recaptured in 1854?" said he, and shook his head. "A while ago. But if we had anything to do with it, I'll find it here somewheres."

It took a wee while. He had to go back into some dark recess beyond my view, and I heard him muttering to himself and the slap of pages being opened and closed. But then he brought it out, an old and tattered book that looked like an accountant's ledger, the pages frayed at the edges and all the scribbled reports written in faded brown ink. He opened it before me on the counter. Yes, there was a drygoods store counter before the only desk in the place, marked with ink spots and some deep-carved initials in the wood.

"Le's see, le's see," he muttered, finger going down the pages, leafing back and forth. "Lotsa action, 1854."

Then a sudden stop of the tracing finger. He bent over the page, the brim of his outrageous hat hiding his face.

"Close by Red River, you say?"

"That's it," said I.

"Woman recaptured, you say?"

"That's it," said I.

He looked at me, the smile broad now, and nodded, shaking the hatbrim like a nervous quiver.

"Old Josh Burnett! He used to be captain of this company."

"Josh Burnett?"

"Sure, his hand, right here."

He shoved the ledger book toward me across the counter, turning it so I could read it. It wasn't easy, that liquid scrawl and words misspelt. But it was there!

Rangers of this company, Bangor Owen second in command, and a group of Tonkawa scouts surprised and attacked a hostile camp on Peace River some five miles south of the Red. Comanche camp burned and destroyed with only one minor casualty to Hicks, an arrow in the left thigh. Seventeen Comanche men killed. Four women using weapons against us killed. A few uncounted children who came into the line of fire. Horse herd destroyed. Some given the Tonkawa scouts and three hundred seventy-four others shot or throat-cut.

Recovered three infant white children, captured along the Brazos earlier this year. All placed in the care of Reverend Charles Reims and wife until claimed by their families.

Recovered was one captive white woman, age unknown, identified as Morfydd Annon Parry, taken captive on an attack against Fort Madoc on the Colorado River in about 1838. Taken with infant girl child who died before rejoining home station. Of natural causes, no wound involved. The woman was placed in the care of Bangor Owen and wife, who had been residents of Fort Madoc at the time of the Kiowa-Comanche attack aforementioned.

This action taken on October 23, a Monday, 1854. Signed and sealed this 31st day of October, 1854, by Captain Josh Burnett.

Standing before those brown ink scratchings, I could see not writing on a page but the village on the Peace.

The people running before the assault, the cries of wounded, the red blood of the dead already turning black, the yammering of dogs, and beyond the smoky-topped lodges the leaves in that October gone to yellow and scarlet. I could smell it. I could taste it, like old brass, and for a moment I had no voice to ask further, but only to think.

Well, there it was. Just as old Sunshade and Otter Tongue had told it, only now the place names filled in by this Josh Burnett. And this Bangor Owen. A good Welsh name, and maybe a sign of good fortune in my search.

"Where can I find this Josh Burnett?" My voice was choked so I could hardly recognize it.

"He's dead," said Ranger Chandler. "Took infection right after the war when a horse fell on him, crushed his leg."

"Then where can I find this Bangor Owen?"

"I don't know. I guess he lit out a while back."

Yes, this Ranger Chandler was too young to remember, and to him 1834 and 1858 were in the dim past, beyond his memory, but to me they were as fresh now as this same day's breakfast, and a lot more exciting.

"But," said he, "there's somebody who'd know."

"Name him."

"William McLean Burton."

At that moment it seemed to me that half of Texas had names that began with *B*. Then the sound of that name struck through my head like a chime in a chapel belfry. Like a clap of Yankee artillery was more like it, firing battery left to right.

"Burton? I knew a Texas man once, name of Burton."

"Well, sir, he's an old man," said Chandler. "There's lotsa Burtons in Texas. This one, he runs a barbershop over on Tarrant Street. He fought with the Fourth Texas in the war."

Scenes came flashing through my mind then, of John Bell Hood's brigade and us billeted in crude huts in the snow behind Fredericksburg, the winter after we went into Maryland. There'd been a man we thought old then, with white hair and beard, and he'd come to our dismal shack on long, cold evenings to cut our hair with a pair of shiny scissors and comb the lice out of our hair with a fine-toothed bone comb, all the while entertaining us with stories about the Comanches and how he was a Texas Ranger once. He'd been from the Fourth Texas Infantry, and standing before that knife-marked counter with the young boy grinning at me under his awning hat, I recalled that man saying many a time:

"Boys, after we've whupped the Yankees and gone home, you come see me sometime, down in old Fort Worth, Jewel of the Trinity!"

Old Burton! It was fifteen years since I'd seen him. We'd always thought him ancient during the war, all of us in our twenties or younger. He hadn't been so old as we'd suspected, but only prematurely gray and long of tooth. When I walked into his barbershop that day in Fort Worth, he looked exactly as I remembered him, the white hair and beard going off in all directions like a frosty forest fire. And the same piercing blue eyes, the same jutting chin that bespoke his no-nonsense view of all things. The same tall, gangling form, loose-jointed and sewn together with the toughest kind of sinew and all covered tightly with a skin that must have been exposed to raw sunlight since time began.

When I walked in and stood there grinning like a schoolboy caught pulling a girl's pigtail, he glared at me a moment, scissors in midair above the head of some corn-haired Texan. His face seemed to flush, the cheeks growing red as a maiden's blush. Then his great voice exploded, making everyone in the room jump.

"Son of a bitch! It's the Black Welshman!"

He made a dash for me, coming past the three chairs in the shop where customers and other barbers were wide-eyed at his eruption, threw his arms about me in a fine bear hug, the open scissors in his hand almost severing my left ear.

"Son of a bitch," he shouted, holding me now at arm's length. "You damned Arkansas hell-raiser! I ain't seen you since that spring we was eatin' them green apples at Gordonsville and all got the Gawd damned flux!"

"I remember. Just before marching off to have a wrangle with Sam Grant in the Wilderness it was."

"You have to mention that bastard's name," he shouted, laughing and showing his fine set of old teeth, brown-stained and sharp. "And right here you done it, in the hallowed halls of tonsorial splendor. By Gawd, Liverpool, most of that black hair's gone to white, ain't it?"

"Everybody grows old, my friend."

"Like hell. I don't grow old. I was borned old!"

"I didn't know if you'd recognize me."

"Recognize you? Hell's sweet sugar, boy, who could forget the best Gawd damned cardsharp and box fighter and woman charmer in the whole Gawd damned Rebel army?"

Well, it was a good feeling, being so fondly remembered.

15

Most often, when old comrades come together after years of being apart, there are a few moments of exhilaration and then a long silence. Each reminds the other of some incident of the camp they both remember, and there is robust laughter, maybe a little forced. And then that fades. And they finally sit and stare at one another and try to think of something to say.

Too many things had intervened. Too many circumstances not shared. And so the silence and wonder in each of them that here before him sat a man who had gone through hell along with him, and yet now there was no common ground. Because the hell was past. They no longer had to think of the morrow together and the mutual danger and the mutual reliance, one on the other.

So when old soldiers met, it was usually a sad day, the only substance holding them together no longer substance at all but only fading memories of those companions torn apart or dead of pox. Or of the days and nights of hunger and cold and marching barefoot over long and cruel roads. So they stared wordlessly and knew they loved each other for those times forgotten now but there were no words to make it all come back again.

But William McLean Burton transcended bad memories.

He was more than anyone's old soldier comrade. He was the Everyman of Texas, bigger than any of his experiences, a barber and Indian fighter and former Ranger and father to many grown sons. And a talker. Most of all, a talker.

Yet there was no word of the strongest thing between us, of friends shot to pieces on the fields above the Rapidan or Chattanooga, blood going black on the ground where a solid shot had taken off some lad's head. Rather, our meeting was a time of rejoicing, when old friends met to blot out all the memories of men gone into the ground of Virginia and Tennessee. As though the bad times never happened and could be wiped out with drunken laughter.

So when we met that morning in a Fort Worth barbershop, there was no sadness. It was celebration, boisterous and rowdy and overflowing with words, many unfit for tender ears.

A man could find it easy to envy William McLean Burton, and not only for his good business and standing in his community and his fine, proud sons. But for his years during the buffalo days, when nothing west of Fort Worth and sometimes not even Fort Worth itself was safe from the Comanches. His life had been arrow wounds scarred over, stalks to camps where white captives were held, the sighting of moccasin prints in a river's sand, showing the little twitch of marking at the heel as though a squirrel had dragged its tail, and the shout of naked men coming on small ponies and shooting arrows from under the horses' necks. All of that and more. For he had seen them in their power, in their time of glory.

Burton regaled his fellow barbers and their customers for only a short time, then sent off the bootblack to alert the wee Mrs. Burton that she must set a banquet for a returning hero. That accomplished, Burton insisted that we see his town, so we set off along Tarrant Street and later toured Main, slipping into each saloon along the way, he slapping my back all the while and introducing me to a lot of men who wore big hats and had horse manure on their boots. And of course explaining to them all that here was a veteran of the Texas Brigade.

Finally, with the sun casting long shadows across the streets, we went home to Biddie, busy with her pots and pans. He lived not far from my hotel, a good thing for the later journey, once we had destroyed the chicken and dumplings. And what a knack Biddie had with the edibles! She was a small, owl-like woman with great black eyes, darting back and forth between parlor and kitchen as McLean Burton and myself rested in horsehair-stuffed chairs trying to outdo each other in the consumption of his sour-mash whiskey, and all the while my nose twitching from the smells coming out of Biddie's domain.

Biddie served the chicken in a vast tureen, delicate and light in its gravy and the dumplings as big as Osage oranges and as light on the tongue as snowflakes. There were snap beans and panfried Irish potatoes and cucumber pickles and spiced peaches. And a large, golden-brown loaf of yeasty bread, taken with fresh churned butter that sat in a plate with beads of moisture dotting it.

"Best Gawd damned cook in Tarrant County," McLean roared, juice running into his whiskers.

It sure as hell beat hotel grub.

Then I was away to my room, staggering with each step, and the shouts of McLean Burton behind me, ringing in my ears, as he shouted his blasphemous farewell from the front porch, loud enough to wake all the good residents of Fort Worth.

He seemed so glad to see me that I hadn't had the heart to tell him I had come to Texas not to visit him but to find a Comanche captive long since retaken.

We spent the next two days without my mentioning Kwahadi's mother, going from place to place and seeing his friends and the sons of his friends and the grandsons of his friends. Liquid spirits were taken all along the way in equal portions with the greetings and back-slappings and arm-squeezings. One evening we went to the theater, taking Biddie along, to watch Mr. Chapin do his rendition of the Danish prince, and another late night, without Biddie, we bent over a green felt table, trying to knock the little ivory balls into pockets. And each night the lovely provender that Biddie put down, first a fine beef stew with parsnips and next a pork pie with carrots and green chilis and a Mexican beer thick as syrup.

"Spending your time on me," I said, "when all the good citizens of Fort Worth are waiting at your empty chair to have their locks sheared."

"To hell with the citizens of Fort Worth," he shouted. "I own that Gawd damned barber shop, and everything in it. If I take a few days with old friends, who's to say me no?"

Not I to say him no, but on the fourth morning, at his Biddie's breakfast table of buckwheat cakes and sausage, I told him why I'd come. He stared at me a long time, blinking and chewing, and his expression told me that from the start he had maybe suspected there was other business in my plans.

"Why, hell," he said. "Everybody in Texas knows about Madoc Fort. And old Josh Burnett bringing back that white woman held all the years by the Comanch'. But I don't know a lot about the details. Bangor Owen? I knew him when he was a Ranger here, and me doin' a little bit of that work myself. Before the war."

"Where is he now? I'd like to talk with him."

"Dead and gone, by Gawd! Killed in some skirmish in your state. Elkhorn Tavern, I think it was. He served with old Ben McCulloch. Old Ben, he died at the same place. Not like Spotsylvania, by Gawd, but more than enough for some. When you go up the flue, it don't much matter where it's at, does it?"

"Ranger Chandler told me this Bangor Owen had a wife. She still alive?"

"Nobis Chandler? Why, that little squeak, hell's fire, he wouldn't make a scratch on a real Ranger's arse, the kind we had back when everybody carried two Walker

Colts and chewed lead for supper. Yeah, Bangor's wife was Mari, a fine woman. I lost track of her.

"After they retook that white woman up on the Peace, her and him went back to live at Madoc Fort. Took that woman with 'em, I recall. Lost track of 'em then. Heard about old Ben and Bangor both goin' up the flue later. But Bangor, before the war, he quit the Rangers and went off to their first home in Texas. Madoc Town, it's called now, on the Colorado."

"I'd like to see that woman."

"Mari?"

"Her and the other one, too. The one they retook from the wild tribes."

"Never saw her," McLean said. "But she was taken off from here by Bangor and his woman. By Gawd, we can sure find 'em, I reckon."

So it was settled, then. Off to the Colorado River, McLean and myself, for he would brook no nonsense about me wandering about his state unescorted.

"Hell, boy, ain't you ever heerd about all the bad men we got down here?"

"Fort Worth's a nice, calm place," said I. "I've seen Ellsworth, in Kansas, when the herds were coming in, and this place here is like church on Sunday beside it."

"Texas boys gets randy once they cross the Red," he said, and winked broadly. "But not here. We got a Ranger company here, you know, and good local peace officers. Oh, Sam Bass filtered through here a couple times before they finally shot his arse off out at Round Rock. And even John Wesley Hardin, before he was sent off to the penitentiary at Huntsville for twenty years. Where he's still at. But by Gawd, no friend of mine is goin' wanderin' around Texas without me to point the way. Hell, boy! What's friends for, anyway?"

Then I found that McLean had offspring scattered around Texas like bluebonnets. There was a son working for one of the Fort Worth newspapers, and from him could be obtained all the railroad passes on the MKT that anyone could ever want, railroads then giving out free tickets to anyone who wrote for the newspapers, in hopes of having good publicity in return. So from Fort Worth to Temple on a handful of those red pasteboards.

There was another pair of sons in Temple who ran a livery stable, and from them a hack and team of fine bays and the back of the wagon for bedrolls and bacon so we could rough it across the prairie the way we once had across Virginia, as McLean put it.

I thought it likely that old McLean welcomed an excuse to be away from Biddie for a wee spell, her cooking like an angel in heaven's kitchen notwithstanding.

Whatever the reason, our trip was joined. When we boarded the cars in Fort Worth and started south, I had the feeling that maybe I would be coming face to face with a red-haired former captive of the wild tribes. It was going fast, too, thanks to Burton and his sons, and there was another tight twinge of guilt, seeing how much I could have accomplished long ago.

West of Temple, in the hack now, it was cold but the days stayed cloudless and the sun was warm toward midday as McLean clucked and chuckled the team of bays along across the unending flats. We traveled a lot of streambeds, mostly dust now and waiting for spring rains.

"All these creeks run east into the Brazos," McLean explained. "They do right up to the time you come to the Colorado, which is west of us here. You got the Gawd damned geography fixed in your mind, Liverpool?"

"Yes," said I, but I could feel it more than see it.

The lift of land toward the west was like a tilting pool table, and I knew that beyond the Colorado was the Edwards Plateau. It was a desolate and almost treeless plain, and we saw roadrunners and a sidewinding rattlesnake or two, all seeming surprised at our intrusion. There were stands of mesquite growing thick together for no apparent reason other than companionship, thorny thickets, and I began to appreciate the heavy leather chaps some of the drovers wore, those drovers who herded their cows past the reservation north of the Red.

I had no idea whether McLean was purposely avoiding any sign of civilization. But for whatever reason, we saw no ranches or farms or settlements but only the wild country, camping twice at night before we reached Madoc. On the second stop, we ate like kings!

He'd brought along a shotgun, and during that day he managed to kill four of what he called scaled quail. We saw more, but he said four were enough. A tiny bird, mostly gray in color but with a white crest and dark brown tail. We roasted them over a mesquite fire, which took a long time to start, but once flaming, gave off an intense heat and seemed to burn forever without going to ash.

Burton made what he called pan bread from cornmeal and water and a sprinkle of salt, flattened and cooked in a skillet on a spider over the glowing fire. There was coffee, the beans crushed in a cloth bag with the butt of the shotgun and dropped into the boiling pot. The smell of it all made my innards ache with anticipation.

The wind laid that night, and it was pleasant sitting beside the fire in the purple darkness of the plain, listening to the stories McLean told about Comanches, and listening as well to the soft snap of the fire. I looked often beyond the boundary of orange light cast by the flames and thought about the war parties that had roamed this land not too long ago. And thought as well of the Spanish and English-speaking peoples who came, a brave people to conquer the brave ones already here. The Spaniards had little luck at it, the Comanches constantly burning out their missions and stealing their mules. But the Anglos, as Burton called them, brought their kids and churches along and were more successful.

Later, as the fire died, I lay wrapped tight in a sheepskin robe provided by one of Burton's sons, and looked at the stars, never understanding their brightness. Then I slept and dreamed of the sea, hearing the blue water on the shores of Gibraltar kissing the rock. I woke in the night and it was totally dark and I felt a strange uneasiness, still hearing the lapping of Mediterranean waves until I realized that what I heard was only the wind come up, murmuring through the scrub like whispering voices of all the ones who had been here before me across this desolate land. I could hear them call my name.

Finally, the Colorado, which was low this time of year, so we had no trouble fording. McLean told me the city of Austin was about eighty miles south, but in that country as I saw it a man could never know there was a city closer than the moon. And he told me the San Saba was nearby, a name famous in Texas history, and he pronounced it with the accent on the first syllable of Saba, in Texas fashion, unlike my Comanche friends, who accented the last syllable as the Spaniards had done. I knew that because I had heard the men on the Big Beaver tell the story of how their grandfathers had once destroyed a Spanish mission there.

The land changed, once we were across the river and heading north, lifting and with more trees. Sycamore and hornbeam along the streamlines, and always the mesquite. Not far from old Fort Madoc, I could feel the wind coming off the Edwards Plateau and from far beyond, the smell of rain in it. Down it came off the high plains, that wind, down off Llano Estacado like the breath of centuries, unchanging, defiant.

Madoc Town was hardly worth the name. A scattering of frame and sod buildings not even so impressive as the cluster of structures around Stoddard & Blanchard's store, south of Fort Sill. And not nearly so many horses. The town was set along the course of a small stream that ran into the Colorado, some distance to the east, down from a plateau to the west on which I could see sheep grazing. The most imposing establishment was a combination stagecoach depot and general mercantile store, and there we were directed to a small cottage on the edge of the settlement, fenced with palings, and the signs of last summer's flower garden in the porch yard.

It was like seeing my mother again when Mari Owen opened her door to us. Only a hint now in her old age of the stout body and limb that had once been hers, the robust health long decayed, yet her eyes still bright and the silver bun of hair at the nape of her neck a saucy reminder of what she once must have been.

"McLean Burton!" she exclaimed on seeing us, and she and my barber friend embraced like brother and sister long away from one another. "I haven't set eyes on you these many years. Dead I thought you was!"

"Not yet, Mari," said he, and stepping back, he waved a hand in my direction. "And this here is my friend from the old Texas Brigade, Liverpool Morgan. We called him the Black Welshman in our days in Virginia, but seems like it's all gone to white, that hair of his."

The light stayed in her eyes as she took my hand, a firm and dry grasp with strength in it, and I suspected she might have sensed I was of her own national blood without McLean's introduction. Well, not national, our people never having had a nation since the Norman invasion or before, but at least the singing between us, which the English never understood.

Just in time for afternoon tea, she said, and invited us into her little kitchen, cozy and warm after the wind outside. It smelled of all the good things I could remember from Welsh kitchens, and the copper pots hung round the walls like the shields of King Arthur's knights. And a fire in her cast-iron stove making its soft sound of welcome.

She served us saffron cookies with the tea, tiny wedges of yellow pastry, and with that a long explanation of how her family had come by these delights through distant cousins who were Cornishmen. And added with a twinkle in her eye that everyone knew the best saffron cookies came from old Cornwall.

The two of them talked together as though this were only a casual visit and they'd seen each other all through the days as close neighbors or as members of the same congregation on Sundays, when in actual fact it had been many years since their last meeting. It came to me that disregard of such long distances in time might be a function of their citizenship in this boundless land, where no matter how far apart, they were still tied always closely together, simply because they were both Texans.

But finally McLean Burton came to it.

"Morgan here," he said, "has come to see what you can tell him about that captive white woman old Josh Burnett and your Bangor Owen retook from the Comanch' before the war."

Those two Rangers and their men had likely taken more than one white captive woman from the wild tribes before the war, but she knew instantly which one McLean meant. There was a sudden stillness in her, everything seeming to stop dead with her cup of tea half raised to her lips, everything stilled except the blue eyes, which probed my face with a deep intensity.

"Morgan here, he says he might know her son," McLean said gently, and Mari Owen shuddered.

"Aye," said she, slowly replacing her cup in the saucer before her on the tiny table between us. "My Bangor said she mentioned a son. But only once, the day they took her from that wild tribe camp. Or maybe the day after. But only once did she mention a son. And never said a word of him again. Josh Burnett said he likely ran off and was et by the wolves on the prairie."

"He got to Palo Duro Canyon," I said. "And joined the Antelope band."

"That was their hangout, all right," said McLean.

"An old woman led him. Only she wasn't old then. Her name was Sunshade. She told me about it."

"How old was this son?" Mari Owen asked.

"I figured from the Kiowa sun-dance calendars that he was about ten in 1854."

She lifted her cup once more and took a wee sip, watching me over the rim. She seemed uncertain, maybe even a little hostile.

"I've been told the girl was taken on a creek called the River of Broken Guns. That's what the Comanches call it," said I.

She looked down into her cup, then, sighing.

"Aye. I've heard it said that's what they call it," she said almost in a whisper.

Abruptly she rose, startling both of us, and took a man's greatcoat from a wall peg and pulled it on, her movements quick now, like a young girl's. And over the coat and her head and shoulders she wrapped a heavy shawl, so she looked like one of the Pope's nuns.

"Come with me," she said, and it was a command.

It had begun to rain, and slanted in the wind were particles of snow, too small to be seen, but only felt against the bare skin of our cheeks. Mari Owen hurried along before us, her head bowed and the man's coat almost dragging the ground behind her. We passed quickly through the settlement, where we saw no one, the people having taken refuge inside their houses with the coming rain.

At the far edge of Madoc Town I looked beyond and saw the stockaded walls of an old fort, long unused. The logs of the palisades were rotting, and a few had fallen out of place and lay on the ground like discarded toothpicks on a tabletop. I knew it was old Fort Madoc even before Mari Owen stopped to point it out before going on.

"They came from all sides that day," said she. "It was just at dawn. We ran to the river and hid until they went away. And coming back, an awful sight we saw. My Bangor, scalped, left for dead."

"Well, I'm damned, I never knew that," McLean said, his white-framed face almost hidden in the upturn of his coat collar.

"Aye, scalped and left for dead. It was only a small patch of his dear hair they took," she said, then hurried on toward the old fort.

Off to the west of the walls was a stand of chinkapin oak and I could see among them headstones, and knew that was our destination. And a hard lump came into my chest. But before we arrived there, Mari Owen stopped once more and turned to us, holding the shawl tight against her face.

"She'd gone for water. Down to the stream, she'd gone. All the children went for water each dawning. The others were back when the horsemen came. But she was still at the water. That's where they took her, I suppose. We didn't see her again until sixteen, seventeen years later, when they brought her back to Fort Worth."

Then, again, she turned and hurried through the wind and rain and snow to the burial ground.

"How old was she when they took her, Mrs. Owen?" I shouted, to be heard above the storm.

"About eleven," she said, not turning, still hurrying on. "Maybe ten. I don't know. It's grown muddled in my old thinking, it has."

We came into the pin oaks, and it was almost like night there with the low cloud cover and the overhanging limbs, bare and creaking now against one another. The headboards of the graves were made of rough timber, many weathered badly. In the midst of them, Mari Owen stopped once more and turned to us.

"We ran away, the ones the savages didn't get. Downriver to the next settlement. But then some of them came back and made Madoc Town as you see it. Bangor and me, we came later, that same year him and Josh Burnett retook her from the wild ones." She laughed shortly, light of remembrance in her eyes. "My Bangor! He said this was the only home he ever knew in Texas, and he wanted to live here all his days. He wasn't a city man, my Bangor. He was a sheep man and for the open country. But I'll tell you true, Mr. Morgan, I think he came back here because of her. To bring her back to the place where she was born."

Then we were standing before it, a grave sunken and with a brown and splintered headboard standing crookedly in the ground. But the legend on that board had been carved deep by loving hands, and was still easily legible without bending to it.

MORFYDD ANNON PARRY.
TAKEN BY INDIANS IN HER BLOOM OF YOUTH.
BORN HERE 1827, DIED HERE 1855.

And Mari Owen had read it too, maybe for the thousandth time and said softly, "Aye. Eleven she was."

Twenty-eight years old when she passed on!

"When the war came, Bangor went off to join Ben McCullock. He'd known him in the Rangers. Then never came back to me. She'd died before that, of course. It broke my Bangor's heart, as the war broke mine. She never seemed to know him after she was retaken. Him that had bounced her on his knee when she was a baby girl, and she'd called him Uncle Bangor."

I expected to see tears on her face, then, but there were none. Only the moist blue eyes, staring at the grave.

"She never seemed to know any of us after she was retaken. Like she was still in that other world, away from us still. She never spoke unless spoken to, and then little she said. And she wouldn't eat. Picking at food like a wee bird. Wasted away, she did. Then died, a young woman but looking old as leather and nothing to live for, we reckoned. I never understood it, and it broke my Bangor's heart. I don't think he'd ever have gone off to the war if she'd been still alive then."

Mari Owen turned toward the stream and pointed, and we could see the dim gray outline of hornbeam and a line of sycamores, the bark patched with white. And in their limbs a few crows, feathers blowing in the wind, scolding the elements with their harsh voices.

"After we brought her back, she'd often come out here beside the old fort and stand for an eternity. Not moving. Just looking off to where she'd been taken that day in 1838. Glassy-eyed. But I never saw her cry.

"No, I take it back," she said, shaking her head. "Did you know she had a daughter with her when they brought her into Fort Worth? A wee baby and already dead when I took her out of the cradle board to wash her body. A wee baby dead. She cried the next day, did Morfydd. Sitting on the edge of the bed and looking out the window. It was raining that day, too.

"A son, you say? And you know of him?"

"I've spoken with him many times," said I. "He calls himself Kwahadi Parry."

"Parry? He calls himself that? Then the rumors are true." And she sighed. "A son among them all these years."

She seemed hostile to any thought of inquiry about that son, of knowing anything about him, no matter who he was or where he was or what he might become. As though it were a part of her memories that she wanted to brush out, those years of Morfydd Annon Parry among the Comanches.

"Does she have any family left now?" I asked.

"None. Her Da was Grandfer Parry, old Madoc himself. Killed along with his wife on that day. And a little brother taken the same day as her, never found again. That Morfydd! What wonderful hair she had when she was a girl. The red deep down in it that came out like fire in the sun's light."

We stood silent awhile, bent against the wind, staring down at the patch of earth. Then, shaking herself as though to rid her old shoulders of sorrow, Mari Owen turned back toward the settlement.

"Cold it is," she said brightly now. "Hurry back to my cottage and we'll have a nice mutton stew for supper and you can sleep in my goat shed. A cozy place, with plenty of straw."

I wanted a few moments alone here beside the grave, and I suppose they understood because they went away without another word, leaving me. I read the inscription again. The wind was lifting, and the howl of it through the bare branches of the oaks was like the spirits calling from the distant past. Some of last fall's brown leaves danced across the grave, past the leaning headboard, weightless and giving off their little rustle of sound like tiny feet running from the cold.

I knelt beside the grave and laid one hand palmdown on the sunken ground and thought, Well, Chosen, found at last.

Old Sunshade's dream had revealed the truth, after all. But now, at least, maybe that chief north of the Red who kept his horses in the wooden house the whites had built for him could sleep more easily at night after I told him where his mother rested.

In Mari Owen's cottage, she and McLean Burton waited. She was still in her greatcoat and holding what appeared to be a piece of cardboard about twelve inches on a side.

"You say you know her son?" she asked, at least now making a concession to his existence.

"Yes. There's no doubt in my mind that he is her son."

"Well, then, for the sake of her memory, he should have this. It only causes me sorrow whenever I look on it."

She turned the cardboard faceup on the table and I saw it was a portrait. The face was weathered and the lips turned down at the corners and the eyes stared out with a cold, empty, bottomless vacancy. The hair was cut at shoulder length, as though hacked off with a dull knife, hanging lifeless and without luster. She was wearing a print dress that looked too large for her.

"Morfydd Annon Parry," she said. "There was a

traveling man came to Fort Worth in a little wagon, just before my Bangor and me left there and came back to this place. He made little prints of people's faces on sheets of paper. Old Josh Burnett brought him around to our house, and us already packing things for the journey. He said it was a part of history."

"Yes, a daguerrean artist," said I. "There were a lot of them traveling around the country before the war."

"Well, he took out all his contraptions and he did this. And she looked so bad that Josh said maybe it wasn't meant to be history. Josh took it as an ill omen on himself that the baby had been brought in dead and that Morfydd was doing so poorly. But no fault of his."

At the bottom of the portrait were words, looking as though they'd been placed there by rubber stamp and fading now, but still I could read them. And did so aloud.

" 'Calotype process of Mr. William H. F. Talbot, Esq.' Calotype. Only a small smattering of Greek I know. But I know that. It means 'beautiful picture.' "

"Not so beautiful was she then," said Mari Owen, with another of her sighs. "A child pretty as sunset. But not when that man did this picture. Life turned a woman to rock, living with the wild tribes."

"After she came to you, did she ever try to escape, to get back to the Comanches?" I asked.

Mari Owen looked at me with a small smile, the lips turned up at the corners into her soft cheeks, as though she were looking at a child who had asked a silly question.

"No. She sat and stared, mostly, she did. She went about like an old spavined horse, doing what she was told to do. Come eat, Morfydd. Go to bed, Morfydd. Take a bath, Morfydd.

"I'd take her in the kitchen, so she could watch me cook. Chattered like a magpie, I did, but all the while she said nothing. Just stared at me with those dead eyes. She could hardly speak our tongue, she had been among them so long. And when it was time to sit at the fire after supper, she'd perch on the edge of her chair, about to take flight, so it seemed, looking at the flames. Then go off to her bed, her feet making no sound, even in those leather shoes we got her, even off the rugs, silent as a ghost.

"No, she never tried to leave. She stayed close to me, like a lost child, afraid to go anywhere, afraid of everything. When our clock struck, she started like a deer about to bolt, eyes wild then. Go back? No. What would she go back to, Liverpool Morgan? From what my Bangor told me, her people were destroyed."

"It seemed, from what I'd heard of her, that she became so much a part of them that maybe she might try to go back. To whatever she thought was left," I said.

"No!" Then she laughed, but there was no mirth in it. "Oh, she was part of them, all right. It was no white woman we had. She gave me the shivers, that thing grown from the darling girl I'd known at old Madoc Fort. But she'd been among them too long. Though my Bangor was never able to believe it in his mind, good man that he was. She wilted like a flower, wilted and died before our eyes, she did. There was no fire in her, and I could remember when she was little those eyes bright and tossing her head when she played among the others. All that gone when she was brought back to us.

"But I suppose it had to be there for a while, didn't it? That high spirit. That grit. Through all the years they had her, it had to be there, else she would have died. But then, brought back to her own people, it flickered out and . . . and . . ."

Mari Owen stopped, her words trailing off with bewilderment, and on her face a look of astonishment.

"I never understood any of it," she said with finality, then repeated, "but life among the wild tribes turned a woman to stone."

Yes, I thought, yet she died from the sorrow of leaving them.

16

It was one of those most wonderful of spring days. The first after a long winter. There had been days before it of sun and the wind blowing without much bite, and there had been green showing in some of the small trees. But this was the first real spring day, with no requirement for topcoat and the breeze warm from the west, not enough of it to ruffle loose hair. The sky was Prussian blue and the larks were out in regimental force and the cardinals fluttering in the low oaks and sandbar willow along the streamlines. There was the smell of new things, and even the dust had the scent of snow-washed earth.

It was a good time to ride out and see Kwahadi. It had taken me a while to make up my mind about what I might say to him. I had the portrait of his mother, framed and heavily wrapped in butcher paper, a chore finished in Fort Worth before I'd said farewell to my friend McLean Burton.

It had been a fitting farewell, too, for ruffians such as we.

Well, sometimes a madness comes on old soldiers after the finish of a difficult mission. A release of steam,

like the pistons jetting hot vapor along the sides of a locomotive following a long climb. It was so my last night
there in Fort Worth.

McLean Burton and myself were having a final go-
round of town, and ended playing pool. By then we had
taken many jots of sour-mash whiskey and rye, and as we
knocked the little balls about, we poured a lot of Mexican
beer down on top of the whiskey. Everything would have
been peaceful, with us ending up sleeping soundly in our
beds, had it not been for the gentleman from Mississippi
and McLean's skill with a cue stick.

This gentleman from Mississippi was large and rug-
ged of frame and visage—a railroader, as he claimed—
and during the course of the evening, on hearing that
both Burton and myself had served in the Texas Brigade,
he began to make loud noises about a certain Mississippi
regiment being the best that ever served with Lee's old
army.

This would have been blasphemy in Fort Worth nor-
mally, but on this night there was a rough crew gathered,
none of whom were tenderly inclined toward McLean
and me because in the first place he had run a string of
balls on one of them in a game of rotation and won fifty
dollars, and secondly because they were all former members of the Twenty-first Texas Cavalry, or some such
thing, which had never served beyond the borders of the
Lone Star State. During the course of the evening, these
gentlemen had become greatly irritated with Burton's
and my own rather superior comments to the effect that
we had marched with John Bell Hood in Virginia.

So when the gentleman from Mississippi gave his
speech about the best regiment of infantry in the old
Army of Northern Virginia, McLean Burton quite naturally laid the butt end of his pool stick across the gentleman's nose with considerable force, and when the Texas
stay-at-home cavalry leaped in to redeem injured pride
and perhaps lost money, I intervened with a brass spit-
toon.

It became a little hazy after that. I recalled later a cigar display covered with glass that was shattered, and a great many beer mugs that found their way against the adobe walls of the billiard emporium. The proprietor had his trousers torn off and ran into the street in his red underwear, waving a nine-ball in one hand and a week-old copy of the *New Orleans Picayune* in the other, and when the city policeman arrived, the combatants momentarily paused in their efforts, and everyone, including the policeman, had a beer at the bar, where the argument started all over again and the policeman was knocked down by the Mississippi gentleman.

After a short and frenzied while, the remainder of the Fort Worth police arrived and the fight moved out into the street, taking both of the pool hall's plate-glass windows with it. A number of passersby who had just come from the theater paused and began to shout encouragement to the various gladiators, and a few even joined in the melee.

Finally, to everyone's relief, Ranger Nobis Chandler and a couple of his men appeared, and once McLean Burton insisted that the next day he would come down and pay for all the broken glass and the owner's trousers, we were told to get off the streets or else be thrown in jail for a breach of the peace. McLean discarded his broken cue stick then, and I cast aside the leg of a domino table, the table having come apart as the struggle moved through the front portion of the hall. The Mississippi gentleman and the people from the Texas stay-at-home regiment and McLean and I shook hands all around and everyone agreed it had been one hell of a good scramble and then it was decided that we'd go back inside and have a few more beers, but Nobis Chandler put the stopper to that.

Biddie patched McLean and me up with carbolic and tallow salve. There were considerable cuts and bruises but McLean Burton was in his glory, laughing and shouting and saying he hadn't had so much fun since the time in sixty-three when he and I stole the jug of apple cider from the old Dutch farmer south of Gettysburg.

"And by Gawd, it's a good thing there wasn't no damned Mexicans in that fracas," he yelled. "Else there'd been a blade drawed, and then we'd go at 'em with this."

Whereupon he pulled from some hidden place under his tattered shirt the largest six-shooter I'd ever seen, and discharged it once into the ceiling before Biddie could get it away from him.

It was a fine sendoff from the Jewel of the Trinity. I was ashamed of myself, yet felt younger than I had in years. But that was before I took the MKT and then little Blue back to Sill, for every mile of that trip disclosed a new ache.

It was good to be back on my windy prairie, with the low spring scrub in the rolling distance looking like damp moss. They'd always told me that in this season the sap rose in a man, but I found as I grew older that, rather than vitality, spring brought only the gentle urge to sit and watch the changing landscape.

While I pondered my visit to the Antelope chief, which would be both gratifying and sad, I made the rounds of agency and fort to pass on my greetings to old friends. Allis Featherman seemed to have aged ten years, such a mature man now, and only yesterday a boy. His wife was already heavy with the child that would come before fall. He told me this glad news with a grin splitting the freckles and his chest thrust out like a bantam rooster let loose in the hen coop.

He said some changes had occurred in my absence. The Antelope band was spreading all along Big Beaver Creek, and many had begun living in the wooden houses the bureaucrats had allotted them. Their herd of Texas cattle was increasing again, and many spring foals were dropping. The Department of the Interior had finally approved an Indian police force, and Kwahadi was heavily involved in the planning, but no action had been taken yet.

Mr. Stoddard welcomed me with a gift bottle of label whiskey from Cincinnati, harsh to the tongue and nostrils but warm in the belly. Agent Belton offered no welcome at all, and hinted that from now on my duties with the agency might not be required, due to my unreliability, disappearing as I did from time to time and spending so many days on the Stoddard & Blanchard stagecoach run. He said I could stay in my miserable agency shack, but that he was thinking about charging me rent, all of which seemed to please Jehyle Simmons, who stood about through the agent's scolding with his ugly teeth showing like those of a jackass.

Adjutant Weslowski had a store of old books for me and a few acid words of his own about going absent without leave from his army mules, yet all of it said with a friendly twinkle in his blue eyes as he wiped his nose, this being the season for nose-wiping in his case.

I paid my respects to the venerable Tracy Shadburn. We spent an evening sitting on the Fort Sill woodpile, sipping some of the Cincinnati whiskey and smelling the beans cooking in the troop messes nearby. Tracy was as spooky as I'd ever seen him, looking over his shoulder at every shadow.

"There's trouble on the way, Morgan, sure as hell," he said. "Out on the reservation, some of them has started eatin' mescal."

"Peyote? Where would they get such a thing around here?"

"Hell, I don't know. It comes from Mexico or thereabouts, they tell me. But there's so much traffic back and forth amongst these heathens, I guess they can get about anything they want."

"I never heard of Comanches using it."

"Well, they are now. They chew this stuff and it makes 'em crazy, they tell me. It's against the law, of course, but what the hell do these red niggers know about the law?"

"Any trouble thus far?"

"No," he said almost reluctantly, and I could feel his impatience with this boring life on an Indian frontier that was no longer a frontier and no action in prospect for the good troopers. "But they'll come a day. They'll come a day."

Well, I supposed that maybe it was just wishful thinking on old Tracy's part, him hoping in his heart that all hell would break loose so he'd have a chance to shoot somebody.

"And some of these sojurs we got now ain't worth mule shit. And we ain't got no ammunition for target practice and half the damned horses oughta be condemned and all the noncommissioned officers ever think about is goin' down south of the Red to fornicate with some slattern that's got seven kinds of pox. All in all, Morgan, it's the same old army."

"It has a familiar ring, Tracy," said I.

"Yeah, it does," he said, and laughed suddenly and slapped me on the shoulder with the force of a kick from an unbroken cavalry horse. "But, hell, let's have some more of that store whiskey and be glad none of us has to worry about gettin' rich!"

Then he started on Rufus Tallbridge.

"He's back on the reservation," Tracy said. "A real scum. He's skulkin' about like a damned coyote, lookin' for horses to steal and runnin' in illegal whiskey for the red niggers. From Kansas and Texas, I expect.

"After you busted him up that time at Stoddard's game room, he lit out a spell. Then in midwinter he showed up at Anadarko, sniffin' around. He comes through here now and again on his way to Texas. You shoulda killed him that night, Morgan."

"And gone to the rope in Fort Smith if I had," I said.

"That Rufus, he'll end on a rope hisself. Maybe not in Fort Smith, though. They got this Federal court in

Wichita Falls supposed to take over this part of the territory. Won't be as good. That Judge Parker, he's my kinda
man, droppin' them scum to hell on a hemp string."

"Well, I suspect you're right. Tracy, wherever they
come from, the law will have our Rufus one day."

"The sooner the better!"

"It's a bad thing to wish on any man, that hairy collar, even our Rufus. Until he's done the foul deed, like
Olin Crater did."

"Why, Gawd damn, Morgan, they always told me
you rebels was bloodthirsty. Now you broke up all my
opinions."

He slapped me again, with another of his grating
laughs, jumped down off the woodpile, and was off to the
officers' mess for his evening beans and pork.

In that time of procrastination, as I worked up my
courage to go out and tell Kwahadi what I'd found, and
that Sunshade's dream had told the truth, Allis Featherman brought me the note. I was bustling about my shack,
dusting off the accumulated grit gathered on the wind
during my absence, when Allis appeared at the open
door, fiddle-footing and blushing. After an abrupt hello,
he thrust a piece of paper into my hand. It obviously
came from a school tablet, the blue lines as bold as
barbed wire, and between them a scrawl in lead pencil.

> We are happy you come back. In my lodge there is
> meat for you when you want it. Kwahadi Parry.

I couldn't believe it! The Antelope chief writing
words on a piece of paper, and in English. Allis seemed
more embarrassed than ever, his face red and his feet
shuffling, his head bobbing.

"I been teachin' him how to read and write," he
said.

"Well, I'm damned! A schoolteacher now, is it? I
didn't even know you could read and write."

"Aw hell, Morgan, I took four grades."

"You tell your pupil that I'll be there soon. I assume you see him every day or so, being wed to his wee daughter."

"Yeah, well, sure, I spend all the time out there that I can when I'm not on a job. It's where I live, you know."

I gave no hint to him of the true nature of my next visit to Kwahadi. Nor had I to anyone else. And the portrait of the chief's mother lay in my cupboard still, the butcher-paper wrapping tight around it.

So, the day after that, I saddled Blue and put the hawk feather in my hat. It was time for the hawk feather, I thought, and with my clumsy fingers and the needle and thread from Augustina's sewing basket, which had scarce been touched since she lay down, I attached the thing to my hatband, on the right side so the vane fell out behind.

It felt a little absurd at first, and although I knew it was only in my mind, the feather felt as though it might weigh two pounds bobbing across the brim of my hat as little Blue took me away from my shack and toward the Antelope camp.

It was a leisurely trip; I was still thinking about what I would say to Kwahadi. But a nice day for leisure, that first real day of spring. I stopped at all the streams to give Blue a little nip of the cold water flowing clear. I watched the birds in the oaks, where the leaves had only begun to make their budding presence known. There were a few pawpaws just beginning to bloom, the purple flowers like pouting lips at the tips of the branches.

Halfway to my destination the strangest feeling overtook me. It was one I had known once before, when Bobby Lee's army was retreating out of Maryland after Sharpsburg and every one of us was expecting the Yankees to follow on our rear to strike a blow. Something behind me, I thought. And had the urge to turn on my backtrail for a mile or so, but then put it off as foolish old-man thinking, my mind wandering back to days gone and never to return.

Yet the feeling persisted. I watched behind and was aware of a nervous cold sweat wetting my sides beneath the arms. Once I saw a single rider, far to my rear, then he was gone in a stand of jack oak. Just a fleeting glimpse. Well, I said to myself, it's only one of the Antelope band returning home after doing some business at the agency. And I tried to think no more about it, but the cold sweat was still there. Like a recruit when he first hears artillery beyond the next hill.

We sat in his brush arbor as we had done so many times before, feeling the soft spring wind and watching his smaller children playing nearby around the tipis and the wooden house. When he came out to greet me, he glanced once at the feather in my hat and there was a subtle change in his expression. As though he knew exactly the reason for my coming. But after that first look, his eyes did not go to the feather again.

And the package in the butcher paper. He looked shortly at that as I lay it on the ground beside me. I felt impelled for a moment to open it at once, but better judgment prevailed as I remembered Comanche courtesy in polite discourse, so I let it lie until the proper moment.

Now, as was usual on our casual meetings, he wore his plains garb and his hair was loose. On that day there were no earrings hanging beneath his hair, and their absence somehow made his face appear more gentle.

He spoke of his horses and of the growing herd of Comanche cattle and of his developing friendship with a number of the head drovers. He said one of his wives had made a good batch of beef pemmican with pecans and wild cherries crushed into the meat, and we would have some with honey during the summer, even though that was usually the time for fresh meat.

"My son Little Horse found a fine bee tree," he said with obvious pride. "I would rather attack a war party of

248 / D O U G L A S   C.   J O N E S

Pawnees than a bee tree. But to him, the taste of honey overcomes all fears."

"And soon," said I, "you will be a grandfather!"

His smile came then, and he looked at the ground before his bent legs and there was almost a girlish embarrassment to his soft laugh.

"Otter Tongue tells me this will be a boy child. He has that knowledge from his wife, who knows about such things."

He spoke then of his son-in-law, Allis Featherman, telling me how the lad was a great help in breeding the Comanche pony herd, and how he was ambitious and hard-working. Then suddenly he turned deadly serious and spoke in a low, hard voice.

"I wish more of my young men were ambitious. But we have bad times now, Liver. The young men don't have enough to do. There are no buffalo hunts anymore to keep them excited. And no war party planning for raids on the pony herds of our enemies. The young men lie around all day with nothing to look forward to, with no inspiration for their living."

He gazed out across his compound, and the laughter of his children came to us. They were running and shouting, the dogs running with them. They rolled hoops of willow, and some of them were completely naked. He watched, smoking one of the Stoddard & Blanchard cigars I had brought him.

"They are losing the old gods," he said softly, almost to himself, and there was a distant look in his eyes. "They are forgetting how to speak with their medicine. They don't know what power is anymore.

"And the missionaries confuse them with words they don't understand and with gods they have never heard of before. I have to do something about that, Liver. I have to find them gods that work in the white man's world but at the same time remind them of who they are. I have to find something to make the white man's road easier for them."

He looked at me directly then, and the faraway glaze was gone, his jaw set and a brittle brightness in his eyes.

"The white man's road is harder than I thought it would be, Liver. Just a short time we've traveled it, and already the old ways of The People are leaving us, with nothing to take their place. The young men are losing their respect for the elders in the band. They buy whiskey and drink it until they fall down, because they are unhappy and search for visions that will guide them. But there are no visions in white man's whiskey. Only puking and sore bellies.

"I'm afraid some of the young men are losing their memory of what dignity is, losing it like they are losing their memory of how buffalo meat tastes. I've got to do something about that."

He'd been thinking about his speech for a long time, I was sure. And I felt great compassion for him, a man who had done so much to keep his people from starving along the white man's road, and now this new thing. This erosion of the old ways among the young, so that nothing was left but the shell of former Comanche greatness. I knew as well that if he said he would do something about it, he would. At least he would try. But I had no idea what that might be. Except maybe the peyote. It was a startling thought.

Coming Back from the Pony Herd brought us meat then. She smiled at me, her face soft, and went away without speaking, except with her eyes. Kwahadi and I sat in silence, enjoying the good beef. And then more smoking, until I knew it was time to tell him.

"My friend, I've done what you asked me to do," I said, and from his look I knew he was not surprised.

"You've been gone a long time. Were you looking then?"

"My mother went to the place beyond the sun, and I rode to the grave where she was laid down. In the mountains, east of here, east of the Civilized Tribes Nations. But only for a little while. It was there that I heard of Sunshade. Allis Featherman sent me a piece of paper with the message written on it. Then I began to look."

"Sunshade. A woman with great power."

"Her dream was true," said I, and now he drooped his eyelids, hiding the light of moisture there. I could see the muscles along his jaw working slowly, and he turned a beef bone in his delicate fingers, as though inspecting it.

"Do you know it as truth?"

"Yes. I went to Texas. I spoke with those who had known her after she was retaken by the white man. They took me to her grave. There were fine trees all around, and the wind blew over the marker that had her name."

"Of her white man's name I know only Parry. What was the rest?"

"Morfydd Annon. Morfydd Annon Parry."

He turned the bone in his fingers, slowly, and I could see no change of expression on his face. Only the muscles in his jaw making little ripples under the brown skin.

"Where did you find her?"

"At the place where your people first took her," I said. "At Madoc Fort, on the River of Broken Guns."

His eyes lifted to mine, then, burning and bright. For a long moment he stared at me, as though trying to see inside my mind.

"In that place, then?"

"Yes. Where your great Sanchess first took her."

"And you tell me from your heart that this was the grave of my mother?"

"Yes, it's true. Everything they told me was right with what Sunshade and Otter Tongue said. They even spoke of the beautiful hair with the red lights in it."

Suddenly he looked away, and I sensed that he could no longer allow himself to see my face.

"Yes," he said, so softly I could hardly hear. "I remember her hair."

The breeze rattled the leaves of the arbor, old leaves from last year, the new green growth not far enough along yet for reroofing. He seemed to listen, his head tilted back.

"And how did she die?"

"They could find no cause," I said. "She died within four seasons of being retaken on Peace River. I think she died of a broken heart."

Kwahadi made a little choking sound, deep in his chest, and was up abruptly, turning away to move from the shade of the arbor. He stood with his back to me, and I could see the glint of copper in his hair where the sun struck it. Arms folded and back stiff, he looked a long time at the line of trees on the Big Beaver.

"It would have been good if she could be here to see her granddaughter's first child," he said.

He stood for a moment longer before turning back to me. As he sat with his ankles crossed, I saw a thick moisture in his eyes. It was time to unwrap my package, and he watched each move of my fingers.

"This is how she looked," said I, taking out the calotype portrait in its broad wooden frame. "A man did this image of her about a moon before she was laid down. It was in the city of Fort Worth, before she was taken back to the River of Broken Guns. A man like Mr. William Soule, who made the impression of you and your wife."

Kwahadi bent forward and stared intently at the portrait of his mother, his jaw muscles working like the current of a river. Then slowly he reached out to take it in both hands, and drew it near, his gaze downward, then pressed it against his breast, arms folded across it. He closed his eyes and lowered his head and I expected him to sing, for there was that poignant pattern on his face which I had seen many times among his people when they were ready to put up a song to their gods. But he didn't sing. Instead he only rocked back and forth, holding the portrait close against his chest.

And I knew it was not a time for words, but only a time for me to leave him.

Everyone had seen that hawk feather in my hat when I rode into the camp. Many eyes were watching as Kwahadi and I had our little visit, Allis Featherman and his wife among them. Leading my pony, I went to their tipi, the same one I had watched them enter on their wedding day.

Padoponi was radiant and smiling as usual, only now with a full bloom to her cheeks that had never been there before, and the front of her smock bulged out. They wanted me to have meat with them, but it was already growing dark and I had to get back to the agency, having a run scheduled for the morrow in Stoddard & Blanchard's coach.

Riding out, I looked back and could see Kwahadi in the brush arbor still, head down, rocking back and forth with the portrait held close against him. In the dusk, when they should have been playing happily in anticipation of evening meat, the children had disappeared from sight and there was no one visible throughout the whole compound except Allis and his wife waving me farewell and the dark figure in the arbor, rocking back and forth, back and forth.

It was a night of new moon, and bright as day. The trees stood out along the ridgelines like black lace on Queen Victoria's petticoat. And the mockingbirds—there must have been a dozen within hearing along every mile little Blue took me toward Fort Sill.

But then I heard something else. Or maybe only felt it. The shuffle of a horse's hooves in the sandy soil, the rattle of a bit chain. I drew rein and looked toward a near ridge, but nothing was there that I could see, even in the moonlight. Nevertheless, I knew I had company with me, only not behind now, but riding alongside.

A few clouds had drifted in from the west, going before the soft wind and smoky at the edges when the moon outlined them, pausing for only a short time, then moving on toward the Nations. While I sat there still, trying to decide whether I had really heard something or was somehow spooked as a new colt, one of those clouds passed, turning the land to darkness. I moved Blue on again, quicker now and no longer tuned to the mockingbirds' songs.

It was about seven miles from Sill, with the moon out brightly again, plain enough to see the cheese, and I was moving along a small creek fringed in willows. Off to the right was a scatter of jack oak, but thick enough so that beneath them the ground was dark with shadow. Blue was expecting another drink, but I held him away from the stream, kicking him toward home, when I saw the dark rider among those oaks. It was just a black form melting into the darkness under the trees, but clear enough to show a hat. Wide brim, high crown.

I started to shout a hallo, then, but my mouth was barely open for it when the flash came, orange-white and brilliant from the trees, and the report coming fast afterward so I knew he was close. There was the thump of something heavy striking against little Blue's flank, like a sack of wet grain dropped on a hard wooden floor, and Blue grunted and staggered and fell into a crooked run. Then came the next flash, and the next, and I'd been shot at often enough to know what was happening.

Blue went down just as a new cloud crossed the moon, and I took a nasty fall in the gravel. There was another shot from the trees, then only the sound of my little horse thrashing about, and I knew he'd been hit hard.

No weapon! I scrambled around in the darkness, feeling for rocks, until I found one the size of a big potato, then crawled back to the horse, who was still now and breathing with a bubbling racket. I lay alongside him and waited, feeling the cold sweat wetting my shirt. In the darkness of passing cloud I could no longer see the outline of the trees, but I heard a horse over there, whistling, and somebody swearing. In English.

Get the hell out of here, thought I, across this creek

and into the far trees and on foot fast back to Sill. I was almost up when the shooting started again, only now the reports had a different sound, and the flashes were not so bright. Then silence, then two more shots, close together, and the cloud passed, leaving me there in the bright moonlight once more.

Blue's body was still quivering as I pressed against him, watching over his shining flank and seeing nothing in the trees now but their trunks. Then hooves pounding fast, roundabout to the stream and then directly toward me, the horse running. I gripped the rock and remembered that I was never much good at throwing, so I'd have to wait until he was close enough to hit with a fist holding the rock. Play dead! Hope he doesn't shoot again before bending over me to inspect his marksmanship.

Then he was on me, riding directly up, and in the bold moonlight I could see no hat on his head. His pony ran almost to Blue's rump before he pulled in, showering me with tiny gravel as the hooves dug in.

It was Hawk! And in his hand a large pistol, and I knew it was mine, the same one I had given Allis Featherman for the buffalo hunt long ago, and he in turn had given to this Comanche. He was down from the saddle in one quick, feline movement, coming to me and pushing the whiskey Colt into the waistband of his leggings. I rose unsteadily to meet him. So sure was I of Kwahadi's friendship that I knew it was not this man of his who had opened fire on me.

"Hawk!"

"Do you have any wounds?" He spoke abruptly, as though the effort of speaking to me was a strain on his temper.

"No."

"Yes, you do."

He squatted before me and I felt his fingers along my right thigh just above the knee, and as he probed, a sharp pain ran up to my hip. I realized then that the bullet that went into little Blue's lung had sliced my flesh as well.

"Nothing bad," Hawk said, slipping the bandanna from his neck and binding my thigh tightly with it, as I stood there trembling in the moonlight. Then he rose and, going to Blue, bent down for a closer look. "But this horse is dying."

I watched him feel Blue's wound, and I began to shake as I had done on a night long ago when we'd made a night attack on Yankee positions around Suffolk. Finished with his examination, Hawk rose above Blue's head and the pistol was back in his hand, gleaming and deadly in the moonlight, and he fired a shot into my little horse's head.

"Now he won't hurt," he said.

"Where'd you come from?" I asked.

"Somebody was riding behind you when you came out," he said. "Little Horse saw him. So I came behind you, too, this time. You better take your pistol back now."

He offered me the gun, and I shook my head.

"I don't want it. Unless somebody's still out there who wants to shoot me."

"He won't shoot anybody now," Hawk said, shoving the pistol toward me. "You take this."

I took it and started to ask him further but he was back on his pony and wheeling away before I could get a word out. But he drew in and looked back at me and I could see the shine of his eyes in the moonlight.

"There's a good horse over there. In those trees. You take him and get on home now."

And then he was gone at a gallop, leaving me standing there holding the pistol by the barrel. It was hot. I dropped it onto the gravel beside poor Blue's body, and looked toward the trees, going out of sight again with the passage of another cloud. In the inky darkness I pondered Hawk's insisting that I take the gun. Maybe he had good reason but I couldn't focus on it, my mind still jumping about like a flea on a hot skillet. It had been so long since I'd been shot at that I was completely unnerved, unable to think.

I wasn't going near those woods, even had there been a dozen good horses waiting. It was shank's mare back to Sill, and not the first time I'd marched with blood running out of me. But before taking the first step, I retrieved the pistol and shoved it into my belt. And for the first time, feeling the still-hot barrel, I really realized that a lot of that shooting in the trees had been Hawk's work. And I knew then, as surely as I was headed in a beeline for Fort Sill, what lay in those dark woods.

Flesh wounds burn like hell's fire, as I knew from experience. As I walked back to the fort that night, the stinging and throbbing pain convinced me there was serious damage until I stopped and took off Hawk's wrapping and felt the wound with my fingertips. The skin was barely broken. Feeling that, I was surprised that Hawk had bothered to bind it. But flesh wound or no, it was sticky and gummy and filled my boot with blood. I began to squish with each step.

It was almost dawn before I came in sight of the fort. I went there at once, knowing that if there was shooting on the reservation, Lieutenant Weslowski should know about it, and I was personally more inclined to report first to the army than to the agent. I seated myself on the edge of the headquarters porch, where a sentry looked at me so casually that he apparently failed to see the blood on my trousers.

It came to me as I sat there that Hawk had handed me the pistol, so I must take blame or credit for whatever use had been made of the whiskey Colt. He knew it would create all kinds of problems if a Comanche was known to be involved.

Would these damned heathen ever stop putting requirements on me? The resentment boiled up like sour whiskey. But after I bent forward and vomited on the ground between my feet, some of the indignation passed and I sat quietly in the cool dawn and waited for Weslowski to appear from his quarters across the quadrangle. My sentry had already moved off behind the headquarters building, which I suspected was his real post, and I was left alone with my shame at thinking of any of the Big Beaver people as heathen.

The fort jumped to life with the first notes of the bugle sounding reveille. The soldiers came tumbling from their barracks, forming their lines as they grumbled and groused the way soldiers always do in the early morning. The first sergeants took the troop reports and were posted by their commanders, and then Lieutenant Weslowski paraded out to stand before them all, a saber cased at his side.

All were present or accounted for down the line, and Weslowski returned the troop commanders' salutes with a quick, chopping movement of his gloved right hand. Then all the lads were dismissed to make ready for the day, to wait for stable call and, after they saw to the horses, mess call. This morning it was fried sowbelly and heavy army bread and scalding hot coffee. I could smell each item as it brewed in the mess halls around the quadrangle.

Coming off parade, Adjutant Weslowski approached me, looking as though he hadn't known all along that I was there. But when he came near and saw my bloody leg, his eyes widened and I was glad to see some small concern in his expression.

"What in hell happened to you, Reb?"

"There's been a wee shooting, Lieutenant," said I. "On my way back from the Big Beaver, where I was on business, somebody tried to pop me up the flue in the dark of night. Whoever it was killed my horse."

"Some of your old friends?"

"Not Comanches, no. I heard Yankee swearing, and Comanches never swear, least of all in English. Maybe a few foul words now and again concerning anatomy or body functions, but never oath-making."

"You're sitting there bleeding like a hog and you give me lectures on Comanches. Who the hell was it, then?"

"Party or parties unknown. He never came close enough to introduce himself."

He saw the butt of the pistol at my belt and thrust his face close to mine.

"You shot back, I hope."

"A few shots were exchanged," I said, and it was not a lie, but I felt it was enough to say at the moment.

"Where? Where'd it happen?"

So I told him as best I could, and he went into action as good adjutants always do, bellowing for Lieutenant Tracy Shadburn. I knew he would send old Tracy and a few dog robbers, disgruntled at missing breakfast, out to see what they could see. And they might push a few of my Comanche friends around a bit in their effort to have the truth. I was well aware of how Tracy and his men could push people around, and the prospect upset me more than my stomach had.

For the moment, there was no time to think of what Tracy and his people might do, and nothing I could change anyway. Weslowski hustled me off to the regimental surgeon, and the good man sloshed a liquid on my wound as hot as boiling gravy, so it seemed, then stitched the slash and bound the whole thing in a massive bandage, as though it were a real injury received in battle.

And a good pair of pants ruined; what the blood and the bullet didn't do, the doctor's scalpel did. By the time I left the surgeon's shop, Shadburn had his dog robbers mounted and riding out in a cloud of grim-looking dust.

It was off to Stoddard & Blanchard's, then, to take up my regular duties, the heavy pistol riding in my waistband like a ton of pig iron. But Mr. Stoddard, when he saw my leg, would not hear of my driving on this day, insisting that I take time for convalescence.

"Be here tomorrow at dawn," he said.

It had been a long time since I'd suffered a gunshot

wound. A long time indeed. It was not a memory I had any reason to want returning, yet there it was, and the pain all up and down my leg. A little breakfast of cornmeal mush helped, and then a nap on my bunk, trying to ignore the new spring flies exploring my nose.

It was midafternoon when one of Stoddard's store Indians woke me, saying the boss wanted me over at his place. The leg had stiffened and it was terrible work, walking that short distance, but there was nothing else for it, my little Blue lying dead alongside the willows out there on the reservation.

As I approached the store and the other buildings I saw a large group of men, red and white, standing about the porch as though there was a dice game. And at the edge of the crowd, Tracy Shadburn and his men, still mounted.

Lying faceup on Stoddard & Blanchard's porch was our Rufus Tallbridge, skin the color and texture of old honeycomb. His eyes were open, and across his checkered shirtfront was a great splatter of dark stain that looked like molasses. I stood there looking into that familiar face for a long time until finally Tracy Shadburn called out from his place at the fringe of the crowd.

"We found the son of a bitch right where you said, Morgan," he said. "You hit him two times where it counts."

"Self-defense, by God," Mr. Stoddard said, glaring at the soldiers. "He got the proper medicine for a bushwhacker."

"We found his weapons, too," Tracy called, lifting two pistols, both of which he held in the crook of one finger by their trigger guards. "Seven shots fired, Morgan. You're lucky all he hit was that leg and your horse."

"Into boot hill this same day, by God," Mr. Stoddard said. "Where he belongs."

So a good, clean killing, all in self-defense. But maybe it would not have been so clean, if they'd known it was an Indian that had done the chore. Even when the victim was a ruffian like Rufus Tallbridge. Hawk had had good reason for letting me shoulder it, and now nobody was the worse for it. So I kept my peace.

Except that now they had me tagged a man-killer. And after I'd thought such things were behind me and finished after Bobby Lee called it quits at Appomattox.

That night I slept the sleep of the dead, hearing nothing, not even my chuck-will's-widow from the trees south of the road. In the morning, still only dimly lit by the coming sun, I prepared to do my run for Stoddard & Blanchard, but before I was away I heard the shuffling of hooves in my horse shed.

There I found the bay, another gelding like Blue had been, only larger and ruby red in the dawn's light. From his mane a feather hung. I knew from whence it came, horse and token as well, and knew that on my next trip to the Big Beaver I would place that whiskey Colt back into the hands of Kwahadi's faithful retainer, where it belonged. And from now on, too, a second feather in my hat.

17

The last time I saw him alive, my old Da said to me, "Memory of recent years goes aglimmer in the confusion of yesterday's details. Yet as time goes down, the images of long ago come clear. The words of your mother in her youth are still clear in mind, but there was something she told me yesterday and I can't remember what it was today!"

It was true with me, as well, and as the years advanced it was a sure sign of winter's approach. Not that I felt the ravages of sinful youth, still in my physical prime as I was, except for the shoulder bad from Yankee bullets. But going longer in tooth, as surely as the turning of the earth.

Still, my heart was fresh each day to marvel at the things that never changed. The brilliance of the cardinals in the white-hanging racemes of the honey locusts in spring, the smell of wind from off high plains, the taste of water cool and clear on hot summer days. The changing color of the leaves among the hardwoods in October, the fellowship of red flames in good oak wood, even when sitting alone before the fire, the bite of cold when the earth took on a covering of snow, and the sound of distant singing.

Maybe that last was only in the head and not the ears. As

time went along, I seemed more frequently to hear Welsh choirs with the haunting harmonies and the throbbing bass, resounding through those green hills of my Da's motherland, even though I had never seen them, their coming to my senses only through his blood.

Those things remained the same, all else taking on new shape and substance, sometimes with startling speed. And as surely as they came at all, the days arrived more rapidly with each passing sun. The recent happenings among my friends the Comanches seemed a blur, a problem of arranging in my thoughts what came first and what second and the total sequence of events among them, but none of it ever so clear in my mind's eye as that day Kwahadi brought his people in, even though it was the earliest recollection of my association with them.

Not that anything was necessarily forgotten. Only their order of appearance on the stage was not clear. How could I forget the great things? said I to myself, only yesterday I think it was. Maybe the day before yesterday.

So most of it I remembered, but whether something occurred in 1878 or 1888 was a detail not available to my poor brain but only to academics, referring on any question to musty ledgers or the various faded reports of bureaucrats.

Ah, the great days! Like the golden autumn morning when Allis Featherman's son was born, the face of Padoponi shining as though no other person in all the world's history had managed to do what she had done. I went to their lodge and she showed me the tiny wrinkled face of her firstborn. He was healthy and loud, with his mother's soft brown skin and black eyes, no hint of his grandfather's gray there. And I was set to wondering about the mysteries of breeding and how sometimes dark flowers come from light.

The boy grew so quickly it took our breaths away, Allis and myself, and he was soon running about among the horses, birth-naked except for the little hide moccasins his mother had sewn for him. And Allis watching him, with pride bursting out of every pore like sweat, and no less so myself, because he was my name-sake. Morgan Featherman!

"How can you place a value on a grandson?" Kwahadi asked.

Maybe most of all I remembered their speaking, the Comanches. The words coming in bits and pieces from the past but always reminding me that here was a people who were called ignorant savages and yet whose language had all the nuance of diplomatic French, all the power of Mr. Henry Morton Stanley's English, all the tones and timbre of exquisite expression.

Oh, it's true they had no words for "locomotive" or "fly-wheel" or "electricity" or any of the vocabulary from the great industrial advancements being made. For those were not of their world. But they had at least twenty words for "horse," depending on its color and size and whether colt or mare or gelding. And they were adroit in expressing fear and anger and envy and hatred and compassion and love. And the abstractions of philosophy. The images in their heads were sometimes brilliant and sharp-edged, sometimes blurred and elusive, as has been the case with all men. But regardless of which it was or whether shaded in between, they could convey its meaning as well as anyone I ever spoke with face to face, or read on printed page.

So much for those who called them ignorant savages!

In those years when the reservation was heading straight for breakup and allotment to the various individual members of the tribes, the world outside was busy being busy. Railroads were springing out all over the plains, and before long one could ride to El Paso or Pueblo or along the Rio Grande or the Santa Fe Trail in the cinder-bombarded cars. And the whistles of steam engines could be heard across the land where only yesterday war parties and buffalo herds held dominion.

Yet somehow all the tracks were laid either north or south of our reserve in southwest Indian Territory, making an enclave enclosed on all sides by the steel, and us still a horse-and-buggy place. And I, through some of those years, driving Stoddard & Blanchard's coach to Boggy Depot. Of course, in that time Blanchard died, never having been seen, as far as I know, in Indian Territory, but making his headquarters in Topeka. Mr. Stoddard retained the old name for the store and all the other enterprises, as though Blanchard still walked on the earth.

"Out of respect for the dead," said Stoddard. "Though I never liked the son of a bitch very much."

Enclave or no, the news of happenings in the other world came to us still, faithfully reproduced in print. *Harper's Weekly* and the grand old *New York Herald*. And there the chronicle of my bridge in Brooklyn, finished at last with a great celebration and fireworks and the boats in the river below letting off mighty whistles and bells ringing throughout all the city of New York.

Often I showed the accounts to the Antelope chief and explained what they meant. Or tried to.

"Immigrants?" he asked me one day as we sat under his summer brush arbor. "What are those?"

"People who come here from far-off lands," said I.

"Ah. As The People came into the Llano Estacado from the north long ago."

"Not exactly."

Slaves, these immigrants were, although not called such because slavery had been abolished with the Thirteenth Amendment to the Yankee constitution. But slaves in everything but name, into the great smoking factories and falling into the hands of land speculators across the northern plains, where the Union Pacific and other railroads shipped them in by the carload to take up homesteads along the iron path's right-of-way, hence providing a population dependent on those same railroads, I explained.

"But if they're slaves here, why do they come?" Kwahadi asked me.

"They're looking for our white man's road."

"They come looking for it?" he asked incredulously. "Some men are crazy beyond my understanding!"

So I gave up trying to explain immigrants, but kept

an eye on them myself, thinking that maybe these slaves were about to revolt, to form unions of workers and ask for decent wages for their toil and ask for living space for their families and demand that their children be able to leave the mines and spinning mills and go to school.

There was a Mr. Sam Gompers who caught my fancy. A great talker, according to *Harper's*, and they ran an engraving of his image. He looked like the kind of man who would make good cigars, which he once had done.

There was a close parallel between Mr. Gompers and my own Kwahadi, each of them trying to organize his people in a world overwhelming to them. As surely as hunters and warriors must find the white man's road startlingly new, so must all those European beet-growers find the belching mills of great Northern cities. But I declined to try an explanation of such things to the Antelope chief.

Old enemies and comrades going down he understood. I remember the exact day I read of General Grant's passing. Not the date but the details of summer dust, me sitting on Stoddard & Blanchard's store porch with my *Herald*, and the flies as thick as lice on the head of a good Confederate infantryman. They were biting, a sure sign of rain, my old mother always said. Some Comanches were running races with their ponies in the street before me, and quite a street it had become. A combination barbershop and bath house; an undertaker's parlor; a pool hall; an enlarged photographic emporium run by someone named Miles, for Mr. Soule had long since departed; and other sundry establishments not meant to be recalled in memory.

And not far off, the new Indian school and other agency buildings, and a new warehouse for storing feed and grain.

But General Grant. Poor man he was, at the end. For after that clouded Presidency and a lot of people wanting to put his associates in jail, he went into banking, where

his partners stole everything from him but his under-
pants, leaving him to struggle for family bread, and then
laid down only four months after the Federal Congress
had restored his soldier's rank, taken from him when he
was elected.

The emotion involved in reading of the death of an
old enemy was considerable. I bore him no hatred, even
though it had been his policy of no exchange of prisoners
that kept me in that devilish prison pen at Fort Delaware
until I was able to swim away. And before that, one of his
soldiers had splintered my right shoulder with a lead ball.

It was natural to remember on that day how we had
heard of General Lee's death, still at his post as president
of some college. That was long ago, only five years after
he had offered his sword to Grant at the McLean house in
Virginia, and when Grant refused to take it, the moisture
had come to Bobby Lee's eyes, so they said.

Well, Sam Grant was a good man. A good soldier.
And dead with scarcely the money left from all his labor
for an ungrateful nation to buy a decent coffin!

There was one old companion of the war not gone
down and still kicking up dust in Austin. It was a delight
to hear that McLean Burton had given up barbering and
gone into politics and been elected to the Texas legislature. He sent me a short note by mail, more to the point
than his conversation ever was, explaining that his major
duties were to smoke cigars and argue with the other law-
makers about matters none of them knew much about.
And that I should come down and view him in his striped
pants and stovepipe hat.

"Bring that big Comanche chief with you," Burton
wrote. "There's plenty talk about him down here now.
Some of my fellow politicos say he's a good one because
he's half white. You might want to argue about that."

And other old friends, too, kicking up dust in foreign
places. Mr. Henry Morton Stanley paddling up unex-
plored rivers in Africa, nosing into lakes never seen
before with white man's eyes. He even helped found a

new country called the Congo Free State, for the Belgians. I suspected there was little freedom about it, what with its being run from afar by bureaucrats in Europe.

And touring the country and the world, Buffalo Bill's Wild West Show and Congress of Rough Riders. I'd always wanted to see that show and stand face to face with the man who became famous for killing buffalo—and not a single one, as far as I could determine, to feed his family.

A bloody riot in Denver, which I remembered as a fine city where I spent a few days in the Brown Palace Hotel before going for elk in the mountains. One Chinaman had been hanged, so the *Herald* reported, a lot more given abuse with clubs and sticks. No end to violence—and no war, at that. A man in Minneapolis who had done rape, so they said, was dragged from the jail and lynched. His name had been McManus, and I'd no idea why, as the years passed, I attached a name to such an incident that had no bearing on my own life. Except that maybe lynch mobs, no matter where found, etch details on a man's soul, like a branding iron on the hide of cattle.

Closer to home, there was all the hoopla about making the western end of Indian land a territory called Oklahoma. Already there was talk of a land rush for settlers into the Unassigned Lands. And that was not far distant, as my bay gelding would go straight across country from the northeast corner of the Kiowa-Comanche reservation. The white man was closing in, creeping closer and clamoring for acres. Break up the tribal tracts, they shouted, allot each Indian a few acres, and let us turn the rest to productive farmland.

Gone the roaming days now, without a doubt. And without sorrow, except in the lodges along the Big Beaver or at the base of the Wichitas or in the breaks of the Washita and all the other places where tipis still stood.

Much of the reservation had been fenced to keep out herdsmen who had not paid lease money for the privilege of grazing Indian grass. The trail herds were gone now, but there were plenty of ranches just south of the Red with hungry cows. The best of those cattlemen knew how to cultivate friendships where it would pay off. Two of them, Messrs. Lowe and Garrison, had seen which friendships to cultivate. They were sweet to the agent, deferential to Lieutenant Weslowski and the other soldiers at the fort, and they were building a large frame house for Kwahadi, already planning to paint black wolf heads on the roof and already calling it Wolf Ranch.

Kwahadi seemed pleased and anxious to move into the place. A wooden house. Gone the old days! And they were digging the well right under the kitchen, as they'd promised they would, the Texas workmen laboring in the sun and swearing and laughing and drinking from jugs and the Comanche children spread around them in a wide circle, squatting on the ground and watching with wondering eyes as the structure took shape before them.

But that fence. It was one of the main concerns of the new Indian police force. At last, all the documents of the bureaucrats had been satisfactorily drawn and signed. Even after that, it hadn't been easy. The young warriors who were no longer warriors hadn't much stomach for enforcing the law on their own people.

"It's a hard thing," Kwahadi said to me. "But I'll tell them as many times as it takes that it's better they make our people behave than have a white man do it."

"They don't like the idea of the agent being their chief," said I.

"Yes, that's the hardest part," he said. "But I'm telling them that Agent Belton will only ask them to do what is best for The People, then hope he does it. If he doesn't, then I'll have a little talk with him.

"It's good, having the people behave. Not each man and each family doing what they please, as they did in the old days. It's a way to keep the tribe a tribe, even if it's on the white man's road.

"In the old days, if a man did something bad for all the others, all the others ignored him for a while, as though he wasn't there. That's a hard thing to take. So finally he'd be ashamed and make it up somehow, maybe with gifts of horses to the injured families. Or else he'd go off somewhere and join another band, taking his wives and children with him. Now we can't do that anymore. There's nowhere else to go. And besides, living so close together now and so few of us left, we can't afford to have a lot of bad feeling going around among us.

"So I'll keep talking to the young men. Maybe I can persuade them the police are a good thing. They like to carry weapons without having the white man suspicious of them. Maybe that might help, too."

And of course, he did persuade them. Or maybe he shamed them into it. But whichever, one of his best tactics was to offer himself as one of the four judges on the new Indian court that was part of the police arrangement. The others were a Paneteka named Hornbeam, and a Kiowa and a Wichita. Kwahadi had a great deal to do with their selection, I suspected. Belton never informed me of the details; I was in bad odor with him still.

At Stoddard & Blanchard's Kwahadi bought them all what he called their "judging clothes." For someone who wasn't supposed to know anything about the white man's road, the Antelope chief was the best manager of his money of anyone I had ever seen.

The judging clothes were very impressive. Black suits complete with vests, and not the ill-fitting agency-issue kind either. White shirts, and narrow bandannas for neckties. High-crowned hats with leather bands, and shoes kept gleaming with tallow and lampblack. And Kwahadi's gold watch chain swinging across his flat stomach.

The first time the judges went into session, coming to the agency where the police barracks had been built and a small courtroom adjoining, they looked as though moving too suddenly might split their tight trousers. But they were soon accustomed to the new garb and became as assured and confident as Chief Justice Morrison R. Waite of the United States Supreme Court. But I doubt that the Honorable Chief Justice Waite ever rode to his chambers on a calico pony with feathers in its mane, or with braids and earrings hanging beneath his hat.

"That friend of yours knows where the power is," Mr. Stoddard said to me one day after we'd heard of the appointment of Kwahadi to the court. "I hear he's been itchin' for this court to get started so he could be a part of it and throw his weight around."

"More than that," I said. "He's doing it for a better reason. So his young bucks will follow the lead and come in to join the Indian police."

"Monkey see, monkey do, huh?"

"No, nothing like that. It's a matter of respect. If their leader comes in to join the white man's road by putting on a black suit, then the young men will be inclined to follow."

"That man's a devious son of a bitch. You know, since that time he came in here a long time ago and threatened to burn my place, he's been back just twice. When he wants something, he always sends somebody after it. But they never fail to remind me that they're buying stuff for their big chief."

"They do that so you'll know it's Kwahadi they're speaking for, and you'll show him respect and not cheat him."

"Cheat him? Gawd damn it, Morgan, I never cheat the Indians in my store."

The day they formed the police force must have been a great disappointment for the dozen or so men who collected at the agency. They were issued old Yankee army uniforms, and slouch hats the origins of which I didn't dare guess. The weapons were a disgrace. Old Remington percussions that had been modified for rimfire, and Spencer carbines. At least the badges were good, newly minted metal shields that gleamed with official brightness in the sun.

Kwahadi began his campaign at once for better dress and more efficient weapons. This took the form of a tax levied on the various bands, from their cattle-grazing money. But not all from that source. I accompanied him to Mr. Stoddard, knowing this was an important thing because it was only the third time Kwahadi had ever been in that store, as Mr. Stoddard had told me. And Mr. Stoddard himself was impressed, in fact for a few moments speechless, when we walked in. The last time he'd seen the Big Beaver leader, the chief had been wearing buckskin and loose hair and paint on his face. Now he was spiffed up in his black suit and leather shoes.

Mr. Stoddard had an interest in law and order, so long as it didn't interfere with his little whiskey business among the white men in his rear room. Then we marched up to the fort and Lieutenant Weslowski, who was anxious to have a civilian police force because he said it was not a fit job for soldiers to be running about the reservation, settling minor disputes between husbands and wives, or else tracking down horse thieves before they could get to Texas or the Nations.

From each of these places came money. Stoddard opened his cashbox to a man who had once threatened to burn his store, which seemed to be eloquent testimony to Kwahadi's persuasive powers. Weslowski's donations came not only from him but from his fellow officers. All of this largesse came as the result of a simple speech Kwahadi made to all who would listen, in English and without a note of begging in it.

"We need young men police," he would say. "To make reservation safe and good to raise children. These young men need respect from all the people who live here or come to see us. You white men give many monies to your religion and your missionaries. Maybe you can afford a little for police to help you."

Thus, hardly a year had passed when the Kiowa-Comanche police force took on the look of dandies among their own people. The old army overcoats and trousers were retained, but now all the young men wore black vests and white shirts with sleeve garters and bandannas, and low-heeled Texas boots and big hats, usually black. And now there were Winchester magazine rifles and Colt revolvers.

They'd seen the drovers during the cattle-drive days, wearing sidearms suspended from heavy cartridge belts. That was obviously better than carrying extra ammunition around loose in their pockets. Besides, the brass and lead shining at their waists looked almost as important as feathers in their hair. So cartridge belts it was.

I had no idea how Indian policemen on other reservations looked in that time, but at mine they were much like peace officers in any white man's town. Except that beneath their hatbrims was the long raven-colored hair and the oak-brown skin tight over the high cheekbones. A no-foolishness bunch of people, this, because they took their duties seriously and wore determination on their faces as plain as the shields on their vests.

And Hawk a sergeant among them! No need there for charity money to buy a pistol. He had the whiskeymaker's Colt again, already proved deadly enough, though this was unknown to any other white man except Rufus Tallbridge, and he was passed beyond memory with the knowledge.

Mostly, Hawk and his fellows were involved with petty crimes among their own people. Family squabbles and nonlethal knifings and disputes over the ownership of certain horses or cows. They brought in disputants in marital affairs as well, and the court made decisions on marriages and divorces.

But there were more serious things. The Indian police patrolled the reservation fences and sometimes came face to face with drovers ready to cut the wire and drive their herds in. Always heavily armed, these Texas men, yet I knew of no single incident when the police had to call on troops at Fort Sill to help them keep out unauthorized cattle. All without a gun going off, too. It was a thing Agent Belton lost some sleep over, the prospect of a shooting between his policemen and the herders. But apparently those Texas men, hard as they looked, were capable of sound discretion.

More serious still was enforcement of the new gun-checking rule. Wooden placards nailed to various trees announced that it was unlawful for anyone to carry arms, and that all weapons had to be turned in at Fort Sill or the agency office by passers-through, to remain there for the duration of their visit. It was a dangerous rule in country where some men felt undressed without heavy metal hanging in holsters at their sides.

It was a warm spring day when the man arrived on the reservation who was to give Hawk his great reputation for law enforcement. Elkins, this man was, riding in a silver-mounted saddle and a handkerchief about his neck as brightly colored as the sweet williams that Mrs. Belton had planted around the agency office. He made the claim all up and down the Strip that he was a first cousin to old Sam Bass, the Texas outlaw. A bragging man, he was loud of voice and obnoxious of mien and wore a large silver-plated pistol and cruel Mexican spurs that jangled like tambourines.

It was ration day, with the usual crowd of people doing their visiting and horseracing and dice-playing. And among them the hangers-on and drifters, the white men who always came to conduct whatever commerce they had with the tribesmen. The gun rack at the agency was heavily burdened with checked firearms, as was the one in Weslowski's guardroom. So the huge revolver suspended at Elkins's waist was more obvious than ever as he swaggered up and down the sidewalk, going into barbershop, then pool hall, and finally into Stoddard & Blanchard's for some cheese and crackers. There he sat on the counter, eating, swinging his rattling spurs, and announcing to all who cared to listen that where he went, his pistol went. Hand in glove, he said.

I'd been watching Little Horse race one of his ponies, a gray stallion fast enough to win me seventeen dollars from unwary travelers who had never seen a Comanche horse run. But after Little Horse made his last dash, I grew tired of the dust and hubbub along the racecourse behind the buildings. On ration day there were always too many people about to run the horses in the street. I returned to my usual place on Stoddard & Blanchard's porch, there to observe the passing scene from the vantage point of a cane-bottomed chair.

That was when I saw Mr. Elkins stroll arrogantly along the Strip and finally into the store for his snack, and observed as well Sergeant Hawk squatting in the open mule shed directly across the way. Most of the people were laughing behind Mr. Elkins's back after he'd passed, but Hawk was not laughing. Even from my distance I could see the smoldering light in his eyes and the firm set of his lips. His usual expression, actually, but now somehow a new deadliness there.

Shortly after the self-proclaimed Texas gunfighter disappeared into Stoddard & Blanchard's, Hawk disappeared as well. I hadn't seen him go, but I suspected his destination and roused myself and went casually into the store myself, waiting a moment inside the door for my eyes to become accustomed to the gloom, after the bright sunlight outside.

There was Elkins, spurs still flapping as he swung his legs, sitting on the counter with cracker crumbs in the fringes of his mustache and sprinkled like snow down the front of his flannel shirt.

"Well, you'd better get that gun checked in at the fort or over at the agency if you intend to stay awhile," Mr. Stoddard was saying. "The local police don't take too kindly to visitors breaking the rules around here."

"Ain't no redskin buck tellin' *me* what to do," said

Elkins. "Let 'em go out on the reservation and play policeman to their squaws and papooses!"

I made myself as invisible as possible, taking refuge
behind a pair of pickle barrels in one corner, where I
could watch the action. I knew it would be finished soon
when I saw Hawk slide into the room from the back door
and come up directly behind the Texan on the counter.

Everyone in the room saw Hawk. Except Mr. Elkins. There was an expectant pause in conversation as he
started another piece of yellow cheese toward his mouth.
Then through the room echoed the loud triple click of a
single-action pistol being cocked, and when Elkins
jerked his head about toward the sound, he was staring
dead into the muzzle of the whiskeymaker's Colt, and
Hawk's frigid face behind it.

Hawk didn't speak much English, but in this case
little formal language was required. As Mr. Elkins sat
with the piece of cheese halfway to his open mouth and
his eyes bulging, the Indian policeman pulled the man's
silver-plated pistol from its holster and shoved it into his
waistband. Then a quick jerk of the muzzle into which
Elkins was still staring, indicating the way to the door.
The Mexican spurs made a loud clatter as the first cousin
of Sam Bass slid quickly to the floor and marched off,
Hawk's pistol gouging the small of his back and everyone
in the place laughing. Except for Hawk and Mr. Elkins.

"Liver, you better come with me," Hawk said in Comanche. "So this man knows what I'm saying to him."

I never understood how Comanche policemen could
sense trouble and collect around it. There had been no
communications between them that I had seen, yet by
the time we reached the sunlight of the porch, three more
Indians wearing badges were coming toward us. It must
have struck Mr. Elkins, as well, because he was making
no more noises about keeping his pistol with him wherever he went, hand in glove.

Where he went now was to the agent's office, and

there Hawk expressed his opinion through me that the Texan should be placed in the Fort Sill guardhouse and held until such time as a Federal marshal could come from Fort Smith or Wichita Falls and cart him off to the mercies of white justice. The other three policemen who had accompanied us nodded their agreement.

But Mr. Belton explained that because Mr. Elkins had made no fuss with his gun, only with his mouth, it would be adequate to send him on his way back to Texas. This was done, the escort of four policemen and myself riding all about Elkins, his pistol still in Hawk's belt. About five miles along Cache Creek, Hawk unloaded the silver-plated revolver and handed it back to the red-faced man in the garish neckerchief, who had said no single word since having tried for a last bite of cheese in Stoddard & Blanchard's store.

Then I told him what Hawk said.

"If you come back to this place and try to walk around wearing a gun, we'll kill you!"

I had no idea whether Hawk meant it, but looking at his face and those of the other three Comanches was enough to convince Mr. Elkins. He took his gun, stuffed it into his holster, and kicked his horse in the direction of Red River. And no one ever saw him again on the Kiowa-Comanche reservation.

There was more to that day than Hawk's ragging a white man off to whence he had come for not obeying the rules. Something more important in my old age and in Kwahadi's. It was the start of a new life for me, and a new mission that would take me back to Texas.

Before we came again into the street at Stoddard & Blanchard's, the long evening shadows running through the dust now, Hawk turned to me and placed a hand on my arm. I thought then that it was important, what he had to say, because he had never touched me before except to examine my wound that night of Rufus Tallbridge's demise.

"The chief wants to talk," he said. "He wants me to tell you it's a very big thing."

Kwahadi had a new brush arbor near the high prairie field where the Texans were building the Wolf Ranch house, a place where he could sit in the shade during the heat of day and watch the pine siding and split-oak shingles going into place. As we sat there that afternoon, he in his old-days hide clothing and me in my feathered hat, he told me about Lowe and Garrison, the cattlemen who were paying for that house.

"They're good men," he said. "They ship that wood on a railroad, to the place where you drive the canvas coach of Stoddard, then on ox wagons all the way here."

Well, there are some Texas men making a lot of money on cows, I thought, but said nothing.

There wasn't much preliminary talk. This was an important meeting. Most of the band members were sitting in a wide circle around the arbor, well out of earshot, but watching us. The only people I could see moving were the white men working on the ranch house; everyone else was as still as a tree stump.

Very important, I knew, because of the pipe. It was a ceremonial pipe, carved and painted and with eagle feathers and otter fur decorating it. I'd seen it only once, on my visit to the Big Beaver a week after bringing Kwahadi the portrait of his mother, the first meeting we'd had after the day I'd left him clutching the picture to his breast.

He was remarking on how good it was that his nice new house overlooked all his pastures. And he made a signal of some kind, I was sure, because a woman appeared from the tipi nearest us, and she held the pipe. As she walked toward us, I could see that she was attractive in a squat sort of way, about twenty-odd years old, with that same soft and gentle face that I'd seen so often among the Comanche women.

She was dressed in traditional clothing, cured hides softly tanned, with long hanging fringes and decorated with brightly colored porcupine-quill beads. Her hair was hanging loose to the shoulders, like a mass of black granite, so thick that the breeze hardly stirred it. Her eyes never met mine, and in fact she acted as though Kwahadi were alone in the arbor as she handed him the pipe, then backed away, turned, and walked with a strange waddling elegance back to the tipi and inside once more.

The atmosphere of seriousness grew while Kwahadi filled the pipe from the pouch hanging at his waist. Eyes downcast still, he touched the bowl with a flaming match that I knew came from Stoddard & Blanchard's mercantile. He offered the pipe to sky and earth and the four directions, and took a few tentative puffs, then handed the pipe to me. Very serious indeed. After a short smoke, I returned the pipe to him.

I was acutely aware that no food had been offered or brought. Unusual! And Kwahadi was staring at the ground before his crossed ankles as though looking deep into a fire. Frowning. The pipe passed back and forth, with no words spoken. Only when he raised his gaze to mine did I know it was time to begin. But to begin what, I had no idea.

"Liver," he said, "in the old days, a man was known

by his father, and everyone knew who his father was. But now we see many strangers and they don't know if a man is from good family or bad. Like your friend Hawk. Nobody except The People know that his father was the great warrior Running Wolf, who fought with Sanchess. And later, when he has sons, no one will know that Hawk, the sergeant of the policemen, was their father."

He sucked noisily on the pipestem, his eyes steadily devouring my face, as though he were looking for signs of tracks made by a wandering pony.

"Now we need to have those second names like you white men have. So a man's son is called as the father is. As I am called what my mother was. Parry."

"Those are called surnames," I said.

"Whatever they're called, we need them. To put on the ration rolls and the census the agent is always asking us to make, counting heads. A man needs a name for himself, but in your white man's world, he needs a name that puts him with his family. I've been thinking about that."

"It's a good thing to think about. It's part of the white man's road, to have two names."

"Good! Then I want you to put down a list of those names on a piece of paper. Enough names so everybody in the band can have one. I want good names that mean something about courage and dignity."

"Well, most names don't mean anything anymore," I said. "They did a long time ago, but everyone has forgotten."

"I was afraid of that," he said. "Well, just names, then. But good names that white men can remember and put down on their ration rolls and all those other places they like to put names."

"I can do that," I said, and felt a sigh of relief go through me because maybe this wasn't such a big meeting after all. But as he continued to stare at me, smoking slowly, I suspected the names were not the real reason he'd called me. And I was right.

"Liver," he said, and his voice had that same resonance I'd heard in the Indian courtroom when he handed down decisions. "I'm going to tell you about an old custom among The People. It's a custom that's good, and I think you'll understand it."

"I'll try to understand."

"Sometimes, when two warriors became close friends, they would call each other brother. I believe we are close friends like that."

If he expected any reply to that one, he was disappointed, because I was for once in my life speechless. To hear such words from his lips was dumbfounding! But he had only begun. In later years, I came to remember all this as coming in installments, like one of those serial stories in the *New York Herald*, each chapter more astonishing than the last.

"We have never stood together against an enemy bearing weapons that might kill us," he went on. "But we have stood against other kinds of enemies to me and my people. White men ignorant of our ways, or those who corrupt the young men with whiskey."

I couldn't recall ever having had anything to do with his fight against evil spirits that came in jugs and bottles. But I remained silent, because it was obvious he was not ready for me to speak.

"And you have made my words clear many times when there was misunderstanding between my people and the agent or the soldiers at the fort or the traders."

Yes, there had been many such incidents, I thought, trying to get ahead of him but unable even to catch up.

"And you have done a quest for me and were successful. You've come to me when I asked you to, once even when it was dangerous for you, though maybe you didn't know that when you came."

Rufus Tallbridge! It was maybe absurd that I should have thought Kwahadi wouldn't know about that shooting almost before the sounds of it died. Maybe it had even been he who sent Hawk to play bodyguard for me. But I didn't ask and I knew I likely never would.

"So we're brothers," he said, puffing his pipe furiously, then passed it to me and I did the same.

"Now, brothers among The People have a special thing between them. In the old days, brothers sometimes shared their wives with one another. It was a thing that came with The People from their life in the far northern mountains."

He had the pipe again by now, and as he smoked, pausing in his speech, I supposed, to allow everything to sink in, he must have noted my pained expression. I could feel it like a mustard plaster pulling at my face. The faintest of smiles twitched at the corners of his mouth.

"Of course, we don't do that anymore," he said. "And even though we may be brothers, I wouldn't offer you one of my wives, because I know it's a thing that might not settle well in your thoughts. In the old days, I would have offered you any one of them. But these are not the old days."

He smoked out the pipe, looking toward his new house. We could hear the hammers of the workers as they nailed the siding to the studs on the near side of the building. Then he lay the pipe across his lap, using both hands as though he were cradling a baby, and looked at me again.

"But because we are brothers, and brothers have great concern for one another, I have concern for you in this business of a wife."

God, I suddenly knew what was coming. Not the details, but the brutal essentials of it.

"Liver, you need a wife!"

There was no way of avoiding an answer now, because I sensed as he stared into my eyes that he would say no more until I'd put in a few words of my own.

"I've had the only wife I ever wanted," I said weakly.

"A long time ago. Now you need a new woman to make food for you and keep your bed warm and sweep the lodge clean and comfort you on rainy days when you can't go out into the sunshine."

So ended that installment! Now he began to speak of other things having no connection with what he'd just said, leaving all of it smoldering for a while in my belly. He talked about his grandson and how well Allis Featherman had pleased him, becoming a part of The People, none of it coming through to my dazed mind until he was well into his speech about the woman.

"You saw her when she brought the pipe," he was saying. "Her name is Quill, because when she was a child she tried to take a live porcupine in her hands and it was very bad getting one of the quills out of her finger. She was always brave, even when she was a child.

"She's the younger sister of my wife Coming Back from the Pony Herd. They have always been very dear to one another. So Quill is dear to me as well. She was married to a man named Black Bandanna, but now he's dead."

"I'm sorry," I managed in a voice no larger than Allis Featherman's son.

He waved one hand impatiently. "It doesn't matter. He's passed on to the land beyond the sun. He liked the white man's whiskey too much. Nothing I could say to him would make him stop drinking it. Last winter, in the coldest time, he went to Fort Sill and sold his horse and bought whiskey with the money. Walking home, he fell down. He was always falling down with the white man's whiskey. He said it gave him good visions. But this time when he fell down he stayed on the ground and froze to death before anybody knew where he was."

"I'm sorry it was the whiskey."

"He didn't get it from your Stoddard. I think he got it from that man who has the house where the little balls run across the table with a green top. But Black Bandanna would find it somewhere. He always wanted it, and there are many white men coming through the reservation or hanging about along the fences who will sell whiskey for a good Comanche horse. So now he's dead."

Then he said, almost to himself as his eyes shifted to the circle of people watching us, "It had something to do with losing the old gods, I think. I've got to do something about that."

Then he leaned back and slapped his knees with both hands, as though the best part of his talk was finished. But it wasn't.

"Now, sometimes among The People a man takes sisters for his wives. But I can't take Quill because I've got too many of them already, according to the white man. Besides, I can't manage the ones I've got.

"But because she's the sister of my wife, I need to do something good for her and not let her roam about like an orphan, a full-grown woman without a husband. Black Bandanna had no brothers left. And Quill's mother and father died a long time ago of the white man's spotted sickness.

"So I need to do something good for her. I've let her come into Coming Back from the Pony Herd's lodge, and I'm treating her as a daughter. So I'm saying all these things to you as her father.

"Now let's take a little walk together. My legs are getting tired, sitting here like this."

We left the shade of the brush arbor, and the sun was warm on my back, but I was hardly aware of it at the time, nor of the spring birds singing, nor, as we drew near the Big Beaver, of the chuckling water going down toward Cache Creek. I was only aware of Kwahadi walking beside me, arms folded, the long fringes of his leggings whispering across the sandy ground. We said nothing until we came under the sycamores that bordered the creek, and there stood to watch the rippling water go past.

"Now I need to do something good for my brother, too," he said. "And nothing is better to do for a man than to find him a good wife. Quill would be a good wife. She works hard and she's clean and obedient and never flirts with the young men. And as her father, I would require no gifts of horses for her, although she's worth at least four."

Across the stream and beyond the low willows I could see a group of young Comanches working with foals, already teaching the band's new horses the feel of something on their backs and in their mouths. At least, thought I, not all the men in this place are back there around the brush arbor, watching this business. It was small comfort.

"I'm not sure this is a good idea," I said.

"She could do a lot of comforting on those rainy days!"

The water's going to run down this streambed no matter what I do, I thought, and the cardinals nest and the redbud bloom in spring and Stoddard & Blanchard's coach go back and forth between here and that dismal Boggy Depot and the evening star shine in the heavens.

"I'll have to think about it," I said finally.

"A man needs to think about such things. You go back to that place of yours and fix your own meat tonight and clean your own floor in the morning and think about it. And think about your empty bed!"

Enough of this, so I wheeled away from him, rudely abrupt, and stalked back to the cluster of tipis where I knew Little Horse would be waiting to hand me the reins of the bay. They were still sitting in their wide circle around the brush arbor, watching, as though they hadn't moved a hair's breadth while Kwahadi and I took our little walk. I passed directly beside Allis Featherman's lodge, and could almost feel his eyes on me. Watching from the darkness inside. Like a denned fox. I wondered how much all of the people in this camp knew about what Kwahadi had said to me.

What the hell difference did it make if they knew? Maybe he wanted to allow them a veto of his little affair. But who in this band would have the unlimited guts to disapprove of anything he did?

I ran the bay a lot going back to the agency, thinking that the jolting of the unfamiliar gait might pound the fuzz out of my brain. Involved before with those people, I thought, and now the chief pulling me in all the way. Well, Allis was doing fine. But Allis Featherman was young and pliable as new mud, and I was set in my ways like sun-baked brick.

A man long on the road has some difficulty turning. True, I'd had much to do with that Comanche bunch, but now Kwahadi was asking that I go whole hog, after almost fifty years a white and good Welshman with some appreciation of my old Da's three-in-one God—asking me now to do more than admire, more than associate, more than be a friend. Now asking me to become more than all that. To join. To become.

Become what? said I. Maybe nothing more than I already was. Yet with prospect of children of a different color.

Never had I known my shack to look so forlorn and smell so unwelcome. My Da once told me that a man can be satisfied with a sorry lot until the possibility of something better presents itself. Then there is no gladness where there had been happiness before, or at least what passed for happiness.

There wasn't much to eat. A can of the new corned beef that Stoddard & Blanchard had just the past week got into stock from Chicago or some such place. I opened it and it looked like red clay, and just as hard and tasteless. I let it get dark around me, afraid to light a lamp to see my thoughts, sitting on the edge of my bunk and pushing chunks of that corned beef into my mouth with a butcher knife. And couldn't stop the thinking.

It was like being trapped with kindness, at least what Kwahadi considered kindness. Yet maybe not so harsh a trap and changing in my mind as the evening turned to night and my chuck-will's-widow began his song down in the oaks.

Once I counted off my jobs of work and my few

friends and the card game in Stoddard's back room, there wasn't much left. And I thought about a warm kitchen in my own house, kind hands tending the meat and potatoes on the stove. A thing long unthought of, since Augustina's passing. And for the only time in all my life I felt desperately lost. And saw ahead more of it than it was possible for any man to endure. And thought about the rainy days with only the printed words of Mr. Charles Dickens to comfort me.

Well, maybe Augustina would understand if she could be here now and see this wretched place and this wretched existence and this wretched loneliness.

It would be a gamble, starting a new life at my age with a young woman for a wife, and a Comanche at that. And I recalled what Kwahadi had told me when I asked him why all the men and women of his people were so addicted to gambling. He had smiled that crooked smile of his and shaken his head.

"Everything we have ever done is a gamble," he explained. "It is not just the games. It is everything. It is living. When we went out to hunt, when we moved a campsite, when we traveled and there was thunder and lightning, when we raided an enemy's pony herd. It has become part of us, staking something of worth against winning or losing. Sometimes we win, sometimes we lose. And when we lose, sometimes more is lost than dignity or power or a good horse. Sometimes we lose life itself.

"That's the way it once was. It isn't so much that way anymore, living inside your reservation jail. But at least there are still the games. Gambling has always made things exciting."

So now he was asking me to join that gamble, among a people I could still hear Phil McCusker describing: "No matter how long you know the Comanche, you will never understand them!" There was a lot more to it than a ceremony of marriage. In fact, the ceremony was the simplest part of it. Out of consideration for my being a white man,

Kwahadi had the same Mennonite missionary do our vows who had done them with Allis Featherman. After the love, honor, and obey part, which I interpreted for my bride, it was over, because all the Comanches required was that I take her to my home with the approval of her father.

I abandoned my shack at the agency, and good riddance, because Kwahadi had moved his horses out of the wooden house the agent had built for him and insisted that I come to the Big Beaver and make a home there. That was the next installment, which I resisted for a moment out of principle.

"I'm driving that stagecoach for Mr. Stoddard," I explained.

"You can still do that," said Kwahadi. "You only do that now and then anyway, not all the time. Those other things you don't need to do."

"Yes I do. I need more money than Stoddard pays me. I need what little I get from the army for driving their wagons, and the money Mr. Belton pays me for helping on ration days with the words."

Then he smiled, not the little twitch at the corners of his mouth, but a broad one, showing his large teeth.

"You said you'd try to understand, Liver, but I don't think you're trying very hard. I want you here at the Big Beaver to help me with the words when I'm with the Texas cattlemen. I've got a lot of business with them, and I need somebody I can trust to do my talking now and then.

"We need my son-in-law Allis Featherman to spend his time with the herds, not teaching me your tongue. I want to speak as well as any white man in his own language. I want to read what he writes on those little pieces of paper, and I want to write some of those words down myself. You're older and have more wisdom than my son-in-law. So you could teach me all those things better than he can. I'll pay you for that, more than Belton pays you for ration day.

"Besides"—and now the smile grew broader still—"when you marry my daughter, you'll be a part of the tribe and have your share of the grazing money. And that's more than the army pays you to whip their mules!"

"You know a lot about what money I make," I said, a mite petulantly.

For the thought had come to me that Kwahadi, regardless of his words about doing good for a brother, never did anything that wasn't good for himself as well. With me, he had his own personal interpreter at his beck and call, like a bellboy in the Brown Palace hotel.

"Yes," he said, and the smile had vanished. "On the white man's road, a man has to know all he can about money!"

Then I was ashamed for assigning selfishness to him. He was many things, maybe even cruel, as a leftover from the old days, but I had seen too often what he did for his people, and knew that selfishness was not there.

So it was done, as surely and businesslike as if I'd been buying a bolt of cotton cloth from Stoddard & Blanchard's store. The missionary came in his black coat on the late evening of the day it happened, and all the members of the band stood around us grinning, Allis Featherman and Padoponi among them. And even Hawk, with the glint of a smile in his eyes if not on his wide mouth, and the glint of firelight on his badge and the big pistol at his belt.

After the Mennonite had gone back to Sycamore Mission and I'd escorted Quill to the little two-room wooden house, all the others had their traditional wedding celebration. The old-men drummers came out and Otter Tongue sang the first song and they all joined in and began to dance. Kwahadi had a bull slaughtered, and they feasted and danced and sang some more and it lasted almost all night, not a hundred paces from my wedding bed. Through it all, Quill had said no single word and kept her eyes from mine. But there was still that softness in her face.

All my personal truck had been carried up from the agency, but there was little of that. Yet all the things required for housekeeping were there, in Kwahadi's former stable. A stove and a table and a new bed with feather ticks that Kwahadi had bought, and a large oval mirror that Allis Featherman had bought, and pots and pans that came from God knew where. Kwahadi had taken me into the little house on the afternoon of the wedding and pointed it all out, proudly, waiting for my approval. Which I gave. And that approval was all I paid him for his adopted daughter, who was worth at least four horses!

We lit no light that night, Quill and I, but went directly to bed as the singing started outside. But it was no marital bed. I lay stiffly, fully clothed, on top of the covers, and she beside me beneath one of the ticks, though it was springtime warm. I stared at the ceiling for a long time, watching the dancing orange light that came from the fires and through the window. Finally I turned my face to her and could see the shine of her eyes, on me now.

"Tomorrow I'll take you to Stoddard & Blanchard's store and buy a scarf for you," I said, and thought, And let them all see my new Comanche wife and get that part finished and over in a hurry.

"I like purple scarves," she said softly, and placed a hand on my chest. "It's all good."

Well, maybe so. I hoped she didn't expect too much.

"I'm not a young husband for you," I said.

"You are husband enough for any woman," she said. "I've seen you many times when you didn't see me, and knew from the first that you would be enough husband for any woman. And he has told me you're a good man."

I knew she meant Kwahadi. And felt reassured. But on that first night I lay on top of the covers until dawn, feeling the light pressure of her hand on me and hearing her gentle breathing, close against my cheek. And knew she was a woman who would expect nothing until I gave it.

It was bittersweet, lying there and for the first time in many seasons having the warm and soft body of a wife beside me, thinking of Augustina and then of this young Comanche bride and how widely separated they were, in time and custom and speech and appearance. But both were women. And I wondered why I had denied myself that presence, that fullness only a good woman can bring into a house.

And so, a squaw man I became. I knew that was what all those at the fort and the agency would call me. And they did, but never to my face, for they all remembered Rufus Tallbridge and what a vicious man-killer I could become. So never to my face.

And now would come the next installment. But that first night, slowly relaxing with the hand of Quill on my breast, I didn't know it, and felt a strange contentment.

19

Kwahadi waited a full year to tell me the rest of it. Time enough for me to teach him much reading and writing in his new language, using lined school tablets and lead pencils. Watching him bend over the page, frowning with the effort, struggling with the letters, I always had difficulty remembering that here was a man who not so long ago had been riding free on Llano Estacado in quest of game or enemies.

The Wolf Ranch house was finished that fall and he moved in with his wives and the smaller children. There was room enough for all. The inside was paneled with tongue-and-groove lumber and whitewashed and already adorned with a collection of calendars from the MKT and Missouri Pacific railroads showing locomotives belching sparks and snaking long strings of window-lighted cars through pine woods, or elk standing on rock outcrops, gazing at far distant snow-capped peaks. And one old Masonic banner with the square and compass, because Kwahadi had liked the design as soon as the Texans showed it to him.

Those Texans had not only built the house, but

furnished it as well. An oak dining table, where we did Kwahadi's lessons, and chairs enough to seat most of the family for a meal, although many of them still preferred to sit on the floor. A well-outfitted kitchen with a goose-neck-handled pump set over the well under the floor, and a sink and the biggest cookstove I'd ever seen, blue and white enamel porcelain across the doors of the two ovens.

"Your women can cook a whole cow in that thing," said I in admiration.

"It's not going to be easy to persuade them to use it," he said. "They still want to cook outside."

The house was a square structure with a wide porch running around all sides. Now Kwahadi could move his rocking chair with the shade in summer, the sun in winter, as the earth turned. And above all, on one of the gables, the black outline of a wolf's head.

"The great Sanchess had wolf medicine," he said. "It's very powerful. He was my uncle before the white man killed him. But in the old days, a lot of the young men wouldn't take wolf power even when they could get it, because it carried a lot of restrictions."

That was the most Kwahadi ever told me about his medicine. But whatever wolf power was, I knew Kwahadi had it.

I met the two men responsible for that house, and Messrs. Lowe and Garrison were good-seeming Texans who wore the usual big hats and high-heeled boots and spurs. I arranged for the photographer on the Strip to come out to the Big Beaver and make a picture of Mr. Lowe and Kwahadi standing before a Comanche tipi, the white man with one hand on the Antelope chief's shoulder.

A strange contrast, Kwahadi in his plains buckskins and holding the same eagle-feather fan he'd held long ago when Mr. William Soule took his image with Coming Back from the Pony Herd beside him. Kwahadi was very serious that day, presenting a face set in harsh lines, his hair falling in braids to his chest. A picture out of the old days.

Kwahadi didn't wear his plains garb much anymore. Now he went about in his judging suit. He became a familiar sight, rocking on one side or the other of his porch, the black hat on his head, his coat hanging from the back of the chair, the gold watch chain connecting the two sides of his open vest. He looked for all the world like an Ellsworth gambler. Except for the long hair.

And my own little house was taking on the shape of a home. I put a fence around the yard to keep out wandering livestock, because Quill wanted to start a garden. It was her own idea. It didn't produce much that first year, but she had hopes for potatoes and squash in the next.

She developed a regular commerce with some of the Wichitas and the few Apache bands who were on the reservation now. Both of these tribes were more accustomed than Comanches to growing things, and Quill knew it. So she went to their women and obtained seeds and explanations of how to make things sprout from the earth.

"Once, our fathers took such things from these other people after they'd grown it," she said one day, in an unusual reference to the old ways. "But now we must grow our own because the white man won't let us raid their gardens anymore."

She always referred to white men as though I were not one, as though they were some breed as separate and apart from me as they were from her.

I never knew a Comanche who took so well to farming. The thought finally arrived in my thick head that she was doing it only for me.

On one of my trips to Boggy Depot, I picked up a crate of chickens, and Quill raised those, feeding them shelled corn I bought at the agency store. I could buy there now, being a member of the Comanche tribe, though I was sure that it didn't set well with Jehyle Simmons. But to hell with Jehyle Simmons, said I.

Kwahadi walked down from the big house one day to view the chickens disdainfully.

"I never liked that bird meat much," he said. "It's more like wet dough than meat. Meat's got to have some red in it."

"Well, I bought the chickens for the eggs," I explained.

"Eggs are all right," he grunted. "If there's not anything else to eat!"

And I taught Quill the mysteries of sourdough. Her first pot was a dismal failure, but then she got the knack and was soon baking biscuits as good as any I'd ever made. Not so good as my old mother had once made, but what biscuits ever were?

I had never seen anyone with such a bright disposition as my Quill. She laughed at everything, like a small child discovering circus clowns. Watching her soft face, I often wondered why so many white men went to their graves thinking Indians were expressionless. Hers was a face as mobile as any I'd ever seen. She put a warmth in my little house that made me glad to share my meat with visitors like Allis Featherman and Padoponi and sometimes even Kwahadi himself and a few selected wives for the occasion.

Explaining that he didn't want any paupers in his band, Kwahadi had given me three cows and a bull so I could begin to breed my own herd. Those Texas cows represented the tribal wealth now, although most white men wouldn't consider it much wealth. The days of going hungry were pretty much past for most of the bands on the reservation, and certainly for the people along the Big Beaver. The Texans were teaching them stock management, and it wasn't difficult because they had a long history of horse breeding. Kwahadi was even looking forward to getting a beef contract from the army in the near future.

I have often wondered about the motives of those Texas cattlemen. They gave more than they got. All they needed to do was pay their grazing fees and let it go at that. But they went far beyond. It came to me that they were proud of being friends with an old enemy, a Comanche who might have had a great deal to do with the slaughter of some of their kind. Certainly his forebears had. But now he was the prodigal come back to the fold. Because he was half white, coming back, although in all his life he had never been there until he decided himself to finally come, that spring of 1875. But because of his mother, coming *back*.

That was the winter I drew up the list of names for the men in each family to select. It was remarkable that often Comanche names were long and intricate and sometimes even obscene, but for their English-language names they opted for simple ones. Like Smith and Jones and Brown. And some kept their Comanche tags for surnames, taking the English ones to go before. Therefore, Hawk became Tom Hawk. By which all his descendants would know him.

Old Otter Tongue refused to take any white man's name at all.

It was a good winter, that cold time after I'd married Quill. No longer did I sleep on top of the covers on the nights when we could hear the wind. She was gentle and patient and warm beyond all reckoning of warmth.

There was meat to eat, and the Indian police were becoming effective enough to cut back on the rustling of Comanche stock. And on each of my trips to Fort Sill, there were books waiting for me, and old issues of *Harper's Weekly* and the *Herald*.

Often I would be reading under the coal-oil lamp, knowing that Quill was watching me from the bed. I seldom saw her sleep. When I was awake, she was awake. Even in the mornings when I rose from my blankets, she would be at our little cookstove, making my breakfast. But never bacon. It was one concession I'd made to her Comanche-ness. I never brought pork into the house, knowing how her people despised the thought of eating white man's pig.

A few times I tried to read things to her from the pages of a magazine or newspaper. She had little comprehension of it, but she enjoyed the engraved pictures in *Harper's Weekly*, especially those showing busy street scenes in some congested Eastern city.

"There are a lot of white people in that place," she'd say.

"Yes, and there are many cities like this there in the East, toward where the sun rises."

"You mean there's more than one of these places with all the high houses and the roads across the river?"

"Yes, many of them, and a lot of white men in each one. Maybe someday I'll take you there to see them."

"No," she said vehemently. "There are so many white people, I'd be afraid they'd step on my toes with their heavy shoes."

So much for Eastern excursions.

From time to time in those days I dropped into the agency to give my greetings to Mr. Belton. He had taken to my marriage with more grace than anyone else among the bureaucrats. Jehyle Simmons regarded me as he would a coiled rattlesnake, and I enjoyed telling about my lovely home life in his hearing, he still living alone and without a woman to prepare his grub. It always infuriated him, yet he stayed nearby, listening because his curiosity would not allow him to stomp out of the agency building, a thing I knew he would have liked to do.

It was on one of those casual trips that I overheard Mr. Belton saying something about measures having to be taken to stamp out the use of mescal on the reservation. I paid little attention to it. I had seen no indication of any drug being used on the Big Beaver, and so naturally I supposed that it had no bearing on anything happening there.

And after the lamp was out and we lay together in our dark home, there was seldom the hot passion I'd

known as a young man. Yet maybe something even better. Sometimes simply feeling the warmth of her body
was passion enough, and there was a tenderness to it that
I suspected could never come with the fire of youth, at
least for me, and I'd known a lot of fire in the old days
when I'd been gadding about from one war to another.

Sometimes, in the night, I hummed Welsh melodies
for her, softly and wordless, and she seemed to enjoy it.
But even my lullabies only put me to sleep, not her, and I
would dream content and secure. It was the best of all
things I could ever expect to know again.

Next best were the evenings Allis Featherman and
Padoponi came and we sat around the stove, feeling its
good warmth and smelling the coffee as it simmered. And
my acting a fool over young Morgan Featherman, bounc-
ing him on my knees and slipping him a cold biscuit with
honey now and again.

It was a hard chore, explaining to Padoponi what a
godfather was, and when I finally got it across, she said
her people had always had such things. Every boy born
called each of his paternal uncles father. So some of them
surely had more of my white man's godfather than any
white child ever had. I let it go at that.

But though the camp was in repose and faring well,
Kwahadi spent that winter in a most decidedly preoc-
cupied mood. Many's the day I saw him walking along
the Big Beaver under the bare branches of the sycamores,
arms folded, head turned down, feet scuffing the snow,
an old buffalo-robe cape across his shoulders. And Coming Back from the Pony Herd, feeding her pet crow at
one of the new brush arbors near the big house, the
leaves there gone to crackling brown, watching her chief
with a serious set to her features. He was always frowning
on those wintery walks, thinking, I supposed, about the
whiskey.

It was getting worse, the whiskey. More and more of
the young men were turning to it. Because of the loss of
the old gods, so Kwahadi maintained. I was sure that on

those lonely walks of his, he was trying to come to grips with the whiskey.

When Christmas came, I explained to Quill and Padoponi and Kwahadi and his wives what it meant. The birthday of a man who had started one of the great religions of the white man, I told them, in a place more desolate and grim than northern Mexico. And to celebrate it, everyone exchanged gifts as an act of celebration and good cheer.

Kwahadi already knew a great deal about Christianity. Many of his people had joined one or the other of the various mission churches on the reservation. The complexion of the tribe was becoming mixed, in a spiritual way. And being the kind of man he was, the Antelope chief was more than casually curious.

So, on those long afternoons when the wind was biting hard and the snow flurries were pecking like my chickens against the windowpanes, he'd pause in his labors of writing, elbows on the huge dining table in the Wolf Ranch house, and tap the pencil on the lined tablet and stare at me and begin to ask his questions.

"How can one god take care of everything?" he'd always start. "The People have always thought there were a lot of gods because it takes a lot to handle everything."

"The Greeks thought the same thing," I'd say.

He wasn't interested in the Greeks.

"One god!" he said. "No wonder it's hard to tell you white men apart. You've all got the same medicine. Now, this heaven the missionaries are always talking about. Why is it a man has to worship their god to get into it? If he's a good man, what difference does it make what gods he takes?"

"I don't know," I said. I was in deep water, and needed my Da for such explanations.

"And why are they always telling us that to suffer in life is nothing, because a man won't suffer in this heaven? Why not make life good here and get into their heaven, too?"

I couldn't answer that one either.

"The People always thought life could be good on Earth Mother's bosom. Then, when somebody went to the place beyond the sun, everything started over. Even the ones who had been mean and done a lot of things the rest of the tribe didn't like. They'd get in like everybody else. It was a new chance that everybody got."

And always more.

"You've told me that all white men don't take this Christianity. There are all those other religions. How does a man know which one to pick?"

"It's mostly the family a man has. He takes the religion of his fathers."

"Ah! You see? That's what we've always done. Now, I hear them call us heathens because we've got a lot of gods. And they say being a heathen is bad. Why is that? They've only got one god and we've got a lot, but we're bad because of that?"

"Let's get back to the writing," I said, in the only way I knew to get out of such discussions. "Write down the alphabet again."

"I just did that."

"Some of the letters I can't read. You've got to work on the letters before you can write the words."

"I like the words better. Show me how to write 'buffalo.' Buffalo means something. All those little marks don't mean anything."

"They stand for the sounds you make when you speak English."

"You white men! You're harder to understand than the Kiowas."

But he bent over the tablet with his lead pencil and did the alphabet.

So I thought those winter walks of his were all about religion and what he could do about the whiskey. I knew he didn't think these new religions would be strong enough to take the place of the whiskey. A spirit people they were, and needed strong spirits, something they could almost touch. A vision people they were, and needed images in their minds. Kwahadi carried his own around with him, but all his young men were not so well endowed as their chief.

All winter he thought about it, pacing back and forth along the Big Beaver, frowning, arms folded. Then when the weather broke and the warm spring winds began, he cloistered himself in the big house and said he'd had enough of the writing and reading lessons for a while. Nobody but his wives saw him for more than three weeks. Then he sent Little Wolf to ask that I come and have a talk. And that was when I got the last installment.

It was my favorite time of year. The greening time. The new calves and foals were frisking around their mothers, and the colts from two years ago were being selected for breeding. It was time when the young men were busy and didn't have time to waste loitering around Fort Sill or the agency, drinking cheap whiskey and falling down in their own vomit. And because of that, I knew it must be Kwahadi's favorite time as well.

Along the Washita the wild plum was blooming, and all across the reservation the honey locust with its little greenish white foxtails of blossom, and on the road to Boggy Depot the redbud, purple as the lilacs of France. Mourning doves were everywhere that year, making their gentle cries after the soft spring rains, and the yellow-billed cuckoo with his rapid-fire cackle like a distant Gatling gun.

I enjoyed the prospect that bright morning of speaking about such things with the Antelope chief, because I knew he watched all these signs of spring as closely as did all the other members of his people, seeing the rebirth of life after a cold winter.

But he was very serious as he received me on the porch of the big house. He was in his rocking chair, with all his family sitting behind him, or crouched against the wall. And he came directly to the point, too, which startled me a little, even though I recognized the seriousness.

"Some of my Texas friends want me to come to one of their cities south of Red River," he said. "It's a big celebration."

"What kind of celebration?" I asked.

"I've got this paper they gave me." He pulled a crinkled envelope from beneath his open vest and handed it to me. "I could read some of it. But they told me what's in it. Garrison gave it to me when he was here the last time."

It was an impressive-looking letter, addressed as it was to Kwahadi Parry, Chief of the Comanches. I slipped out the single sheet of foolscap and saw that it came from the City of Fort Worth. They were inviting Kwahadi, and any of his elders he wanted to bring along, to a county fair. And as guest of honor! I translated all of it, word for word, every member of the family watching each movement of my lips.

There were murmurs of approval from his wives, and I knew Kwahadi had not until now revealed the contents of the missive. But he quickly raised one hand and there was silence again among them.

"This is a great honor," said I. "It's called a county fair because people bring in what they've grown during the year so other people can see it. In October."

"A celebration of farmers?"

"Well, more than that. There'll be plenty of good things to eat. There'll be plenty of fine horses."

His eyes lit up at that, and he showed the trace of a smile. Then he rocked rapidly, rubbing the point of his chin with those long, delicate fingers.

"You think I should go?"

"It would be good. You could make many friends among the whites."

"Maybe they'll put me in a cage and let the little children throw food to me." His smile broadened.

"They won't do that. Your Mr. Garrison and Mr.

Lowe are powerful men in Texas. You're coming as the guest of the whole city. They'll treat you with honor."

"Well, there was a time when we were enemies of the Kiowas," he said. "Then we made peace and often went to their sun-dance celebrations. So maybe it would be all right if I did the same thing with the Texans."

I knew then that he was teasing me, that he had already made up his own mind to go, and had asked me to confer only out of courtesy.

"It says to bring elders," he said, now serious once more. "I think maybe I'll take Otter Tongue and Hornbeam, the Paneteka judge on our court."

"I think you should take Tom Hawk, too."

"Why? He's not an elder in the tribe. The letter says elders."

"A bodyguard."

His eyes widened and he stared at me, the rocking chair still now.

"A bodyguard? You think I'll need a bodyguard among these Fort Worth white men?"

"No. As a symbol of your prestige. To impress them."

He grunted and started rocking once more and he thought about it for a long time. All the members of the family watched him expectantly, as though he were making a decision to raid somebody's pony herd.

"Maybe so. Hawk's an impressive-looking man, all right."

"Of course, he wouldn't carry that six-shooter. Just his badge."

"The pistol's part of being a policeman."

"It might make them nervous. Besides, he's not a policeman in Fort Worth."

"All right. Then he won't have the badge, either. I don't want to make those people nervous about anything."

He slapped his knees, and all the members of the

family began to smile, knowing it was settled to his satisfaction.

"Of course, you'll be there," Kwahadi said. "I want you to help me with the talk. Can Allis Featherman show us how to get there?"

"Yes, but I can do that. I've been there before."

"Sure, but I want you down there before us," he said, and then went on to some detail of the trip which was of no consequence, leaving it to dangle and letting me know that there might be more to this than just visiting the Texas fair. I had no idea what. But it was a little astonishing that I had come to anticipate this strange man, maybe see a wee bit of his thinking. It wasn't very satisfying. In fact, it was completely unsettling.

"We'll have to get Otter Tongue one of these white man's suits," he was saying. "I don't want anybody down there thinking he's an old barbarian, like a Lipan."

"They might want to see at least one of you in plains clothes," said I.

"No. If we're going to white man's cities, we ought to go looking like white men. We don't want to make them nervous. But getting Otter Tongue into white man's clothes may not be too easy."

"You said I'd be there before you," I said, unable to wait for that part of his design. And I was amazed at how far I'd come with him, never before having had the audacity to push him.

"Yes. You told me a long time ago that you knew a man there, in this Fort Worth."

"McLean Burton. An old soldier with me a long time ago."

"Yes, you told me all about that," he said, a little impatiently. "You said he'd become one of their chiefs."

"Well, he's in the state legislature. That's like a council of elders."

"Good! I've been talking to Garrison and Lowe, and they say we might need somebody like that to help us. I want you to go down there ahead of me and talk to this old soldier of yours and tell him we need his help."

"What sort of help?" I asked, knowing he was stringing this thing out to build the suspense. And I knew he was enjoying it!

"Well, Liver, now that you're part of the family, you ought to know that we've got to get our mother back up here and bury her among her own people!"

Our mother? My mouth gaped open, but no sound issued. Until finally, his eyes on me, the name passed my lips.

"Morfydd Annon Parry!"

"Yes. Our mother!"

There was no earthly connection between me and that red-haired little girl who had been taken by these people when I was a two-year-old toddler. And here he was, calling her *our* mother! I was married to his adopted daughter, sister of his eldest wife, and nothing more. Then I realized he was doing it to seal my place in his band. To show me that he considered me not only son-in-law, but brother.

Well, hell, he'd called me brother. That was what had started this whole business. Leading to Quill, and that to this, placing me in such a position that to refuse to help in such a thing would mean a great loss of dignity, not only to me, but to him!

I often wondered how far into my head Kwahadi could see. Maybe a lot deeper than I suspected. Digging up dead bodies and transporting them was not a particularly joyful prospect for me, and maybe he knew that. So getting me a wife was an accommodation to a lot of people, and most of all to him. But it was also the tie that now bound me to him and his purpose. Maybe the whole lot of it was for that purpose alone, having nothing to do with my former loneliness or the welfare of his favorite wife's sister.

It only came to me when he spoke of how much Quill had come to mean, how much affection and love there was between us. In that moment I saw her as a talisman placed on my side of the board to ensure this further design of the chief, to reinforce his imperative concerning the white woman who was his mother.

Yet, as always when he did something that infuriated me because I felt used, there was about it all a certain thrill in his recognition of my value to him, of my power, of my medicine. And thus it was irresistible.

"It may not be easy, taking a body out of the ground in Texas and bringing it to the Territory," I said, and he could sense the petulance in my tone.

I was sitting on the edge of the porch before him, and now he bent to me and placed a hand on my shoulder. His fingers may have been long and delicate, but I could feel a hot strength in them.

"Liver, that's why we need the Texas chief," he said. "I've been thinking about it all winter, how your friend has become a chief down there. So maybe he can show his friendship now, when you tell him we're brothers. Maybe he can help us get our mother back where she belongs."

Getting old Otter Tongue into a vested black suit was both funny and sad. He was at first adamant in his refusal to have anything to do with such a thing. But finally Kwahadi explained to him that he wouldn't go to Texas without it. It was obvious that the old man wanted to go, and equally obvious that he would accede. But not without a further show of resistance.

"I've been in Texas many times," he grumbled. "The place where I was born, they call that Texas now. I lived most of my life there. And always when I was a man, I carried weapons in my hands in Texas!"

"The time for weapons in Texas is past," Kwahadi said, not too gently. "And for hide clothes as well. We need to show them how far we've come along the white man's road."

"I haven't come very far," Otter Tongue muttered, his bloodshot eyes gleaming.

So he agreed to the black suit and the hat and the boots, but only if he didn't have to go himself into Stoddard & Blanchard's store to try everything on. Kwahadi said he could use the Wolf Ranch house as a dressing room where no one would see him until he was satisfied with his appearance.

So into the Strip, Allis Featherman and I, Kwahadi's gold coins in our pockets, there having to guess at sizes, holding up trousers and coat and shirt and cocking our heads to one side. I found it completely incongruous that such clothes should ever cover that old man's body.

Otter Tongue was very apprehensive, the day we all collected in one of Kwahadi's bedrooms at the big house. Allis and Kwahadi and myself were there, but the old man would allow no one else in the room. He kept glancing nervously toward the window to see that none of Kwahadi's children were peeking.

He stripped down to his loincloth, but would not hear of taking that off. It wasn't modesty, for I knew that Comanches placed little store in such things. It was because inside the loincloth was his medicine bag, containing his power, and everything protecting his manhood as no white man's clothing could ever do. So into the underwear anyway, the loincloth underneath.

Then into the white shirt and the trousers, and rebelling again at the stockings. But Kwahadi insisted. Then the boots, and Otter Tongue sweating and glancing repeatedly toward the window. The vest and coat, and at last the black hat. It sat atop his head, the dark dome of some church held up on either side by his ears, like flying buttresses. And behind, the thin scalp lock hanging.

We all exclaimed at how wonderful he looked, and he stared down at himself in utter disgust. He moved cautiously about the room, stiff-legged. He ran his fingers across the vest, and a sudden gleam came into his eyes.

"Maybe one of those little chains would be good," he said.

"You can have mine," Kwahadi said. "A gift so that the white man in this Fort Worth will be impressed with the greatest elder of the tribe."

But even with the gold watch chain, Otter Tongue would not leave the room so the people could see him. They were all gathered outside the front door, waiting silently in the sunlight beyond the porch, watching the house, waiting for the old man to appear in his new white man's clothes.

We left him and waited with the others. We waited all afternoon and into the setting sun and beyond, until the bright evening star was out and there were whippoorwills calling from the trees along the Big Beaver. And still he did not come out.

"How can we expect our young men to take the white man's road when the elders make such a bad example?" Kwahadi said, finally exasperated, and he stalked around the house and into the kitchen through the back door, his wives following.

Otter Tongue slept that night in Kwahadi's bedroom, alone, for no one would go in and make him come out. He slept in the white man's clothes, and even the hat, leaning stiffly in one corner. And in the dawning he woke and hurried from the house when no one would see him, going quickly to his own tipi, a short distance off, and carrying the bundle of hide clothing under one arm.

He stayed inside his lodge for a week, never appearing even for food, his old wife feeding him as he sat before a small fire, clad only in his loincloth, the white man's clothing to one side of him, his own buckskins to the other.

And then, on the seventh day, he came out. Suit, shirt, hat, boots, and all. And more. The old pipestem-bone breastplate was neatly tucked under the coat at its edges, and hung just above the watch chain of his chief, which drooped in a golden half-circle across his vested belly!

About Otter Tongue's emergence as a white man I heard later from Allis Featherman. For by then I was in Texas, talking with McLean Burton. I'd sent him a telegraph message beforehand, and he met me at the MKT depot, loud and boisterous as ever, explaining that the legislature wasn't in session at the moment and we'd have a hell of a good time for as long as I stayed. And so began the negotiations to have Texas give up the remains of Morfydd Annon Parry.

"I never had any truck with diggin' up old graves," said McLean Burton. "And I don't know what the God damned legalities might be. But me and the governor get along pretty well, so we can work it out. But it might take all summer."

"Well, she's got more family in the Territory than she has in Texas," said I.

"Hell, boy, she ain't got *any* family in Texas anymore. The Comanch' took care of that a long time ago."

"The governor should appreciate it, then, her going back to her own."

"By Gawd, I like it, Liverpool!" he bellowed, clapping me across the shoulders. "This Kwahadi gives us some peace after all those years, and now we give him back his mother!"

"Shrewd traders the Comanches have always been, McLean, shrewd traders indeed!"

And who should know better than I?

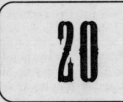

Father Peyote!

I had to explain it that summer to McLean Burton in the best way I could, but, not being a Comanche, I fear my best efforts were completely unsatisfactory.

It's always been difficult for me to understand another man's religion. No small wonder, what with never having been able to define my own. But maybe the Comanches had as good an idea as any. It had to do with power, that was plain. As far as I could tell, they believed that every man had this power. It was a matter of his finding it. And once found, whether it was put to use for good or evil was up to him.

Well, actually I had no notion of a Comanche definition of evil among The People. I'd heard Kwahadi speak many times of this or that thing being good, but I could not recall his ever using the word *evil*. But at least I knew about the search for power, and how each man must find it and use it as he saw fit.

As with so much about them, it seemed so simple and straightforward, yet with a closer look it became more complex, like learning from the simple fact of learning how much was still left unlearned. That summer in Texas I made my first attempt at putting it into words for another white man. It was my last attempt, as well. Because the more I talked about it, the more mysterious it became.

So if I succeeded only in confusing myself, what a muddle McLean Burton's mind must have been. Good man that he was, and even sympathetic to my friends north of Red River, he was still a white man, and maybe because of that, he was beyond understanding.

"It scares hell out of everybody," he said one evening over a bowl of Biddie's oxtail soup. "The Comanch' up there in the Territory, chewin' mescal and goin' crazy!"

"No such thing," said I. "It's a religion to them. At least it seems so to many of them. It has no war talk in it."

"Then what *is* in it?" he asked, mimicking me as he had fallen into the habit of doing, by way of teasing me about my strange speech, and leaning over his soup, eyes blinking rapidly.

"It's about power," I said. "It's hard to explain what power means to a Comanche. They once had it from their spirit gods. But none of the spirits work anymore. None of their old power can control the white man or bring back the days when there were buffalo."

"Hell, there may not be any buffaler left, but they get fed on the government dole, don't they?"

"Sometimes not too well," said I. "Sometimes, even now, there are hard winters when rations get short and they suffer a great deal."

"The hell you say!"

"If it weren't for your Texas cattlemen and sometimes a generous army commissariat, a lot of them would have starved. And maybe some did, despite good intentions. But that's not the point here, McLean. It's more than having a full belly. It's the way they have to live, remembering the way they once lived. Did it ever come to you that there's a great indignity in having to depend on charity to feed your children?"

McLean Burton blinked more rapidly still, thinking hard about it now and spooning soup into his mouth with a sound like a cow's hoof in sticky mud.

"But where does the mescal come in?"

"It gives them power. It gives them visions. Some of them joined the white men's churches on the reservation. But for a lot of them, that's not enough. They need something left of the old power. And they say peyote gives it to them."

"And what does our man Kwahadi say about all this?" he asked, still spooning soup between words.

"He encourages it. I think he believes it will help the young men stay away from whiskey."

"Gawd damn it, Liverpool, what are you talking about? Power and spirits and the old ways and now whiskey. What the hell's whiskey got to do with it?"

"Maybe a lot. Remember, no more war parties, and this a warrior people. No more buffalo hunts, and this a hunting people. So the men sometimes turn to whiskey to forget, to get falling-down drunk. There's not much else to do, anyway."

"Well, now you're talkin' about something I can understand," McLean said. "Remember all them times when we had the chance we'd get so drunk we couldn't talk, just to forget the boys we'd seen blowed into smithereens at the last go-round with the Yanks?"

"You see? Maybe it helps them forget the white man's road. Listen, whiskey's a bad thing in the Territory. And Kwahadi thinks it's a big thing in destroying his people. He's fought it ever since the band came in."

"All right! Then this mescal—what's it do? Worse than locoweed, so they tell me. Where the hell does it come from? It don't grow north of the Red. It don't even grow around here."

"I don't know where they get it. Except that I've got suspicions. Now and again, one of them goes on a trip to

New Mexico. He comes to Texas and takes a train. Or else rides all the way horseback. Sometimes the agent says these visits are authorized. Sometimes he doesn't, but nothing he can do to keep them there if one or two of them want to strike out and go."

"Wanderin' across Texas without permission!"

"Sweet Jesus, McLean, it's still their country, as far as they think about it. And no harm done. They go and come without hurting anybody. Or maybe sometimes a man comes up through the Territory, like one of the old traders, carrying something he knows they'll pay for. Or maybe even for friendship alone. I don't know. I've given this thought, I have, and I can't tell you how they get it. But they get it. And nothing the bureaucrats can do to stop it, so it seems."

"Well, you say it don't make 'em crazy. What the hell does it do? I suspect they've told you, being married as you are to one of their own kind."

"Maybe a mistake, telling you about my wife."

"Oh, Gawd damn, Liverpool! I don't give a good hang who you're married to. A woman's a woman. But now, tell me, what does this stuff do? You know that?"

"Yes," I said, drawing a deep breath, and plunged in. "I've taken it myself."

McLean Burton stared at me incredulously, his spoon drooping from his fingers. So I tried to explain it all to him, too deep now to extract myself gracefully, and sorrier with each word I spoke that the subject had ever come up. But it was bound to sooner or later, I supposed, because of the innate curiosity of all barbers and some politicians. And he was both.

"Father Peyote," I said. "This little cactus with a rosette of blue buttons, pale blue. And when you eat it, it gives you supernatural powers. A way for the Comanches to communicate with their spirits, so I understand it. Even sometimes with their departed ones. It gives them a sense of the old ways, when their gods were everywhere, guiding them day and night, hour by hour."

"A lot of hawgwash," McLean Burton said. I ignored him and went on.

"Yet different. Because the peyote rituals preach peace and harmony, not war and raiding other people's herds. Friendship and family the thing, you see? Family care and self-support through hard work."

"Work? A Comanche, work?" McLean shouted.

"And staying away from whiskey!"

"Well," he said, drumming his spoon now on the tabletop. "I can understand a little of that. It makes some sense, because everybody knows they can't any of 'em hold their whiskey. Like you and me can do."

"And wreck a pool hall?"

"Well, that was just a little fun. It cost me three hundred dollars, too. But go on about this mescal, Liverpool, it's beginnin' to get my interest."

"Known it for many years, they had, but seldom used it. This old man told me it had been known as far back as his grandfather's time, when they first came south. From the Apaches. Old enemies. But they never needed it before. Sometimes, so I'm told by this old man, a young warrior might chew a button or two before a big raid. But it was just a part of his own medicine then. Now it's got to be a community thing."

"Community thing? Hell, sun dances were community things, too. And they scared the horseshit out of everybody!"

"Yes, but the Comanches never held sun dances."

"I heard they had one not too long ago."

"They tried one, some of them, because they were willing to try anything to help bring back the power. But it didn't work. Besides, it's against the law."

"So now they're trying mescal," McLean said. "And you tell me you've tried it, too. You're gettin' too Gawd damned old to be messin' in such business, Liverpool."

"A man gets roped into a corner sometimes, he does."

"Horseshit! I never seen a corner you couldn't

wiggle out of in the old army days. Wonder you wasn't shot by a firing squad."

"McLean, watch your tongue," said Biddie, bending to take a deep-dish apple pie from the oven. Its aroma was as solid as the oak table.

"Well, Kwahadi thinks it's good. And he knows more about what his people need than I do. All of peaceful intent it is, in that way a lot like Christianity."

"Well, God damn it, tell me about when you ate some of that stuff. Did you talk in tongues? I've seen white men get religion so full up at revival meetings they spoke a language nobody ever heard before, and rolled on the ground."

So I plunged on again, with great misgivings, but here was a man willing to use his influence to help me get Kwahadi's mother back to the Territory, so what better place to tell it?

It was a Saturday evening when Kwahadi came to me. A little surprising because he was dressed in the old fringed hide smock and leggings and moccasins, and his hair was flowing loose and he was holding the eagle-feather fan.

"Liver," he said, very seriously. "Brother. I want you to come with me to one of our ceremonies. At the painted tipi in the blackjack oaks along Big Beaver Creek."

"What kind of ceremony?" I asked.

"Just a little ceremony of brothers," said he. "A thing to bring us together now and then, when all the bands are breaking up and the families are going off to make their own farms and ranches. It's good, this coming together. Besides, it's all about power."

That painted tipi had been up for some time. Everybody knew about it, but nobody except a few of the men ever went there, and that on evenings just like this one. Allis Featherman had said he'd heard singing from the tipi, many times lasting all night and into dawning. So now I had my own invitation and jumped at the chance.

Besides, it was a good night for a short stroll, with the mockingbirds singing across the Big Beaver, and the smell of cedar on the land under a pale, star-bright sky.

Kwahadi didn't say another word as we walked along the stream in growing darkness. We were joined by Hawk and Otter Tongue, like shadows drifting into our path by accident. They were silent, too. As the big painted tipi loomed ahead in the night, I could see other men there, waiting, most of them blanket-wrapped and all in their old plains dress and a few with feathers in their hair hanging down behind.

Far to one side was a woman. I didn't recognize her in the dark. Then a few murmured words passed among the men, and everyone filed into the tipi, Hawk taking my arm and guiding me, as though he thought I might bolt at the last moment. There was a small blaze in the usual fire hole at the center of the ceremonial lodge, and at the far side, across the fire, sat a Yamparika Comanche named Thunder Voice, whom I knew only slightly from seeing him at ration day. Everyone took a seat in a wide circle, shoulder to shoulder, Thunder Voice and Kwahadi side by side and myself between Otter Tongue and Hawk, near the tipi door flap.

Thunder Voice made a little song of welcome as a pipe was passed around the circle. A prayer was offered up by a man I didn't know. It was about doing hard work to keep the families fed. Everything had a mystical flavor, and the scene came to my memory in later times in flashes of color. The firelight flickering across the brown faces, the decorated hide smocks, the dark shine of black hair, the white vanes of feathers. And then the blue of the peyote.

Directly at Thunder Voice's feet was a small leather bag. After a few more prayers by other members of the circle, he opened it, singing now to Father Peyote. Thunder Voice asked the spirit of Father Peyote to bring power and to help everyone love his brother. He began to pass the little peyote buttons around until everybody had one. In my fingers I could feel the smooth texture of it, and the firmness. Yet somehow, it seemed as though it were living. Like holding a warm, unmoving mouse in my hand.

Holding that mescal button, I wondered what strange route it had taken to this place in Indian Territory, over many miles from where it grew in northern Mexico. I had no idea how that commerce, possibly between old enemies, had come about or how it functioned, nor did I ever learn. As though Father Peyote appeared when needed.

But I knew there was a practical reason for its being there near the banks of the Washita, and I suspected strongly that Kwahadi was at the root of it. But I never learned.

Everyone around the circle was eating his mescal. And although none of them looked directly at me, I knew they expected me to do the same. Well, many things had passed my lips. So now this.

It had a slightly bitter taste, yet not unpleasant. But as the prayers continued, it seemed to become larger inside my belly, the sensation of a warm little mass growing there. I could feel no effect. Except that after a while, everything seemed to be moving more slowly. And some of the words said in song and prayer were blurred in my ears like the hum of a gentle honeybee. Fuzzy and more color than sound.

Then Thunder Voice was passing more buttons around the circle, one for each man seated there.

I became very thirsty. After the second button, the woman I'd seen outside the tipi came in to pass around water for everyone. It was Kwahadi's wife Coming Back from the Pony Herd, and she was gone again almost before I realized she was there.

Then more chants were offered up to Father Peyote, and more singing, the voices now coming to me through a great distance so the words were unknown. Coming to me through a veil of swirling color and soft ringing in my ears. And sometimes sharp-edged, like the clang of tiny tambourine cymbals. My body seemed weightless, and the sight of my own hands before my face was like seeing the hands of some other man, as though they were not attached to me, but were part of the whole group of men in the circle with me.

The sense of smell became sharp almost to painfulness. For the first time since walking into the ceremonial lodge, I knew the wood burning in the fire hole was locust, and with that odor the scent of tanned buckskin, and somehow the smell of water running in the Big Beaver.

Everything moved so slowly! Yet it seemed no time at all till the night was finished, the ceremony as well, and everyone filing out of the lodge. I had never felt such a sense of profound peace and comfort and warmth, everything from within, but shared with all these others.

McLean Burton was staring at me pop-eyed, waiting, I was sure, for something terribly dramatic.

"Well?" he finally said.

"That was all of it," said I. "Some praying and singing and some water and the buttons."

"God damn it, you mean to say there was no dancing?"

"No. There were long periods of complete silence, each man staring into the fire."

"And that's supposed to give 'em this power you talked about?"

"It's a hard thing, explaining what happened," I said. "It was like a bright fog coming across my mind. I could see yellow and red and blue and great balls of light, growing slowly, brilliant beyond all reckoning, then fading to the soft colors again."

"Did you hear voices?"

"Yes," said I, most reluctantly, because I knew he might think me daft. "Yes. I heard voices. Maybe it was just their voices, praying. Like a dream it was, when you wake and can't remember. Then it was finished."

I didn't tell McLean Burton about having heard my old Da's voice. But at some point during that night, he spoke to me as clearly as he ever had in life. Oh, I'd heard those others, speaking in Comanche. But Da came to me in English, and he long in the ground. For all the seasons of my life, I remembered his voice and remembered it that night at Biddie's table in Texas. Yet I could not recall a single word he'd said!

"How many times you eaten these things?" McLean Burton asked.

"Only that once. They never invited me back again."

And I thought, Nor do I want such an invitation. It had unnerved me completely, once the effect of the drug wore off. Most especially when Coming Back from the Pony Herd asked me how I'd enjoyed the meat she'd brought during the ceremony, and I could not remember having eaten.

Maybe Kwahadi was reading my thoughts more clearly than I could myself. In an apologetic tone for not having asked me back to Father Peyote a second time, he once said to me, "Liver, I think you ought to find your own power. I think you find it somewhere I don't know about. Every man has to come to his gods in his own way."

A thousand times I'd heard the Antelope chief say that. But it was only after the peyote ceremony that I came to understand the truth of it. Those hallucinations were not for my poor old head. But I could understand how they might be a powerful medicine for someone with the deep spiritual leanings of my friends the Comanches. And maybe even a force against the whiskey.

"By God, Liverpool," McLean Burton said, "I never heard such a story in my life."

"Well, now that it's becoming well known, the bureaucrats are going to make laws against it, I hear."

"Bureaucrats are always making laws against something," said he, motioning Biddie to produce her chopped-apple pie from the sideboard. "Hell, I ought to know. I've helped make a few laws like that myself."

"I expect it to happen," I said. "Since we've known them, everything we haven't destroyed of their life we've made against the law."

"Well, by God, they give us a lot of bad times, those Comanch'!"

"And us them. And in their own country."

He opened his mouth to respond, spots of angry red appearing above his whiskers. Then he clamped his jaw tight shut, good man that he was, and unable to deny what I'd said. And slapped a plate of pie before me.

"Well, eat your pie!"

It gave me an intense sense of guilt, rubbing this old man's nose in past wrongs. But my amends were feeble at best.

"But then, McLean, it wasn't always their own country, either. Passed from hand to hand it was, like the isles that were once Briton and then Saxon and then Norman."

He had no idea what I meant. I had no idea where the words sprang from, but maybe that was what my Da was saying to me in the painted lodge beside the Big Beaver on the night I saw Father Peyote.

21

Celebrations I'd seen, but never one like the Fort Worth Fair in the year we began to make arrangements to have Kwahadi's mother brought back to the Comanches. The fairgrounds were west of the city, and there the canvas was raised. There were small tents, large tents, square tents, round tents, and long tents with brightly colored pennants flying from each of the pole tops. These last were called revival tents by McLean Burton.

"We saw plenty of revivals in the old army, huh, Liverpool?" he asked.

"Yes, but never under a canvas cover. Only the winter sky to cover us."

"You ever wonder why there was so much religion going around in the cold months, and not much in summer?"

It was the kind of question to ponder in the long afternoons while we enjoyed the marvelous Fort Worth beer.

The fair had many imported attractions, the most noteworthy being a dime show at one end of the fairway. At the other end was the world-famous B. E. Wallace Circus, featuring the world's greatest bicyclists, or so the placards proclaimed. This was a family group of seven, with the women wearing bloomers and shocking pink stockings. The dime show ran to freaks and acrobats and a fire-eater, the last of whom, when one came within ten paces of him, smelled like old coal-oil cans.

At the center of the midway was a carousel with a steam calliope inside the turning wheel, belching smoke and giving off tunes nobody could recognize, as the little gondola-like seats went in their constant circles. It was billed as the world's largest merry-go-round, but I'd seen larger in Palermo years before. There was a fascinating machine that bubbled forth what they called cotton candy, a pale pink like the lady bicyclists' stockings, and sweet to the taste, like morning mist flavored with brown sugar.

A great pit had been dug for roasting beef and hogs, the carcasses spitted above the red-hot embers. Barbeque they called it, and a slab of that with a mess of Mexican brown beans cost ten cents, on a metal plate and eaten at rough board tables and benches, all set out under the Texas sun. Nearby was a small tent fly with a plank bar set on barrels, and kegs of beer on sawhouses, where the foam came out warm as fresh cow's milk. That was the most popular place on the midway for the menfolk, but the women and children walked a wide circle around such a den of wickedness.

There was a tent with a lantern slide show, swelter-ing hot inside once the flaps were all lowered to produce the necessary darkness. Well, more like gloom than dark-ness, and the spectators had to lean forward and squint to make out the tinted images of snow-covered Swiss moun-tains, the gush of water over Niagara Falls, and strange caravans of camels going Indian-file across the sands of the Sahara.

"Remember when the Yankee army tried to use camels out here?" McLean Burton asked. "I wonder what ever happened to all those poor damned camels."

There was a performing bear with a heavy leather muzzle on his ugly snout. There were trapeze artists under the Wallace tent. There were roasted peanuts and a steam tractor that moved along with a great noise and vomit of smoke, and at night a minstrel show with white men putting burnt cork on their faces, pretending to be something they were not and saying things that were supposed to be funny.

An upright wheel of chance spun for those interested in wagering, but it was closed down the first day of the fair by city policemen because there were Fort Worth citizens who had the same kind of contraption in their Main Street establishments, and felt they should have a monopoly on wagers. There was a puppet show called Punchinello, straight from Italy, so they said, and the favorite of youngsters next only to the cotton candy.

The real purpose of the fair was set well aside from the midway, the tents and corrals and sheds where the livestock and produce were on display. Rows of preserved peaches and strawberries in those new glass jars. Blue and red and white ribbons with rosettes hung on boards, awaiting judges' decisions as to what was best of everything, hogs or sheep or calves or ears of corn, dry now but golden, row on row of kernels on the cob. Cabbages and late watermelons and early pumpkins and squash and green beans and chili peppers dangling from peeled poles like strings of green and red firecrackers.

And horseraces! Straightaway for a quarter-mile, just like the Comanche races in the Territory, but here the riders wore silk shirts of many colors, as though it were old England, and Victoria herself was there to see from the temporary grandstands. Each afternoon the horses ran, after the first show in the Wallace circus tent. They ran until dark, when the fireworks began, rockets and Roman candles and pinwheels throwing off their fire and evil-smelling smoke across the cheering crowds.

The town itself was decorated in red, white, and blue bunting, slung over the streets and across the storefronts. The flag of the old Texas Republic floated out in many places with its lone white star, and there were brass bands playing and a parade each morning, with the dime show's contortionist on a flat wagon bed, twisted and bent into shapes impossible, standing on his hands with his face where his arse should have been.

It was all a delightful time, with everything foolish and serious about the ways of a people living on the bosom of the earth, dirt under their fingernails and calluses on their hands, taking holiday as seriously as they took their struggle to bring sustenance from the ground beneath their feet. A hardy crowd. A howling mob. And myself among them, drinking beer with State Senator McLean Burton.

Kwahadi and his party arrived at the MKT passenger depot one morning, and I was more than a wee bit apprehensive about how the Comanches would react to all that was happening. I wasn't alone in my anxiety.

"How are these red heathen of yours going to take to all this white man's hoopla?" McLean Burton had asked at breakfast that morning of their anticipated arrival.

"They'll endure it, they will, or I miss my bet," I said, sounding more confident than I felt.

"I read in the newspaper that not too long ago one of 'em went to Washington City to see the Great White Father Yankee, and the first time the train went through a tunnel, he fainted from pure fright."

"That was Ho-Wear. He's a Yamparika. I know him only slightly, but I suspect he's a very brave man. Railroad tunnels have never been a thing their medicine had to deal with. And there are no tunnels between here and Boggy Depot."

"Yeah," McLean said around a mouthful of Biddie's buckwheat cakes and molasses. "But I dunno. Maybe it's like whiskey. They can't stomach anything of the white man's without goin' a little crazy."

We met them at the train, having been informed of their time of arrival by a telegraph message from Allis Featherman. An impressive welcome it was, with Lowe and Garrison and McLean Burton and Nobis Chandler, now a sergeant of Rangers, his mustache even more elaborate than ever, waxed at the ends to needle points. A brass band was playing across the switching tracks, and most of the people who were not on the fairgrounds were surely there, gawking and pointing and some of them waving handkerchiefs.

My conductor friend, Keims, on the MKT, had been aware all along of what was happening. He put his distinguished savage passengers in the last car so they could exit on the back platform, giving them a chance to look about before stepping down. And giving the burghers of Fort Worth a chance to look at them.

So they appeared, like candidates for office, on the rear platform. There was Kwahadi in his judging suit and holding his eagle-feather fan. On either side of him were Hornbeam and Otter Tongue, in their best bib and tucker, but Otter Tongue still looking a little stiff and embarrassed, even with the glint of the gold watch chain across his middle below the old bone breastplate.

Behind them was Allis Featherman, grinning like a young imp, and beside him was Hawk in his usual police garb of Texas hat and vest and army trousers. But on his feet he wore Comanche moccasins, tasseled front and rear, a kind of defiance of white man's clothes. And without his pistol and badge. His face was impassive, as though every day of his life he had viewed such splendor as the bunting-clad Tarrant County seat.

Kwahadi showed interest but no surprise. Hornbeam alone among them all seemed startled and ready to bolt back into the car, had not Hawk been standing directly behind him. Otter Tongue held his head down, that faint smile on his face, his hands clasped before him as though he were praying. Allis Featherman grinned and waved to me.

They stepped down from the platform, and Kwahadi began shaking hands with all the greeters, violently, as he always did. So violently with McLean Burton that the good legislator had to grab his stovepipe hat to keep it from falling off.

"You're the friend of Liverpool Morgan," said Kwahadi in English, and I was taken a mite aback because I'd never heard him utter my Christian name.

"Yes, a fine man, that Morgan," McLean shouted, clinging for life to the Comanche chief's hand. "I welcome you to Fort Worth and to Texas. The governor sends his greetings."

"I've been in Texas before," Kwahadi said. "But the governor never gave me much hospitality. It's good he does now."

McLean flushed a little, but I had to give him credit. His smile remained wide and toothy.

They were led directly to the Cattlemen's Rest Hotel, near the depot, where there were rooms waiting for them. McLean Burton had wanted a separate place for each of us in Kwahadi's party, but with the influx of fair visitors, even his influence was not enough to bring that off. So it was Kwahadi and Otter Tongue in one room, Hawk and Hornbeam in another, Allis Featherman and myself in yet a third.

"Hell, you can keep stayin' with me," McLean had said. "Where you was at all summer while we was doing this Morfydd Annon Parry business. You tired of Biddie's grub?"

"No, never tired of such delights," I'd said. "But I belong with the chief, in case he needs me for the words."

"By God, he's gonna have that other fella."

"Allis Featherman."

"So you told me. You said he was all right with the words."

"Yes, but maybe the chief needs me close by."

"You do as you please, Liverpool. Never knew the time you didn't!"

So it was settled, and I moved that morning into the hotel before the train arrived, knowing the pot roast there would never be as good as Biddie's.

It was a fine hotel, mahogany furnishings in the lobby and a grand staircase leading to the second floor and all the brass spittoons shining like squat suns along the walls between the urns of peacock feathers. In the rooms, wide windows looked out onto the town and there were beds with good, strong mattresses and everything lighted by the new gas-jet lamps bracketed to the walls.

It was a strange procession from the train to the hotel, the Texas men leading the way, with Kwahadi walking beside them, holding the eagle-feather fan in front of his chest like a Spanish dancer. Behind him came Otter Tongue, head down and clasping his hands and smiling, his eyes shifting from side to side to see the people who were watching. Hornbeam tried to maintain his dignity as the blaring sounds of the brass band assaulted his ears. I wondered if he had ever seen a wooden house of more than one story. Certainly never such an imposing structure as the Cattlemen's Rest, which boasted four floors.

And Hawk, impassive. I found myself wishing he would show some small bit of astonishment, some surprise. But he didn't.

Finally, Allis and myself bringing up the rear, like Comanche lads watching the pony herd.

"Your wife wants you to come home," he said, giggling. "Now she's in a family way."

"Soon enough," said I.

"Well, her being in a family way," he repeated.

"I know. And you all along thinking this old man incapable of powers of that nature!"

"I never said any such thing," he said defensively, so I slapped him across the back roughly and we laughed, the both of us.

We were into the great lobby then, the manager himself bowing and scraping as though he were entertaining a caliph of Baghdad. And reporters from the two Fort Worth newspapers running alongside, posing their discreet questions about how the trip seemed thus far, and Kwahadi ignoring them. And well back from it all, some of the city's fine women in feathered hats and full skirts, watching with large eyes and holding small purses before their breasts, tense and ready, I supposed, to ward off scalping attacks.

At the ends of the halls on each floor of the Cattlemen's Rest were the latrines, called convenience rooms, but latrines they were. The most modern west of Memphis, so said the hotel manager, showing them proudly, one for ladies, one for gentlemen. They were zinc-lined and sat four bottoms in a row, walnut seats with oval holes. By pulling a chain, water flushed in a rush through the thing, one flush accommodating all holes. And away everything went, down a drain that led I had no idea where.

It took some time to explain to Otter Tongue the purpose of all those seats with the holes in them. He'd seen privies, but mostly one-holers and never any with water running in them. Once the light of understanding lit his old eyes, he was delighted.

"Right inside the lodge," he exclaimed. "It's as good as that metal thing in Kwahadi's house that pumps up the water."

"This water comes from above," I said, as Otter Tongue pulled the chain a second time. "There's a tank of water on the roof."

"It runs like a spring flood!" he said. "It's clear and cool looking."

"It's not for drinking," Kwahadi said with gentle impatience.

"I know," Otter Tongue said. "Only for defecation and urinating. What a waste of fine water!"

There was little time for inspecting the hotel. We

were quickly led off to the fair by our hosts, who outnumbered us four to one, having been joined by the mayor of Fort Worth, his chief of police, a representative from the governor's office in Austin, a bishop of the Methodist church, and a few others I never could identify.

We rode a massive open coach with seats upholstered in leather, drawn by a team of four large horses of a honey color, with manes and tails like wheat straw. I could see Kwahadi eyeing them with approval.

First we stopped at the tent of the Wallace Circus, where the performance had been delayed until our arrival, and there into the reserved seats along the front row, which was set off with more of the red, white, and blue bunting. Throughout the show, most of the people were watching the Comanches instead of the bicyclists or the trapeze artists.

Then onto the midway. Hornbeam rode on the carousel, sitting with solemn mien, going round and round, gripping the sides of his little gondola car as the calliope puffed out its discordant music.

On Hornbeam's third revolution, the operator stopped the contraption and all the rest of Kwahadi's party boarded, except for Otter Tongue, who refused to come any nearer the thing than ten paces. He stood watching with his little smile as we revolved past him. We were the only patrons on the carousel at the time, all the whites standing well back and watching us.

Everyone had a plate of the barbeque, and Kwahadi even drank a small bucket of beer. Otter Tongue drank three. At the freak show, everyone stared in revulsion at a man who seemed to have his nose on upside down. We watched the lantern slides and the acrobats and the giant tractor with its iron wheels that cut deep into the ground, a thing of little beauty. We watched the performing bear do his elementary tricks. We passed the exhibited vegetables without pause, and the hogs as well. But then came the cattle and horses, and I could see from Kwahadi's eyes that these alone were worth his trip.

Most of the cattle the Comanches had seen on the trails to Kansas had been longhorns. But at the Fort Worth fair they saw crossbreeds. Durham and Hereford mated with the Texas cattle. Shorter horns, shorter legs, bigger barrels where the meat was. Kwahadi was most taken by a purebred shorthorn, compact as a tube of pemmican, and roan-colored.

"We need some of those," he said to me in Comanche, and I saw another mission for myself taking shape in his mind. And was irritated enough to respond.

"Why don't you speak English in front of all these people?" I said, also in Comanche. "To show what a civilized man you are."

He turned to me and smiled and placed one of those slender hands on my shoulder.

"I don't speak as well in that tongue, Liver. You don't want me making a fool of myself, do you?"

Well, hell, if he wanted shorthorns, I'd get them for him.

Best of all were the horses. Our large party stood at the racecourse, but the Comanches had seen many races and this was nothing new. Except for the jockeys.

"Those men riding wear very unusual clothes," Otter Tongue said. "They are bright enough to blind the ponies."

When I interpreted that for our delegation, the Texas politicos laughed heartily and rolled their eyes.

Going through the horse pavilion took a long time. There were the small drays and the fine trotters and the plains workhorses, built for pulling plows.

"What a waste of horses," Otter Tongue said.

The Comanches admired them all, but they'd seen some of each before. What they hadn't seen were the big European workers, most impressive to them the pair of French Percherons. Kwahadi stood in awe beside them, feeling their gray flanks to assure himself that they were real.

But Otter Tongue was unimpressed.

"That may be a good horse for the white man," he said. "But I'd hate to try running down a buffalo on such a thing."

I felt such comments were better left uninterpreted for our illustrious white friends.

"What did the old man say?" the governor's representative asked.

"He said he'd like to have another bucket of beer," I said.

"I'll send someone!"

Then into the evening minstrel show, which none of the Comanches understood. Otter Tongue drank more beer and had to go many times to the makeshift, canvas-enclosed latrines. And everywhere we went, the Texans and their families, dragging their children by the hand, followed at a discreet distance, staring. To be looked at so long and so intently becomes irritating after a while, yet my Comanche friends seemed completely unaware of it. But I knew this was nothing more than a courteous façade.

We rode back to the hotel finally in the great open coach, and there in each room McLean Burton had insured a bowl of cheese and apples and a pitcher of iced lemonade, in case our bellies were not already full of the barbeque. Or beer. Hawk had to support Otter Tongue up the stairs, the old man beginning to giggle as much as Allis Featherman, and making remarks all the while about those big horses.

Allis Featherman and I sat for a long time, talking about the fair and munching the crisp little red apples and nibbling the yellow cheese like mice. We agreed it had been a fine day, the weather not too hot, and our reservation companions conducting themselves as gentlemen—even old Otter Tongue, who toward the end had become a little drunk on the beer. But always Hawk had stood near him to guide him away from any foolishness.

"Some men seem designed to look after their fellows," said I.

"Well, we sure done a good job on Kwahadi," Allis said. "He can talk almost as good as some of these Texicans."

"A quick mind, your father-in-law," I said. Allis grinned crookedly. He'd been at that beer keg a few times himself and was somewhat out of focus in the eye.

We were ready for bed, I in my underwear and Allis as well, when Kwahadi came. He opened the door and walked in without the hint of a knock, and he was still clad in his complete judging suit. He was frowning, and not the expression of concentration I'd seen so often.

"My head hurts," he said. "We blew out the light a long time ago for sleep, but my head won't let me. Maybe all the dust and noise today. They make a lot of noise, don't they?"

"Have a glass of lemonade," I said.

He shook his head and settled on the floor, cross-legged, still frowning and now taking off the hat and rubbing his forehead.

"No," he said, "I had some of that already. A strange-tasting thing, that liquid. Worse than the beer. But now I want to talk with you. A family thing, Liver."

I knew what was coming, for I had been expecting it since he stepped down off the rear platform of that railroad train.

"I want to talk about this thing you've been doing for the family."

"Everything is done. Except for hiring the men to take her up and have her carried home."

"I'll pay them a lot of money."

"No. Your Texas cattlemen friends will do that. They want to do that for you as a gift."

"Those are good friends," he said. "One never refuses the gifts of good friends, because it causes a loss of dignity for both sides. When will it be?"

"Just a short time," I said. "McLean Burton will see

to all the details. But I'll be here to help and come back with her body to the Territory."

"Yes, someone in the family should be with her always, from the time she's taken up."

"I'll be there. McLean will see to the details. His friend the governor has given his approval."

"Good. That friend of yours, McLean, is a good man. But he hurts my ears sometimes with his loud talking."

We talked a while longer, the night going down, Kwahadi still fascinated by those big French horses.

"A man told me," he said, "their foals are as big as some of our ponies. I'd like to see that. I'd like to see one of those big mares foaling."

Then he was off to bed, his headache fading now, and Allis Featherman and myself alone once more and taking a final few nibbles of the cheese. I turned out the gaslights at last and climbed into bed, where I lay awake a few moments before sleep, thinking of the task ahead. The grave-robbing. Well, not really *robbing*, yet it seemed so to me, even with the blessings of the governor of Texas. As I started to drop into an exhausted sleep, Kwahadi's first words when he entered our room came to me with a sudden vividness.

We blew out the lights!

"God Almighty," I shouted, and leaped from bed, causing Allis Featherman to start up from sleep wild-eyed, his face illuminated by the light from the hallway as I threw open the door.

At that moment I supposed I would have to break down Kwahadi's door, but then realized that the Antelope chief had likely never used a lock in his life. I tried the knob and the door swung open and a blast of evil odor struck my nostrils, like the faint scent of rotten eggs. Into the room with a leap, then, and they were on the bed, Kwahadi and Otter Tongue, both fully clothed except for their hats.

As I grasped his shoulders, Kwahadi's eyes came

334 / DOUGLAS C. JONES

open, opaque and misted with sleep. But with more than sleep. He made no sound, no outcry at my abrupt handling of him, trying to get him up. His movements were uncoordinated, like a rag doll, and I lifted him bodily and ran into the hall with him, where Allis Featherman stood in his underwear, looking as though he thought I'd gone mad.

Laying the Antelope chief on the floor, it occurred to me in disjointed thought that he was very light in my arms. Almost like a young girl, for all his height and seeming muscle.

"Get downstairs and tell whoever you can find to get a doctor up here," I shouted, then ran back into the room as Allis disappeared headlong down the stairs, still in his underwear.

In the wee light from the open doorway, I fumbled along the walls until I found the lamps. The petcocks were full open and there was a faint hissing. I turned them off and then threw open the windows. Then to the bed, where the old man still lay. I knew as soon as I peered into his face that he was dead!

Many times I'd been in the company of tragedy, and many times seen friends gone of unnatural causes. And most often these scenes came to memory as a kaleidoscope of movement and faces, of voices and scents somehow detached from reality. So it was that night in the Cattlemen's Rest Hotel, when Otter Tongue went to the place beyond the sun.

Leaning against that hallway wall, I remembered as though it had been yesterday the time in Richmond when my comrades and I were enjoying furlough and were warned by the lady in the pleasure house where we were spending our leisure and our money that one must never, never blow out the gas-jet lights, on penalty of death. But my Comanche friends had never been in a place where anything other than coal oil was used for the white man's night illumination. So now, for Otter Tongue, total darkness from the white man's light.

There was Allis Featherman, chalk-faced and trembling, still in his underwear with the back flap gaping open, leaning against the wall opposite me. Kwahadi was sitting on the floor, bent over as though he might throw up, holding his head in his hands. And hotel people were washing his face, or at least trying to, with cold water.

Hawk was moving up and down the hall like a great brown cat, looking as though he wanted to kill somebody, but had no idea who. Hornbeam stood at the far end of the hall with a hotel bed blanket across his shoulders, bewildered and keeping his distance for fear of catching some white man's disease.

From the open door of Hornbeam's room I could see light shining, so I knew why he and Hawk had not been victim to the gas, as Otter Tongue had. Old Hornbeam was unsure still in this white man's world, and had wanted to keep a light going through the night, I suspected, and hence, without knowing how, had saved his own life and that of Hawk.

Three doctors finally arrived before we wrapped Otter Tongue's body in his own blankets and carried him back into the now well-ventilated room. And there we pulled one of the Cattlemen's Rest sheets over the long, still form. I'd brought him out into the light of the hallway to be sure, and his face was the most intense blue color I'd ever seen on human flesh. After they carried him back into that death room, I could still see in my mind the wrinkles on his face, like furrows etched on a wet canvas thick with pigment, but all still and cold, and the plucked brows standing out like ridges of some flint ridge along the approaches to Palo Duro Canyon.

Allis Featherman stood back with gaping mouth as I sat on the floor of the hallway, bent over and crying as I had not cried since Augustina. That old Comanche man, I kept thinking, that old Comanche man. Nothing more than that in my mind, yet the choking sobs making my body shake and finally Allis coming over, still in his underwear, and touching my shoulder gently.

"Morgan?" he said, and I looked at him and saw no tear on his face, and that somehow made me duck my head and cry more. But the grief lasted for only a short, violent time.

Somehow I dredged up the presence of mind to get myself and Allis into our clothes, Kwahadi having been moved by then into our own room and sitting on the bed and one of the Fort Worth doctors spooning hot tea into his mouth.

"That's a strange-tasting soup," he kept mumbling. "That's a strange-tasting soup!"

I sent Allis along to fetch McLean Burton, and he was away for only a moment before he was back, explaining that he had no idea where McLean Burton lived. So I went myself on that sorry chore, to tell the good legislator that his festival to honor my friends the Comanches had ended like this, with one of them blue and dead in a strange room and among strangers.

"Asphyxiated?" asked McLean, dumbfounded, standing in his red flannel night shirt in the light of Biddie's upheld lamp. "My Gawd, Liverpool, what have I done to that good old man?"

At first it astonished me that Kwahadi would agree, in the wee hours of dawning on that terrible day, that the most honored elder of his band should be buried there in Fort Worth. But slowly it came to me. He wanted no white man doing all the things they do on embalming slabs. I could only assume that he had some knowledge of such things from the Fort Sill mortuary.

Still suffering from the effects of the gas he'd inhaled, he was nonetheless adamant about what he wanted done.

"A man doesn't get into the place beyond the sun if he's been mutilated."

"They won't mutilate him."

"Yes. They will take things from him, and his body will not be the same."

So quickly into the ground went Otter Tongue, even though in the old days Comanche war parties had often carried their dead long distances to get them back to friends before burial. Yet sometimes dead warriors were buried on the trail home. So into a little graveyard next to the Trinity before the setting sun. And there I learned more about Kwahadi's thinking.

He and Hawk and Hornbeam prepared the body, binding it in blankets and tying all secure so that Otter Tongue was in a sitting position when he was lowered into the grave, facing the east. At the last moment, Kwahadi dropped his eagle-feather fan into the raw hole.

More and more I was impressed by my friend McLean Burton. He had arranged everything, and quickly, as was required.

"Whatever the Comanch' want, they get, by God," he'd said. And he'd hired the undertaker and his mule-drawn black hearse with glass windows on the side, and selected the gravesite, well away from all the other headstones of white men, and overlooking the river.

As the men who were paid to do such things shoveled dirt back into the hole and onto old Otter Tongue's body, I stood beside the Antelope chief. He was looking across the river at the flat expanse of mesquite-covered land. He had loosened his braids, and now, with his hat off, the wind blew his hair across his face. I was reminded of the day he came into Sill to surrender his people, even though now, below that flowing hair, was the white man's black suit. But without the gold watch chain, for it rested in the grave.

I supposed he must have sensed my question: Why had he laid Otter Tongue down in this place, while at the same time he was planning to move his mother's body back to The People? As he looked across the river, he spoke to me. Softly, and only to me, because all the others were standing well back from the grave, Hawk and

Hornbeam and Allis Featherman and the worthies of the state who had hosted the Comanches at the fair.

"In the old days," he said, "Otter Tongue rode along this river. When he was a boy, driving the pony herd for the war parties coming here. And later, in the full growth of manhood, with a lance in his hand. Now his spirit can be here with his brothers, those who came once, a long time ago. Because they are still here. The white man has built his town and the white man has put his cattle in the places where the buffalo once were and the white man has driven all our old beloved enemies away. But Iron Shirt and Sanchess and now Otter Tongue still ride here. If you look across the river, you can see them."

But there was no need to look. I knew that only Kwahadi could see them.

22

Morfydd Annon Parry came home to her people in the fall, when the gum trees were blood-red and the sycamores were touched with gold and silver in the late sun. When I'd left the reservation, the honey locusts had been hanging their creamy Chinese-lantern blossoms down, but when I returned with the tiny white casket, the grass had turned brown and the wind in it made a dry rustle of sound, like Queen Victoria's petticoats when she walked her little black dog.

A time of color and scents and tastes it was in memory, more of that on backward look than impressions of shape. And there were voices.

The day we stood under the chinkapin oaks once more near old Madoc Fort and the River of Broken Guns, and the men dug into the grave, there was the voice of McLean Burton. He looked older that day than I'd ever seen him look, his skin almost matching the color of his white beard.

"After thirty years or so," said he, "there won't be much left. I expect they put her in the ground natural as she died, without any of that undertaker's juice in her."

"Only bones now, bless them," Mari Owen said, herself as ancient-looking as the oaks and standing, head bowed, in the latticework of shade from the branches above, where the stubborn leaves still clung to dapple everything beneath with sunlight and shadow.

And only bones there were. Not a trace of the shining red hair. Only splinters of the rough casket in which she'd been laid down. Only a few faded fragments of the cloth she wore, the same as that showing in the portrait I'd taken to her son. And leather shoes, looking grotesquely large on the long, slender bones that had been her feet.

"I burned those savage moccasins she was wearing when my Bangor brought her in," said Mari defiantly. "And we could never find real shoes small enough for her dainty feet."

It was a funeral in reverse, taking out instead of putting in, with all of us standing about bareheaded, myself and McLean and Mari, Garrison and Lowe and a few of their men in cattlemen's gear.

McLean had provided a child's casket, angel-white and with brass handles on the side and lined with purple velvet. Into that the bones were placed, as I watched with disbelief that such a thing could be happening before my eyes, and McLean and Garrison gave soft-voiced instructions to the men doing the dreadful work.

"How you want 'em laid in here, Senator?" one of the diggers asked.

"Top to bottom, as near as you can tell," McLean said.

"Well, this here box ain't long enough to lay it out like it was a real body."

"Just the head at one end, and all the rest around them ribs," McLean said, and I knew it was only through great self-control that he didn't turn loose a line of blistering oaths.

And I thought, All I'll ever see of this woman who

has had so much to do with my life in recent times—this pitiful arrangement of white on purple velvet.

"And leave those old shoes in the grave," said McLean, and I'm glad he did, because I was thinking of how it would look when Kwahadi opened the casket, and open it I knew he would.

Then McLean, thinking as much like a Comanche as a Comanche might, after all his years of fighting them in his youth before the war, said there'd be no railroad trains.

"She never rode on one before," said he, "and won't now."

So we'd traverse the distance between Madoc Fort and the banks of the Washita with horses and wagons, in the old way.

But before we left, Mari Owen placed her gentle hand on one of my arms, smiling and looking up into my face.

"Liverpool Morgan," she said, "come back under better circumstances sometime, and I'll make some more of those Cornish cakes for your wee mouth."

"You'll always be the very sight and sound of my own people to me, Mari Owen," said I, and kissed her on the cheek she turned to me.

"God keep you from those savage heathen," she said.

And so we went, Garrison and Lowe's men riding escort to us, although none was required now in a land that had a heritage of violence but was now pacific. We had an old-fashioned trail-drive chuckwagon from Lowe's outfit, and a cook who dished out the toughest beefsteak I'd ever tried to eat, and beans with so much Mexican chili in them that they scorched the tongue. And a tack wagon with night gear and the little white coffin, the brass handles along the sides gleaming in the sun when the canvas top was rolled back to air out the bedding each day.

We drove across the Colorado and north to the Brazos, which we forded about eighty miles west of Fort

Worth, so McLean told me. Then on to the West Fork of the Trinity and a camp outside Wichita Falls, all the riders going into town to get drunk, but McLean and I staying in camp with the surly cook, because I'd told Kwahadi that I'd stay with her all the way home. And McLean stayed because I did.

McLean Burton left us at the Red. Somehow I knew he would. He bent toward me and I took his hand and somehow knew that I would never see this old soldier comrade again.

"The rest is up to you, Liverpool," he said. "I got no part in the rest of it. One of these boys has said I could use his saddle pony to get home to Biddie. So go on, take her home to your friends."

"You're welcome to come."

"No. You just tell that chief of yours that if he'd like to come back to Fort Worth sometime, I'd be pleased to have him stay in my lodge."

"I'll tell him."

"Good-bye, Liverpool. Someday maybe I can cut your hair again."

It was less than a year later that I heard he was dead.

Our little cavalcade crossed Red River at a shallow ford, and then went on to Fort Sill without pause, and right through the agency area and on to the Big Beaver.

There was an ancient feeling about all this, as though we were a raiding party coming in from a battle with the Utes, the whole band coming out to meet us. They stood in silent lines, many for the first time in years wearing their old plains garb, most of it in tatters now.

Hawk came to meet us, his face painted black, and led us through the camp and on to the Sycamore Mission. I had no idea why. I have never been able to understand why. But to the mission it was, and there we carried the little casket inside the church, where already two chairs with spool legs had been set facing one another, and on the seats we placed the casket. Hawk ushered us out then, and we waited in the sun, all the band standing in two lines, making an aisle to the mission church door.

Until finally he appeared, walking from the Wolf Ranch house along the stream to the mission, hatless, but with his judging suit brushed, and for the first time I could remember, no scalp lock hung from the back of his head; the hair was all pulled tightly together in two braids along either side of his face, and there, too, hung the silver Mexican pendant earrings.

For a time he paused before the door, all of us watching silently, the Mennonites and the people of his band and the Texans and myself. Then he made a small movement of one hand, and his daughter Padoponi walked from the side of Allis Featherman to join him. But before he turned inside, his eyes met mine, shining, telling me as surely as with words that my duty to him had been done.

It was hot, standing in the October midday before the place where Kwahadi had gone in to see his mother. As the sweat began to collect in tiny beads of wetness across the back of my neck, I tried to imagine the scene inside. But I could not. Only in my mind was the picture of the room where the little casket lay on its resting place of chair seats, near a simple pulpit. And behind, the whitewashed wall where lithographs hung, showing Jesus reaching out to touch a kneeling pilgrim, or talking in the temple with the Jewish elders. And there, too, hung a small clock in an ornate wooden frame, its pendulum long since stopped and the hands showing now and at all hours an eternal eleven o'clock. And beside that, a paper Christmas star of faded red.

It seemed to take a long time. But everyone stood motionless throughout, as though some oration of great import was being pronounced and heard only by the deaf. Then Padoponi appeared, and at once—all prearranged, I supposed—Hawk and Little Horse went inside, and they, along with Kwahadi, carried out the casket. From the rear of the lines of people, some of the old women began a gentle keening, like mourning doves in chorus, wordless and rising slowly to a high pitch of grief.

They carried Morfydd Annon Parry to a waiting open grave behind the church, in the place called Sycamore Cemetery, and there lowered the casket by ropes into the ground. The people flowed around the grave like water, but stayed well back, except for Kwahadi and Hawk and Little Horse. It was at that time that my wife, Quill, moved beside me and I felt her hand in mine. She gave me a quick smile, and I could hardly keep my eyes from her, this being the first time I'd seen her since the spring, and it was now October and her smock was bulging out in front. She was as beautiful as spring.

At graveside, Kwahadi took a small knife from a vest pocket and cut a lock of his hair from the trailing end of one braid and dropped it into the hole where the white casket lay. Then he and Little Horse went to their knees in the loose dirt, Hawk backing away. The keening was more intense now, most of the young women joining with the old. The kneeling Antelope chief and his son shoveled earth into the grave with their hands.

Alongside Morfydd Annon Parry's final resting place was a sunken rectangle of ground, the last bed of old Sunshade. And when Kwahadi's work was done, he rose and lifted his earth-soiled hands and spoke so softly that only a few of us heard.

"Now my two mothers are together, where they belong, close beside each other and among their own people."

I don't know if Sunshade heard, from her place beyond the sun. But I heard. And it gave me some intense, secret exhilaration. As though some great circle was finally closed.

Afterward, as we walked back along the Big Beaver to our homes, Allis Featherman and I, with our wives just behind, I heard Padoponi speak as though to herself.

"He caressed each bone," she said. And she was crying.

EPILOGUE

From the faded reports of bureaucrats and the musty files of academics. And from the pages of many newspapers, coming into the Indian country along with all the other trappings of the white man's culture.

Liverpool Morgan was wounded by a shotgun blast from an assailant unknown, on the evening of June 4, 1905, a Sunday, while riding to Lawton, Oklahoma Territory, from the place known as the Wolf Ranch, where he had been visiting his wife's relatives, she remaining at home that day to prepare a sourdough shortcake with some of the strawberries she was growing in the dooryard.

The old reservation had been dissolved and opened to white settlement, and all along Morgan's route he passed the new farmsteads where corn was planted and milk cows grazed and sod houses stood like dark warts across the rolling, sandy land. It was early evening, the light of the sun still on the clouds above the Wichita Mountains. He could hear a churchbell in the town, faintly, and all about were the cardinals, making their last calls before nightfall. The sound of the gun sent flurries of meadowlarks up from the fields alongside the road.

He was returning to his home in the newly named town, a house behind his place of business, the Stoddard & Morgan Mercantile, where he had purchased a partnership three years earlier in consideration of the one hundred and sixty acres of land his wife had received from the Federal government as her allotment of tribal land.

Morgan was found the next day by two officers of the Fort Sill garrison who were out hunting for quail in the dawning. Brought to his home, he was nursed by his wife and other members of the Antelope band, who came in with their chief from the farms along Big Beaver Creek. But complications of an unknown nature set in, and he died in four days.

Survived by his wife, three sons, and a daughter who would one day marry a United States congressman, Morgan was laid down among his old friends in Sycamore Cemetery. He was sixty-eight years old, and the headstone placed on his grave, ordered and paid for by the Antelope chief, was engraved as follows:

LIVERPOOL MORGAN,
A SOLDIER OF THE WHITE MAN,
A BROTHER TO THE PEOPLE.

The murder was never solved, but old man Stoddard, confined now to his chair with gout, was heard to say that the son of a bitch who had done the shooting was likely some relative of one Rufus Tallbridge. None of the new white immigrants had ever heard the name.

The Territories of the Five Civilized Tribes and of Oklahoma survived Liverpool Morgan by a single year. And then, in November 1907, the two became a single state of the Federal Union, the forty-sixth star on the field of blue and eventually nicknamed the Sooner State in honor of those white men who had come to take the land before it was officially theirs to take.

OBITUARIES

OCTOBER 17, 1913

KWAHADI PARRY, COMANCHE COUNTY.

Mr. Parry was a prominent Comanche Indian of the Lawton area, and is said to have been the last chief of the Comanches. He died in his sleep at his ranch house late yesterday afternoon, of natural causes. Although there is no record of his birthdate, he was said to be about seventy years old.

Mr. Parry was the son of an Indian warrior and a white woman who had been taken captive in Texas as a child in the decades before the Civil War. His mother, Morfydd Annon Parry, died in Texas, but her body was disinterred for reburial in what is now Comanche County.

Mr. Parry rose to the zenith of his leadership after reservation days were begun, bringing his people into the new culture and eventually becoming known statewide and nationwide. By special invitation, he attended the Inaugural of President Theodore Roosevelt in 1905, and rode in the parade there. He was accompanied to Washington on the railroad train by a number of Texas cattle barons who were his friends.

Three years before his death, Congress awarded him an official seal and placard indicating that he was recognized as a chief among his people. This award and a portrait of his mother were said to have been his most prized possessions.

He is survived by seventeen children and an unknown number of grandchildren.

Funeral arrangements were completed by his eldest child, a daughter, Padoponi Featherman. Burial will be in the Sycamore Cemetery, near Lawton, at noon tomorrow, where he will be placed beside the grave of his mother. A large crowd is expected.

They had brought some Apaches to the old Kiowa-Comanche reservation before the turn of the century. Among them was Geronimo, who, after they let him out of the Fort Sill guardhouse, spent a lot of his time growing pumpkins. The Apaches were held in southwestern Oklahoma until the year of Kwahadi's death, although there was no connection. At that time they were allowed to stay or remove to a reservation in Arizona.

Of the few who stayed, some came to the Sycamore Cemetery two days after the burial of the Antelope chief. They stood near his grave, their white man's loose shirts blowing in the wind, their white man's hats held in their hands.

They stood for a long time as the shadows ran toward the east, listening to the whisper of October's leaves. They didn't say anything to one another. They had no need for words. They were there to pay final homage to the memory of old and respected enemies.

And after a while, they went silently away.

Little Horse Parry, Jr., enlisted in the Marines in June of 1917, and served with the Second Infantry Division in France. There he won a Distinguished Service Cross for valor at Belleau Wood. After the Armistice, he came home and The People had a little celebration for him, with dancing and a whole steer roasted over an open-pit fire.

They were celebrating something else, too. The state of Oklahoma had just granted a charter recognizing the Native American Church as a constitutionally protected religion.

Little Horse Parry, Jr., and Father Peyote, all in the same celebration!

In 1967, a great-grandson of Kwahadi Parry was commissioned a second lieutenant of artillery at the Fort Sill Officers' Candidate School. In that same year there was a great gathering of whites and tribesmen in Baxter County, Kansas, to commemorate the signing of the Treaty of Medicine Lodge exactly a century before. Maybe the connection was more real than apparent.

In the little town of Medicine Lodge there was a great carnival. Everyone wore the clothes his or her forebears might have worn one hundred years ago. There was a parade and fireworks. The main street was blocked off at night for square dancing. In the city park was a village of canvas tipis where stayed the visitors from all the various tribes who had been in this same basin of the Timbered Hill River to touch the feather and make peace with the white man, when Mr. Henry Morton Stanley came to report on the great event.

Of course, there had been a lot of grief and fighting after the treaty was signed, but now, a century later, nobody gave that much thought.

Each night, at a softball field, the representatives of the tribes danced for the white spectators. The sound of drums throbbed through the low trees beyond the foul lines, and the singing voices echoed hauntingly under the glare of floodlights. At home plate each night stood a young Native American, microphone in hand,

*explaining the dances to all the glowing white faces in the grand-
stands.*

*And without fail, he told of each generation of young men
who had gone to answer their country's call to arms. They had
fought in the uniforms of all services during World War I,
World War II, and the Korean War.*

*"And now," he would say, "our people are fighting in Viet-
nam."*

*There was, each night, a resonance of pride in his voice and a
shining in the faces of those waiting to dance, because it is hard
for such things as warrior traditions to die. And maybe they
never do, so long as the people who have them live.*

In the seventh decade of the twentieth century, two
Comanches attended the graduation ceremonies at the
United States Military Academy at West Point. Their
names are not so important as the fact that they were both
descended from the great leaders of The People.

One was old, wearing civilian clothing with a bright
sash, and in his hand was an eagle-feather fan. The other
was young and in the cadet gray of West Point and receiving his commission in the white man's army, the first Comanche ever to do so at the high and honored citadel
above the Hudson.

In the cadet chapel, the sunlight shone through the
stained-glass windows in colors like the coming of autumn's leaves along the Washita. And there the old man
charged the young, just as the chiefs of long ago had
charged the warriors going out against traditional enemies. He spoke in Comanche, so all the other cadets and
their parents and the distinguished visitors had no idea
what he was saying.

But then the old man, holding the eagle-feather fan,
explained in English, as he was well able to do, for he had
himself served as an officer at Normandy and later on the
battlefields of France, in World War II.

"It was all about dignity and courage," he said. And

one observant newspaper writer at the rear of the crowded chapel noted in his report that there were many tears on the faces of people who had never heard of Llano Estacado.

And some of Kwahadi's people prospered and wore double-knit suits and sedate neckties and drove Cadillac cars. And others did not prosper and could afford only denim and walked. And some graduated from the University of Oklahoma and some never graduated from high school. And some of them found their medicine, even on the white man's road, but others never did.

And it was often repeated, what Kwahadi had always said: "Each one has to find his own power in his own way."

But no matter what they did or how they were forced to live, they remained Comanches. They remained The People.

And all of those who had never stood in the chapel at West Point knew in their hearts the meaning of the words. The meaning of dignity and courage!

DOUGLAS C. JONES has written thirteen highly praised historical novels. He received the Friends of American Writers award for best novel of the year for *Elkhorn Tavern*, and was three times the recipient of the Golden Spur Award for Best Western Historical Novel. He lives in Fayetteville, Arkansas.

HarperPaperbacks *By Mail*

Experience sizzling suspense in the breathtaking Southwest by *New York Times* bestselling author

TONY HILLERMAN

Master of suspense Tony Hillerman weaves Native American tradition into multi-layered mysteries featuring Officer Jim Chee and Lt. Joe Leaphorn of the Navajo Tribal Police. Brimming with rich detail and relentless excitement, each of his twelve gripping mysteries defy being put down before the very last page is turned.

The Blessing Way
Lt. Joe Leaphorn must stalk a supernatural killer known as the "Wolf-Witch" along a chilling trail of mysticism and murder.

A Thief of Time
When two corpses appear amid stolen goods and bones at an ancient burial site, Leaphorn and Chee must plunge into the past to unearth the truth.

Dance Hall of the Dead
An archeological dig, a steel hypodermic needle, and the strange laws of the Zuni complicate the disappearance of two young boys.

The Dark Wind
Sgt. Jim Chee becomes trapped in a deadly web of a cunningly spun plot driven by Navajo sorcery and white man's greed.

Listening Woman
A baffling investigation of murder, ghosts, and witches can be solved only by Lt. Leaphorn, a man who understands both his own people and cold-blooded killers.

People of Darkness
An assassin waits for Officer Chee in the desert to protect a vision of death that for thirty years has been fed by greed and washed by blood.

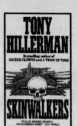

Saddle-up to these

THE REGULATOR by Dale Colter
Sam Slater, blood brother of the Apache
and a cunning bounty-hunter, is out to
collect the big price on the heads of the
murderous Pauley gang. He'll give them
a single choice: surrender and live, or go
for your sixgun.

THE REGULATOR—Diablo At Daybreak
by Dale Colter
The Governor wants the blood of the
Apache murderers who ravaged his
daughter. He gives Sam Slater a choice:
work for him, or face a noose. Now
Slater must hunt down the deadly rene-
gade Chacon…Slater's Apache brother.

THE JUDGE by Hank Edwards
Federal Judge Clay Torn is more than a
judge—sometimes he has to be the jury
and the executioner. Torn pits himself
against the most violent and ruthless
man in Kansas, a battle whose final ver-
dict will judge one man right…and one
man dead.

THE JUDGE—War Clouds
by Hank Edwards
Judge Clay Torn rides into Dakota where
the Cheyenne are painting for war and
the army is shining steel and loading
lead. If war breaks out, someone is
going to make a pile of money on a river
of blood.